MAY 1 0 2007

PLEASE LEAVE CARD
IN POCKET

DISCARD

THE DEAD HOUR

By the same author

GARNETHILL
EXILE
RESOLUTION
SANCTUM
THE FIELD OF BLOOD

THE DEAD HOUR

Denise Mina

BANTAM PRESS

LONDON · TORONTO · SYDNEY · AUCKLAND · JOHANNESBURG

TRANSWORLD PUBLISHERS
61–63 Uxbridge Road, London W5 5SA
a division of The Random House Group Ltd

RANDOM HOUSE AUSTRALIA (PTY) LTD
20 Alfred Street, Milsons Point, Sydney,
New South Wales 2061, Australia

RANDOM HOUSE NEW ZEALAND LTD
18 Poland Road, Glenfield, Auckland 10, New Zealand

RANDOM HOUSE SOUTH AFRICA (PTY) LTD
Isle of Houghton, Corner of Boundary Road and Carse O'Gowrie,
Houghton 2198, South Africa

Published 2006 by Bantam Press
a division of Transworld Publishers

Copyright © Denise Mina 2006

The right of Denise Mina to be identified as the author of this work
has been asserted in accordance with sections 77 and 78 of the Copyright,
Designs and Patents Act 1988.

All the characters in this book are fictitious, and any resemblance
to actual persons, living or dead, is purely coincidental.

A catalogue record for this book is available from the British Library.
ISBNs (hb) 0593051424
9780593051429 (from Jan 07)
(tpb) 0593051459
9780593051450 (from Jan 07)

All rights reserved. No part of this publication may be reproduced, stored in a
retrieval system, or transmitted in any form or by any means, electronic,
mechanical, photocopying, recording, or otherwise, without the
prior permission of the publishers.

Typeset in 12/16pt Garamond by
Falcon Oast Graphic Art Ltd.

Printed and bound in Great Britain by
Clays Ltd, Bungay, Suffolk

1 3 5 7 9 10 8 6 4 2

Papers used by Transworld Publishers are natural, recyclable products
made from wood grown in sustainable forests. The manufacturing processes
conform to the environmental regulations of the country of origin.

For Owen,
who knows how to make
an entrance.

As ever, many thanks are due to the wonderful Selina Walker, a patient, kind and honest editor who has an invaluable eye for the rhythm of a story and is always a good laugh. Also, to the home team of Rachel Calder, Henry Dunow, Camilla Ferrier and all at The Marsh Agency who have bought my houses for me.

I have to give the Transworld editorial, marketing and misc. people their very own paragraph to say a fat thank-you for all the effort and help given for little return and little acknowledgement. Many of them are known to me, some not, but I still appreciate all their work and want to buy them a drink. Sadly, I'm tight, so I probably won't.

To my Mum and also to Louise, Amy and Sam for translating this and other books into Bromley.

The bloody Considines have managed to elbow their way in here yet again, thought God knows how they did it, because they weren't at all helpful to me with this book.

Lastly, to Fergus, Stevo and Ownie, who fill my days with gold.

1

Not Like Us

1984

I

Paddy Meehan was comfortable in the back of the car. The white noise from the police radio filled the wordless space between herself and Billy, her driver. She had only just warmed up after a bitter half-hour standing in sheet rain at a car accident and didn't want to step out into the cold February night, but a handsome man with an expensive striped shirt and a ten-quid haircut was standing in the doorway of the elegant villa, holding the door shut behind him. There was a story here. No doubt about it.

They were in Bearsden, a wealthy suburb to the north of the city, all leafy roads and large houses with grass moats to keep the neighbours distant. After five months on the nightly calls-car shift it was only the second incident Paddy had been called to in the area, the other being when a night bus had staved a roundabout and burst a wheel.

The address was off a side road of old houses behind high hedges. Driving past two granite gateposts, Billy followed the gravel driveway up a sharp bit of hill. A police car was badly parked in front of the house, hogging the space. Billy pulled the car hard over to the lawn, the front wheel dipping into the carved canal between grass and gravel.

They looked up to the door. A policeman had his back to them but Paddy still recognized him. The dead-of-night shift was a small community. Dan McGregor was standing under a stone porchway, jotting notes as he questioned the householder. The man was in his office shirt, his sleeves carefully folded up to his elbows. He must have been cold. He kept his hand on the door knob behind his back, holding the door closed as he smiled patiently at the ground, arguing for the police officer to go away.

Cursing the cold and the night and the feckless man, Paddy opened the car door and stepped out on to the gravel, conscious that the glorious warmth in the cabin was being diluted with cold. She shut the door quickly and pulled the collar of her green leather up against the rain.

Back inside the car Billy reached for the cigarette packet on the dashboard. Paddy and Billy spent five hours a night together, five nights a week, and she knew his every gesture. Now he'd flick his finger on the backside of the disposable lighter tucked into the cellophane wrapper, pull it out and, in a single gesture, flip the carton lid up, take a cigarette out and light it. Paddy paused long enough to see the burst of warm orange flame at his window, wishing herself back inside as she turned towards the house.

Across the slippery, rain-logged lawn the Victorian villa had a pleasing symmetry. Large bay windows on either side of the front door were dressed in old-fashioned frilly net curtains and heavy chintz curtains, still open. The window on the right of the door was dark but the left-hand window was bright, light spilling out on to the gravel, harsh as the ugly lights in the dying half hour of a disco.

Paddy smiled when she saw Tam Gourlay, the other police officer, hanging around by the squad car, blowing on his hands and stamping his feet. When they were called to the rough estates on the outskirts of town one of the officers always stayed back to guard the patrol car from angry residents, but it was hardly necessary here. Paddy imagined an unruly gang of doctors running up the driveway, ripping the wing mirrors off and tanning the windshield. She giggled aloud and caught herself. She was acting odd again. Night shift was getting to her.

Long-term sleep deprivation. It was like a fever, shifting the turn of her eye, moving everything slightly sideways. The bizarre nature of the stories the shift threw up appealed to her but the news editors didn't want surprising, surreal vignettes. They wanted flat, dull news stories, the who, what and when, rarely the why or the guess-what. Her exhaustion coloured everything. She found herself a foot in the wrong direction to meet anyone's eye, her own lonely heart alone in the universe, a beat out of step with everyone else.

She caught Tam's eye as she approached the panda car.

'Meehan,' he said.

'All right, Tam? Is that you back from your holidays?'

'Aye.'

'Nice time?'

'Two weeks with the wife and a six-month-old wean,' sneered Tam. 'You work it out.'

He was the same age as Paddy, in his early twenties, but monkeyed the genuine melancholy of the older officers.

'So.' She took her notebook out of her pocket. 'What brought you out here?' She'd heard the call on the police radio in the car: the neighbours were complaining about a disturbance. It wasn't a neighbourhood that would tolerate much night life.

Tam rolled his eyes. 'Noise complaint: cars screeching, front door slamming, shouting.'

Paddy raised her eyebrows. Noise complaints took two minutes: the householder opened the door, promised to keep it down and everyone went home.

Tam glanced at the door. 'There's a woman inside with blood on her face.'

'Did he hit her?'

'I suppose. Either that or she's been punching herself in the mouth.' Tam chuckled at his joke, but Paddy had the feeling he'd made it before. Or heard it from someone else. She didn't smile back.

'Not really the right neighbourhood for a noisy party on a Monday night.'

Tam huffed. 'Seen the motors?' He nodded to two shiny BMWs parked in the shadows around the back of the tall house. One was big and imposing, the other a sports car, but they matched somehow, like his-and-hers wedding rings. Paddy didn't know much about cars but she knew that the price of one of them would pay her family's rent for three years.

Together they looked at the man. 'Is Dan going to lift him?'

'Nah,' said Tam. 'The woman wants us to leave it. Vhari Burnett. She's a lawyer. One of us.'

Paddy was surprised. 'She's prosecution?'

'Aye.' He pointed at the police officer at the door. 'Dan knows her from the high court. Says she's decent. But, you know, why doesn't she want him prosecuted?'

Paddy thought it was pretty obvious why a woman wouldn't want to bring a criminal prosecution against any man who had a key to her front door. Her oldest sister, Caroline, regularly turned up at home with big bruises on her arms and went mad when anyone mentioned them. The family were Catholic; leaving wasn't an option. Paddy could have put Tam straight, but it was two a.m. and she heard the same lazy, simple-minded shit from officers attending domestic incidents every night. She depended on them for stories and couldn't call them on it. Despite her courting and never contradicting them, the night-shift guys still sensed her distance and went behind her back, feeding the best stories to other journalists, guys they watched football or drank with. Banishing thoughts of her fading career, Paddy turned towards the house.

The first thing she noticed about the dark-haired man was his mouth-watering figure: tall with long legs and slim hips. He stood

4

with his weight on one foot, hips to one side, tolerating Dan's chat. His lashes were long and dark and he kept his eyes a little shut, as though the weight of his lashes forced him to look languid. The conservative white shirt had a thin salmon-pink stripe. Over it he wore black braces with shiny steel buckles, and he had expensive black shoes and suit trousers. It looked like a work uniform. His face was calm and smiling, although his fingers fidgeted nervously on the door handle behind him. He was beautiful.

Paddy sauntered slowly over to the door, keeping in the shadows at the side of the house. Dan was nodding at his notebook as the man spoke.

'. . . Dan, it won't happen again.' He seemed quite casual and Paddy could see that Dan had no intention of taking him in, not even just to lock him in the cells for a couple of hours and teach him a lesson about being a snotty shite. She had seen Dan and Tam at many midnight disturbances and they weren't known for their tolerance. Dan was a fit man, for all he was thin and older. She'd seen him being cheeked up, and using his wiry frame to introduce a couple of faces to the side of his squad car.

Dan scratched something into his pad with a stubby pencil. Thinking himself unobserved, the man dropped his guard and Paddy saw a twitch of excitement as his hand tensed over the handle.

'OK,' said Dan. 'You'll need to keep it down. If we get another call we'll have no option but to take some sort of action.'

'Sure. Don't worry about it.'

Dan shut his notebook and backed off the step. 'Maybe you should get her seen to.'

'Definitely.' He seemed to relax for a moment. Paddy stepped into the circle of yellow light in front of the door. 'Hello. I'm Paddy Meehan from the *Scottish Daily News*. Could I talk to you about the police being called here?'

The man glared at Dan, who shrugged and backed away to the

panda car. Up close his eyes were Paul Newman blue and his lips pink, fleshy. She wanted to touch them with her fingertips. His eyes read Paddy's second-hand green leather coat, the spiky dark hair, beige suede pixie boots and large gold hoops. She saw him notice the red enamel thumb ring on her right hand. It was cheap, bought from a hippy shop, and the blue speckles of enamel were crumbling and falling out.

'Like your look,' he smiled, but she could tell he was lying.

'Thanks. Your look's a bit "business", isn't it?'

He swept his shirt front straight and tucked a thumb under his braces. 'Like it?' He shifted his weight, drawing her attention to his hips. It was a bit too explicit, too overt to be casually flirtatious. She didn't like it.

'So, have you been beating your wife?'

'Excuse me . . .' He held his left hand up and showed her his bare third finger in defence. He wasn't married.

'Do you know Dan?'

He looked her square in the face, eyes clouded over. 'I don't know Dan.'

She frowned and raised a sceptical eyebrow. '*Dan?*' The familiarity of the first name gave more away about their relationship than his manner towards the policeman.

He shrugged as if he didn't care whether she believed him or not, and ran his fingers through his black hair. She could hear the crisp crumple of the fine starched linen of his shirt sleeve.

The door fell open a foot behind him. Paddy saw an imposing Victorian hall stand, dark oak with hooks for hats, a stand on the arm for umbrellas and walking sticks. In the middle of the dark wood frame was a large mirror, and reflected in the glass she saw a woman's frightened face.

The pretty blonde was standing in the door that led to the living room, listening. Slim necked and fine featured, the tips of her bob were stained pink with blood. As she watched Paddy in the mirror her slender fingers cart-wheeled the curtain of hair behind her ear, revealing a bloody jaw. A thin slash of scarlet ran from the side of her mouth to her chin, down her neck and over her collarbone, soaking into the wide Lady Di lace ruff on her white blouse.

For a sliver of a moment their eyes met and Paddy saw the vacant expression she'd seen many times at car crashes and fights, a look saturated with shock and pain. She raised her eyebrows at the blonde, asking if she wanted help, but the woman gave a half shake of the head and broke off eye contact, sliding backwards in the doorway and out of the mirror.

The man saw Paddy looking and pulled the door closed at his back. 'We're fine, really.' He smiled warmly and nodded, as if thanking Paddy for coming to a party. The porchway light was weak and yellow but she saw it suddenly: blood on his own neck, in among the short black hairs. They were spots, flecks from spray. He smiled at her. She could see the glint of flint in his eyes.

'Have you beaten her before?'

He was getting irritated, but only a little bit. He glanced over at Tam and Dan by the squad car and Paddy followed his gaze. Dan shook his head, giving the man an answer, sending a signal Paddy didn't understand. He took a tired breath. 'Won't you wait for a moment, please?'

Opening the door less than half a foot, he slipped inside. For a moment, as the door fell towards the jamb, Paddy thought he had done the sensible thing and shut her out, but he came back smiling a second later.

He leaned forward and put something in Paddy's hand. 'I can't stress enough how important it is that this doesn't get in the paper.' It was a fifty-pound note. 'Please?'

The note was damp and pink with blood.

Paddy glanced around. Both officers were standing by their panda car with their backs to her. The windows in the house across the nearest hedge were black and blank and empty. Her cold fingers closed over the note.

'Good night.' He slipped back into the house and shut the door firmly but quietly.

Paddy looked at the grain of the oak door, worn yellow where habitual hands had felt for the handle or fitted a key. The large brass handle was smeared with blood. She had fifty quid in her hand. She squeezed it just to be sure it was there and the wetness of the blood chilled her. A little excited, she crammed her fist into her coat pocket, turning stiffly and crunching back down the perfect driveway. The wind ruffled her hair. Somewhere in the far distance a car rumbled down a road, pausing to change gear.

At the police car, Tam shrugged. 'It's important to them. She's a lawyer,' he said, inadvertently letting her know that they'd been paid off too.

Dan slapped the back of Tam's head and tutted. As she passed she overheard Tam defend himself in an undertone. 'It's only wee Meehan.' They climbed into the police car and started the engine, Dan backing carefully out of the driveway, reversing past Paddy at the side of the calls car.

As she opened the passenger door she glanced back at the brightly lit window of the big house. For an instant she saw a movement behind the net curtains, a swirl of light and motion. She blinked and when she looked back the room was still.

Billy watched her fall into the back seat in the rear-view mirror and took a draw on his cigarette. He had seen her take the money, she was sure of it. She could have offered to share it but she didn't know what the etiquette was, she'd never been bribed before. Besides, fifty quid could solve a host of problems.

Billy reversed out of the drive but Paddy's eyes lingered on the house. In the coming weeks and months she would recall the skirl of light she had witnessed at the window, how glad she had been to be back in the warm car and how thrilling the note had felt in her pocket. And she would burn with shame when she remembered her absolute conviction that the bloodied woman in the mirror was nothing whatever to do with her.

II

Billy drove in silence down the black glistening road towards the city, listening to the pip and crackle of the police radio. Paddy could hardly look at him in the mirror.

Even if Billy had seen her take the money she knew he wouldn't ask her about it. They were careful what they asked each other because the truth was difficult. Injudicious questions had told her that Billy and his wife were fighting all the time, that he didn't like his son much since he had become a teenager. She had told him that she felt disgusting and fat, that her unemployed family resented living off her wages and the unnatural power it gave her in the house.

Billy and Paddy had never developed a workmates' rapport of comforting lies. The police radio was on all the time, forming a wall of static that stopped them talking in anything more than staccato bursts. They never spoke long enough to let Billy hint that his son was basically a genius who hadn't found his niche, or for Paddy to suggest that her weight was a bit hormonal. All that lay between them was a raw stretch of truth. At least they were kind to each other. It would have been unbearable otherwise.

'Hey, you'll like this one.' Billy turned the radio down for a second. 'What's a domestic altercation?'

'I don't know, Billy, what is a domestic altercation?'

'A fight in a hoose in Bearsden.' He turned the radio back up and smiled at her in the mirror, telling her it was OK.

She looked sadly down at her hand as it uncurled in her lap. Her palm had blood on it. 'You're right, Billy, I do like that one.'

She needed the money. Her father had been unemployed for two years. There were four children living at home and she was the only one bringing in a wage. She was the youngest and now the major earner. It gave her an unspoken veto in family decisions; her mother told her how much every item in the shopping cost and emphasized her frugality with food. It left Paddy with nothing for herself and she couldn't fathom how to rectify the power imbalance at home. Still, the Meehans were relatively well off: one in three adults were unemployed in many parts of the city. Her mother wouldn't notice the blood on the note as long as she left it to dry and brown.

'Was it a couple?' Billy wound his window down an inch, dropping the end of his cigarette out of the crack. It bounced off the sill, giving off a burst of red sparks, before disappearing over the edge.

'She had blood on her. I don't know if we should have left her there.'

'Don't feel too bad. They're not like us, rich people.'

'Aye.'

'She could leave him if she wanted.'

'So I suppose.'

The domestics they usually saw were in tiny flats on sink estates, of necessity public events because the couples had to go out into the street to get a good swing at each other. Husbands and wives could languish on the council list for years while they waited for separate houses to come up, festering in small rooms. Blow-ups were inevitable.

Billy caught her eye again. 'We gonnae phone that story in then or just leave it?'

If she didn't think Billy had seen her take the money, she would have moved on to the next call and the next incident, but she didn't want him to think badly of her.

'OK,' she said. 'Let's find a phone box.'

'Then we could try up at Easterhouse,' suggested Billy, letting her know that he doubted the story would make it to print. 'There's been a lot of swordplay in Barrowfield as well.'

All over the city nutters and gangsters were getting hold of machetes and swords and claymores and attacking each other. Sword fights had been going on for years and the moral panic they generated had been mined to death. It was a tired story, but it was still a story.

'Aye, some bastard must be killing somebody somewhere,' said Paddy, hating her job and all the places it took her to.

2

Living on His Knees

When Paddy left work the sun still wasn't due to rise for three hours. The few early-morning commuters on the street scurried along, heads to chests, keeping warm and keeping going, determined as clockwork mice. She was the only person sauntering through the icy city centre, head up, the only person watching. She had discovered that in the mornings, particularly when it was dark, no one looked up – they scurried along with their minds elsewhere, rehashing fights or rehearsing their day ahead, sometimes talking to themselves. She alone was present in the street, alone in the fleeting moment.

She walked slowly. She didn't want to get to Sean's too early or she'd have to sit while his mum walked around in her slip and skirt and ate her breakfast, passing on stories, most of them malicious rumours about women in the parish.

Taking a long, wandering way down to the station, Paddy doubled back up Albion Street and crossed the Siberian expanse of George Square. She was warm in her green leather. It was a knee-length fifties coat with a round collar and three big green buttons. It was a jumble-sale buy, bought for a pound, made of buttery calf-skin. Best of all it hung straight at the back with no waisting at all and disguised her bum a bit. It was roomy enough to allow for a jumper underneath. She slowed to a stop, pulling her red scarf up from the back of her neck to cup her head, covering her ears to stop the icy wind giving her earache.

A man in a green boiler suit and heavy work boots hurried across her path. As she watched him make his way towards the City Chambers it occurred to her why she liked green so much: it was because of Betty Carson and Paddy Meehan's prison release day. She hadn't made the association before. Maybe that was why she'd been so drawn to the green sleeve on the rack at the jumble sale.

Patrick Meehan's story was through her like weft through a weave. Telling details came to mind at the most unlikely times, bubbling up from her subconscious just when she was least expecting them.

Paddy Connelly Meehan was a career criminal, a small-time safe-blower who had spent more of his life in prison than out of it. If he wasn't cooking gelignite in frying pans in deserted tenements he was boasting about his exploits in the Tapp Inn. He had been found guilty of a high-profile murder when Paddy was just a child and the accident of their names meant that she followed the story all through her childhood, hearing before most people in the city that he was innocent, that the real villain had tried to sell his story to the Sunday papers, that a famous journalist was writing a book about the case. Growing up faithless in an obsessively Catholic family, Paddy had looked to the outside world for models on how to behave, and somehow she'd replaced the New Testament with Meehan's story. It wasn't that unusual a thing to do, she realized: many failed Catholics became Marxists because of the perfect fit of mental infrastructure. Both had a single text and their own saints and fallen heroes. Both demanded time and money and evangelizing and both looked forward to a future when justice would abound and the meek would inherit the earth.

She had become obsessed with the Meehan story, finding bravery and dignity there, nobility and perseverance, integrity and loyalty. The only detail spoiling it for her now was Paddy Meehan himself: after his pardon he had stayed in Glasgow, hanging around the pubs and telling his story to anyone who'd listen, falling out with journalists and barmen and everyone. He had lived past his moment of glory and couldn't stay a hero in the workaday mess of getting by.

He was the reason she became a journalist, why she wanted the crime desk and saw glory and dignity in a job most would see as a career compromise.

A green coat.

In Paddy's imagination Betty Carson's flame-red hair was brilliant against the cream wall, her skin as pale as white bread. Betty and Patrick Meehan were both eighteen, both taking shelter in the same dark close, waiting for the rain to go off. They spoke for a while and he walked her to the bus stop, waiting with her, watching her wave from the retreating tram with his heart beating loudly in his throat.

Betty was from good people. Her staunchly Protestant family were surprised when she came home a few months later and announced that she was married, but, in a bigoted city, they were open minded and accepting of the young Catholic man. They gave Meehan every chance to do the right thing. Each time he came home from prison they welcomed him, expecting it would be different this time because he said so.

Prison release day. According to his own account, Betty met him outside the gates at the end of every single prison sentence. Every time she would be outside, standing in rain or wind or in the biting dark of a long Scottish winter. And she'd be wearing a new green coat or dress or suit, green for new beginnings, green to set off her red hair.

Meehan and Betty kissed, Paddy imagined – kissed and wrapped their arms around each other, squeezing a little, delighted to be together, and they'd set off, arms linked, walking calmly as she did through the early-morning rush of people hurrying to work, head-down people talking to themselves and hurrying through a grey morning. On release day Betty floated through the town with her man, taking him home to a hearty breakfast.

Betty, a happy fleck of festive green and red in the great grey city.

II

Paddy stepped off the train on to the windy Rutherglen station platform, bleary eyed, with dry powdery baked potato coating her teeth. Her head was too scrambled to stick to the High Fibre Diet, but she was still trying and always kept a cold baked potato in her bag. She had put on weight in the last few years, on her hips and her chest. Any faith that she could stick to a disciplined regime had deserted her, so she ended up applying the principles in a half-arsed way, supplementing meals with baked potatoes or cold beans eaten straight from the tin, feeling tired and guilty all the time and shamefully scuttling off to corners to pass stinking wind.

As she climbed the long flight of stairs from the platform to the street, compound tiredness made her back curl over, her hands slapping on the steps in front of her. She needed a big starchy sugar lift and knew there would be porridge and honey at the Ogilvys'. As she walked down Rutherglen Main Street, passing the commuters spilling out of the bus shelter, she swithered over the promise of porridge. Being fat was holding her back at work. She didn't have the confidence to put herself forward or take the initiative and apply for better jobs in London. If she was thinner she could do it. She was just twenty pounds away from the life she should have been living.

On the other hand, she wasn't at work this morning and she was tired and sorry for herself. She could give in and gorge herself on warm porridge and mugs of milky tea.

Rutherglen Main Street was in the calm lull between the morning rush to work and the gathering of old people and young mothers for ten o'clock Mass at St Columkille's. They would be making their way there slowly, coming through the shopping arcade and heading downhill from the small housing schemes dotted around the Main Street. All her elderly relatives would be coming. Her sister Mary Ann would be walking the straight road from Eastfield. Paddy kept her head down and hurried through the back streets to Sean's house in Gallowflat Street. She'd hide at Sean's until well after the Mass came out, or suffer a hundred inquiries after her mother, father, brothers and sisters as she tried to make her way to her warm bed and a long, creamy sleep.

The Ogilvys' kitchen window was steamed up, the living room dark. The light would be on if Sean was up – he liked to watch the school programmes while he ate his breakfast. Paddy turned into the close, almost bumping into a young woman with a screaming baby in an old-fashioned Silver Cross pram.

'Fiona O'Conner, how ye doing?' said Paddy, though she had never liked her at school and vaguely remembered being insulted by her. 'Is this your wee one?'

Fiona raised red smarting eyes. 'Oh, yeah, hi. Help us down with the pram.'

Paddy took the front axle of the pram and lifted it down the two steps to the street. Fiona looked annoyed. 'I thought Sean was going out with Elaine McCarron now.'

Paddy winced a little at the mention of Elaine and wondered why she did. 'Aye, they've been together for a year now. Seem to be getting on well.'

'Oh, right,' said Fiona slyly. 'You're always here, but, eh?'

Paddy gave her a stiff smile and slipped past Fiona into the close.

She could have been married to Sean by now, they might have had a family and a house of their own. She had chosen instead to continue working at the *News* and hope for a career, to dream one day of a house of her own that didn't smell continually of soup and potatoes. Making the difficult choice wasn't enough. She was still at home, her family of five reliant on her wages. Her clothes were cheap, came from What Every's and lasted no more than two washes. A place of her own was a long way off.

She had started going with Sean at school. They were close and both came from big families so neither of them bothered with other friends. It was too late now – the lifelong friendships that trail on after school, that made for best men and holiday companions, were out of reach for them now. They found themselves stuck together, not engaged or even dating, just hanging around during the day watching *County Court* on TV, or grainy pirate videos of the three films his brother owned: *Airplane*, *Evil Dead* and *The Exorcist*, or else going for pointless walks up the Brae.

Mimi Ogilvy was pulling on her coat as she opened the door. 'Come in, Paddy, wee hen, good of you to come.'

Paddy stepped into the hallway, into the warmth and the homely smell of toast and strong tea. The holy-water font inside Mimi's door was large enough for a small chapel: a Disney-ish Our Lady gazing lovingly down at a fat baby Jesus who was holding a pink oyster shell full of holy water. Paddy dipped two fingers of her right hand and dabbed her head, her breastbone and both shoulders as she crossed the threshold. It was an old habit she couldn't shake. She had no faith but knew the gesture soothed her mother's fears about her. Every time she did it she felt like a hypocrite, but a hypocrite with a calm mother.

She noticed a new set of leaflets stacked under the telephone table. Black text on red paper this time, proclaiming Callum Ogilvy's innocence. It cost a lot of money to print them – she wondered where the hell Sean was getting it from. But just then Mimi ambled out of the kitchen, peeling two pound notes from her purse, and laid them on the telephone table, answering her question.

'That's for his ciggies and a pint at teatime. And,' she pulled out a fiver and three more pound notes, 'he's got his last driving lesson later.'

17

It was meant as a compliment that she did it in front of Paddy, a mark of acceptance. Paddy looked away. Mimi had paid for so many lessons that Sean had his test in a few days. Sean didn't need to drive – he wouldn't be able to afford a car. And anyway, no one was paying for her driving lessons.

Mimi glanced at the clock on the far wall of the galley kitchen and stepped past Paddy to the door. 'There's porridge in the pot for ye and the honey's in the cupboard next to the fridge.'

She was gone, leaving Paddy in the hall listening to her ex-fiancé snoring and trying to resist the pull of warm porridge after a long night shift. Sean didn't take porridge for his breakfast. Poor Mimi had gone to all that trouble just for her. It would be unkind to leave it.

III

He was awake. His breathing had become lighter, but he was still facing the wall and keeping his eyes shut, curled up to hide his morning glory.

She rapped on the open bedroom door once more. 'Get up.'

Sean stretched out under the blankets, savouring the hazy sleep in his limbs. He was wearing his brown pyjamas with the yellow trim on the pocket. He looked like a six-foot-two ten-year-old.

'Hey, smelly boy, wake up. Come on, you need to sign on.'

'Yeah, yeah.' He clasped his hands in front of himself and gave a luxurious stretch, smiling at her standing in the doorway, his eyes puffy with sleep, his lashes pressed this way and that by the pillow.

Paddy felt a burst of righteous anger. Both she and his mother were working hard at thankless jobs and cooking and caring for him. She knew his brothers gave him money on the fly as well, two quid here, a packet of fags there. One of them had bought him a season ticket to Celtic Park so that they could all go together. Paddy came straight over from work every two weeks to make sure he got up and went to claim his Supplementary Benefit. He couldn't even do that himself.

'You're a lazy bastard. You want to get on your bike and look for work.'

They locked eyes and grinned at each other across the soft darkness of the bedroom, a look that lingered too long. Ambushed by the sudden moment of tender connection, their smiles slid gently into awkward until Sean stretched his arms behind his head and broke it off. 'Anyway, milk and five sugars, love.'

'Fuck you.' It was a little too angry for a play fight and he was surprised into looking at her. She wasn't angry at Sean, she was angry at herself for eating the porridge and then going back for more porridge with more honey and then standing, watching old ladies with string grocery bags passing by the kitchen window, picking at the papery skirt of dried porridge around the rim of the pot, eating it and wondering why she was doing it. It didn't taste of anything. It didn't even have a pleasant texture. But while she was eating all she thought about was eating. She didn't worry about work or her family or her weight. Even unpleasant food made her feel happy. Except cottage cheese with pineapple. She could hardly look at it now, after a reckless week-long attempt to eat nothing else.

Sean kept her eye and rolled away from her, farting lightly in her general direction. She tried not to smile.

'Saw this in the hall.' She held up the Callum Ogilvy pamphlet.

'Yeah, a woman took one from Elaine's salon yesterday.' He propped himself up on an elbow. 'She's a reporter from the *Reformer*, said she was interested. It could be the start of something.'

Paddy grunted. *The Rutherglen Reformer* was an advertising paper. They covered local swimming galas and wheelie-bin controversies. They wouldn't touch a story like Callum's but Sean was trying to worry her, make her write about his campaign for the *Daily News* before someone else scooped the story.

Callum was eleven when he and another boy were convicted of killing a three-year-old they had taken from outside his front door. Looking back, it seemed bizarre that Paddy alone was convinced that there must have been an adult hand in the killing. The rest of the city settled happily on the two boys as lone culprits.

Paddy had found the man behind the killing – she still had the mental scars to prove it – but even she knew that Callum had killed the wee boy. He might have been driven to the spot and terrorized into doing it, but Callum Ogilvy was still guilty. He'd had blood on him from the baby, his hair was found at the scene and Callum had more or less confessed.

Only Sean wouldn't accept it. Callum's innocence had become an article of faith with him and she thought he had half convinced Callum now too. The Ogilvys had abandoned the wee cousin to his fate once, leaving him to be raised by an unstable mother, and Sean wasn't going to betray him again. The adamancy of his conviction and the sincerity with which he wrote letter after letter to MPs and journalists and anyone who might be able to help were starting to have an impact.

'Sean,' she spoke with forced patience, 'there's no new evidence—'

'The old evidence could be made up.'

'Mrs Thatcher could be an evil robot, but she isn't. Just because something's plausible doesn't make it possible.'

They looked at each other again. All it would take, she thought, was for one of the animals at work to see a career boost in the story and Sean would be eaten alive.

'You'd be better off dropping it. No one wants to keep this story going but you.'

'Pad,' he used the fond diminutive of her nickname but sounded serious, 'it's not just a story to me. I won't side with the world against that wee guy. I'm all he's got.'

'Couldn't you be all he's got and still accept that he did it? Does he have to be innocent for you to like him? He was ten years old when he did it. Who knows anything at ten?'

'Don't start that.'

Resigned, Paddy nodded. 'Come on anyway, get up.'

Sean stretched back. 'Put the kettle on, eh? And a couple of slices.'

'*Playschool*'s on in a minute.' She backed out of the room and hesitated at the doorway between the living room and the kitchen. She had come here straight from a night shift, but she drew the line at cooking his breakfast. She chose the living-room door, fell on to the settee and looked around the room.

The Ogilvys were good little soldiers of the Church, just like her own family. Their furniture was nice enough, built to be hard-wearing but not to look nice or feel modern. All the pictures on the walls were either religious or sacrament-related triumphs of the various family members: Sean's parents at their silver wedding anniversary, the ordination of a distant cousin, one brother's small wedding to a pretty girl from Hamilton and the subsequent christenings of their four children, all outside the same ugly little chapel during different seasons. Paddy and Sean had been engaged for two of the christenings and she was pictured in the family group, although, in her only expression of annoyance at Paddy breaking the engagement off, Mimi had framed one of them so that she was sliced in half by the edge of the frame.

Paddy took a copy of the *Daily News* out of her pale leather backpack, frowning heavily to stop herself grinning at the second page. Her insert was printed there: Police were called to a party at 17 Drymen Road, Bearsden, after neighbours complained of the noise. A woman was found to be injured but police made no arrests. It was her first piece of copy in four night shifts.

Putting down the paper, she listened for noises from the hall. Nothing. 'Sean,' she shouted, irritated. 'They won't let you off with it any more.'

'I'm eating a fry-up in the shower.'

She could tell by his voice that he was still lying down. If he was late again they wouldn't process his giro cheque until later in the afternoon, which meant the cheque would arrive in three days instead of two. They did it to punish latecomers and Mimi needed the money.

'Your mum's behind on all her catalogues. Mr McKay'll come and repo all your underpants.'

She heard the clip-clop of high-heels in the close and a key rasping into the front door. She hoped it was Mimi, but knew it wasn't. Guilty, as if she had been caught skiving school, she tucked her hands between her knees and sat up straight on the settee.

Elaine McCarron stepped into the hallway, mac on over her blue work pinny, smiling to herself. Elaine had been two years below them at school, slim, slight and fine featured. She hated Paddy but was too dainty to ask Sean to stop hanging about with his ex the whole time. A junior hairdresser, she worked hard on her feet during the long afternoons that Paddy and Sean spent watching telly or wandering around Woolworths eating pick and mix and playing with the toys.

Paddy let herself be known by a stage cough. Elaine spun round, infuriated, and Paddy tried a smile.

'I wouldn't have come,' she whispered. 'Only Mimi asked me.'

Elaine pursed her lips hard, draining the blood from them, and looked away to Sean's bedroom door. She pulled her pinny straight, composing herself before knocking prettily.

Paddy sat sheepishly back on the settee. She couldn't leave immediately. It would look as if she had done something wrong. She felt a familiar hollow sense of guilt, as if she had eaten the flake out of Elaine's ice cream and no one knew it but the two of them. She could blame Mimi all she liked, she could deny it to everyone, but Paddy knew that she was clinging to Sean because he was the only person she felt completely comfortable with. She needed him even more now because she missed her sister, Mary Ann, so much.

From across the hall she heard Elaine give a sexy giggle, louder than she needed to – for Paddy's benefit, she was sure. She stood up suddenly and turned the telly on to the news. Unemployment was running at one in ten. The Scott Lithgow shipyard was threatening to close with six and a half thousand redundancies. Boy George was pictured arriving in Paris, Charles de Gaulle with his Japanese girlfriend. Then the local news.

Mist rose from a lawn. In the distance was a Victorian villa with serious policemen in front of it, their frosted breath silver in the brittle morning air. It was the house she had stopped at last night. The home owner, Vhari Burnett, had been found this morning by a colleague who had come to give her a lift to work. They showed a grainy photo of the woman Paddy had seen in the mirror. Her hair was shorter in the picture and she was outside, her blonde hair wind-ruffled, smiling crescent eyes.

Paddy sat upright: the good-looking man had killed her. She remembered the flurry of light at the Bearsden window and it seemed to her now that an arm swung in a punch, a machete strike, a death blow. She recalled the night cold on her cheeks, the wind brushing her hair back, and saw again the fingers clench the door handle, holding the door closed, keeping the woman inside.

Burnett had been a prominent member of the fiscal's office, unmarried and a political activist. In the wide shot Paddy noticed that both BMWs were gone from the side of the house.

As Paddy sat on the settee, slack and horrified, vaguely aware of the sound of voices out in the hall, she shifted and felt the fifty quid crumple in her pocket. She should phone the police and tell them about it. It could be important – not many people had the odd fifty-quid note sitting about in their hall. But the police would gossip about it. Her first and only bribe would become public knowledge.

The front door clicked shut and Sean said something. She'd be known as corrupt and the note would end up in some policeman's pocket. Evidence was misplaced all the time, generally money or other valuables – it never seemed to happen to mouldy jam sandwiches or hats with holes in them.

'Did ye not make tea?' said Sean, repeating himself. He was standing at the door of the living room.

Paddy pointed at the telly. 'He killed her.'

'Who?'

'I was at the door of that house last night and they've just said a woman was murdered after we left. I spoke to the guy who did it.'

Sean glanced at the television. 'Creepy.'

Paddy drew a long breath, balancing the news of the fifty-quid note on the tip of her tongue, unsure if she wanted to commit herself to doing the right thing. She looked at Sean's face and gave in. 'He gave me money, a fifty-pound note, to go away.'

'Fucking hell.'

Paddy cringed. 'Shit loads, isn't it? Mum'd have a field day with a note that big.'

Sean's eyes widened, thinking of all the things he could do with fifty quid. It was five weeks' worth of benefit for him. He could send his mum to Rome on pilgrimage. Buy shoes that fitted him. Get new carpet for the threadbare hall.

'Ye need to hand it in to the police though, Pad.'

'Aye,' she agreed quickly, as if that was what she had been going to do all along. 'Aye, I know.'

'You'll get it back, I'm sure.'

'Oh, aye.' She turned back to face the telly and nodded, a little too vigorously. 'I'll get it back.'

3

Home

Kate had been awake for almost two days. Sitting behind the wheel of her smart new car she felt panicked and buzzed at the same time, giggly almost, when she thought about the value of what she had in the boot, frightened when she thought about the consequences of what she had done. She turned a corner and saw a lorry lumbering along in front of her on the straight road. She stepped on the brake, touching it lightly, curling her bare toes over the soft leather insole of her navy-blue court shoe, and the sensitive car slowed on the wet road. Beautiful motion. Reflexively, her thumb stroked the enamelled BMW badge at the centre of the wheel. The blue matched her woollen Chanel suit, her earrings and watch. Lovely to be surrounded by lovely things.

The Loch Lomond Road was quiet this morning. It was too cold for tourists, too rainy even for Germans. The summer crowds were hardly even a memory now. As she drove through the little settlements dotted along the bare road all the bed and breakfast signs had 'No Vacancies' attached at the bottom. Kate had come here every summer when she was young and knew the rota of visitors to the Loch, from the pasty-faced city-dwellers who came on the bus for a day in a tea shop during the drizzly, midge-infested summer to the other old established families who, like hers, came to their holiday homes for Christmas and Hogmanay, trooping from one house to

GIBSONS AND DISTRICT
PUBLIC LIBRARY

another bringing season's greetings and good bottles of malt with them.

He would probably suspect she'd come to the Balmaha cottage, and look for her there. She didn't have keys for the front door but could easily break in around the back. She imagined herself in bra and stockings and suspenders, sitting on a chair inside the front door, seductively smoking a cigarette as he opened the door. He'd love that, she smirked to herself, he'd go mad for that. She imagined the scene again: lowering the lights, pulling her curly blonde hair up but letting tendrils tumble about her shoulders and putting her glasses on. Sexy secretary. He loved that look. Unfortunately she didn't have any of that sort of underwear with her.

She was overtaking the lorry, a third of the way up the side, flicking the wipers on to smear away the spray from the tall tyres, when she saw the red car coming straight towards her, twenty feet away and closing.

'Shit!' Eyes wide, suddenly awake, she took her foot off the accelerator, slammed the brake and managed to pull in behind the lorry so neatly that the red car narrowly missed clipping her near corner of the bonnet.

'Shit!' She shouldn't be driving, suddenly doubted her perception of space and time and safety. The lorry pulled ahead of her and Kate let the car slow to a stop, pulling in to the side, not even waiting to find a resting place, just letting the car roll to a halt and crunch into a bank of shingle, the bonnet dipping into the ditch.

Ahead of her the windscreen view was filled with sheer black rock, jagged and wet, covered in netting to stop loose boulders tumbling on to the road and making it any more treacherous than it already was.

She had been driving around for most of the last two days and now realized that it was a wonder that she hadn't killed herself. She needed to sleep. She hadn't eaten either, now she thought about it.

She would get to the cottage and have a bath. There were always some tins of ham in the cupboard. Some dried milk, too – she could make up a jug and have some tea. She took deep breaths, well practised at bringing her heart rate down. She was trembling. Her fingers were actually trembling with fright.

Reaching over to the well of the passenger seat, she pulled up her navy-blue handbag and sat it on the seat, feeling blind for the packet of cigarettes. She lit one. It wasn't what she really wanted but she needed to slow down, calm down, keep steady. Get it together and drive to the cottage. Have a bath. Eat some ham. Make milk from the powder in the cupboard. The police might pass her here and come to talk to her because the car was parked strangely. They'd recognize her, maybe, check the car, go into the boot.

Kate took a drag on her cigarette and reminded herself that those things hadn't happened. She had just imagined that they had. They hadn't happened. Realizing that she didn't know if she had been parked for a second or an hour, she turned the radio on to give herself a measure of the passage of time. Duran Duran. She liked them. Lovely suits. Tans, nice suntans. Princess Diana liked them, too. She took another draw on her cigarette and imagined herself at a smart party in Chelsea, with Sloane Rangers in hairbands and guys in suits who worked in the City. Rich, rich people. Lot of money, champers, no one eating because they were all as coked up as she was. A room full of striped furniture and lovely things, well made. Italian things.

She felt warm and comfortable. She drew on her cigarette again and smiled at the passenger window as though it were a fellow guest at the party. She nodded at a woman across the room. A titled woman. Someone who had house parties in her country place. People could stay all weekend because the house was so big they'd never run into each other. Never get sick of each other. She invited Kate away for the weekend. She'd invited half the party, but only half, and Kate was included. Kate smiled over at her again. Hi.

Duran Duran stopped and the news announcer came on the radio. Vhari Burnett. Kate heard the name and for a millisecond thought Vhari had done something lovely. Been proposed to by a Royal, given an MBE, won a big case. Vhari Burnett had been murdered in her home. Her body was found by a colleague arriving to give her a lift to work. Her body. Murdered. Kate took three sharp, consecutive drags on her cigarette until she was almost certain there was no corner of either lung unfilled by smoke. She tried to see the titled woman from the party again, but couldn't.

She punched the radio off. It was impossible to imagine Vhari being dead. Vhari being away on holiday was possible, she could imagine that, but not dead. Not murdered.

Kate rolled her window down a fraction and felt a swirl of bitter wind against her cheek as she pushed the cigarette out into the road. She wound it up again and restarted the car.

A hot bath and a tin of ham and a think about things. She watched the road behind her, turning, her right arm slipping over the seamed cream leather seat-back. Lovely thing, the car. Lovely things.

II

Paddy put her key carefully in the front door and pushed it open. In front of her the stairs were still, the bathroom door on the landing lying open, the light off. Through the living room to her right, she could hear the burble of the radio coming from the kitchen. Two plates crashed together, louder than was necessary. A cup hit a saucer.

Trisha was smashing around in the kitchen, washing and putting away, wiping up and preparing breakfast for a family with nowhere to go. They didn't know whether it was the change of life or the family's circumstances, but Trisha was as likely to shout over nothing as burst out crying and Paddy was worried about her. The news was full of stories about families breaking up under the strain of the recession, of mothers being found dead in spare bedrooms with bottles of pills next to them or fathers disappearing off to London. But no one else seemed to have noticed. Con was a shadow and everyone else was distracted by their own worries.

Paddy took her leather off and hung it up in the cupboard under the stairs. She imagined she felt the crumple of dry paper from the pocket and blushed that the bloody note should be so near her mother. She walked through the living room, leaning in the kitchen door and hanging on to the door frame, trying to communicate the fact that she wouldn't be coming in.

The table was set for two people to have breakfast together: Paddy and Trisha. Martin and Gerard were still in bed, though it was ten-thirty. Mary Ann would be out at Mass. Her father, Con, was sitting at the table, flushed with the weather, having been out walking for a couple of hours.

'Been out already, Da?'

Con nodded, stroking his little David Niven moustache. He used to colour it, she knew he did, with some powdery concoction Trisha bought in a paper bag from the chemist's, but he'd stopped recently. Now it was turning grey, disappearing against his grey skin apart from a little patch of red making itself known at the side, looking like a trace of ketchup from a distance. Con had been made redundant two years ago and had lost faith that he would ever find work again. Force of habit made him rise at seven every day, take the breakfast Trisha set in front of him and then, abruptly, find the whole hollow day staring him in the face. He took long walks across the industrial desert between Eastfield and Shettleston. Inside flimsy security fences ran miles of Armageddon fields, pitted with tangled metal and abandoned buildings, and Con picked his quiet way, carrying home scraps they might have a use for.

'Find any goodies?'

He shook his head, turning back to his tea. 'Nothing.'

Beyond the kitchen window the sharp, low daylight sliced across the grass tips of the overgrown garden and cut through the kitchen. Trisha was at the empty sink, her face screwed up tight against the bright morning, wiping down the metal until it sparkled. She looked up at Paddy. 'I've put your cereal out.' She pointed to a box of pressed high fibre that tasted like malted paper.

Paddy yearned for bed. 'I had something at Sean's, Mum.'

Trisha looked at her, barely suppressing a pang of fury. 'OK then, but you'll have tea.' She turned to the worktop and pulled off the knitted tea cosy, pouring two mugs of strong tea from the steel pot. 'And how was last night?'

'Oh, quiet,' said Paddy, watching the tea pour and hanging firmly on to the outside of the door frame, as if her mother's need for company would be strong enough to suck her into the kitchen. 'Missed the big stories again.'

'Did ye hear about this girl killed up in Bearsden? A lawyer, nice girl. A Protestant, but a nice girl. It was on the radio.'

Paddy smiled at her mother trying to show she wasn't a bigot. 'How do you know she was a Protestant, Mum? They hardly announced that, did they?'

Trisha poured milk into both cups of tea. 'Yes, Miss Smarty-Pants: they always mention it when someone's Catholic. Anyway, she lives in Bearsden and her name's Burnett.' She held out the mug to Paddy, just far enough beyond the reach of her fingertips so that she would have to step into the kitchen to take it. 'The news'll be on again in a minute.'

Paddy was being sucker-punched and she knew it. Trisha lifted the mug of strong hot tea a fraction, releasing a puff of comfort. Paddy could smell it at the door. She reached for it and no sooner had her fingers curled around the handle than Trisha pulled a chair out.

'Isn't Caroline down today?' Paddy only asked the question to upset her mother and they both knew it.

Usually Caroline would be in when Paddy arrived home late and it was ominous that her seat was empty. Baby Con had started school and Caroline came home most days. When she didn't get the two buses down to Eastfield it was always because of her husband: John'd either given her a sore face or he'd raised hell about the housework and she'd had to stay home and scrub.

'She called from the phone box. She's got too much to do today.' Trisha raised her mug to her mouth. 'Sit. Just give us your chat for a wee minute.'

Feeling small and unkind, Paddy sat down. 'Well, first we went to this car crash, but no one was hurt, and then we went over to the police station in Anderston.' She monologued as she knew her mother wanted, giving her the highlights of the night shift but skipping the visit to Bearsden.

Like all her women friends, Trisha's life was vicarious. Paddy heard them in the Cross Café and outside the chapel: they passed on second-hand stories about their kids' friends, got angry about fights their husbands had at work, boasted about their families' achievements, while they themselves stayed in the kitchen. With an unemployed husband and three of her kids sitting at home waiting for the recession to abate, Trisha had very little material. She couldn't talk honestly about Caroline's home life and Mary Ann spent all her time in the chapel. Marty and Gerard were mono-syllabic at the best of times. If Paddy didn't take the time Trisha wouldn't have anything to offer.

She was gibbering about last week's newspaper awards and JT's prize, when the news came on. The Bearsden murder was the first item. The police had attended a call at the house earlier in the evening. An inquiry was being called to investigate why the officers left Vhari Burnett in the house. Trisha was right: Vhari was from an aristocratic family, the villa had recently been left to her by a grand-father and she had only just moved in. She was an active member of Amnesty International and the Campaign for Nuclear Disarmament.

31

'There,' said Trisha. 'You should go and ask about her, get a story. Then they wouldn't be able to keep you back.'

In a paranoid morning of exaggerated despair, Paddy had confided in her mother her conviction that the editors hated her and wouldn't print any story she phoned in anyway, so it was all pointless. It was really just the tiredness talking but Trisha took it literally. Paddy suspected that Trisha had told some of her lady friends about it: she often asked about the conspiracy and suggested reporting the editors to the union. Paddy didn't know how to take back the allegation without making herself look foolish.

'It's political.' Trisha pointed at the radio. 'You wait and see. She knew something important and they killed her. You should question the folk she was in the CND with.'

'CND don't meet that often. Amnesty do, but everyone else'll think of it first. They'll be out this morning.'

'Well, go earlier then. Go today. Go just now.'

'I need to sleep, Mum.'

'Fine.' Trisha stood up and began to wash her mug without pouring the last bit of tea out.

Con smiled quietly into his mug. Paddy knew she was cheating her mother of a triumph. She finished her tea quickly and sloped upstairs to sleep.

4

Closing Credits

I

It was like watching the closing credits to an action movie. Every time Paddy came in to work on the night shift she had the feeling that anyone exciting and interesting was floating out of the door. Around the desks, people were gathering their coats and fag packets, turning off lights, looking relieved and happy that it was home time.

An air of damp disappointment clung to the night-shift workers. It was so all-pervasive they didn't even really want to associate with each other.

Paddy kept her flattering coat on as she walked across the floor to the blacked-out office door. The long copy-boy bench seemed very low to her now. When she first started at the paper she used to take her place on the bench and run her thumbnail along the grain of the wood, gouging little channels into the soft pulp, and imagine seeing the marks in the future, when she had reached the heights of a junior reporter and was remembering her former self. Seeing the marks now never gave her the buzz she had expected. They made her feel disappointed and despise her former naivety.

Behind the bench a glass cubicle had black Venetian blinds covering the windows and door, the plastic fading from a decade of being wiped with abrasive solutions, looking as if grey mould was creeping over it at the edges.

The paper's editor, Farquarson, had big hair. His pomade had worn off during a long day of head holding and his hair had risen like warm white dough. The skin below his eyes was very blue. He had his coat on and was pulling his office door shut just as she caught up with him.

'Boss, can I talk to you?'

'Not again, Meehan.'

'It's important. And personal.'

Reading her face and seeing that she wouldn't shut up and piss off, he opened the office door again and flicked on the light, dropping his briefcase and holding out his hand to invite her in.

The messy office charted a long day shift, from the cups abandoned during morning and afternoon editorial meetings to page plans scattered all over the floor. The bottom drawer of the filing cabinet next to the door was open and Paddy could see packets of sweets and boxes of biscuits in there. Murray Farquarson had the diet of a housefly: he survived exclusively on sugary foods and alcohol and yet was still rake thin. His hair had turned white over the past few years.

He followed her into the room and pulled the door shut behind them. He didn't bother walking around the long table that served as his desk but slumped against the electric-crackling Venetian blinds, keeping his tired eyes on her shoes.

'Quick.'

'I need a move.'

He rolled his eyes, 'For fucksake.'

'Boss, I'm going stone mad—'

Farquarson sagged against the blinds, each slouch articulated by the snap of unhappy plastic. 'That's neither important nor is it personal.'

'Please?'

He sighed at the floor, his head hanging heavily on his limp neck. She knew not to interrupt him. Eventually he spoke. 'Meehan, just keep your head down.' He lifted his tired eyes to her and she thought for a moment he was going to confess some awful personal secret. She flinched, blinked, and when her eyes opened again he was looking past her to the door. 'Keep on the shift for another wee while, OK, kiddo?'

And then another bizarre and frightening thing happened: he cupped her elbow and gave it a little squeeze. 'You'll be fine.'

In a crumple and snap of blinds he stood up straight and reached for the door. Paddy, rigid with alarm, stood as still as she could. He pulled the door open and the bottom of it hit her hard on the heel. She had to shuffle to the side to let him pass.

'It doesn't need to be a promotion . . .' she said.

'Yeah.' He rubbed his eyes. 'Bollocks anyway. There was a call from Partick Marine police station. They saw your para about the house call in Bearsden last night. Want you to go in, tell them what you saw. She was pretty, the dead girl. Can't you think of anything there you could write up? No obvious hook we could spin from?' Farquarson's bloodshot eyes were sympathetic for a moment, but it passed. 'You were the last person to see her alive, I think. Do me a hundred-word description – scene at the house, atmosphere, book-end it with facts. I want it before you go out in the car. Finish it by nine thirty and I'll tell the night desk to use it as an insert in the coverage. Anything else?'

She shook her head. If she was a male reporter who had come up with nothing from a scene like that Farquarson would have said she was fucking useless. A fucking waste of fucking space.

'Well, piss off and get it done then.'

She turned to go, bumping into Keck from the sports desk. He brushed past her dismissively, snorting at the miserable look in her eyes.

'Hoi,' Farquarson shouted, always looking for an excuse to tick him off. 'Mind your fucking manners in front of a fellow professional.'

Keck tried to make a face that would simultaneously convey mannerliness to Farquarson and superiority to Paddy, his face quivering between the two. Farquarson raised an eyebrow. Paddy nodded and backed out.

It was eight thirty in the evening, and she had an hour to write one hundred words. She went to the stationery cupboard and made a coffee, checked out the biscuit situation and chose two shortbread fingers that she meant to eat at the desk as she was writing. She found an empty typewriter at the end of the news desk and spooled in three sheets sandwiched around carbon paper.

Still wearing her coat, Paddy stared at the angry blank page, eating the buttery biscuits and sipping her coffee, sifting through the incident for what to put in and what to leave out. If she mentioned the fifty-quid note she'd have to hand it in to the police. They'd get the murderer anyway because Tam and Dan had seen him, and it didn't make sense to hand the note in and let it disappear in a police station when it could disappear into her mother's pocket and take the weight of worry from her for a while. But the story didn't make much sense without her and the police having a reason to leave the house. They had to believe the woman would have been safe, and the more Paddy thought about it the clearer it became: it was obvious she'd been in a lot of trouble.

Paddy felt a pang of anger at Vhari Burnett for retreating back into the living room, slipping out of the mirror, instead of pushing past the man at the door and walking away to freedom. It was the same anger she felt towards Caroline for staying, a bewildered furious pang, as if by passing up the chance to leave they were letting other women down, making men think it was all right to beat them.

Paddy took another sip of coffee and battered out the paragraph, re-reading it to see if the facts were as jarring as she expected. A woman covered in blood and everyone had left. Actually, depressingly, it read perfectly well.

II

Shug Grant was watching Paddy across the table, pulling on his leather. He was flanked by Tweedle-Dum and Tweedle-Dee, a couple of sideliners who always hung around newsroom bullies, sniggering at their jokes. All three were ready, jacketed and going for a drink, she could tell by the excitement in their eyes and the fingers jingling loose change in their pockets.

'You, Meehan, what fucking use are you?' Shug drawled at her. 'One para of copy for four nights in calls car? What, are ye driving round and round George Square with your eyes shut?'

Paddy shrugged, feigning good nature and letting it go. 'If it doesn't happen it doesn't happen.'

'You want to start making yourself useful, woman.' He licked his lips, pausing before the delivery of a cherished killer line. 'At least bend over and give us somewhere to put our pens.'

They sniggered at her, three malevolent sets of bared teeth, breath choked out of their throats in little forced puffs.

Paddy rose to her feet as the skin on her neck prickled and her lips curled into her teeth. 'The phrase is overworked, Shug. Been up all night practising that line, have ye?'

Dum and Dee shifted away when they saw the muscles on Shug's face tighten. He could see that Paddy was livid, mad with tiredness and had lost her sense of proportion.

'Did ye lie awake last night, Shug, staring down at your fat, ugly wife in the dark, wondering why your kids grew up to hate ye?' She was going at it too hard, hitting too low, but the fury warmed her. 'And ye don't have the guts to leave her or kill her so ye think what I'll do is, I'll go into work and pick on someone to make myself feel big.' She needed to calm down. The three men across the table were beyond uncomfortable: Tweedle-Dee stepped sideways out of the group and Tweedle-Dum was trying to shift behind Grant's shoulder. But she couldn't stop herself. 'Lying awake in the dark, hoping to glean a last shred of self-respect from the good regard of your peer group. Look at your peer group, Shug. Dum and Dee. That's your audience.'

As if from nowhere, George McVie appeared at her side. 'Enough now,' he muttered.

But she kept talking. 'You're a menopausal cliché. Margaret Mary said you're impotent.'

She heard a gasp from the sports desk behind her. Margaret Mary was a time-faded redhead who hung about the Press Bar and over the years had woken up next to almost every man in the office. She was famously indiscreet, but most morsels of information weren't passed on because every faction in the office had one member of the Margaret Mary club to protect.

McVie took Paddy's arm and guided her out from behind the chair to a corner. 'Shut it, you stupid cow. Don't act as petty and vicious as them.'

Dum and Dee shuffled out of the door to the news room. Shug Grant had more balls about him and lingered, complaining about his treatment to one of the photographers.

Despite it being the end of his shift McVie was wearing ironed clothes and a smart pair of shiny trousers. His clothes were always clean nowadays, in sharp contrast to his crumpled hang-dog face. Some of his outfits were veering close to fashionable: he had a grey leather bomber jacket that he sometimes wore with matching grey loafers with toggles. A few weeks ago he had been seen in the town carrying flowers.

He was going through something of a personal renaissance. Having languished on Paddy's calls-car shift for years he had finally found a story that got him moved. The death of a nineteen-year-old boy from heroin shocked the city and McVie had interviewed his mother before anyone else. He was so sympathetic that she allowed the *Daily News* to photograph her dying boy in hospital, as a lesson to other young people. McVie was now the drugs correspondent, a position that was becoming big news as cheap and plentiful class-A drugs, once the preserve of glamorous pop stars and Americans, flooded into Glasgow. 'You went too far there.'

'Sorry. I'm tired. I just asked Farquarson for a move and he touched my elbow. It kind of threw me.'

McVie looked surprised. 'Did he say anything?'

' "Keep going kiddo", something like that.'

'See,' he nodded seriously, 'sales took another drop, the board are looking for people to lay off and you're not handing in. There's only so much he can do.'

Everyone was nervous. Print workers no longer took constant tea breaks or called for strikes at the first sign of a dispute. The board and their new chairman were trying to make cuts and increase the slow decline in sales with promotional give-aways and competitions and constant demands to Farquarson to drop the highbrow nature of the paper and give them a sex scandal every so often. The chairman, nicknamed King Egg, had made his money in chickens before moving into publishing. He bought a couple of magazines first and discovered a flair for interfering. Having bought the *Scottish Daily News* he was holding her close, peering over her shoulder to the south of England, cutting his teeth on a Scottish paper before he moved on to a national.

'You never took me up on my invite,' said McVie. 'I've been expecting a visit to my new house.'

Paddy tried to think of something positive to say. 'Billy's boy has got a try-out for the Jags junior team next week.'

McVie and Billy had worked together for three years. They stopped talking after the first few months but over the years their genuine loathing had mellowed into a pantomime. Paddy knew they missed each other, and passed on information each way without making them ask for it.

McVie's face said he was impressed by Billy's boy. 'The Jags are shite.'

'Aye.' Paddy didn't want to get trapped in a football

conversation. 'I heard you were seen with flowers in the town.'

'So?' McVie looked suspicious, tilting his head back and looking down his nose at her. 'Who told you that?'

She did it back. 'Have you got a girlfriend?'

They had a momentary stand-off: she tried to read his face and he kept it blank, flaring his nostrils at the deception. She burst into a wonky smile and McVie got to 'Ha' in her face. His breath smelled of an expensive, slightly flowery breath-freshener.

Suddenly, gracelessly, JT slithered between them, staring at Paddy though his face was inches from hers, his eyes bright and shiny. 'All right, Paddy? How are you?'

JT hadn't managed a career as chief news reporter by being gracious or having manners. He was drawn to good stories, had an astute nose on him. Only last week he'd won the News Journalist of the Year award at an annual industry celebration that Paddy wasn't invited to. He never did anyone a favour if he could possibly get out of it. She had once seen him sit at a crowded table and eat an entire packet of Polo mints without offering one of them.

'What is it, JT?' She shoved her hands into her coat pockets and pulled them out as suddenly. The fifty-quid note was still in there, untouched since last night, crumpled in among the biscuit crumbs and bits of grey pocket fluff. She was waiting for a blistering fit of conscience to tell her what to do, hoping that if she waited long enough the police would catch the guy and she might not have to hand it in.

'Saw your in-brief this morning,' said JT. 'Did you and Billy stop there?'

'Aye, yeah, for a few minutes.'

'And the police walked away and left her with her killer in the house?'

Paddy shrugged.

'Why did they leave? Were they in a hurry? Were they called to something else?'

'Dunno.'

JT moved in close. 'See anything else?'

'Nothing. It was just a domestic.'

'But the woman was bleeding when the police were there?'

'Aye.' Paddy touched her mouth. 'I think she'd cut her lip or something.'

'Well, you're wrong. She had teeth pulled out all along one side of her jaw. Then they caved the back of her skull using a hammer. Left her for dead, but she wasn't. She managed to drag herself twenty foot in four hours, out to the front door. Trail of blood all the way through the house. Found her behind the door, curled up, like she was waiting.'

Paddy cringed. 'He took her teeth out?'

'Didn't you notice?'

'No, I didn't.'

Both McVie and JT looked at her, one gleeful, the other saddened by her incompetence.

JT slid out from between them, holding up a hand as though, regretfully, he would have to leave them alone, JT-less until the morning when his star would rise again.

She waited until he was gone. 'I did so notice the blood. I just didn't want to give anything away to him.'

But McVie wouldn't look at her. 'Guy's a dick,' he muttered.

5

Fucking Hell Almighty Fucking Shit God

I

Kate looked out between two rotting planks of wood. She could see the cottage from here, though the drop to the loch side was so steep that she was almost invisible. A stranger, someone who had never visited before, wouldn't know the boat house was part of the same property. She was chewing her tongue again, knowing she could gnaw it raw again if she kept it up. She stopped herself, stepping back from the rotting boards and opening her mouth wide, rolling her unnaturally pink tongue around in a wide circle.

A small yellow rowing boat hung high above the lapping water, tethered to the ceiling. The oars were fixed to the wall, everything where it should be, nothing changed in the two decades she had known it. She should sell the cottage, advertise it in *The Times* and sell it to a Londoner with bags of dough as a Highland retreat. She had only owned it for three months but the caretaker had handed in his notice and the property was already falling into disrepair. The garden was overgrown, the mint in the back had tumbled over everything else, choking all other vegetation as it crept towards the house.

She drank some more watery powdered milk out of the measuring jug and looked out through the crack again.

She had the tin of ham with her but no can-opener. Stupid. She needed a bath as well and hadn't even turned on the immersion heater before she had taken sudden stomach-churning fright and, grabbing what she could, run out of the cottage and come down here to hide. She had brought the jug of reconstituted milk. It tasted nasty but she drank it down like medicine for thirst. It was good but not what she needed. Even knowing that she was about to give in to her craving made her shoulders relax away from her ears and her face soften, her outlook calm.

She put the jug down carefully and took a flat silver box from her handbag. It had a secret compartment in the side and she stroked it with her thumb, reminding herself of all the good times. Looking around for somewhere to sit, she chose the big orange plastic box they kept the lifejackets in. She sat down, wiggling backwards one buttock at a time, imagining how pretty she looked while she did it. She smiled as she opened the box.

'Fucking hell almighty fucking shit god.'

It was all gone. Every grain. Even the corners were empty and she couldn't get in there with her spoon. She must have hoovered it up with a note. She didn't like that. The spoon was the mark of a lady. Sad addicts used notes. She tried to think who else had been there so that she could blame it on them, but she had been alone for days and days.

Angry and disappointed at her lapse in manners, she wiggled off the orange chest, the heels of her court shoes landing on the wooden deck with an emphatic clack-click. All sense of danger was lost now that she had promised herself relief and been denied it. She walked quickly along to the door and pulled it open without even listening for cars or people outside, her heart skipping a beat when she realized what she had done. She paused and heard nothing. The water lapped against the shore outside. Wind ruffled the trees. Stupid.

Hurrying and breathless, heart racing, Kate scuffled sideways down the steep incline to her car parked at the water's edge. She fitted the key in the boot and opened it in a single, graceful motion.

The bag of coke was as big and full and welcoming as a freshly plumped pillow. She smiled down at it.

Working carefully, her hands suddenly steady as a surgeon's, she unpeeled the tape from the top seam of the bag and dipped her snuff box into it, scooping, over-filling it so that the gritty powder spilled over the sides. She was being anxious and greedy about it. That was very sad addict. She poured a third of the powder back into the pillow and snapped the snuff box shut again, reapplying the tape to the open wound, smoothing the edges down. She couldn't stand the thought of the pillow coming open during a drive and her not knowing until it was all blowing out of the back and gone.

He had left a lot of tools in there, heavy-duty things for heavy work. She wondered what he needed such things for and why he needed to hide them in her car, before the familiar trapdoor shut in her head. He did a lot of odd things. Men who made money like he did couldn't go about explaining themselves all the time, silly girl. None of my business.

She shut the boot, holding her snuff box tightly as she tiptoed back up the muddy slope and along to the boat house. She sat the snuff box on the orange box and opened it, pulling the spoon out of the little compartment on the side, scooping a single portion for one nostril and breathing it in like powdered oxygen.

Her head rolled back on her slim neck, her eyes tickled. The first spoon took the edge off the world, restarted her heart so that she could hear it pounding and nothing else. The second spoon would give her the buzz and bring the noises and colours of the world alive again, but she lingered between the cold of the deep water and the ragged heat of the dry shore for a moment, thinking of nothing, remembering nothing, imagining herself nowhere but here, present in the moment and content to be there.

She didn't even need to open her eyes to fill the spoon again and find it with her nostril. The cocaine fired her up, making the blood too warm, lubricating it so that her brain slipped its moorings and slid sideways, crashing into the wall of her skull. She collapsed on to her side, her blonde hair fanning out around her head, her legs bent and to the side, perfectly parallel with one another in a symmetry she would have found pleasing. A trickle of dark blood ran from her left nostril, crossing a white cheek and disappearing into her yellow hair.

II

The sun had been down a long time and the night had plummeted into a bitter, bone-cracking cold. No one lingered in the streets or bared any part of themselves to the elements that wasn't essential for navigation. Orange-lit taxis were hunting for fares in the city centre, crawling past bus stops and slowing to tempt the few walkers. It was early evening and everyone in Glasgow had decided to stay indoors.

The station at Partick Marine would have been one of the stops they called at on their rounds anyway as they trawled all the city police stations for the latest stories, so Paddy told Billy to make it the first of the night. She didn't see why she should go and see the police on her own time. It was *News* business, anyway.

It occurred to her that they might want to talk to Billy as well – he'd been there, after all. If anyone had seen the money change hands it would be him.

'By the way,' she said, trying to be kind, hoping he would be if they asked him about it, 'I told McVie about young Willie and the Partick Thistle try-out.'

'Oh, right, yeah. What did he say?'

'Said the Jags are shite.'

Billy smiled fondly at the road and looked at her in the mirror. 'I like that.'

'I think he misses you.'

'Yeah, well, maybe we'll get engaged.'

They were travelling west, passing the gothic university perched high on the hill. They took Dumbarton Road, a broad thoroughfare that cut through the west of the city. At one point the fast road became Partick high street. Billy called it the shooting gallery because the pedestrians would throw themselves across the road, defying buses and cars. It was deserted tonight, the only bright light from a chip-shop window.

Billy pulled into a side street and drew up outside Partick Marine. The building looked like a mock-Georgian office block. The pale-blue door was wide and rounded at the top, with a row of matching windows to the left. On the right side of the door, a blank wall was topped by a stone balustrade interspersed with wild shrubs and stringy tufts of grass. Behind, visible only now because it was so dark in the street, tired yellow lights leaked from tiny barred windows.

The Marine was once the busiest police station in Glasgow. It was a base for policing the river back when Partick and next-door Anderston were stop-offs for fishermen from the North and the world community of sailors. Immigrants from the Highlands and Islands had settled in Partick. The older policemen tended to be from among them because, in the not-too-distant past, it had been an important skill for a Partick officer to be able to break up a fight between Gaelic-speaking sailors and immigrants.

Now the river had died and the Marine was separated from it by a motorway. The shipyards lay empty, rotting back into the river they had grown out of. The Partick Marine was a landlocked anomaly, a drunk tank for students from Glasgow university.

It looked quiet tonight. Lights from the tall arched windows glinted on the wet street.

Paddy opened her door. 'Come and get me if anything comes over the radio, eh?'

'Sure thing.'

Paddy held her leather coat closed against the rain and ran across

46

the deserted street to the door of the police station. She pushed it open and found herself in a noisy bacchanalian crowd of drunks in shiny suits and best dresses. She looked around, bewildered by the press of people waiting to be booked by the three uniformed officers working at the wooden front desk. Then she saw the carnations in the buttonholes.

She pushed her way to the front of the queue and caught the attention of Murdo McCloud, a neat white-haired man with a soft Highland accent. The rostrum he sat on night after night was a long wooden desk on a three-foot-high platform, built so that the officers could oversee the waiting room. Behind the desk the platform developed into a series of glassless windows. A corridor ran behind it that efficient ghosts scuttled along on their nightly journeys. On a quiet night Paddy could hear footsteps and wooden creaks in the waiting room.

'Good evening.'

'Miss Meehan, how are you this very fine evening?' He burred his 'r's in a way that made the tip of Paddy's tongue tingle.

'Is this someone's wedding?'

He nodded solemnly. 'The Curse of the Free Bar.'

Next to her a drunk man in grey pleated trousers, skinny leather tie and wedge haircut was swaying wildly in the arms of a small elderly woman, possibly his mother. She hoped it was his mother.

'Someone from this station phoned the paper and asked me to come in. It's about the thing in Bearsden.'

Murdo gave her a look, as if the home team were under attack, and stood up, opening the door into the corridor behind the desk. He leaned through, leaving his feet in the waiting room, and called to someone that she was here about the Bearsden Bird. The name sounded like a character from a children's TV show. Paddy had noticed an inverse relationship between the silliness of names and the brutality of the cases. 'The Razor Attacks' was a spate of knife fights between drunks in pubs which usually resulted in cuts to hands and fingers. 'The Bunhouse Guy' was a vicious rapist who operated in or around the waste ground on Bunhouse Lane and bit his victims until they bled.

Murdo came back to the desk and smiled at her, thumbing over his shoulder. 'In you go. Sullivan's waiting on you.'

Paddy took the steep steps up at the side of the desk, feeling as if she was climbing on to a stage, and walked through the door behind Murdo.

Behind the partition wall was a rickety wooden corridor running parallel to the desk. The walls had been painted white, giving a nautical impression. The black paint on the floor was peeling and chipped so that splinters of bare wood were visible below. There were three windowed doors in the facing wall. She guessed which one Murdo could have leaned into without leaving reception and, pushing it open, peered into a small office.

Down three steps, the small, grey office had a large window looking straight out on to a wet brick wall. At a desk in front of the window sat two men in loosened ties and shirtsleeves, smoking and staring perplexed at a form. They looked up when she came in.

'I'm Paddy Meehan.'

'Ah.' The younger man stood up, smoothing his short brown hair back with the flat of his hand. He had a blotchy skin and a square face, with hands and body to match. His partner was tall, white haired with sun-leathered brown skin. He had been slender once, before middle age. His frame was slim but odd pockets of fat sat on his chin, his belly and the tops of his legs. He still moved like a young man, leading with his hips as he stood up to greet her with his hand out.

'Here, sit down.' The younger man pointed at a chair on the other side of the table and the older man tipped his chair back, leaving the group, giving his colleague room to do the questioning.

Paddy sat down and shed her coat carefully over the back support. 'Paddy Meehan,' she repeated. She leaned across the table to shake hands, to make them introduce themselves and look her in the eye. It was a trick she had learned from long experience. No one would look her in the eye unless she made them: she was short and looked younger than her twenty-one years. She reached towards the older man first, making him right his chair.

'Gordon Sullivan,' he said, letting his eyes disengage from hers as soon as he could.

The geometric younger man held her gaze for longer. 'Andy Reid.'

'Pleased to meet you. I'm from the *Daily News*.'

Gordon Sullivan wasn't letting her tip the balance of power in her favour. 'We know where you're from.' He suppressed a smile. 'We told you to come in.'

Paddy suppressed a smile too. 'Just introducing myself, being polite. Having manners. You remember manners?'

He tilted his head. 'That was a sixties thing, wasn't it?'

''S that the last time you were civil?'

Reid watched Sullivan and Paddy playing, inexperienced and sensing, but not quite understanding, what was going on.

'Well, then,' Sullivan took over the questioning and Paddy liked to think it was because he was going to enjoy it, 'Miss Meehan. It is "Miss", is it?'

'No,' said Paddy. His eye flickered to her ring finger. 'It's "Ms".'

Sullivan laughed in her face. ' "Ms"?'

'Yeah. Are you married, Mr Sullivan?'

Sullivan had a paunch and an ill-defined chin but his white hair was thick and carefully coiffed into a late-Elvis bouff. He'd have been attractive in his day and she guessed that he was fond enough of the ladies to enjoy casting a veil over his status.

His mouth twitched a pout. 'So,' he said, 'your reputation goes before you. I know what you did on the Baby Brian case.'

She sighed and patted the table patiently.

Sullivan nodded heavily. 'I know, I'm just saying, you're not as

49

daft as ye, um . . .' Uncomfortable and a little lost, he flicked his finger up at her. 'Ye know. Anyway, so, you were at the Bearsden call? What did you see?'

She hesitated, knowing she should tell them about the fifty-quid note. 'I spoke to the guy at the door. Did Tam and Dan give you a good description?'

'Yeah, don't worry about that. Did you see the Burnett woman?'

'I saw her in the mirror. She had blood all over her neck, all down her shoulder. So she was found by someone who came to give her a lift to work? Was the door left open?'

Sullivan ignored the question. 'What else?'

Paddy thought back to the Bearsden driveway and the dark, remembered the rain on her face and the terrible coldness of the night.

'Lights were on in the hall. And in the room on the left, as I was facing the door. The room on the right was in darkness. The man had braces on and an expensive shirt. He was talking to Dan at the door, and Tam Gourlay was guarding the car, which I thought was funny because of the area.' She looked at them. They didn't find it funny at all. 'The man kept one hand behind his back, keeping the door closed, like he didn't want anyone to see in. I caught Vhari Burnett's eye in the mirror and I sort of went –' she raised her eyebrows. 'You know, like, "D'you want a hand?" She shook her head and kind of –' Paddy slipped her chin to her chest and sat back in the chair, miming Vhari slipping out of view. Neither policeman seemed interested in the minutiae of their interaction. 'I saw two BMWs parked there.'

Both men sat forward. Sullivan tapped the desk. 'Where?'

'Round the back. I came up the drive, passed the squad car and saw round the side. Tucked in behind the house. Where it's dark.'

'Are you sure it was two cars?'

'Certain.'

Sullivan took a sheet of paper out of a drawer and pushed it across the desk with a pencil. 'Could you draw them?'

She sketched the rough shape and he asked her about the details – how high off the ground was that one, this one, any idea of the licence-plate number? What made her notice them if they were tucked around the back?

'Aye, well, Tam was talking about them. He pointed to the cars and said how flash they were. That's why I thought Burnett and the man at the door were married, because of the matching cars.'

The officers glanced at each other and Andy Reid, not versed at hiding his feelings, raised an eyebrow.

'Wasn't it her car?' asked Paddy.

Reid shook his head, 'She'd hardly need a lift to work if she'd a BMW round the back, would she?'

Sullivan cleared his throat and watched his hands folding a sheet of paper as he spoke. 'There's going to be an inquiry into what the officers did at the house and why they left. You'll be called so you better, you know, be available.'

''K.' Paddy took a breath and looked around the desktop.

Now was the time to say it, but telling them about the fifty quid would be more than a confession; they would guess that Dan and Tam had been given money as well. Policemen stuck together like cooked spaghetti. Threatening one of them meant threatening all of them and she was already regarded suspiciously because of the Baby Brian case.

Paddy looked around the desk: two packets of cigarettes, a lighter, a form, two sheets of carbon paper and a small bald circle on the wood to the right of the form where a previous occupant had placed a hot cup and burned through the varnish. She could just blurt it out.

'You can go now.'

They waited for her to get up but she sat there, trying to think of a way to tell them.

'I said you can go.'

She took a breath and stood up. 'OK,' she said finally. 'See you later.'

Gordon Sullivan waited until she was at the door before calling goodbye.

Paddy Meehan stepped down from the front desk rostrum into the mess of the waiting room, knowing she had done a cowardly thing.

6

The Trick of Being Brave

I

Mark Thillingly stood in the dark shadows of the bridge watching the thick grey river slide past. He had never been in the river but had watched it from here so often that now, sitting here on the grass with the smell of damp soil in his nose, it felt like the times in his life when he had stayed away were silly pointless interludes. His father had brought him here when he was a boy. Their family firm of solicitors had offices in the building just behind him, and they came out here in the summer for picnic lunches. He'd brought Diana here just before they married, but she didn't really get it and he should have known then that it was a mistake to marry her. Poor Diana. She thought she was marrying the next leader of the Labour Party and instead she got fat Mark who killed his friends.

He was too tired to cry any more, bored by his own inadequacy and misery, too bored by grief to even allow that it mattered or could be remedied. He was not the man he had hoped he could be. He wasn't brave or selfless or strong. At the very last he had let Vhari down.

Up on the bridge a car sped past, trying to beat the lights and failing but running through just the same. It reminded him of himself in the car park outside work. When he realized they were going to hit him, when it became clear that they were definitely going to use violence, he had run for it in a mad panic, running for his car, stupidly running towards the thugs who had come to frighten him.

Mark flinched at the memory. He'd never been a brave man, not physically. At school he banded together with thick bully boys so they wouldn't pick on him, and despised himself for it. He avoided sport because he was afraid of physical pain, and even chose to follow his father into law when he wanted to teach, because he'd heard that some of the school kids were handy. It was a weakness he had tried to organize out of his life, that he was ashamed of, and now it had cost Vhari her life.

The admission horrified him afresh and he covered his mouth with his hand and sobbed. She was dead. Because of him. He heard what they had done to her, he'd called a contact in the police. There was blood all over one side of an armchair where the guy had held her down and pulled her teeth out with pliers. Then they'd hit her hand with a hammer, broken two fingers so that they were swollen to twice their normal size. She hadn't told them what they wanted so they hammered her head and left her to drag herself through the living room to the hall, blond hair smeared scarlet, leaving a long, bloody red smear through the familiar drawing room, past the dark wood archway to the Victorian hall and out towards the phone. Bit of bone in her brain. They couldn't have saved her if she'd managed to make the 999 call. The detective remembered then that Thillingly knew her. Didn't you work with Burnett or something? Years ago, said Thillingly, trying to keep it light.

He fumbled to pull a cigarette out of his packet, his cold hands clumsy and trembling. He lit it and dropped the lighter in the grass. He didn't need it any more. There would be no more cigarettes, no more large dinners or football matches on TV, no more fights with Diana, no more smiling through the disappointment he found himself, and God it was a relief.

Holding the cigarette between his teeth, he stood up and walked towards the river. A small muddy incline led to the waterside. He imagined himself stepping delicately toe-first, like a nymph going for a midnight dip, into the great grey slug of water. He'd chicken out if he tried to do it that way. Try and flap his way to the bank or call for help. He was a fucking coward. That's why he was here in the middle of the night.

Shutting his eyes to squeeze out a final tear, he backed off from the water and walked up to the bridge, looking to make sure he wasn't looking down at land. He was too close still: his body might spin and he'd land on the bank. He took five sideways steps, climbed up on to the railing, thought of Vhari wearing a summer dress and touching her hair, and toppled off the bridge.

He wasn't frightened as he fell. He knew the water would be piercingly cold, that he was dropping from high enough for the landing contact to break bones, but he convinced himself that he would land on a bed of cushions and his body relaxed into the drop, expecting softness. He fell happily.

A second before he hit the rush of greedy black water, Mark Thillingly realized that he had learned the trick of being brave.

7

The Sad Fate of the Late and the Lost

I

Kate awoke with a start. She had been dreaming that a giant insect was sitting on her throat, its hollow proboscis burrowing into the soft skin on her forehead, sucking out a blackhead that turned into a reservoir of pus. She woke up slapping at herself, her elbows rattling noisily against the wooden floor of the boat house, frightened and bewildered as to where she was and who had put her there. She sat up against the orange box, looking around in the near dark and realizing how cold it was. She was lucky not to have frozen to death in the damp. She could see her breath and had nothing on but a linen suit and a blouse. She was missing a shoe.

Her eyes adjusted to the light and she realized she was in her grandfather's boat house. Loch Lomond, for God's sake. She reached blindly up over her head, feeling on top of the box, and smiled as her hand felt the cold of the snuff box kissing her fingertips. But then she heard the engines and froze.

Two cars, quiet, good engines, good motion. Driving slowly along the road, looking, definitely looking for something. One set of wheels coming off the smooth black tarmac and crunching over the dirt drive in front of the cottage. Only one set, though. If it was them they'd both want to be off the road in case she was there, so that they would be less visible to passers-by. The second set of wheels crunched slowly in a turn. She stood up unsteadily, shedding her one shoe, and looked out of the crack again.

Two BMWs parked side by side. It was getting dark outside but she knew him from the shape of his head. She could have recognized him from part of an ear, a shoulder, a toe, because she'd spent so long watching him sleep and eat and make love. She remembered every corner of him. From the second car came two men, neds, one wearing a sheepskin. Cheap gangster look. He was letting himself down being seen with men like that. He didn't need to employ cheap-looking men. There had to be well-dressed gofers, surely.

He'd have laughed if he heard her say that. Once upon a time he'd have laughed, but maybe not now.

She had left the cottage door unlocked and they didn't knock, just pushed it open and walked in. She watched as the light went on in the hall, a bright-yellow light radiating out into the cold night. She should be sitting inside the door in her underwear, waiting to greet him.

She thought of the two men coming in through the door and giggled, imagining them embarrassed, overwhelmed by her sexiness. God, he'd say, you are stunning, and look at her with the shining-eyed, hungry admiration he'd had that night in Venice.

She looked fondly towards the cottage, thinking of him in there, looking for her. She almost went to him, but a small window of insight opened up in her coke-scrambled head and she remembered that Vhari was dead, murdered.

Kate watched the cottage through the boat-house window and wondered what she had done wrong. She stumbled noiselessly over to the orange box and opened her snuff box again, finding the spoon sitting inside, covered in powder, where it shouldn't have been. She helped herself to a half portion, a maintenance sniff. She was rubbing her nose when she started crying, because her nose stung so much and now she couldn't think straight or sort anything out.

II

Her luck had changed. Paddy could feel it as a vibration coming off the city, buzzing off the grey concrete and the wet tarmac. She sat in the back of the car, bright-eyed as each dramatic call came in: a fight between neighbours that ended with a stabbing, a motorway pile-up with two dead, and now a drowning. None of the stories were big or significant enough to be taken away and given to a better journalist. Her copy would be all over the paper.

They were cruising along empty roads to the south bank of the Clyde where a body had been seen floating in the fast-moving water. A cold mist began to descend on the midnight city, a stagnant exhalation that clung to the tops of passing cars. Yellow street lights jostling hard against the thickening dark.

Billy pulled up under an iron railway bridge and yanked on the handbrake, switching off the engine, anticipating a long wait. Paddy sat forward and together they looked across the road, beyond the marble handrail of Glasgow Bridge. They could see the tops of black police hats, all facing the river.

'Dead then,' said Billy, seeing no ambulance had rushed to the scene.

'Aye, another poor soul,' said Paddy, hoping it was an interesting story. 'God help us.'

Billy was watching her in the mirror, sceptical at her pretence of emotional engagement. He could see how excited she was by the course of the night. Paddy dropped her eyes, opened the car door and got out.

As she crossed the empty road droplets of cold mist burst on her warm skin, catching on her black woolly tights and darkening the toes of her boots. The swirling river cast up the smell of decay as she crossed the empty bridge to the high fence.

The riverbank was cut off from the street by a high Victorian railing, painted black and glistening wet. Through the fence she could see a crowd of black-coated policemen standing on the grass, looking down a gentle grassy slope, watching someone in the water.

A tall fence was necessary because beyond the inviting slope of green lawn the ground suddenly fell away into a black cliff. For ease of access, a little wooden stepladder was leaning against the railings and a wooden box had been placed on the far side. The railings would have been a steep climb, even for a super-fit policeman. Happily not all the policemen were super fit and they kept the small wooden stepladder hidden nearby. Paddy never found out where they stowed it. She climbed up the five steps now, swinging her legs over the spikes at the top and dropping down awkwardly on to the box on the other side, toppling on an ankle as she stepped off but righting herself before anyone noticed.

The dank fog was thick on the water, so close to the swilling surface that the far bank was hidden, back-lit and glowing yellow. At the foot of the cliff a lifejacketed man in a wooden rowing boat was prodding at something on the surface with a long pole. It looked like a submerged black balloon, bobbing in the fast-moving grey water, tugging the hook on the end of the pole, trying to free itself.

The boatman poked and prodded the object, moving it towards the riverbank. Employed by the Glasgow Benevolent Society to dredge the river for bodies, he patrolled every morning looking for unlucky drunks and suicides from the night before. It was a rare occasion when he was called out of his hours.

Paddy walked over and stood behind the policemen, watching the show on the river. The pack of policemen glanced back, noting that she was there but so used to her appearing at their backs that the storyteller holding their attention didn't bother to temper his chat.

'She'd her shirt over her head and he's standing there giving it ho ho,' he said and the others chuckled.

Paddy had seen the guy before. Every time she met him he seemed to be giving a command performance to a group, usually telling a long story that involved a woman taking her top off. He was funny; she'd laughed at a couple of his stories before and she'd meant to tell him about Dub and the comedy club.

She felt she should announce her arrival. 'What's the story here, then?'

'Ah, some guy dead in the water,' said the joker.

Paddy looked around at the empty street and heavy fog.

'How did anyone know?'

'A couple coming from a nightclub stopped at a phone box. They saw him splashing about.' He nodded over. 'Saw him from the bridge.'

'Take it to the bridge,' called a policeman, trying to mimic James Brown and failing. There was a small bleak pause.

'Aye, right enough,' said the funny one, smiling but not laughing.

The boatman had pinned the bobbing body to the bank and shouted up to them to come and get it out of the water.

'Ah, Christ,' said the joker. 'We'll be stinking of the fucking river for the rest of the shift.'

The river was swollen by the heavy rains and the steep cliff was only three foot deep. As they edged gingerly down to the water's edge Paddy stepped to the side to get a better view. She had never seen a drowning victim before. They were usually found during the day when her shift was finished. Teenagers and disorientated people favoured the river – jumping from a bridge was an impulsive act – but this body looked too big to be a young person. The black balloon bumped between the boat side and the riverbank.

The joker and the not-funny one grabbed the wet material with both hands, lifting on a count of three. They rose for a moment and then fell back as the weight of the body came out of the water. One more surge of effort and they pulled him on to the muddy bank.

The body rolled over on to its back and everyone recoiled at the sight. It was a man in his thirties, clean shaven, eyes open, the bridge of his nose burst open from a blunt hit. His cheek had burst, flesh blooming outwards like a meaty flower. The rip was so deep that Paddy could see flashes of his white jawbone. His ear was slack, hanging too low towards the back of his head. It turned her stomach and she was repelled, but found her eyes drawn to it, racing across the mess, doing a mental jigsaw, trying to make sense of it.

'What do you think?' The joker stood back and looked at the body. 'Someone put him in there or a suicide?'

The policemen closed in around the body.

A stocky policeman who hadn't spoken yet bent over the body and flicked at the messy tear with the blunt end of a biro, dropping the flap of skin back to where it should have been. The ear twisted like a door knob coming back to true.

'Yeah, something in the river got stuck in his face and ripped it open. The nose looks like a straight punch. I'm guessing suicide.'

Paddy didn't want to give away her fright so she focused on his eyes. They were open, staring blankly, black speckles of mud filigreed over from the drag up the cliff face. His skin was a terrible vibrant white, and when her eyes strayed back to the cheek again, the face resolved itself and she could make out a messy tear, now just a puffy black crease across the cheek. His nose was swollen between his eyes, the bulbous skin split in a thin crack. He'd lost a slip-on loafer shoe and a wet silk sock perfectly outlined his toes. A sharp big toenail was slicing against the material.

'That's enough,' said the stocky policeman, stepping back. 'I'll phone it in as a possible murder, just in case.' He pulled away from the crowd and made his way back to the car and the radio.

Paddy kept looking, memorizing the details for the piece in the paper. The man was in his thirties, a bit pudgy and self-conscious about it: she knew the tricks. He wore a vertically striped shirt under a long straight overcoat. Paddy could spot someone who hated their body across a room. The overcoat was straight cut with rolled-back cuffs and thin lapels, diagonal pockets. Under the coat his pale-grey trousers were pleated and baggy coming into a narrow ankle with a thin turn up.

The joker rifled through the man's pockets, pulling melted clumps of paper hankies out of one. He found the wallet in the inside pocket and flipped it open.

'Money not missing. Twenty quid in here. Lived in Mount Florida. Thirty-two years old.' He pulled cards and sodden paper out of the wallet, flipping them dismissively on to the ground after he read them. 'Visa card. Member of the Law Society. Chairman of the local Amnesty International chapter, and the Child Poverty Action Group. Our Mother Teresa's name is Mark Thillingly.'

'Maybe someone killed him for having a dick's name,' said the not-funny one but everyone laughed anyway, just for relief.

The boatman didn't laugh. Still sitting in his boat at the bottom of the cliff, he used a single oar to negotiate the water, remaining steady despite powerful eddies. Paddy caught his eye over the heads of the policemen. She could see that he hadn't lost his compassion for the people he dredged out of the water. He'd been doing the job for ten odd years and she knew his father had done it before him. If anyone needed a laugh for relief at the sad fate of the late and lost it was him.

'Thillingly,' repeated Not-funny, chuckling again and enjoying his triumph. 'And he was a lawyer.'

'I'll go, then.' The boatman raised a hand and the wooden rowing boat slid back into the bank of fog.

The policemen stared down at the body lying limp on the frozen ground, waiting until the boatman was out of earshot and hesitating because they were unsure when that would be. The joker spoke for everyone but Paddy.

'That guy's a creep.'

III

Kate had been watching through the dark wood for over an hour, listening to the noises of smashing glass and breaking furniture coming from the cottage. A lot of the furniture had been custom-made for the house in the late 1800s when it was built as a holiday home for her great-greats. The dresser in the kitchen was irreplaceable. She wouldn't get half as much for the place if they ripped it apart.

It was bad of him to do that when he didn't need to. She would hardly have stashed the pillow in the cottage and left on her own. It was bad of him not to know that.

Her eyes were getting tired, focusing through the bald trees on the cottage so far away. She'd seen them going back to the cars a couple of times to get things and assumed that was what the man in the sheepskin was doing when the yellow light from the hallway was interrupted by his big frame. He passed the car, not turning to the passenger door or the boot, but walking straight past, pausing at the side of the road to look up and down. He stood, turning his head slowly, scanning the wood for movement of any kind. Kate held her breath.

He spotted the boat house and stopped scanning. He stuck his head out and looked again. Crossing the road, walking lightly for such a big man, he held his arms out to steady himself as he tiptoed over the muddy ground, hesitating when he snapped sticks before taking the next step, always coming straight for her. She recoiled from the rotting wooden boards, feeling for the orange box lid and her snuff box. She needed to hide. She looked up at the boat hanging from the ceiling. She was slight but didn't think the ropes and ceiling would hold her. She tried the orange box lid, knowing it was kept locked, had always been kept locked and the key was in the cottage pantry, hanging up behind the cups.

She looked up at the oars on the wall but they were too

unwieldy. By the time she got a good swing he could have grabbed her arm. She picked up her one shoe, hugging it together with her snuff box, flattening her body against the wall behind the door.

She could hear him approaching through the sticky mud and wet mulching leaves. He was outside the door and had stopped to look around. He wouldn't be able to see her car from there but if he took ten steps north he'd see the bonnet and know she was there for sure and call the others.

He took a step – towards the boat house, she was sure – then another, definitely towards her. The round handle turned silently and slowly and after a moment the door swung open. He hesitated before stepping into the dark.

The wooden floor groaned beneath his weight and no wonder. He was a big, big man. Six foot to her five foot five, shoulders broad and sloping as a buffalo's. He stood with his feet apart looking away to the right, taking in the boat attached to the ceiling, the oars, the lip of floor that sat over the water. He stepped forward to look underneath it and Kate sensed that her only possible moment was now.

She lashed blindly at him with her court shoe, holding it by the sole and flicking the heel at him sideways. She might have tapped him on the shoulder with it but as it happened he turned to look to the left just as she attacked. The reinforced three-inch heel plunged through his eye and beyond to a thin wall of bone. The sensation was like punching a drum of paper with a pencil.

With the grace of a felled bull, the big man dropped to his knees, swayed and toppled to the side, twisting the shoe in the socket and shutting the door hard. His shoulder twitched in a shrug.

Kate opened her snuff box and took a trembling sniff right there, freestyle, standing in the damp dark of her grandfather's boat house, over the corpse of a dead stranger. Then, newly steadied, she pulled the shoe out of his eye and slipped it on her foot, dragging him away from the door and, opening it, stepped out into the wood.

She headed down to the car and found her other shoe by the boot, sitting in the mud as if an invisible one-legged woman was standing there. Shocked into an unfamiliar stoicism, she calmly fitted the shoe on her other foot and climbed into her car, backing out of the dark deep little valley on to the road in a smooth movement.

She left her lights off until she had safely passed the cottage and, unnoticed, headed back down the loch side to Glasgow.

8

Homeland of Tramps and Whores

I

It was two thirty in the morning and the streets were so quiet that they didn't need to stick close to the squad car to follow it. Paddy sat in the back, half listening to the radio. She couldn't believe the police had invited her to go with them at the start of a murder inquiry. Usually they kept journalists away from families they had to deliver bad news to, but, as they left the scene at the river, the not-funny policeman had spoken to someone over the radio and then suggested that she tag along. If she was interested.

It would be her first death knock. Calling on a bereaved family and trying to cajole or steal a photo of the loved one was the most soiling, horrible thing a junior journalist had to do. Grown-up growling journalists remembered their own early death knocks with a shudder.

'You're not going to annoy the wife, are you?' Billy asked from the front seat.

'I won't annoy her. It wasn't my idea. The police told me to come along.'

'They suggested you should come?'

'Yeah, it was their idea.'

Billy nodded, raised his eyebrows and fell quiet again. She could hear his reproach through the white noise of the radio: she should have been reluctant to do a death knock, should have been sent by a bastard editor who gave her no option, and anyway, decency commanded that she leave it for a couple of hours after a victim's family heard the news. She could see why McVie had lost patience with Billy and found him irritating.

They followed the squad car to Mount Florida and turned left into a wide curving road of large semi-detached houses, each with a garden at the front and bushes blocking the view from the road. The squad car they had been following pulled up behind another police car already parked at the kerb.

Billy pulled up behind the second squad car and turned to look at Paddy.

'I'm not going in to hassle the guy's family, Billy,' she said defensively. 'But if I need to I need to. It's my job. I can't refuse because it's a little bit rude.'

'It's not a *little* bit rude.'

At that moment the passenger door on the front squad car opened and she saw why the police had insisted she follow them. Tam Gourlay got out. He must have heard she was at the river from the radio calls and asked them to bring her. Tam walked over to the car, uniform jacket unbuttoned, hitching his trousers up by the belt. Without looking into the car for her, he knocked on her window, three harsh raps commanding her to get out.

Paddy opened the door and stepped out on to the pavement, leaning back into the cab,

'OK,' she said, hoping to give the impression of an ongoing conversation. 'Give me a shout if anything comes over the radio, Billy, eh?'

Billy nodded and looked bewildered. He would have called her back anyway but she wanted to emphasize that she wasn't alone. She shut the door.

Tam looked in the window at Billy leaning forward to the dashboard for his packet of cigarettes. 'Was he the driver from the other night as well?'

Paddy took Tam's elbow and pulled him away from the car, over to the dark shadows of a wet, dripping hedge.

'He's nothing to do with the likes of you, so just leave him alone.'

'Who is he, though?'

'Billy's been the *News* driver since Moses was a boy. Leave him out of it.'

Tam looked over at Billy, narrowing his eyes, trying to look scary.

Two officers got out of the second squad car: the not-funny one and another guy, but not the joker, who'd gone elsewhere.

A small 1930s cottage stood at the end of a long strip of garden. Paddy looked through the hedge as the two uniformed policemen tramped up a grey gravel path running diagonally across a busy bushy lawn, their heads hanging heavy with the awful weight of what they were about to do.

'Nice house,' she said, hoping that Tam being there was a co-incidence and she was still on for a story.

'The dead guy's a lawyer and comes from money. No kids.' Tam sounded bitter. 'Must be rolling in it.'

'Didn't kill himself over a debt then?'

Tam turned his attention to her. 'You saw Sullivan and Reid at the Marine. Heard you were talking about the motors.'

His tough-guy act was starting to grate.

'"Motors"? What d'ye mean by that? "Cars"? Is that what ye mean?'

Tam nodded, a little sheepish.

'Why didn't you tell them? Shouldn't we tell them everything to help them catch the animal that killed Burnett? Didn't they find him yet?'

He sneered down at her. 'Did you tell them *everything*?'

Beyond the hedge and over the lawn, Paddy heard a woman's voice cutting through the still night, rough with sleep, keening a desperate 'No.'

Tam was staring at her. The fleshy leaves on the hedge glistened behind his head and a drip of sticky dew dropped on to his shoulder like a gob of saliva.

'Tam, why did you tell them to bring me here?'

He looked over his shoulder. 'You keep your mouth shut,' he muttered, 'because we know as much about you as you do about us.'

Tam knew she had taken the money, and was implying there was more to know. But there wasn't. He couldn't possibly imagine how mundane and uneventful her life was. She grinned at the thought. Being threatened with exposure seemed unbearably funny and she laughed to herself, shaking and holding on to the tip of her nose to hide her mouth.

'You know about me?' She pushed past him. 'Tam, you're a fucking idiot.'

She climbed back into the car, glad to be away from him. Her hand was on the door handle, pulling it shut when she heard Tam quite clearly through the burr of the radio.

'We'll get you.'

II

Paddy stood in front of the electric kettle and watched droplets forming around the spout. A rush of steam followed, rattling the base and threatening to flood the fridge it was sitting on before turning itself off and calming down.

They should have arrested the good-looking guy from the door by now. Tam and Dan would have been able to give a good description, and she was sure Dan knew him.

She still had the fifty-quid note. She could hand it in to Sullivan, but he might not be discreet about it. If she insisted on getting the note back afterwards it might force him to keep it quiet. After all, the best way to keep a station load of police officers from lifting a note was not to tell them it was there. Policemen were famously light-fingered. She had read somewhere, in some newspaper she was poring over in the middle of some night, that at university the worst people for stealing books were divinity and law students. It was presented as a surprise fact but it made sense to her. They were closer to asking the why-not questions, after all.

She poured hot water on top of the coffee and milk. It was a pint mug, extra large. She'd brought it into the office and kept it hidden away in the stationery cupboard. She sat at a desk and took out all the well-thumbed editions of different newspapers from the day before, opening each to the Bearsden Bird story and spreading them out on the table next to her, promising herself a nice read once she had done the chore of typing up the copy about Thillingly.

No interesting details went into the story: not Thillingly's ripped cheek or his trendy coat or his tidy little house at the end of a lawn that must have swallowed up his weekends. All she had to tell his story was a dry four lines, barren of humanizing details. She could try to write it another way but dry was the house style and nothing else would get past the editors. It took her nearly half an hour to get the dull four lines down.

Carrying her copy, she padded across to Larry Grey Lips. Larry was reading a black-spined Penguin Classic and didn't look up as she approached across the cavernous newsroom. She waited at the end of his desk for a moment before exclaiming 'For fucksake' so loudly a man sleeping on a nearby desk stirred momentarily, lifting his heavy head and splitting puffy lids open to see what was going on. Without lifting his eyes from the page Larry pointed at the spike on the end of his desk. Paddy tutted, skewered the copy on it and walked away to make another pint of strong coffee.

The news room was the heart of the newspaper. A vast room with desks arranged into three sections: news, sport and features. Each section was a horseshoe arrangement of tables with big steel typewriters perched along the legs. Paddy had learned shorthand but was afraid to type well in front of anyone: it was hard enough

70

not to be taken for a secretary as it was. Rumour was that typing through three sheets and two carbons was a dying skill anyway. A new national daily was being set up in London using computers, editing on screen and sending it all down a phone line to be printed up off-site for a fraction of the cost.

At each section editors sat on the curve, giving out orders and chopping up the work or sending it back for rewrites. To the left of the room was Farquarson's office, behind the protective solid-oak copy-boy bench.

The room was quiet. The people sitting at the desks breathed in unison, like a sleeping pack. The worst hours on the night shift were between four and six, when time and space played tricks. Moments uncoiled into infinitely long pockets of waiting, and then, unexpectedly, a head-turn would take up three-quarters of an hour. There was rarely any real work to do, but the *News* still had to remain staffed in case the Queen Mother died or war broke out.

Red-eyed men wandered through the half-lit news room with newspapers and novels. Some of them turned lights off and had a pragmatic hour's sleep, slumped over desks so that the room became a hastily assembled dormitory. The snoring and soft light made it harder for everyone else to stay awake and it was common for the kippers to wake up to find their sandwiches eaten or Tippex in their hair. Ill-paced drunkenness caused the occasional fracas, when a man would throw things around and make grand statements of the I'm-leaving, those-bastards variety. The rest of the night shift understood the paranoiac need for an outburst and covered up kindly, getting the cleaners to pick up anything broken and saying nothing the next night when everyone assembled at their desks for another frolic in sleep deprivation.

Paddy blinked hard to soothe her burning eyes and took a long drink of milky coffee before beginning to read about the Bearsden Bird.

Vhari Burnett came from a lot of money. A vast fortune had been made in textiles way back and slowly frittered away by the following generations. The death of Burnett's grandfather three months ago had been expected to free up a lot of money. Instead it uncovered a huge hole in the family funds.

A file photo of the grandfather's funeral accompanied the story. A flurry of people in stiff black mourning clothes stood on the steps outside a small grim chapel, shaking hands with a gothic-faced minister. Vhari stood close to a young square-faced man. Her hair was much longer in the photo than when Paddy had met her and was curled into a horrible poodle perm that tumbled about on her head, pinned up here and puffed up there. Her face was hardly visible under the mess of it – just her sharp chin and slim neck were recognizable. She must have had all her hair cut off since the funeral. But she'd had a sleek bob when Paddy saw her and it would take longer than three months to grow a perm out. Maybe she'd had it straightened. A perm like that had to cost more than fifty quid and a good straightening job cost a fortune again.

Paddy had assumed that Vhari was someone's wife, a spoiled and cared-for princess who'd never have to save up and pay for her own driving lessons, a woman devoid of social conscience. But Vhari had studied law and worked at the Easterhouse Law Centre and later for the Fiscals Office as a prosecutor. Her political involvement and choice of job clashed with her big house and hairdo.

Paddy photocopied the picture of the funeral, folded it when the toner was dry and slipped it into her pocket. She was standing in the photocopy room, dizzy from the adhesive stench of toner that always hung there, when it came at her like a truck doing ninety: Burnett and Thillingly were both lawyers and both in Amnesty. They'd have known each other. And they had died within a day of each other.

III

It was busy at the Brigate. Everyone was going about their business, paying no attention to the crumpled lady sitting at the corner. She had leaves in her hair, and a trail of blood from her nostril to her hair line. The suit she was wearing was expensive but had seen better days and she was giving off a bizarre smell, like dirt and curry, as if she had been wearing the clothes for a week, sweating into them when she slept.

A fat waitress with corned-beef legs came to the table and took Kate's order without looking at her or reacting to her appearance. She tipped her head back a little as she wrote 1 $\times$ tea and 1 $\times$ egg roll in her order pad, stepping out of the field of the smell. But it wasn't the first time she'd done that. The Brigate was in that part of the city that belonged to people who were down on their luck. Tramps and whores and miscreants of all kinds gathered there, between the flea market and the morgue and the cheap cafés selling fish teas and pig feet. Since the Middle Ages it had been their bit of the city, an area where they could walk tall and not be stared at, a homeland for lost people. Kate had never been here before. She'd driven through it often on her way to other places, watched the safari through the window, fascinated but unmoved.

The ugly waitress brought her tea in a stained mug, dropping the plate with the egg roll on to the table so that it rattled as it spun to a stop.

Kate couldn't bring herself to eat it. She didn't belong here, she was sure of it. She'd tidy herself up in the loo and hang about for a bit, waste time reading the paper. Then she'd go to Archie's. Archie'd help her.

IV

Paddy dropped her head into her hands and rubbed her eyes. 'Please can I go? I haven't slept.'

She was back in the little grey office in Partick Marine, back with Sullivan and Reid, both of whom had the pink-faced freshness of men who had slept well and breakfasted. Behind them, out in the corridor, Paddy heard the noises of a busy police station firing up for the day. The wooden platform creaked as personnel scurried along it and the other desks in the room filled up with police officers coming from a morning meeting.

Reid and Sullivan nursed their mugs of tea and looked at the clear evidence bag sitting on the desk. The blood had dried on the fifty-quid note tucked inside it, creating a rusty residue which sat in the seam of the plastic. Paddy's attention was more drawn by the packet of digestive biscuits sitting next to it, the wrapper messily ripped up the side, scattering crumbs on to the paperwork. The tantalizing brown edge of a biscuit peeked out of the red packet, promising Paddy a logy carbohydrate euphoria. She wished she was alone with the packet.

'Why didn't you tell us last night?'

'I didn't know how to bring it up. I tried. I was hanging about at the door, d'ye remember?'

Sullivan glanced up at the doorway as if she might still be there and nodded softly.

Reid tried to take charge. 'How do we know that you didn't get this fifty from someone else?'

It was a preposterous suggestion but Paddy didn't want a fight, she just wanted to go home. She took a deep breath. 'I was reluctant to tell you because I don't want it to get out.'

She looked up at them but they averted their eyes. Sullivan suddenly straightened his straight tie and Reid watched him, studying his senior partner for tips on how to behave.

'Look, it'll get out eventually,' said Sullivan. 'There's going to be an inquiry into the call to the Bearsden Bird's house. They'll want to talk to you. No one can keep a secret in the police. You might want to tell your boss before he hears it from someone else.'

Paddy's stomach cramped at the thought of having to tell Farquarson what she had done.

'Let's go over this again,' said Reid. 'You still printed the story after taking the bribe?'

'Well, I didn't really take the bribe. The guy just put it in my hand and shut the door in my face. It's a lot of money.' She looked longingly at the fifty-quid note and then up at Reid, angry, as if he was trying to steal it from her. 'I want that back, by the way, especially if it's no use, and if you can't use it I want it back in jig time.'

'You'll get it back,' said Sullivan, blinking slowly as he spoke.

Paddy held a finger up to get his attention. 'Please don't think I don't mean that. I'll be phoning every day until that money is released into my hand. Where does the evidence get kept?'

'There's a constable upstairs,' he said. 'His job is to be the production keeper. He'll trace it coming in and out of the lab and keep it in a safe.'

'A constable? What does that mean? Someone who's nineteen?'

Sullivan looked offended. 'McDaid's fifty-five. A lot of the old constables never changed rank.'

'Can I ask him about getting the note back?'

Reid curled his lip. 'You want a fifty-quid note covered in some dead woman's blood. What are you going to spend it on? Make-up?'

Paddy felt a hot spark at the nape of her neck. 'I've got rent on a four-bedroom house to pay for my mother who's never owed anyone in her life, so no, I don't think it'll be getting spent on make-up.'

Sullivan pulled himself straight. 'I've got three brothers at Scott Lithgow, been there all their working lives.'

Scott Lithgow shipyard was about to shut and when it did thousands of workers knew there were no jobs waiting for them elsewhere. The dole money was so low it was effectively a life sentence. Mrs Thatcher had publicly insulted the workers and when a committee of wives travelled to London with a petition she'd refused to meet them. Nor would the deputy prime minister or the chancellor. The beleaguered women had gone to Number Ten Downing Street.

Sullivan was flushed and angry. 'The doorman wouldn't even take the petition through the door. What would it have cost him?'

It was unusual for a policeman to speak against the government. Sullivan smoothed his hair back. Paddy suspected he was regretting what he had said in front of Reid.

'Anyway,' Sullivan changed the tone, 'I'll give you the production number and you can call the lab about it, and the evidence room as well. Once it's in the evidence room there's a wee old guy in charge and he's the most trusted man on the force. You'll get it back, don't worry.'

Reid glanced nervously at him and took over. 'What made you come back?'

'I met Tam Gourlay and it reminded me.'

'Where did you meet him?'

'I was at the house of a drowning suicide in Mount Florida and ran into him.'

She looked straight at Sullivan, hoping they wouldn't press her further.

Sullivan tipped his head back. 'You ran into Tam Gourlay on the south side in the middle of the night?'

'Aye.'

'Tam who works the north and never goes south of the river?'

'Look.' She rubbed her eyes again. 'Can I go home? Or at least have another biscuit to keep me awake?'

She could feel Sullivan watching her, willing her to look at him. She didn't.

'I don't think biscuits keep you awake,' he said. 'But wire in, wee hen. We need to speak to someone.'

They left her sitting at the desk for ten minutes, alone with the biscuit packet. She had one digestive and then another. The sugar give her a little lift so she had another. The rhythmic chewing became hypnotic after a while and she stared at the desktop, eyes unfocused, munching and munching. Policemen came and went from the office. An officer at a desk across the room sniggered lasciviously down the phone. A young officer in Sta-prest grey slacks came and left some papers on each of the desks in turn.

When she came to she found she had eaten two-thirds of the packet. She brushed the crumb trail from the packet to her lap on to the floor and pulled the sides of the packet straight, to hide the meagre contents.

Sullivan and Reid came back carrying their jackets over their arms, smiling and nodding over at her as they snaked through the desks, licensed to be pleasant and friendly.

'So.' Sullivan's glance lingered on the erect packet for no more than a second and she knew he hadn't even noticed. 'Thanks for coming back in. We'll drive you home, but first we'll take the note upstairs. You can come with us if ye like, and meet McDaid.'

Paddy bounced to her feet and grinned. By the time Sullivan and Reid got back to their desks they would blame the missing biscuits on a greedy passer-by.

9

Colum McDaid

I

The station stairs were busy. Reid and Sullivan glanced back at Paddy periodically, checking she was behind them as they fought their way against the flow of officers coming down.

'So,' she said, 'have they found the guy who killed her yet?'

'Aye.' Sullivan turned back. 'They've got the guy, yeah.'

She felt a wash of relief. 'Brilliant. Is he in the cells here?'

Sullivan shook his head and beckoned her to follow him. The stairwell was painted like a close: thick green gloss to shoulder height and then white. Judging from the skid marks and the chunks out of the green, Paddy imagined the stairs had seen a lot of action and scuffles. The dark wood banister had been broken on the first landing and mended with a two-foot length of wood that was a bad colour match. Paddy touched it as she passed, her finger noting the bump in the join. She thought of one of Terry Patterson's articles about the torture techniques used by the Argentinian military. They threw unconscious political prisoners from helicopters into the sea so that the bodies would be found drowned and responsibility couldn't be traced back to the army. She had heard unprintable rumours that the British government were dropping blindfolded suspects out of helicopters in the North of Ireland. The helicopters were only five foot off the ground, but the accused didn't know that.

Sullivan dropped back to level with Paddy. 'The guy who murdered Burnett's dead. They pulled him out of the river last night.'

'Out of the river?'

'Aye.'

'Was his face burst?'

Sullivan stopped and looked down his nose suspiciously at her. 'Why?'

'The drowned man was identified as Mark Thillingly.' She dropped her voice to a mutter. 'Sullivan, I saw the guy at the door: it wasn't him.'

Glancing at Reid, Sullivan nudged her to fall back out of earshot. 'But he knew Burnett – knew her well. They went out together, grew up near each other. They were engaged.'

'I can only tell you what I saw,' she whispered. 'Even with the ripped face, I'm sure he wasn't the guy who answered the door. That guy had her blood on his neck.'

'It can't just be coincidence, though, him dead within twenty-four hours of her murder.'

Paddy nodded. 'It might not be a coincidence, but it still wasn't him at the door.'

Sullivan sighed through his nose. 'If I could get you in for another look at Thillingly, would you come?'

'Aye.'

Reid stopped and looked back at the two of them ten steps behind him on the final flight of steps. '. . .'s a welder, apprenticed since he was a boy,' said Sullivan, hurrying her to catch up with his partner. 'And there's no work anywhere. Man, he's got no chance of another job if the yard does shut.'

Paddy caught the thread of the lie quickly. 'They're just wicked bastards, I know. They're goading the coal miners into a summer strike as well, loading up stocks of coal so they can ride it out. It'll be a disaster for the miners if they fall for it.'

'You two and your politics,' said Reid indulgently. He led them along a corridor with a low ceiling and windows set deep into the wall.

They stopped at a door and Reid nodded a jaunty little rhythm, glancing at Sullivan and smiling, anticipating the answer. They heard it as a cheery call from far away,

'Hello out there?' A man's voice, a Highland accent like Murdo McCloud's, in a high register with burrs and wide-mouthed vowels.

Reid opened the door into a small attic office. The back of the room was walled in with padlocked chicken wire, fencing in two grey filing cabinets and an open set of shelves. A large blue steel safe stood next to the plump, white-haired man sitting at a desk. His eyes were warm and kindly, Santa Claus in a police uniform.

The room was warmer than the rest of the station, pleasantly so, and smelled of polished leather and tea. On the desk was a blue teacup in its saucer with a small matching plate of gingersnaps at the side. He was holding one to his mouth, a crescent bitten out of it already.

'Oh, no,' he said, looking crestfallen. 'I'm just having my tea. Can you not come back later?'

Sullivan held up the plastic bag with the fifty-quid note in it. 'Important production. Needs to be filed right away. You can drink your tea in a minute.'

PC Santa dropped his biscuit hand to the desk, rolling his eyes theatrically and pretending to be very angry. 'I'll have to make another cup and start all over again. Who is this fine young lady?'

As if remembering that she was there, Reid and Sullivan parted and looked at Paddy with renewed interest to see if she was either fine or a lady. Uncomfortable at the assessment, Paddy took the initiative, stepping across the floor and holding her hand out. 'Delighted to meet a man who takes tea and biscuits seriously. I'm Paddy Meehan.'

The constable stood to meet her hand and shook it firmly once. 'Ah, *Meehan*. Now, what county would your people be from?'

Normally suggesting that someone with an Irish name wasn't Scottish would be tantamount to hinting at repatriation, but Highlanders were as obsessed with their ancestry as the Irish.

'Donegal, I believe, around Letterkenny.'

'Not Derry?'

He was right. She was surprised and smiled. 'Aye, the Meehans tend to be from there but ours were from Donegal.'

'And you didn't go to New York with the rest of them?'

Paddy's jaw dropped. 'How would you know that?' Con's glamorous cousin lived in New York, in the Bronx, where the cheers came from. The family talked about them as if they were movie stars.

He winked. 'Lucky guess, actually. I'm a McDaid.' He shook her hand once more and let go. 'Colum McDaid.'

He was letting her know he was Catholic too. A lot of the Western Islanders were, having never converted during or after the Reformation. Paddy was ashamed that she cared which religion he was or that it instantly made her trust him more. She was barely Catholic herself.

He sat back down and looked at the two policemen. 'Now, what's important enough to interrupt my tea, you godless pair?'

Reid chortled and put the plastic bag on the table, prompting Colum McDaid to put his tea aside and open a drawer next to him, pulling out a large, black leather-bound book. Half the pages were rumpled and crisp from having been written on, with the facing pages flat and new. From the shallow drawer above he took out a thin ring-bind folder and opened it to a page of stickers. Seven-digit numbers were penned carefully in a tiny script above the empty spaces where white labels had been peeled off.

Colum McDaid opened the leather book. A margin and columns had been drawn in using a ruler and a red biro. A third of the page was filled in, again in tiny perfect writing. Paddy couldn't read it upside-down but she could just about make sense of it. Each row had a paragraph of jagged capitals describing an item, next to an entry for the case number, the location, a policeman's name and rank, a date and, finally, a seven-digit number to match the sticky labels.

Sullivan leaned forward and placed a note on the end of the desk. It was a scrap of paper torn from a ruled jotter with a seven-digit case number on it. McDaid read and understood it immediately.

'Bearsden?' he asked.

Sullivan nodded. 'Miss Meehan's very worried about getting her fifty-quid note back.'

McDaid looked at her and poked the bag with his finger. 'So this is yours?'

'Aye.'

'Well, you'll certainly get it back but it might take a wee while. Depends on how important it turns out to be to the case. Rest assured, though: this production will be escorted by me to the laboratory and back, and the rest of the time,' he pointed to the blue safe behind his desk, 'she'll be keeping warm in there. And I'll be sitting here watching everyone who comes in.'

'No one else can get in?'

'Not a soul. Top of the police station, manned twenty-four hours.' He patted the safe door. 'And you'd need a lorry-load of dynamite to open this door.'

'Can I phone you every so often to find out where it is?'

'Miss Meehan, I shall eagerly anticipate your call.'

II

Paddy sat in the back of the police car and tried to imagine how angry Farquarson would be when she told him about the fifty quid. She'd tell him when he was tired – when she got in tonight it would be the end of his shift. She'd seen his blistering morning attacks, when he was full of sugary coffee and vim and hadn't yet blunted his temper at the morning editorial. She never wanted to witness it again, much less be the focus of it.

'Here?' Sullivan was cruising up the Cambuslang Road, watching out of the corner of his eye as the house values progressively declined, finally tumbling into a black hole.

'No, it's on a wee bit yet. Go right here,' said Paddy. They took the lights and headed up the hill. 'And first left here.'

Paddy used to feel proud when people from work dropped her home, but not any more.

The Eastfield Star was a small estate on the edge of the countryside. The central roundabout was broad and the houses on the radiating streets were cottage-style, some four to a block, some detached houses for bigger families like her own. The estate had been built for a colony of miners, but the Cambuslang seams were thin and the mines had shut down long ago. Residents were council tenants and workers in heavy industry, the very sector that had been decimated in the recent recession.

An atmosphere of despair hung over the small housing scheme. Stick fences hung drunkenly on rusted wires and the grass and bushes on the roundabout were full of litter. Kids from the scheme further up the road had scarred the gable-ends of houses and garages with messy graffiti supporting splinter factions of the Irish troubles. The porridgy protective coating the council gave the houses was due to be renewed and had weathered badly, flaking off in big patches and exposing the weak brickwork underneath.

Mr Anderston, the gardener on the roundabout, had died of a heart attack in his kitchen. He had been replaced by a family of drinkers who fought loudly with each other in the street and attacked anyone who asked them to keep it down. For the first time in their lives Paddy's parents were afraid of their neighbours.

The only person on the street this morning was Old Ida Breslin. She was standing in the long wild grass in Mrs Mahon's front garden as they approached, wearing a child's green parka with the hood up, looking at something on the ground. They couldn't see her face past the furry rim but Paddy prayed that she had her teeth in. When Ida heard the noise of the approaching car she turned, still as a startled gazelle, her tongue running along her collapsed lips.

'Here.' Paddy let Sullivan glide past Quarry Road. 'You can just stop here.'

He looked out at Ida and Mrs Mahon's pink nylon curtains. 'Is this your house?'

'Um, no, not really.' She didn't want them to go past her own house; stray vegetation and long grass had overrun the front garden and their gate was held shut with a rusting bit of wire hanger.

'Well, which one is yours then?'

She realized that Sullivan wasn't driving her home to be polite; he was there to see where she lived, so that they could keep tabs on her. He turned back to look at her. 'You live here?'

'Aye.' She glanced out of the window to the hillside overlooking the estate. A stolen car had been abandoned and set on fire. Lazy smoke crept out of smashed windows while the bonnet smouldered.

'For goodness' sake.' Paddy tutted as if it was a misplaced tablemat. 'Who put that there?'

III

The clock said four and it was dark outside. Paddy sat up with a start, thinking for a moment that it was four a.m. and she'd been asleep at work. She swung her legs over the side of the bed and stood up before her legs were awake, staggering off to the side, and heard a giggle from her sister's bed. Mary Ann was sitting in the dark, holding a set of plastic pearl rosary beads. She watched Paddy stagger back to the bed and kneel on it before carrying on with her prayers.

'It's a bit dark, isn't it?'

Mary Ann smiled as her fingers automatically clicked on to the next bead.

Unreasonably angered at the sight, Paddy climbed across the beds and took hold of her sister's feet, lifting them up and down and whistling, 'Strangers In The Night' because their granny told them that when nice girls whistled Our Lady cried. Her sister smiled a little, looked down at her rosary beads and carried on.

Paddy bounced to a stop on the bed and watched her sister repeating the ancient prayers by rote. 'Don't shut your eyes, Mary Ann, look up.'

But Mary Ann ignored her.

Since they were children Trisha had prayed every night that one of them would find a vocation and join a religious order. She'd set her heart on her eldest son Marty being a priest, but Marty wasn't very nice or religiously inclined, and Gerald wasn't smart enough.

Mary Ann's side of the bedroom didn't have posters of heart-throbs any more and the chest of drawers at the end of her bed no longer had make-up on it, but holy books and novenas. It started when Pope John Paul II gave a Mass at Bellahouston Park. Even Paddy was impressed by the spectacle and the pomp. They were an immigrant minority and the generation of young people at the open-air Mass had grown up ashamed of their primitive Catholicism. But John Paul II dignified religious defiance. He had remained Catholic under a brutal communist regime, openly pro-claiming himself and ministering to anyone courageous enough to follow him. Young Catholic Scotland suddenly rewrote the mean-ing of their journey and felt proud that they had kept the faith despite being denied work and houses and being marched against by the Orange Order.

When the Pope took the stage they stood shoulder to shoulder with two hundred thousand fellow faithful, the hot June sun warm-ing their backs, applauding until their hands were scorched, clapping themselves as much as their priest.

Paddy went on the parish bus to please her mum but drifted off as soon as she could, standing at the back with the loose crowd of sceptics. She felt something in the summer air: a power, maybe, the energy of conviction. The thrill caught the back of even her unbelieving throat. She could share in the pride of her people even if she didn't share their faith. She never went to Mass any more, but did her parents the courtesy of pretending she might by always being out on Saturday evenings during the hour of the teatime Mass when the Sunday obligation could be fulfilled.

Mary Ann left the park deeply changed. She became a devout daily communicant and spent her days praying at home or passively engaged in the business of the Church. She had tried the Charismatic Renewal, a highly emotive movement within the Church that invited the Holy Spirit to manifest itself by making people behave in faintly ridiculous ways, like falling over, talking rubbish or crying in public, but she was too giggly and shy for it.

A priest with a twitch at St Columkille's was trying to get Mary Ann a place at Taizé, an ecumenical camp for young Christians, so she could try out the religious life and see how it suited her.

Paddy stood in the dim light at the end of the bed, watching Mary Ann's lips tremble in the dark as her fingers found their mark on the row of beads. The light seemed to leave the room as she looked at her. She loved Mary Ann more than anyone alive and she didn't want her life to consist of prayers in grey halls or being nice to people in trouble, an awful, humble half-life. She wanted Mary Ann to have great dangerous adventures in wild sunshine, trips to America, a passionate love affair that ended in tears on a bridge in Paris.

Mary Ann bowed her head to the grey beads, her fingers moving on to the next obligation. The toilet out on the landing flushed and their mother's soft step padded back downstairs to the kitchen.

'I wish you wouldn't,' Paddy said.

'Leave me alone, Paddy,' Mary Ann answered quietly. 'I let you be how you are.'

Paddy stepped down from the bed and snapped on the light,

pulling her nightie over her head, walking bare-breasted to the chair, facing into the room as she pulled her jumper and trousers on. Mary Ann ignored her. Paddy shuffled past the tightly fitted beds and sidled past the wardrobe blocking the door, sliding into the hallway and down the stairs.

10

The Brigate Morgue

I

The house was full: Trisha was scrubbing the oven angrily, sweating and flushed but pretending she wasn't. The boys were slumped in the living room, watching television.

Paddy made a plate of toast, took a mug of tea from the ever-full pot and picked up the *Daily News* she had brought home with her. Out in the hallway she sat the plate and mug on the stairs as she pulled on her outdoor shoes, a pair of gloves and a coat. She opened the front door and walked down the path. A lone car parked at the end of the street made her stop.

It was a red Ford Capri, quite new and very clean, the roof glinting from a recent wax. She couldn't say why it caught her attention, other than that she'd never seen it before. The Eastfield Star was a dead end; it wasn't a place drivers passed through by mistake. She shivered lightly and stopped herself. She had been followed by a van during the Callum Ogilvy case and strange cars still frightened her sometimes, when she thought she'd seen them before or suspected the drivers of looking at her. It was the private space that scared her, the dark five-foot-square inside where passers-by wouldn't interrupt a man beating a woman to death.

As she looked she saw a shadow shifting in the Capri. The engine suddenly fired to life, headlights coming on as the car hurried backwards, reversing left and then shooting forwards, taking the roundabout the wrong way.

Paddy stood on the path and watched the car drive away. It had left because she'd seen it, she knew it had. It wouldn't be a burglar – there was no money here. It might be Sullivan, sitting in his own car: he'd insisted on dropping her home, after all, and knew where she stayed.

Worrying about it and wondering if she was right to, she crossed the garden and lifted the key out from under a brick, unlocking the garage side door and opening it, stirring up the musky smell of rotting paper. A damp fug hung in the air.

She knew before she flicked the light on that the neighbours hadn't been to take their stuff out. The pile of rotting cardboard boxes by the door made her feel a lethargic spark of annoyance.

She lifted the plate of buttery toast off her mug, sat it among the pencils and pens lying on the wooden box by the damp armchair and fell into the seat, pulling the wooden shelf that fitted across the arms. She put her toast and tea on it and began to eat, looking around the room.

She had set the garage up as a study, to finally get down to writing her book about Patrick Meehan's wrongful conviction. She kept every scene of his story in her head, from the night the old lady was battered to death in Ayr to his release on a Royal Pardon. She even knew the details of his time in Communist East Germany as a young man, his trip to Moscow, and his family life and his background.

It should have been an easy book to write, but at first she couldn't get going because the garage was too cold.

Her father had found a wood burner on one of his long walks around the old industrial wastelands. He fitted it on a slab of concrete and fed a snake of aluminium tubing out of the window for a chimney.

Then she was uncomfortable in the wooden chair. Con found

her an old armchair and made her a wooden shelf that sat over the arms for a table.

Having resolved the major impediments to writing the book, she sat there afternoon after afternoon, winter light dying outside the small window, surrounded by research and fresh stationery lifted from work, still as a corpse, alone with her own resounding shortcomings. She spent a lot of time there, wishing she could write the book, but the pet project had turned into a monster. It felt like trying to swallow an elephant in a gulp.

Paddy chewed her toast and knew that today would be no more productive than all the other days past. She tried to fire her interest by imagining Meehan in an interesting scene from his life: his interview with MI5 in West Berlin, when he explained his brilliant method of springing spies from British prisons; the riot outside Ayr High Court when he was brought there to be charged with murder; the afternoon in grey Peterhead Prison when he broke the seal on the vellum letter that contained his Royal Pardon. Still, flat images all. The characters in her mind struck cardboard poses: no one moved or spoke. If she couldn't write this she couldn't write anything.

Her dejected eyes strayed to the copy of the *Daily News* she'd dropped on the floor next to her. She lifted it on to the table. The Bearsden Bird was on the front page again. This time they were poring over her family history and had printed a picture of her old school. She'd been engaged once, to Mark Thillingly, but was single now.

Paddy considered the engineering feat of pulling the teeth out of someone who was wide awake and not consenting. It would take two people: one to hold her and the other one to pull. That would explain the two cars parked around the back of the house. He must have already pulled one or two teeth out by the time Paddy spoke to him at the door. Vhari must have been in agony.

Paddy saw her face in the mirror again, sliding back into the living room. Vhari could have walked away. She could have pushed past the man at the door and climbed into a safe police car. Women stayed with men who hit them, she knew that. Leaving a husband was much more complicated than picking up a coat and leaving. But the man wasn't Vhari's husband. His name didn't seem to have come up in the police investigation yet so he probably wasn't even her boyfriend. She must have had a good reason for staying.

The police were useless. Neither Dan nor Tam was admitting that Mark Thillingly wasn't the man at the door, and they weren't talking about the BMWs parked around the back either. They had taken money and they knew the guy, she felt sure they did.

She was sitting back, wondering, when her eye fell on a page-two story. There was a picture of Patrick Meehan in a small living room, grinning bitterly and holding up a letter. His skin had a heavy smoker's yellow tinge, dying from the outside in. The criminal injuries board had paid him a lump sum of compensation for his wrongful conviction. Meehan said he was accepting the money because he owed a lot of people and wanted to do the right thing by them, but fifty thousand pounds wasn't enough.

He didn't look anything like the one-dimensional Meehan in her weak imagination. She looked at his watery eyes and saw traces of bitterness, impotent anger, a tinge of self-disgust. She had heard gossip about the damage the case had done to his children. He was holding the letter too tightly: his fingernails were white at the tips. He must have been holding it for a while; the photographer probably had trouble with his lights.

Meehan had always been part of her life but he had never seemed like a real person before.

II

Paddy hesitated at the mouth of the dark cobbled alleyway. Brigate lanes could be used for a lot of things, and being mugged for her monthly Transcard, the only thing of value she owned, was the least of her worries. A few of the lanes had mattresses in them, put there by forward-thinking prostitutes who still had the sense to attend to their own comfort.

She took a step into the lane and felt herself swallowed by the darkness. She could smell a wet mattress on the cobbles and imagined the sickly scent of formaldehyde. Cardboard melted slowly into the stone. It smelled like the neighbours' debris in her garage.

She was ten yards into the inky dark when she saw his shadow. Sullivan was waiting for her at the side door to the morgue, just as he said he would be. He had asked her to come at about six thirty or quarter to seven. He couldn't say it but she understood the implication: police shifts changed at that time and most officers would be getting briefed for their shifts; they wouldn't be coming past the morgue on routine business.

Sullivan nodded at her and kicked his heel back, pushing the usually locked door open into the bright white-tiled corridor. Paddy shut the door behind her.

Wordlessly he led the way along the corridor. Glassy Victorian tiles covered the walls and floor. The overhead striplights glinted yellow off the glaze. She could smell bleach.

'Thanks for coming,' he said. 'I'd appreciate it if you didn't mention this wee visit.'

'You're sticking your neck out here, aren't you?'

Sullivan shrugged, reluctant to voice his suspicions. Paddy touched his back, telling him to lead on, that she would follow. He was a brave man.

They came through a reception area with a vacant desk, a grey school cardigan slung over the back of the office chair. Behind stood a stack of oak boxes of index cards, each fronted by a letter of the alphabet written in gothic script. Sullivan stopped at a set of double oak doors and looked back at Paddy.

'You been in here before?'

'No.'

He didn't offer her words of comfort or warning and she appreciated it. He took a deep breath, rolling his finger to warn her to do the same, and then pushed the door open.

The sharp compost smell was tempered by the cold, but not enough. Across the tiled floor, a cold steel wall of big drawers splintered the overhead light, and standing in front of it was a man in a white coat, facing the door expectantly. He was young but bearded, his moustache grown down over his top lip, wet at the tips. He smiled shyly, trying to be welcoming, but his teeth were stained and broken. Sullivan looked away and Paddy saw the sadness in the man's eyes.

'All right, Keano? Here's the wee lady I was telling ye about.'

Shamed, Keano pressed his lips together and nodded at Paddy. 'Don't get many birds in here.' He tapped a fingernail against the metal drawer behind him. 'Don't mean in *here*. Birds die just the same as us, eh?' He looked to Sullivan for confirmation that women couldn't cheat death.

'Oh, aye, they die just the same.'

Keano cringed, aware that he sounded stupid. 'Die just the same.'

They were looking at Paddy, expecting a response. She gave Keano an unthreatening smile. 'Good,' she said, wanting it to be all right for him.

Sullivan leaned in confidentially. 'Is our guy handy then?'

Keano took two steps across the steel wall and took hold of a handle. The drawer slid open easily, a narrow seven-foot-long tray. Mark Thillingly's corpse was wrapped tight in a crisp white linen sheet, patches of the material translucent where water had dampened it. The earthy smell of river water rose as soft as mist.

Keano flipped the sheet open left and right. Thillingly was naked, his skin waxy and luminous. Paddy tried not to look further down than the nipples but she could see Keano's hand reach out and pull the sheet back over the genitals.

A raw T-incision across the chest and stomach had been sewn back up with big stitches and thick thread. The rip on his cheek had been sewn more carefully, but still puckered around the heavy thread. Thillingly was fat. Paddy looked at his sagging stomach and slight breasts and felt for him, imagined all the times he had avoided taking his top off in front of others; how, like her, he must have dreaded hot weather and avoided going swimming.

She knew one thing for sure: he wasn't the man at Vhari Burnett's front door on the night of the murder. She looked up to speak but Sullivan was shaking his head softly.

'Keano, my man,' he said cheerfully, stepping away from the tray. 'Thanks, pal.'

'You owe me a drink then, eh?' Keano forgot himself and grinned again.

'Sure do.' Sullivan backed off out of the room, taking Paddy with him. 'Sure do, my man.'

'Aye.' Keano watched them leave. 'We don't get many women visiting, is what I mean.'

'Right enough,' called Paddy as the door swung shut behind them. 'Sullivan, that's not him.'

'OK.' It wasn't what he wanted to hear.

She tried not to sound excited. 'This is a big story. This is going to be massive.'

'OK.' He led her further down the corridor and when he turned back she could see how troubled he was. No policeman wanted to take a stand against another. 'The board of inquiry into the Burnett call are meeting next week. They're calling witnesses. You'll get a letter but they've got you pencilled in for Tuesday afternoon. You'll have to tell them about the fifty quid then. I can't guarantee word won't get out after that.' He was reminding her that she had a lot to lose too.

'Fair enough. I'm going to need this story then. I'll wait for it, but I really need it.'

Sullivan nodded. 'Pet, if the story is what I think it is, I'm going to need you. Do you know what I mean?'

They looked at each other: neither of them favoured by colleagues, both in need of a boost and someone at their back.

'Hundred per cent.'

II

It was still dark outside the car but Kate had been awake for ten minutes. She smoked a breakfast cigarette and looked out of the window at the car park. She had slept in the driver's seat, arms folded, her chin on her chest, secure in the bad area as long as the doors were locked. She'd taken a small sniff too, just to give the cigarette a nice morning edge.

She shook her right hand again, irritated, banging her fingertips off the steering wheel. A sharpened pencil through a drum of paper; she could feel it in her fingers, the sensation of resistance followed by a snap and give. She blinked hard when she saw the man on the floor with the shoe heel in his eye. Her coke-widened eyes shut tight and opened again, hoping the image burned on to the back of her retinas would change. She couldn't take the image in, it felt like two distinct pictures overlapping. A shoe and a man. Not a shoe in a man. A shoe and a man. Even through a fog of drugs and tiredness she sensed the world moving beyond her capacity to grasp it. She had killed a man.

Kate did know not to park the car outside the restaurant. She wasn't a complete idiot. She drove the car three streets away and pulled up in the dark far corner of an office car park, turning off the engine. She drummed her fingers on the leather-clad wheel. If she left it here, in the dark, all alone, it would certainly attract attention. It was a new BMW, for God's sake. Most of the people around here had never seen a new pair of shoes. She wouldn't mind them taking the actual car itself, but the parcel in the boot was another matter.

It came to her very suddenly: if she was to stay alive she had to get the pillow out of the car and plant it somewhere safe. That way, if they came for her – and she knew they would eventually – she would have a negotiating tool. She felt like an ex-wife trying to make a deal, driving around with a car stuffed with collateral, art or bonds or share certificates or something. Alone in the dark car park, with nowhere to go and brain tissue from a stranger on her heel, the thought made her smile.

But where to leave it. She rolled through possibles: a safe deposit box. She'd be too easy to trap because she'd have to go back again and again to fill up her snuff box. Who did she know that could keep it safe without knowing what it was? Her parents, but she dismissed the idea immediately. She hadn't seen them for over three years and it would take too much explaining. Alison, her best friend at school. She had two kids, though, and might not be sympathetic to a party girl. She thought about people Vhari knew, old old friends from back when they were so close most of their friends were sort of mutual. The Thillinglys. But he had a dreadful wife and Mark was too strait-laced. Bernie. She loved Bernie, even if he wasn't nice to her. His garage/shed thingy was down by the motorway and would be empty at night.

Kate looked around the car park, realizing that it was overshadowed by the office buildings above. She could have a little snifter quite safely here, she thought, but she was super thirsty and definitely needed a drink first. Or after. After would do too.

She felt naughty as she took the snuff box out of her handbag and detached the little spoon, dipping it into the powder as her other hand flicked the lid open.

It hurt. For the first time in a long time the inside of her nose burned white hot. She had the presence of mind not to drop the snuff box, even though she had the pillow in the boot. Eyes shut, she snapped the box shut and put it in her handbag, keeping her other hand on the bridge of her nose as she doubled over her knees.

She rubbed the bone vigorously as if that would make the pain go. Her eyes were streaming, her nose running. It must have been a big crystal. A big solid coke crystal had landed in her nose and it was tickling like a complete bugger. She gasped a smile, squeezing a tear out of her eye. Complete bugger.

11

Archie's Place

The moment she stepped into the news room Paddy knew some terrible, seismic shift had occurred. The last pages of the paper had gone to stone, but instead of the usual haemorrhage of staff the news room was full of people behaving as if they were extremely busy.

A senior editor on the news desk was talking seriously on the phone while a couple of guys stood behind him, glancing nervously around to see if they were being watched. Even the sports desk looked busy. One reporter was typing and three others sat next to him reading the rival papers. No one read the rival papers except first thing in the morning. They were filling in time, waiting for some great event to unfold.

The photographers were all hiding in their office at the far end of the room. The door was ajar and Paddy could see Kevin Hatcher, the pictures editor, standing by a chair, looking out into the busy room, waiting. Kevin drank bigger quantities more often than any- one else at the paper: that he was standing up at seven o'clock at night was a minor miracle.

She shirked off her coat, and as she was hanging it up saw that the two copy boys on the bench were sitting tall, their attention not on the news room but behind their backs, listening hard to what was being said in the editor's office.

Paddy watched Reg, a sports reporter, who was apparently enthralled by a *Daily Mail* report about the Spud-U-Like shops. He felt her gaze on him and looked up, eyes red and open slightly too wide.

'Farquarson's getting the bump,' he said quietly. 'They didn't even call him down to editorial to tell him. They came up here and did it in his office.'

Paddy looked at Farquarson's closed office door and suddenly understood the air of shock and horror in the room. The board were making changes. Farquarson had been in the job for four long years so it wasn't because he wasn't fit for the job: they were making changes because the paper wasn't making money. Any one of them could go next.

'Who's coming in?' she asked. 'Do we know yet?'

'A bastard from London.'

'How do you know he's a bastard?'

'Because he's from London.'

At the far end of the news room the door of the office opened and Farquarson stepped out. Behind him a dejected crowd of his favourite editors and sub-editors had gathered, his star columnist and a couple of red-eyed PAs.

Farquarson cleared his throat. 'Right.' He paused as if the room needed a chance to turn its attention to him, as if they weren't waiting for him. 'Well, I don't need to tell you what's happened today. If I do you shouldn't fucking be here.' A polite laugh rolled around the room and stopped abruptly. He held his hands out, like a fisherman describing a fish, but stopped, shaking his head at the floor. 'You've been . . .' He stopped again, swallowing hard, looking as if he might cry. He took a deep breath and when he spoke again his voice was loud. 'Let's all go and get pissed.'

A great roar of approval rose from the room – largely, Paddy suspected, gratitude at Farquarson managing not to break down in public. Everyone stood up and began to applaud him as he made his way through the room, shaking hands and accepting grand statements of loyalty.

Paddy stayed by the wall as he came past, keeping out of the way. He had been kind to her but she meant nothing to him. He'd known most of the men in the room for ten years or more. His PA carried his coat and briefcase as she followed two steps behind him, smiling at the kindness of those he passed, gracious as a politician's wife.

The room quickly emptied as everyone was carried through the double doors in the wake of Farquarson's departure. Paddy heard the loud burble in the stairwell and went over to the window in time to see Farquarson and his coterie burst through the fire doors, leaving them swinging open as he walked down to the Press Bar, shaking hands with the van drivers and the print setters gathered in the street. His grin was forced.

Paddy turned back to look at the suddenly empty room. It was a shabby mess. The walls were marked where chairs had banged into them, the tables were scuffed, and the great grey typewriters all looked ancient and tired. The first thing the new editor would ever hear about her was that she took a bribe. In times of economic crisis they always sacked the women first on the grounds that they had no one at home depending on their wages.

Paddy shook her head, her mind rolling over an endless *Oh no*, in panicked certainty that she'd be out of a job before the summer was over. There was nowhere else for her to go. She didn't have much experience, her shorthand was so crap even she couldn't understand half of it. It wasn't just a career and a future she had to lose. They needed the money. Her mum needed the money.

She looked up and saw Reg still sitting at the desk, his head in his hands, staring terrified at the table-top. She'd seen the same look in her father's eyes.

She walked over to him and tugged his arm to make him stand. 'Reg, 'mon,' she said briskly. 'Up.'

The red-eyed man got to his feet, looking to her for further instructions.

'Everyone's shitting it, Reg, you're not special.' She gestured to him to follow her and prodded and waved him through the double doors and downstairs, into the street and along the pavement.

She opened the door to the Press Bar. A wall of mildly manic cheerfulness met them. Farquarson was drinking in the middle of the room, surrounded by concentric circles of jolly men, all raising glasses and making a loud happy noise, their eyes sad and frightened.

Paddy felt the emotion catch in her throat. A great man was on his knees and no amount of chirpiness would make it anything but another fucking economic tragedy. She pushed Reg in front of her. Farquarson looked to the door and saw her there, his face a little lost, unsure.

Paddy grinned a big cheerful lie for him and he returned the kindness. She pushed through the crowd.

'Boss,' she said, slapping his arm as hard as she could. 'Did they sack ye 'cause you asked for my move?'

He nodded. 'Aye, so you owe me a drink.'

She hit him again and pushed her way to the bar, concentrating so hard on getting through the crowd of men that she washed up between Father Richards and Half-Assed Willie, a notoriously pedantic editor who was having the arse bored off him by Richards ranting about Tony Benn's leadership bid in a husting-steps haranguing bawl. Half-Assed sipped his beer, increasingly desperate for a break from Richards' tub-thumping. True Socialism, the great promise of the Benn candidature: a return to nationalization and full employment.

Paddy stepped back to see if she could skirt around one or both of them but found herself penned in. Richards was the head of the union but was rarely in the office any more. He spent most of his time off on union junkets, planning a new Socialist Republic.

People were hungry and disgusted at the callous government of grasping capitalists. Revolution was inevitable now.

Half-Assed, usually a mild man, snapped quite suddenly, reaching across Paddy and punching Richards in the face. She jumped back as the two men tumbled off their bar seats to the sticky floor, pulling at each other, a jumble of flailing hands and legs. The crowd gathered around, delighted at the drama.

As Richards rolled past him on the floor, Farquarson aimed a toe tap at his back, starting a game so that soon everyone was kicking Richards, some joking, some vicious. Paddy watched Farquarson and saw that he was happy his party was going so well, pleased that it had that essential, slightly brutal tone that the news room had. It was more than fitting.

She felt a tap on her shoulder and looked up to find McVie's miserable face behind her. They nodded to each other. He had a clean starched shirt on.

'You never came to see me at my new flat,' he said.

Paddy wasn't sure she wanted to be alone with McVie, but he'd given her the address weeks before and was being quite insistent.

All pretence of playfulness had gone from the kicking game. Richards was getting quite badly hurt. He shouted at them to stop it and tried to sit up to defend himself, but Half-Assed was enjoying the fight and pulled him back down again, eliciting a cheer from the crowd.

Farquarson looked over at Paddy, a big jolly grin on his face, and nodded her towards the door. She thumbed back to the bar, that she hadn't bought him a drink yet. He held up a whisky in each hand and nodded her away again, still her editor, knowing that Billy would be waiting for her by the car.

It was only because she knew she would probably never see him again, but Paddy did something very out of character: she covered her mouth with her hand and blew him a kiss. Farquarson accepted it graciously, as a friend would, with a slow blink and a big grin.

Paddy made her way to the door and looked back at the closed circle of men. Farquarson's hair rose above the line of men like a puff of smoke from an encampment. She smiled sadly and pushed the door open, stepping out into the bitter cold.

II

Billy had worked under Farquarson for four years and was expressing his indignation through the art of bad driving. He veered the calls car around roundabouts and sped towards orange lights, letting the world know he wasn't happy. A thick smog of radio hung between them in the car, making consolation impossible. Paddy didn't really want to talk or rehash the injustice. She had enough worries of her own.

They were sliding through the wet town, the deserted streets washed clear of litter and dust. It had been raining in the city for two weeks now. Paddy liked the rain, the privacy of everyone walking with their heads down and the wild wind skirling in back streets and alleys.

Thillingly wasn't the man she had seen at Burnett's door, but she wondered if he could have been the man in the second car. She imagined him, wet and chalk-faced, sitting in Vhari Burnett's brightly lit living room staring at her malevolently, his limp fingers, dripping foul river water, rising up to touch the raw ripped flesh on his cheek. It didn't feel right. She might have been prejudiced in Thillingly's favour because he was fat, but viciously torturing an ex-fiancée didn't seem in keeping with his chairmanship of Amnesty.

Billy pulled the car to a stop at a set of lights and the radio noise dipped, blocked off in the valley between the high office buildings.

'Billy, how did your boy get on in his try-out for the Jags?'

Billy nodded sadly. 'Wee bastard passed an' all. He's joining the junior team.'

'Isn't that good?'

He looked at her, mournful. 'I'm a Gers fan. I saw ye take money

103

off that man.' He slipped the comment in at the end, blind-siding her. 'Have ye done that before?'

'I didn't really take it. He pushed it into my hand and shut the door.'

The lights changed and Billy pulled away, swaying his head sideways, only half believing her. They passed through the valley and the disabled radio blurted sharp cracks and waves of noise into the cab. Paddy sat forward and touched his shoulder, making him flinch. 'I handed it into the police this morning. I could just have kept it.'

He nodded heavily, avoiding her eye, checking the mirror. She was going to spend as much time as possible out of the car tonight.

The Marine looked warm and inviting as they pulled up outside. Yellow light from the windows cut through the rain needling puddles in the street. Paddy had the door open before Billy had pulled on the handbrake.

Her boots were squelching by the time she reached the door of the police station. The suede was developing a tide mark because she kept getting them wet. As she brushed the rain from her hair she saw Murdo McCloud at the desk again. The waiting room was empty. The warmth from the radiators had had a chance to build up without the door being opened over and over again and it was cosy inside.

Two officers came through the door from the back offices, one slapping McCloud on the shoulder as he passed him, calling him 'Cloudy, ye old shite' and making him laugh. Still tittering, he spotted Paddy and called to her as he flipped open the incident book, gesturing for her to come up so that she could see the book entries for herself. It was a mark of respect. She jogged up the stairs, her footsteps cracking loudly on the wooden boards.

McCloud was talking her through all the gimcrack calls of the night, shavings from other people's lives, when the door behind them opened and Sullivan emerged, still in his shirtsleeves, clearly not expecting to get home for a while. He was surprised to see Paddy and pointed at her significantly.

'You,' he said, as if she had just been on his mind.

Together, McCloud and Paddy gawped at him for a moment.

'And you,' replied McCloud on her behalf.

A sharp crack from the wooden floor made all three of them start. Newly awakened, Sullivan waved her into the white wooden corridor behind him.

Through the back wall she could hear that the quiet room she had been questioned in by Sullivan and Reid was now bustling and full. Officers were laughing and cheerful despite the hour.

'You're working late,' she said pleasantly, trying to sustain the chumminess she'd had with McCloud.

But Sullivan was too excited. 'Thanks for coming . . . to see Keano, you know, earlier. Outside the door at Bearsden, did you see anyone in the room – a shape through the curtain, anything?'

She cast her mind back. 'What sort of shape?'

'A big guy, bald, big on the shoulders.'

She shook her head, trying to match the description to Thillingly, but he had a good head of hair. She remembered a wet fringe falling over a half-opened eye, and shuddered at the thought. Sullivan was watching her, willing her to confirm the description.

'I told you about the braces guy.'

'Aye, we can't find a match for him.' He still seemed excited.

'Did you get something off the fifty-quid note?'

He crumpled his chin, thrilled and happy, looking away.

'Blood group?' she guessed.

He shook his head. 'Cocaine. Covered in it. And—'

He wanted her to guess, so she did. Fingerprints took weeks for a match because the files had to be trawled through manually. 'Well, not prints anyway,' she said, but Sullivan raised his eyebrows and waggled his head in a tiny figure of eight.

'You got fingerprints off the note? And a match for them – a name – on the first day? Is Deep Blue working for you?'

He grinned at her, biting his bottom lip hard.

'So,' she found herself smiling back, 'did they match the braces guy?'

'No. There's two sets on it: one of them must be his, from when he handed it to you, but we don't have him on file.'

'But you can use it for confirmation when you get him, can't you?'

He smiled again, looking past her.

She asked him a question he could answer. 'Did the other set match prints from the house?'

'No, we didn't get anything from inside the house.' He let his face split into another grin. 'It was wiped, thoroughly cleaned.'

'But why did they go to all that trouble and not bother about the note?'

He raised his eyebrows and Paddy nodded. 'They thought I'd go out and spend it, didn't they? They thought I'd break the note up.'

'The other set match a known name, a heavy, someone Mark Thillingly would never have gone with. Supports the idea that it wasn't him after all.' Sullivan clasped his hands together, delighted with himself. 'You can't use any of that, obviously. Not yet.'

'You know I couldn't even if I wanted to,' Paddy said. 'The lawyers won't let us print anything that could prejudice a trial.'

'Aye. We don't want these people walking because you put their name in the paper before they get to court.'

'What sort of names would I be not putting in the paper?'

Sullivan leaned towards her and whispered a single word before pulling away. 'Lafferty.'

III

Kate had been waiting in the car for what felt like months, sitting doubled over her knees with her eyes tightly shut as they streamed with tears, trying to flush the solid crystal from the mucous membrane. As she sat there she swore she would cut the powder with something. She should have brought the milk powder from the cottage, but who thought of these things?

When she finally sat up she felt refreshed and sensible. She had dealt with a medical emergency calmly and on her own. Well done me, she thought, and started the engine, backing out of the space slowly, crossing the empty car park and pulling out on to the road.

The restaurant belonged to Archie, and although Archie wasn't really her friend he had always made it clear that he liked her. He had tried to grope her a couple of times, running his fat American hands over her backside when he thought they were alone in the back corridor. Sometimes he followed her to the toilet during late-night lock-ins and once she had let him touch her breast and kiss her neck before fighting him off. Archie liked her a lot.

She cruised slowly past the crescent of shops until she saw the 'Tusks' sign and the bright window with its lowered white blind. It was a wine bar really, but they did little dishes, tapas, small morsels of delicious food. She'd tasted a couple of things and they were really very good. Chips and an egg thing. Lovely.

She passed the street nearby that they usually parked in before going to Archie's. She found a space and was about to reverse into it when she remembered she was trying to sneak around. If she knew to look there for his car, he'd know to look there for her car. Well done me.

A sharpened pencil through a drum of paper. She shook her hand as if trying to fleck off mud. Nasty feeling. She drove around the corner and parked there, on a suburban road, tucking it in tightly behind a big van so that if he was driving past her car would be hidden.

She would have a dry white wine, large, cold, and a giggle with Archie. She might let him seduce her. He was old and unattractive but she might let him anyway. It had been days since she had even spoken to anyone else and a night with a kind friend would be nice.

Feeling slightly squeamish about it, she put her handbag over her shoulder and stepped out of the gorgeous car, locking it and trying the door handle out of habit, just to be sure. She brushed her blonde hair roughly with her fingers, tucking it loosely behind her ears, and did up the gold buttons on her navy suit. As she walked along the road to Archie's she became more aware of being seen and started to sway her hips, roll her shoulders and pout a little. She'd have a drink with Archie, scout the place, see if she could leave the pillow there somewhere, and maybe let Archie have his way.

The heat was radiating through the glass of the large window. She remembered a hundred nights here, all conflated into one door being opened for her, one table heaving with the most expensive wines and Archie pressing dishes on them all to complement the wines and enhance the experience. She smiled along with all the guys as they laughed about something, a joke she was half listening to, a pun about types of French mustard. Smirking smugly, she pushed the door open, clip-clopping down the glazed terracotta stairs into the circle of tiles that marked the reception area.

The restaurant was only half full but every single person there dropped their cutlery and stared at the door. Puzzled, Kate smiled faintly and turned back to look over her shoulder. There was no one behind her. She turned back and realized that they were all staring at her, gawping, being very very rude.

She tutted and adjusted the strap on her handbag, moving it up her shoulder and looking around for Philippe, Archie's maître d'. She didn't have to wait. Archie himself came straight out of the back room, barrelling across the floor when he saw her.

Kate flung her arms up in a great big glorious greeting. 'Hello, darling.'

Archie took hold of her wrist, twisting it so that it actually hurt a bit and pulled her outside, almost dragging her up the three semi-circular stairs to the street. Her handbag slid down her arm, bumping heavily on the tiles.

Outside, Archie turned to her, pressing his face an inch from hers. 'Go away. I never want to see you here again.'

She dipped her chin down and looked up at him coquettishly. 'Don't be a meanie, Archie. I've had a rotten couple of days.' She ran her finger down the buttons on his shirt front. 'Be nice to me.'

'He's after you, you know that?'

'I know, I know, it's a misunderstanding. He thinks I did a naughty thing but I'm only naughty in a good way.' She smiled up at him, hoping he would get the sexy hint and take her home with him, look after her. She didn't care that he was old tonight. She didn't care that hair grew wildly out of his nose and the neck of his shirt. She didn't care that he only had a restaurant. She wanted to touch someone and be touched. She needed human contact and a place to go.

'Archie.' Her hand slid up his shirt to the shoulder. It was a cheap shirt, she could hear the nylon fibres letting off a rip-zip sound as her fingertips slid across it. 'You like me a lot, don't you?'

He put his hairy fingers over hers and peeled her hand off his chest. 'You know, Kate, I don't like you. I think you're a vacant twat. But there was a time when I'd have fucked you.' He held up his finger, drawing her attention to the salient point. 'See, that's different. I'd have fucked you because you were with him. But now,' he flicked his finger up and down her, 'now I wouldn't let you pay to suck my dick.'

It was the rudest anyone had ever been to her. Kate stepped back and stared at him. He was fat and old and wore cheap shirts and had hair everywhere. She was the prettiest girl in her year, the best-looking woman at the Marina Club, the biggest prize at each and every ball she had ever attended. She made a face like a little fist, knowing it suited her, playing her best card, and swung an open hand at his great fat head.

Archie grabbed her wrist and held her arm high. He was utterly unmoved. 'Fuck off and don't come back.'

Kate bit her lip. 'You're rude and vulgar,' she said and turned away, walking along the row of shut and shuttered shops: a designer clothes shop, a tobacconist's that sold excellent cigars, an estate agent's. Lovely shops. She should come back here when they were open.

She felt Archie's fat puffy eyes on her back all the way to the corner but she didn't look back. She wouldn't give him the satisfaction.

She retained her composure until she climbed back into the car and locked the door. No one had ever spoken to her like that and she couldn't believe he'd had the nerve. Rude, fat man. She'd let him touch her breast once, slip his fat hairy hand into the silk blouse she was wearing and give her a squeeze.

She flipped down the sunshade over the passenger seat and turned it towards her to check her hair and make-up in the mirror. She was far enough away from the strip of mirror to see the reflection of her whole face in it.

Kate gasped. It was too dark for colour but she saw black tendrils coming from her nose, a thin black mess with bits, like an octopus climbing out legs first, a black string across her cheek into her hair, black into her mouth, black all over her chin. Her hair had black in it, in a lump over her ear. The skin under her eyes was puffy and blackened, as if she had been punched. She smiled hopefully at herself, a thin, nervous parody of the glorious smile she habitually gave herself in the mirror. She was missing a front tooth. She didn't even remember losing it. She looked like a tramp.

No wonder Archie had told her to leave. She looked awful, and she *was* awful, and in a sudden moment of clarity she knew Vhari was dead because of what she had done. Unable to take it any more, she looked away from the mirror and saw the car slice down the empty street, not seeing her tucked in neatly behind the van. A BMW, a big model, with two men inside.

12

Like Shit to a Sheet

I

Paddy sat in silence at the kitchen table with her oldest sister. Caroline was openly smoking a cigarette, watching through swollen black eyes as their brother Marty chased Baby Con around the tall grass in the back garden.

None of the Meehans knew anything about gardening. They were a bit afraid of the countryside and nature in general, and the garden was usually only used for visitors to smoke in or for storing broken furniture or washing machines. Only the choking plants survived, eating up all the colour. Their other brother, Gerard, had moved the washing poles nearer the house so that Trisha wouldn't need to wade through the long grass to hang up the wet clothes.

No one smoked indoors at the Meehans', yet Caroline sat smoking in full view of her mother, who stood over the cooker, tending the broth she was making. Caroline's eyes were puffed shut, bruised black and so swollen that the skin had split on her right cheekbone.

Paddy watched her mum at the cooker, stirring in a cheap gammon cut and potatoes for bulk, and wondered how the hell they were going to manage now, with only her small wage to feed another two mouths, for the time being anyway, until Caroline went back to John and made her marriage work.

II

Nervous but curious to hear about the new editor, Paddy was two hours early for her night shift.

She found a letter in her pigeonhole by the door, a formal letter typed on to creamy grey paper with a watermark in it, informing her that the official police inquiry into the Drymen Road call was being convened to start its investigation tomorrow and she was being summoned to give evidence next Tuesday at two thirty in the afternoon. After Tuesday everyone would know about the bribe. She re-folded the letter, running her nail hard across the seam, trying to seal it shut as she looked around her.

The news room was bustling with fake activity: everyone was reading furiously with big frowns, or walking around, holding bits of paper, nodding during phone calls to friends or family. Farquarson's office door was lying open and Paddy could see that the filing cabinets were empty, the walls cleared of pictures, the big long desk he had used for editorial conferences had been moved out. She gawped into the empty room, taking in the dents in the carpet where the massive table had stood for all the years she'd been there.

'Where's it gone?' she said almost to herself.

A copy boy, skinny as a match, who watched her often and blushed when she looked back, stood up off the bench. 'New ed's called Ramage.'

Ramage had come in, introduced himself and announced that there would be changes, big changes, the first raft of which had been announced that morning. Four new editors and a sub were being drafted in from other papers. Which meant four old editors were being demoted. One of them had accepted it and the other three were leaving. The new printing presses they had been promised were being cancelled and they'd have to limp along with the equipment they had. The presses themselves weren't as important as the promise of a future that they represented. The day shift had already dubbed the new boss Random Damage.

She spotted McVie across the room and nipped over to him.

'Have you ever heard of a thug called Lafferty?'

'No,' he said curtly. 'Did you hear about this guy? He's moved his office downstairs in editorial. He's got three rooms to himself.'

'He's not going to be in the news room?'

'He was up and gave us a talk earlier about how he's here to make us profitable. He's changing the tone of the paper and anyone who doesn't like it can fuck off. No one walked, though. He's trying to outrage us into leaving so he doesn't have to shell out the redundancy.' He dropped his voice. 'He's from the *News of the World*.'

Paddy's mouth dropped open. 'Bloody hell.' It was a rag, a scandal tabloid, as different from the *Daily News*'s dry fact-laden style as shit to a sheet.

'He's coming to see you lot later. You've all to be here at nine thirty. You'll be all right though, you're crime.'

She'd be all right if they didn't hear about the fifty quid. Her long-despised calls-car shift was suddenly one of the few secure jobs left. But if a light-fingered policeman had walked with the note everyone would want to cover up the fact that it ever existed.

She went over to a news desk and picked up a phone, calling Partick Marine and asking for Colum McDaid.

'Hello Constable McDaid, Paddy Meehan here. I met you the other day.'

'And I was delighted!' he interjected.

'Any word about the friend I left with you?'

'Ah,' she could hear McDaid smiling, 'yes, there is indeed. Our friend has come back from her short holiday in the fingerprint lab. She travelled by car, escorted by myself and is now back at home enjoying the facilities.'

'What sort of facilities would those be?'

'A cosy safe, my company, her own plastic bag.'

'Lucky her.'

'Yes, she's very snug and happy so you don't need to worry about her at all. Now, you don't need to phone after her all the time because she's tucked up tight here and won't be going out until a court case.'

'PC McDaid,' she said miserably, 'thanks.'

She hung up and looked around the office. Her future was falling away from her, a cliff sliding into the sea. McDaid was a man of integrity. She was fucked.

III

A late train rumbled across the high Victorian arch, following the rail line along to the west. Behind Kate cars flashed past on the busy motorway. The road in front of her was quiet: the occasional passer-by tended to come from the concrete-block social club down the road, wild-kneed small men staggering home, passing her car, oblivious.

Kate had the fears badly now. Every person in the street and every shadow that shimmered across the road was the first sign of an imminent attack, foreshadow of a gang, a team of Archies, men over whom she had no pull and no power.

Without her looks and the good regard of every man she met to play on, she was nothing but a sad coke-head, past her prime. For the first time in her life she would have to look after herself.

The social club was a grey concrete box with a red and white brewery sign hanging outside like a red cross. Three old men in baggy trousers and dirty suit jackets helped each other along the road and up to the tenements.

Kate waited until the street was empty before opening the car door and stepping out, daintily fitting the strap of her handbag over her shoulder. The exposed metal heel of her court shoe skidded on the wet cobbles and she almost lost her footing, but grabbed the car door to steady herself, leaning all her weight on it. Two days ago she would have stopped and checked the door, making sure she hadn't damaged it by grabbing it like that or pulling at it, but now she didn't care what happened to the stupid car. It belonged to a different Kate. She leaned into the back seat, lifted out the blue-handled bolt-cutters she had found in the boot, shut the door as quietly as she could and stood to listen.

Beyond the darkness of the railway arch was a wasteground. Jagged muddy hills were punctuated with tufts of grass and beyond that a red tenement, with dark windows and a bright light at the opening.

Somewhere in the far distance a dog yelped in pain and stopped abruptly. Fired by the sound she slipped her shoes off and left them by the car, walking to the end of the arch, keeping close to the wall. The frost on the cobbles numbed her soles but she hardly felt it. She'd tried to have another wee sniff after Archie. God, she needed it, but it had stung too much to sniff so she'd resorted to rubbing it on her gums. It wasn't as pleasant but it worked: it woke her up a bit and took the edge off.

Bernie's garage had a sign above it. It was cheaply done and badly hung. No logo, no design consultant or marketing manager, just 'Bernie's Motors' in black paint, handwritten. It was so simple and plain and like Bernie that she smiled as she walked along the shadows towards it. She'd love to see Bernie now, to sit in the garden in Mount Florida and drink Pimms or something delicious, Bucks Fizz, something summery. Normally a thought like that would lift her spirits. Normally she would taste the drink, her skin would warm with the sun and she would feel Bernie nearby, but it wasn't working tonight. She knew what was real tonight. She felt the weight of the bolt-cutters hanging at her side, her bare feet and numb toes on the time-smoothed stones, the cold spittle of rain on her ruined face.

Bernie's arch had been bricked up with grey breezeblocks and petrified grey mortar that oozed like ice cream between wafers. In the centre of the high bricked arch two red metal doors were padlocked together with a chain so that they swung a few inches either way but wouldn't open. She lifted the bolt-cutters and fitted them around a hoop of the chain, spinning the screw tightly into place and squeezing the hands together. The metal held out for a moment and then snapped open.

Grinning, Kate pulled it from the handles, opened the doors just enough to step inside and pulled them shut behind her.

The darkness was absolute. She had never visited, but if she had been blindfolded and shoved in here she would have known Bernie's scent, the smell of motor oil and builders' tea. A little frightened of the oily black dark, she felt inside her bag for her lighter and broke into a sweat of sheer relief when she found it.

The ceiling above her was cavernous, a red and yellow brick patchwork with shadows flickering over it. A train passed overhead and the arch shuddered like the belly of a brooding animal. Kate hurried over to the wall and flicked the light on.

The striplight hung on two chains, swaying at the memory of the last train. She spotted a sink over in the corner with a plastic-framed mirror above it and hurried across. No plug. She let the tap run – even the water smelled of motor oil – and used a bit of orange towel to wash her face. She gasped when she looked in the mirror.

Her nose had flattened at the bridge; a glacial deposit of scarlet and white skin sat on her top lip, dried and hard. She prodded it with a fingertip. Solid. No wonder she couldn't sniff or breathe out of her nose. She turned sideways and looked at her profile. Flat as a wall. She took a deep breath and squared her shoulders. She'd get a nose job later, when things got ironed out. They could do amazing things now.

She dabbed at the mess with the wet towel and finally picked the huge scab off her lip, leaving the worst of it up her nose to save the raw skin from contact with the air. Finally clean, she gave her customary hopeful little smile, but turned away in disgust.

It was a large room. The floor space was quite big. Parked neatly in a row were an old green Jaguar, an MG and a rust-spotted green

Mini Cooper. Cloths and dirty spanners and bits of metal were strewn across the floor. Bernie was a messy little bugger, always had been. Next to her, along the wall from the sink, sat a table encrusted with cup marks and splodges of white paint and receipt books, a pile of brown envelopes for sending out bills, and a filthy, filthy flask with a tartan pattern on the outside and a thick rim of dried brown tea on the inside. Tucked neatly under the table was a red metal toolbox. Kate walked around to look at it from the front. It had long slim drawers for keeping tools and things in. She walked around to the other side. The table and toolbox were flanked by a filing cabinet, no taller than the table, blocking the view of the back of the toolbox from anyone not standing flush to the sink.

She switched the light off before she opened the doors again and scuttled carefully along the wall to the car. She opened the boot and lifted the pillow out, carefully keeping the slit uppermost, carrying it like a sleeping child back to the garage and in through the doors.

She sat on the floor, unpeeled the tape over the slit and filled up two brown envelopes from the table, sealing them and sitting them upright on the table-top so that the rim of little white dunes showed through the address windows. She pushed as much air out of the pillow as she could, trying not to lose the fine dust, resealed the slit and folded the empty corners down to make it as small and compact as she could. Then she leaned down by the side of the sink and fitted the pillow behind the toolbox.

She stood up and looked at the space critically. Even from the side of the sink she couldn't really see the pillow. She stepped in front, walked around the side, tried it from the other side of the room. It was invisible.

She loved that little parcel. She could use it to bargain her way out of trouble, but didn't want to hand it over. It was valuable, sure, worth a lot, but he wouldn't appreciate it the way she did. She needed another chip. And then it occurred to her – Knox. She knew about Knox and she could use that information instead. She gasped at her cleverness. Knox would matter much more to him than the pillow. All she had to do was work out how to make the most of what she knew.

Excited and buoyed by the thought that she wouldn't need to hand the pillow back, feeling pretty smart for a party girl in need of a nose job, she scrambled around in the debris on the table and found the keys to the Mini Cooper. It started first time. Good old Bernie. She left the engine running and tiptoed back to the table, fitting the two brown envelopes inside a bigger one to allow for spills. She picked up a stubby pencil from the table and jotted on the top border of an old copy of the *Scottish Daily News*, 'Sorry, Bernie.'

It was a bit feeble. Flaky. She wanted him to know she was different now and knew what she had done. She added, 'So, so, sorry.' But it didn't seem any more sincere. She tried again. 'I love you.' She wondered why everything she wrote sounded like last words.

She turned off the lights and opened the doors. She took her bolt-cutters and climbed into the Mini, fitting the precious envelope under the seat, and heaved the steering wheel around to drive out of the garage.

Outside she stopped, afraid to turn the engine off in case it didn't start again, and shut the doors, refitting the padlock so that a casual observer would think the door was still sealed. She drove down to the BMW, got out and picked up her shoes. She opened the driver's door of the BMW wide and put the keys in the ignition, turning on the lights before retreating to the Mini. The arch was in a quiet corner of the city but she knew someone would see the car. It would take at most a few hours for someone to help themselves.

The Mini rumbled along the cobbles until she finally reached a proper road. Even then she could feel every lump and bump on the road surface. She headed west, taking the deserted road out to Loch Lomond and the cottage.

13

Ramage

I

The night shift were herded together in one corner of the news room. They stood unnaturally close to each other, an ill-assorted crowd, nervously straightening ruined ties and clearing smoky throats. Everyone was trying to hide behind someone else; all avoiding eye contact with the man in front of them.

Andrew Ramage was delivering an address to the troops. Paddy could see immediately that he was from the same place as them. He was working class, like most of the journalists and subs. He'd had the same paltry chances as them and despised them for not getting on as he had. She could hear it in his rounded London accent, see it in the expensive cut of his clothes which he touched every so often, stroking the seam of his steel-grey suit jacket, touching the perfect cuff of his white shirt. She could see the thickness of a neck that had done hard physical graft at some point in his life. Farquarson had been privately educated, a middle-class boy who understood that he was from a privileged social stratum compared to the men who worked for him and had tried hard to compensate. He always had a gentler air about him.

Ramage paced the news room, crossing back and forth in front of the open door of Farquarson's empty office. His hands were clasped behind his back in a Napoleonic gesture, uncoupling occasionally for an adamant wave or air splice.

The night shift on any paper were the front line, he told them, the commandos. The night shift formed the back-shop boys, and girl, he nodded at Paddy, a lopsided smile on his face. They caught the unexpected stories as they came in and without them the paper would be far, far less something or other. Paddy's attention wandered. Neither she nor, she suspected, anyone else from the night shift recognized their jobs from Ramage's description. They were only employed because missing the huge story that broke in the middle of the night every ten years or so – an earthquake in Armenia that killed tens of thousands, the unexpected death of a Soviet leader – would ruin the paper's reputation and advertisers would stop buying space. The night shift knew they were nothing more than an insurance policy against Suits For Sirs and Bejam's Freezer Stores moving their accounts to the *Glasgow Herald*.

Ramage raved on, shaming them with hyperbole until many of them began to wonder if they should have been doing something very noble at night instead of dozing or scratching their bollocks or fighting among themselves like kids in detention. He wanted them to know that the entrepreneurial spirit sweeping Britain was going to be welcomed at the *News*. Anyone could come straight to him with a story suggestion. Any time of the day or night, just knock on his door. It's about selling papers, and stories sell papers. Let's never forget that.

Then Ramage gave them the death blow: slightly less than half of them would be superfluous. The tight crowd drew in a collective breath, but no one complained or spoke. Someone at the back sniggered and someone else struggled to clear an unclearable throat. The *News* needed producers, product. Come up with product and you'll be safe, he said. Anyone who didn't like the new regime could fuck off. Clear? He fixed them carefully with his gorgon gaze, hoping someone would go and get their coat and save him a big pay-out. The room was still.

He reminded them again that stories sell papers and left, walking through the silent room with every eye following him.

They stood for a moment, stiff-necked, watching the door. A tentative voice from the back of the room muttered 'cunt'. Ramage didn't fly back into the room and sack the voice, so it was said again, louder, and another faceless voice agreed. Paddy looked around. Eyes were wide and frightened, falling on their neighbour, assessing where they each came in a ladder of indispensability. Paddy had no direct contemporaries. Her job was a one-off so she was probably safe. Unless they brought in someone from the day shift to replace her. Or used an agency.

The miserable group dissolved, floating slowly back to their desks. Most of them were exiled to the night shift because they were unpopular and unsympathetic. Richards wouldn't fight for them. Allowing Ramage to decimate the night shift could well be Richards' price for concessions on the changes to the day shift.

Paddy spoke to the retreating crowd. 'Shouldn't we do something about this? Object or something?'

A sub turned back to her. 'Either they cut the staff or the whole paper goes down. Richards knows that. The NUJ knows that. There's nothing we can do.'

'Won't the print unions do something?'

The sub stopped and looked at her sadly. 'Meehan, that's why the management are refusing to buy the new presses. If the technology comes through the print union'll be dead in five years and we'll be doing all this ourselves. New editors like to slash and burn and make their mark anyway.' He flicked a finger at the door. 'He's making a list of everyone who doesn't come up with a story idea. It could be a massacre.'

She was halfway down the stairs before realizing she hadn't any ideas for any stories about anything.

Ramage's office was on the editorial floor, one level below the news room. Because no one but the board and admin staff came to editorial during Farquarson's reign, the corridor always seemed to have the heavy scent of lemon in it, as if the cleaners had just been and no one had passed through to stir up the air. But doors were opened into some of the rooms now and boxes piled up along walls where people were laying claim to the space. It felt like the emergence of a new class under a new regime, splitting off from the old journalistic camaraderie and barricading themselves away from everyone else.

Ramage's name was on a door that Paddy remembered from a scary incident a long time ago. Standing looking at it now made her feel sick and frightened. She knocked, waited for the call and then opened the door to the conference room, the biggest on the floor.

Ramage was sitting a mile away, watching the door from behind a massive dark oak desk. The desk was built like a small castle: solid, square and elaborately ornamented with finials and carvings of apples and oyster shells, all topped with a lush green leather top. It shamed the nasty industrial carpet and navy-blue hessian walls. All he had in front of him was a telephone, a leather-bound notebook and a gold ink pen. His chair was red leather, mounted on an oak frame that tipped back. He wore a crisp blue shirt under black braces and leaned back in his seat, tapping his teeth with the gold pen as he looked her up and down.

'I'm Meehan, calls-car night shift.' She didn't like him looking at her. She'd have been rude if he wasn't sacking people all over the place.

'What do you want?'

'I'm on a story, Strathclyde police're claiming the Vhari Burnett murder was committed by a guy who committed suicide the other night. I saw the guy at Burnett's door and it wasn't him. The police saw him too but they're sitting on the evidence.'

She saw an excited flicker in his eyes but he sat forward and blinked, hiding it from her.

'Thing is, the story isn't ready yet. It's my word against theirs and I need to get some other evidence before I run with it.'

'Good. Good story, it's got legs. Burnett was a good-looking bird, it'll keep going.'

She couldn't disguise her lip curl and he saw it.

'Meehan, don't give me any women's lib *shit*.' Ramage hissed the word. 'I haven't got time for that crap.'

'No, Boss.' She spoke so flatly, eyes half closed, that they both heard her telling him that she hated him.

'I had a girl working for me in the last place. She had bigger tits than you, but I like girls on the floor, gives the place a different atmosphere. I'm a definite fan of the female species.' He smiled a toothy smile that never got anywhere near his eyes.

Paddy smiled back, matching his warmth, and considered stabbing him in the face with his letter-opener.

III

Both of the drivers involved in the crash stood sullenly on the steep motorway grass verge, arms crossed, twenty foot apart, ignoring each other while the police and firemen and ambulance men chatted around the fused cars. The whole west carriageway was shut down, a cordon further back keeping the few midnight motorists waiting until all the debris could be safely picked off the road.

The driver of the Mini Metro said it was an unfortunate mistake; according to the Ford Anglia it was an act of vicious stupidity. The two cars moving along the motorway at two thirty a.m. had made contact in the middle lane after the Metro, realizing that he was about to miss the sliproad for his exit, slid across from the inside lane without looking or indicating. The cars had some-how locked flanks and waltzed across all three carriageways, failing to turn over because they were stuck together.

When the police arrived the men were jammed in their cars, side by side, screaming abuse at each other. They didn't shut up until the firemen threatened to piss off and leave them like that. Once they'd been cut out and the ambulance service had had the chance to examine them, neither man was found to have a bruise or a mark on him. Both cars were write-offs.

It was a nice call to be on. There were no fights to break up, no one had died, and the emergency service lingered on the empty carriageway in a moment of unexpected camaraderie, as if at a town fair held on a frozen river.

Half an hour ago Billy had gone to find a phone box to ask the office to send the photographer out. Frankie Miles had turned up with a ton weight of photographic equipment in a shoulder bag and then realized he didn't have a *News* chitty for the return taxi ride. He couldn't walk far with the heavy bag and wouldn't find a roving black cab at this time of night. Billy and Paddy offered to run him back, so now he and Billy were standing by the car, smoking silently as they rested their bums on the warm bonnet and waited for her.

Paddy was finishing up her notes, checking the junction number on the overhead sign, when she noticed the funny officer from Thillingly's drowning holding forth to a crowd of uniformed officers. Remembering Dub, she walked over and joined them, momentarily distracting his audience and causing him to mis-time an important line. She held up her hands and waited for him to finish his story.

'So I go, "That woman's had more miscarriages than the Argentine judiciary."'

The men laughed dutifully and drifted off.

'Thanks very much; you just ruined my story.'

'I didn't know you were in full flow. I wanted to ask you something. The river death the other night – is it definitely suicide?'

'Well, yeah, that's how they're dealing with it.'

'What about the torn cheek? Wasn't it a wound from something?'

'Nah, they found a bit of stick in there from the river. The guy was functioning fine on the actual day, his wife said. But he left a note in his car, didn't say why really, just blah blah, can't go on.'

'What kind of car was it?'

'A Golf GTi, top spec.' He nodded approvingly. 'Nice.'

'Right, right.' Paddy glanced down the road. 'Ever heard of a thug called Lafferty?'

'Bobby Lafferty?'

She wasn't sure of his first name but repeated Sullivan's description. 'Big guy? Broad shoulders, bald head?'

'Aye. I arrested him for drunk driving a few years ago. He was so pissed he was in the back seat looking for the steering wheel.'

She laughed loud, pleasing him enough to prompt another story.

'I was lucky he was too pissed to fight me. He bit someone on the eye, ye know. Blinded the guy. He'll do anyone – his relatives, his school pals, anyone.'

Paddy watched him, an obsequious smile on her face, privately observing. Lafferty was a known criminal and Vhari Burnett was a prosecutor. There had to be a link between them. She might have been prosecuting him for something, something that would cause him to attack her.

'He killed his own dog. Can you imagine the mentality of the man? Threw it out the window, from twenty up.' His eyes were shining – if she blocked out the words, he could be talking about a great sportsman or a war hero.

'Anything recent? Has he been charged with anything?'

'Nothing I've heard of. Doesn't mean anything, though. They're always up to something. Animals, these people, animals.' He nodded at her to concur, but she was thinking about Lafferty and Thillingly and Burnett and she missed her cue by a half-beat.

'Aye,' she said. 'Aye, right enough.'

He looked wary. 'You don't know Lafferty, do you?'

'Like you, I also believe violent people to be animals.' She was talking like a bad robot. She giggled, looking away down the glistening black motorway to the three-car police cordon. 'Oh dear. Have you ever done continuous night shift for months on end?'

He frowned. 'We do rotation shifts.'

'Well, this is my fifth consecutive month. If I seem a bit odd or my timing's off, it's not because . . . I don't mean anything by it.'

'Yes.' She could already see him forming a story about the journalist who couldn't speak. 'You seem to be aware of English yet not familiar with it. Is this your first time in our country?'

She laughed so hard her head reeled on her neck. 'OK.' She calmed herself down. 'Right, let's give up on conversation and just get to the important bits. Does Lafferty work alone?'

A policeman by the squad car twenty feet away called across to them.

'Nah, he's a hired hand.' He looked over her shoulder to the squad car and saw that he was being shouted back. 'I need to go.'

She meant to grab his arm and stop him slipping past but she misjudged the distance and took hold of his two forefingers, then squeezed to check if she was indeed holding his hand.

They were standing shoulder to shoulder, like flamenco dancers. He smiled down at her, not displeased at the intimacy. Opening her fist and releasing his fingers, she considered acting as if the flirty gesture was deliberate. He was attractive and funny, he was tall and he wasn't Sean, all good things, but she imagined touching him, kissing him and being kissed, and nothing stirred anywhere. All she felt was a little bit hungry. He was definitely funny, though; she should tell him about the Comedy Club and invite him to meet Dub McKenzie.

'My friend . . .' She hesitated, wondering if it was a good idea to invite him out after touching his hand, and realizing that she sounded as if she was addressing him as 'friend'. 'Um, my friend's a comedian. He's doing a stand-up gig tomorrow night at the comedy club in Blackfriar's. You should come and meet him.'

Surprised, he raised his eyebrows, smiling as though he had just seen her tits. 'OK. Maybe see you there.'

'I'm just saying. Comedy's a good thing. I'm not asking ye out on a date.'

'Course not.' His glance flickered down to her neck and he licked his bottom lip, leaving a glistening trail that glinted silver in the dark. 'Course not. Mibbi see you there then.'

There was no saving the situation. He smiled at her, eyes narrowed so that she couldn't see what was in them. He swaggered back to his colleagues who were watching him, curious about wee Paddy Meehan grabbing his hand.

The cold white motorway lights glinted at her from his left hand and it took her a moment to realize that it was a ring. The joker was married.

14

George Burns

Kate was surprised that the Mini held out as well as it did. The tank was half full when she left Bernie's garage but the needle kept slipping down towards empty and she thought the tank was leaking. She drove slowly, far more slowly than she had in the BMW, missing the suspension of the big German car.

The pre-dawn wind was gently stirring as she neared the corner before the cottage. She held her breath when she passed it, expecting to see cars outside, but there were none. She stole a glance towards the boat house on the left side, down by the water's edge, but there were no signs of anyone there either. She slowed and took another deep breath as she pulled the car over to the verge. Better to park in the road, she might need to get away quickly.

Inside was a turmoil still-life. They had broken everything: smashed everything that wasn't attached to the walls, pulled cushions off the sofas, yanked the mirrors and all the photographs off the walls, leaving them face-down where they lay on the floor. It was worse in the kitchen. Every shelf had been emptied on to the floor, heavy stoneware jars had been dropped into the Belfast sink so that a giant crack skittered across it. The table had been overturned. She could hear the message clearly. We will do this to you.

Kate lifted a wicker hen basket from the floor and filled it with all the tins of food she could find. She had left the cardboard box of powdered milk on the worktop when she ran off to the boat house and they had knocked it over but left it. She folded the waxed paper over at the top and placed it carefully in her basket. She could use it to cut the dunes in the brown envelopes. She could stay up here for weeks if she did that.

She looked out of the kitchen window, up the hill to the chimney of her nearest neighbours, knowing their house would be empty until May when they always came back from Kenya for the summer, watching for smoke to be certain she was right. The house was still, the ochre of the chimney blending perfectly into the green of the conifers in the foreground. A casual viewer would never know it was there.

She was smiling to herself when she realized that something had changed in the garden. A patch, a big patch, of disturbed earth lay by the back wall.

She knew exactly who it was and knew how easily it might have been her.

II

It was her night off and Paddy had considered skipping the comedy club at Blackfriars this week, nervous that the married policeman might turn up. But she'd slept well during the day and been sitting in the living room watching *Junior Superstars* when she realized that she'd be up all night anyway, sitting on her own, worrying about Ramage hearing the details of the Burnett call after next week's police inquiry. She might as well go into town.

The pub was on the edge of the old warehouse district. Most of the buildings were high-walled, small-windowed storage facilities for tobacco bales and mountains of sugar, monuments to the end of Empire, now empty rat-runs.

It was reported to be up and coming as a residential area. New York-style lofts had been carved out of rat-infested grain stores by developers who didn't really understand the qualities of the space. They had crammed small new-town houses inside the grand walls of the warehouses, cutting windows in half and leaving cast-iron pillars in the middle of kitchens and hallways.

The regeneration had only just begun and the council had put in a lot of street lights to make the new yuppie residents feel confident about leaving their Volvos and Saabs in the street. It still felt like a well-lit ghost town. Paddy knew that McVie's flat was here somewhere. She was curious, but afraid he meant to try and touch her or something. McVie was a strange man, sometimes avuncular, sometimes leering, sexual signals shooting out every which way.

Blackfriar's was smoky and full of good cheer. A crowd of psycho-billys were gathered at a table near the bar, all wearing denim and battered leather, every one of the girls with a slash of scarlet lipstick, regardless of their colouring. Three hard-looking Mohican mullets were playing on the puggies, their pints of snakebite and black delicately balanced on a thin shelf.

Paddy made her way through the throng. In a narrow corridor leading to the back exit, a small black door sat open in a wall pasted with posters for events past and future. A girl sat guarding it from a small console table. She had a dainty face and pretty brown corkscrew curls that she wound endlessly around her finger. Miserable, she tapped the table-top with a thick black marker pen.

Paddy took her scarf and mittens off, tucking them inside her coat pocket, and then she saw the sign that made her heart sink. Open Mike Nite. In two years of hanging about comedy clubs Paddy had never ever seen an open-mike spot go well. Any idiot with a nervous complaint could get up on stage and die and have it witnessed by a paying audience. Dub said she was a jinx: he'd seen people storm at an open mike and sometimes established comedians using it to showcase new material, but whenever Paddy was there it was always gut-shittingly awful.

Lorraine saw Paddy grimace at the blackboard. 'One, is it?'

'Hi, Lorraine, how are ye? I'm on the guest list. I'm here with Dub McKenzie.'

Lorraine nodded uncomfortably, pulling the lid off her black marker pen with an adamant 'phut'. Paddy held her fist out and Lorraine scribbled her initials on the back of her hand.

'I like your leather.' Paddy pointed to Lorraine's brown coat. It wasn't nice at all. It was made of stiff, shiny PVC and didn't fit around the shoulders.

'Thanks.' Lorraine shifted in her cardboard coat. Paddy smiled and stroked her own soft green leather as she traipsed downstairs.

The cellar doorway opened out into an oppressively low-ceilinged room. The bar ran at ninety degrees from the entrance. To the right was the smaller stage area with collapsible chairs in a few rows in front of it.

In among a thin crowd of milling drinkers, stooped over the bar, was Dub McKenzie. Since he had left the *Daily News*, skinny Dub had taken up smoking and had actually managed to lose more weight. He was wearing a pair of red checked trousers, a blue surfer shirt and blue suede shoes with an inch-high crepe sole. He turned to the door as she stepped in, raising a hand and letting his long fingers unfurl into a greeting.

'You might have told me it was an open mike,' she said, pulling her bulky scarf out of her pocket. 'I wouldn't have come. It's inhuman.'

Dub took her scarf out of her hands, bundled it into a ball and threw it into a corner behind the bar where the coats were kept. The barman caught her eye and she ordered a half-pint of shandy for Dub and a Coke for herself.

'I wasn't sure you'd come tonight,' he said.

'Where else am I going to go? The Press Club? You're the only man I know who isn't thinking about leaving his wife.'

'Apart from Sean.'

He always sneered when he said her ex's name and Paddy didn't really know why. It wasn't as if they'd ever met or anything. 'Who's up first?'

'Some guy, does a bank manager with a lisp.'

'Funny?'

He shrugged. 'Punters laugh and clap. It's not comedy-song clapping either, it's all the way through.'

Dub had a theory that comedy songs were never funny and audiences were applauding with relief when they finished. A comedy theologian, he had formulated innumerable laws of comedy and had an encyclopaedic knowledge of comedy history, could trace a joke through a hundred incarnations. He had an amazing library of comedy albums ranging from early Goons to bootlegged Lenny Bruce tapes and early Ivor Cutler. Paddy had been to his house many times to listen to them in Dub's cramped bedroom in his parents' bungalow. They sat on the bed drinking tea and smoking, his mum didn't mind, listening and laughing at the wallpaper. Occasionally Dub lifted the needle off to explain why it was funny. She could count the number of times she'd seen Dub laugh on the fingers of one hand, but nothing engaged him like comedy. She'd seen him in a trance watching a good visiting act.

The club began to fill up for the nine o'clock start and people approached Dub, complimenting him on his performance the week before, asking favours and passing on messages from comics they ran into on the circuit. Paddy stayed in his gangly shadow, glancing nervously at the door every time she saw a shape that looked like the funny policeman. He wouldn't come, she felt sure. If he did turn up she'd try to give him the impression that Dub was her boyfriend. She'd hang close to him and laugh at his jokes or some-thing. Maybe touch his arm.

It was the usual sort of crowd: a lot of friends of the acts, a few genuine punters, some terrified, sheet-white boys there for the open spot. The few punters were pretty straight looking, guys in shirts or C&A jumpers with girlfriends wearing lemon-yellow knits or kitten-bow blouses, all shop-bought style. They had heard about the comedy scene and had come in from the suburbs to spot the next Ben Elton. They were pleasant, amenable people, looking for an excuse to laugh, not the famously intolerant Glasgow Variety audiences who had bottled off most of the great British acts of the last half-century.

Somehow, without being called, everyone drifted over to the collapsible chairs in front of the stage and sat down, resting their drinks on the floor and arranging their coats over their knees. Dub slipped away to check the speakers and leads and Paddy glanced at the door one last time. He wasn't coming and she was relieved. She sat down at the back, in an aisle seat where Dub could see her face in the light from the stage. He didn't need a smiling pal in the audience any more but she did it out of habit. He hadn't always found it easy.

The lights dropped and Paddy just had long enough to consider the fire hazard involved in blacking out a cellar full of smokers before Dub came rushing up the aisle, brushing her shoulder as he passed. The stage lights came up, Dub lifted a gangly leg up the two-foot step on to the stage, took the mike from the stand and launched into his why-don't-you-just-go-and-live-in-Russia bit.

III

It was like making vegans watch a seal cull. The audience had travelled to get here and they were nice people, choosing to giggle their Friday night away instead of getting drunk and fighting with their loved ones or neighbours. Yet here they were, sitting looking at their knees, glancing back at the fire exit while a young man had a low-grade nervous breakdown on stage.

Muggo the Magnificent described the symptoms of his anxiety as they arose: his throat was drying up and now he was shaking – look at his hand, look, he was shaking, it wasn't like this at parties when he stood up to talk, honestly. My feet are stuck, he told them,

I can't move and I'm sweating. I think I'm going to cry. It would have been a kindness to shoot him.

Dub bolted from the shadows and picked him up like a bit of scenery, carrying him off down the aisle to the bar. Paddy initiated a round of applause.

The next open-mike volunteer came on without an introduction from Dub, who was busy in the back room feeding a sugary drink to the dying man. He was wearing a brown suit and a jester's hat, was sweating and excited, trembling a little. He leaned too close into the mike, making an ear-raking 'pop'.

'OK,' he said. 'Listen up, arseholes, because this is funny.' Somewhere in the world this would have got a laugh. Sadly, that place was not here.

'Christ,' muttered Paddy and got up to go to the toilet for a break from the carnage.

'Hoi, fatso!' The guy on stage had spotted her. 'What do you do for a living?'

She turned on him with a look she had learned on the newsroom floor. He flinched, knowing that he might be holding the mike and have the benefit of amplification but he had picked on the wrong fat bird tonight. He buckled and the audience saw it. Some of them turned and looked back at Paddy.

'What do you do?' he repeated.

'I book comedians,' she said loudly.

The audience laughed with surprise at the level of aggression, snowballing into gratitude that she had given them an excuse to let off some energy, which was what they had paid their money for. Paddy used the noisy hiatus to slip off to the empty ladies' loo.

She checked herself in the mirror. Across a darkened room a bad comic could see she was overweight. She took hold of the pocket of fat under her chin and gave it a vicious little squeeze. She wasn't trying hard enough. Everyone was losing weight on the F Plan but she was dreaming of sugary icing on sticky buns and chocolate, hoovering up calories. She hadn't enjoyed a guilt-free mouthful for months. She didn't know why she couldn't have been born slim like Mary Ann.

Back-combing her hair with her fingers at the side where it had gone a bit flat, she ran a finger under her eyes to straighten her chewy black eyeliner and stepped back out just in time for the break.

The joking policeman was standing at the bar, looking as much like an off-duty polis as was possible without swinging a truncheon. He was dressed in Sta-prest slacks and a smart V-neck jumper over a shirt. The barman brought him a long clear drink with lemon and ice in it and he sipped it, smiling faintly at the stage area of the room.

Paddy considered bolting back into the ladies' and staying there until he went away. But Dub would come looking for her. Worse, the policeman might ask for her and then everyone would know he was there to see her. She took a deep breath and walked over.

'All right there?'

'Hi,' he said, smiling a crocodile grin. 'Hi. You look nice.'

She noticed with horror that he had taken off his wedding ring.

'Did you catch any of the acts there?'

'No.' As he looked her up and down his smile slipped to the side of his face and nestled there. 'Can't say I did.'

'They weren't very good.'

It was half time and members of the audience gathered around them, pressing for the bar, repeating Paddy's assessment of the quality of the acts. She looked over and saw Dub skulking in the doorway to the keg cellar, an area jokingly referred to as backstage.

Below the level of the bar, in the dark at pelvis height, the policeman's hand found Paddy's. He took hold of her fingers, pressing meaningfully. Shocked, Paddy yanked her hand away and muttered 'No!' in a manner that conveyed her disgust so fluently there could be no going back or dressing it up.

He turned on her. 'You fucking invited me here,' he loomed over her.

Paddy grabbed his sleeve and pulled him out of the crowd. She led him over to the audience seats. A couple of them were still occupied, people keeping the places or watching their friend's belongings, staring at the empty stage, taking in the ripped curtain and the broken chair half hidden behind it.

She sat him down. 'I invited you here because you're funny, not because I fancy ye. I don't. It was the middle of the night and I got confused and grabbed your hand by mistake. You're very funny. You should know that this comedy club is here. Because you're funny.'

It was like a rejection wrapped in a compliment. He looked at the blank stage and the punters watching it, looked at Paddy again. It seemed to Paddy that he remembered he didn't really fancy her anyway. He decided to let it go. He nodded. 'I *am* funny.'

'Yeah, you are.'

'And what're you after? You want to manage me or something?'

'I don't want anything from you. I don't even want to be friends with you, but I come here every week and watch six unfunny comics for every good one. I thought you'd like to know about it.'

Dub appeared at Paddy's side, staring at the policeman, who stood up and held his hand out.

'Right, pal? Are you one of the comics?'

'Yeah.' Dub shook his hand firmly once and let go. 'I compère here. Dub McKenzie.'

'I'm George Burns.'

Dub reeled as if he'd been slapped on the back of the head. He shook his head at Burns. 'No, pal,' he said. 'What you are is comedy fucking gold.'

15

A Bad Time for Big Girls

I

The audience had gone home. The comics and bartenders were all sitting at a corner table in the empty cellar, sipping their staff drink. For the open-mike attempters it was the only kind of payment they'd get for their efforts, one shitty drink, a pint of the cheapest lager or a sweet wine. Paddy thought they were being overpaid.

Lorraine was two giggles and a hair flick away from offering herself there and then to George Burns. Paddy watched him, noting that he was pleased at the girl's attentions but also somehow detached, observing Lorraine's behaviour and thinking about it. Lorraine listened to his stories along with the rest of the table, laughing extra hard at the punchlines, sitting forward to fill his line of vision, touching her hair, her lips, her décolletage, drawing his eye to them.

Burns held the table rapt. He had never done a gig, yet almost every comic at the table was listening to him talk. Usually, Paddy had noticed, when one comedian told a joke another would tell a better one, or interrupt to rewrite the punchline, but they were all deferring to Burns, laughing at his stories and enjoying him. It wasn't because of his age, either; it was because he was a great storyteller and the police force was the perfect place to pick up material. Even Dub listened, smiling at the table and nodding occasionally, mentally charting the technicalities of what Burns was doing instinctively.

Paddy downed the last of a flat Coke she had bought an hour ago, pulled her scarf on and stood up, announcing that she would need to leave now for the last train. Normally Dub walked her to the station, but before he had the chance to reach for his coat Burns shot to his feet, knocking Lorraine as he got up.

'I'll run you home.'

'No,' she said. 'No, I've got a Transcard anyway. It's not costing me.'

'I need to talk to you about the guy you mentioned the other day.' He glanced at the adoring clowns around the table and decided to risk the indiscretion. 'Lafferty.'

Dub dropped his hand to his lap and conceded to him. He could only offer to walk her to the station. He didn't have a car.

'Oh,' she said. 'OK.'

Burns looked at everyone. 'I'll see you next week.'

'Brilliant,' said Muggo the Magnificent.

Burns and Paddy gathered their things and said their goodbyes. She felt proud being escorted out by him. She didn't like him or want to spend time with him but she loved the idea of Lorraine and the others watching them leave together. Lorraine looked crestfallen that he was leaving with someone else. Even Dub, who had just been usurped as their leader, raised his hand in salute. 'See ye, Paddy.'

Paddy led the way upstairs, aware that Burns's eyes were watching her fat arse. She found herself putting an extra bit of swing in her walk, swaggering almost, not ashamed of her body the way she usually was when she felt observed.

Upstairs in the pub the staff were cleaning up, washing ashtrays and loading dirty glasses on to the bar. One guy dragged a bin bag after him, gathering rubbish from the tables. No one acknowledged Paddy and Burns as they walked to the far doors and let themselves out into the frosted street.

Burns rolled his shoulders back proudly when he reached his car, a Triumph TR7 sports car, beige with black trim, the roof sloping backwards as if bent by the incredible high speeds it routinely reached. Through the window she could see bucket seats upholstered in black leather, designed to curl around the body, with matching lush headrests and a leather-coated steering wheel. She was impressed but determined not to comment on it.

'I stay in Eastfield, know it?'

'Yeah.' He looked a bit surprised. 'Had you down as a Pollockshaws girl, to be honest. Somewhere a bit nicer.'

'Eastfield is nice, it's just fallen on hard times.'

He unlocked the passenger door for her, giving her a frank look that lingered too long to be innocent. He skirted around the bonnet for the driver's door as Paddy climbed into the low seat. The interior of the car was immaculately clean; she could imagine Burns lovingly oiling the leather on his days off.

He opened his own door and dropped in next to her, smiling to himself, anticipating his return to the comedy club next week. 'You watch a lot of comedy, tell me this: what goes down better, characters or observational stuff?'

She thought about it. 'Well,' she said, 'character does well initially, but observational has a longer life. You can keep the same act for years with observational, but it's easier to make a breakthrough with a novelty character.'

He smiled at the road as he started the engine. 'Which attracts the most birds, though?'

Uncomfortable, she arranged her narrow black skirt to hide her fat legs. 'So,' she said, 'how long have you been married?'

He tutted sullenly and looked at her. 'You don't mess about, do you?'

She shrugged. 'I'm just asking.'

Burns flicked on the indicator and checked the empty street, looking over his shoulder, avoiding the straight answer. 'Why? Are you married?'

'Burns, if I was married I'd wear my wedding ring all the time and everyone would know.'

They drove on in a heavy rankling silence for a few minutes, negotiating their way out of the deserted narrow valleys between the buildings. The pine air freshener swung rhythmically from the mirror, the cellophane envelope hanging off it like a pair of trousers dropped to the knees. She should have taken the train.

They hit the main thoroughfare and the Friday-night traffic. Closing-time drunks littered the streets, staggering out in front of the traffic and causing trouble among the bus-stop queues. A woman wearing a flying suit and gold belt with strappy high heels swung her handbag playfully at her boyfriend. Paddy saw short ra-ra skirts and ski pants and nipped waists. It was a bad time for big girls. She suddenly thought of Vhari Burnett and remembered that she had to get Burns talking if she wanted to find out who Lafferty was.

'The town's been quieter in the past month or so,' she told the window. 'Or maybe it just seems that way.'

'It is quieter. Do you want to know why?'

'Go on then, why?'

'I'll show you.' Burns swung the car in a sharp U turn, doubling back through the Trongate in a highly illegal manoeuvre and cutting through a red light. He drove on to the Gorbals, taking the Rutherglen Road and a sliproad to St Theresa's Chapel next to the high rises. For a moment Paddy thought it was a bad idea to be alone with this man, there was a frightening energy at his core. If he did anything to her she wouldn't be able to go to the police: he was the police.

II

Burns pulled over and stopped the engine, sliding down in his seat.

'Watch,' he said.

They were across the road from the shopping centre, a tall wide alleyway straddled by massive stilts supporting the high flats above it. The breadth of the building was picked out in wide stripes of grey and black. The underbelly of the flats was a stained concrete slab. Between the stilts was a row of squat, shuttered shops.

It was a familiar scene to Paddy. The next-door police station was a nightly stop for her and Billy. It was usually the last stop before the death-burger van at two thirty, and the lit blue 'police' sign hanging over the door made her feel hungry and a little bit excited at the prospect of a cheeseburger. The incidents in the station were usually drink-related family fights.

'Why are we here?'

'Just watch.'

'Are you going to tell me about Lafferty?'

'Seriously – watch.' He pointed at the block of high rises looming over them. A lot of the windows were open, she noticed. An unusual number for February. She'd heard the heating was sometimes controlled centrally in the older council blocks and they could easily overheat if the system went berserk. But not all the windows were open.

She thought it was something falling slowly from a window on the third floor at first, but it was a bit of paper being lowered softly on a string. When it was five feet off the ground, a tiny shadow figure materialized from behind one of the stilts, tugged the paper free and melted away again. The string hung there, billowing gently until another young man ducked out and tied a note to the end, watching as it rose above his head. Further down the block another weighted string was lowered from a first-floor window and someone else stepped out of the shadows, caught it and tied a paper to it.

'What's going on?' whispered Paddy.

'That's money going up, heroin coming down. It's the reason the town's so quiet. The people used to be in the town on Friday nights having knife fights. Now they're around one another's houses, jagging up and watching telly.'

She thought about the traces of cocaine Sullivan had found on her note, currently sitting in PC McDaid's cupboard. 'What about cocaine? Do they sell that here?'

'No, that's the other end of the scale. Rich people. They never really catch those ones; they're too well connected. See, we can't search the flats without a warrant and the tenants won't open the door unless they know who it is. This way they can deal without opening their front doors.' Burns paused. 'I asked around about Lafferty, by the way. He's up to his elbows in all of this.'

'Really?'

'Yeah.' He pointed to the shadows and the strings. 'He's a known face, but no one knows which outfit he's working for and there aren't any charges outstanding against him.'

'Did Vhari Burnett ever prosecute him?'

'The Bearsden Bird?'

She didn't want to give Sullivan's lead away and half wished she hadn't mentioned it, but nodded softly.

'Not that I know of.' Burns stroked the leather steering wheel. 'Someone else was asking about that. Have you heard something we should know about?'

'No, name just keeps coming up, that's all.' Paddy looked and found his eyes drinking in her bare neck and her mouth. He didn't stop when he saw the coldness on her face either but smiled ruefully, as if he knew he'd never touch her and regretted it.

He turned the key, starting the engine and startling the buyers so that, black on black, they scattered like a flock of bats under the dark belly of the building.

16

Better to Burn

I

Kate sat at the table in the small green kitchen, frozen with terror, repeating Knox's name under her breath in a mantra, trying to feel safe. She couldn't bring herself to turn around and look back at the man peering curiously in through the window. She could hear his hand brushing dirt from the small pane above the sink, feet crunching on the dead plants below the window as he swayed from foot to foot. He must have been as cold as she was.

And it was cold in the house. She had found logs under the back porch and coal in the cellar but didn't dare build a fire. She didn't know who was watching. Luckily she had found a wardrobe full of woollen jumpers and trousers in the back bedroom and now wore three layers, none of which suited her. She didn't care. She had turned all the mirrors to the wall. She couldn't bear to look at herself.

The light hit the table at an angle and she could see long, tongue-shaped trails through the dust. She had licked it last night, trying to be frugal and not waste a spilled drop because the envelopes seemed to be emptying by themselves. She had mixed the contents of one of them with the milk powder but it just meant she had to get more into herself to achieve the same sense of comfort and it was hard because her nose was so sore and raw. She had to hold the tip of it out from her face to sniff. The second envelope wasn't mixed with milk but the contents were still evaporating. It seemed inconceivable that she was taking it all. There was no one else in the house, even though she had been convinced for a period last night that there was, so it had to be her.

Kate imagined that the face at the window had blurred features because of the soil stuck to his pale skin. There would be a deep bloody black hole where his eye should have been. His fingernail scratched slowly down the window, a high-pitched shriek, running down her spine vertebra by vertebra.

Kate covered her eyes and tried to breathe. It didn't matter which room she went into, where she sat in the house, the man from down the hill would be behind her somewhere, singing sometimes, a vague tune in a low growl, trying to get her attention. Every spare corner of her head was filled with him; every time she shut her eyes she recalled the sight of him, her fingers tingling with the sensation of a pencil punching through paper.

Since last night he was becoming confused in her mind with Vhari. She saw them as a couple, happy together, malevolent only to her, the cause of their troubles, the cause of their deaths. Vhari hadn't had a boyfriend since fat Mark Thillingly dumped her, but now she was drawn to the one-eyed man by their shared hatred of Kate. The couple lingered in the shadows, became more confident at night, tiptoed across landings, laughing behind doors, playing whispering tricks on wide-awake ugly Kate.

To be ugly. She was now ugly. It had never seemed possible. Maybe at sixty or fifty, but not at twenty-two. She caught her reflection in the windows during the day and saw a stranger, so thin she might have been a boy, her nose flattened, widening her face, making her look more freakish than plain. She grew up knowing she was beautiful. Her looks invited privilege and she took it wherever she went. She left school at sixteen and never worked, never wanted, never even had to ask for favours, just got given everything. People liked having her around. Not any more.

She looked at the almost empty second envelope. There was no one at the window despite what she could hear. She still knew that much anyway. She had to get the fuck out of here. She had to get back to the city and visit Bernie's garage.

If she didn't get up from this chair soon and move she'd be found next May, swinging from the stairwell.

II

Paddy smarted at Burns parking a little bit down from her house and turning off the engine. It wasn't for him to decide they'd stay and talk for a while. And yet they lingered, a combative silence hanging between them. They were both in the middle of a stretch of night shifts and neither of them was anywhere near tired.

The Meehan house squatted like a fat frog in the overgrown garden. Only the living-room light was on. Marty and Gerard would be watching late-night TV. They'd have to share a room tonight, as they did before Caroline got married and moved out. They would have spent their evening being directed by Con as they moved Gerard's bed back into what was now Marty's room and brought Caroline's dusty single bed down the narrow ladder from the attic. The camp bed, a death trap for anyone over four stone, would have been unravelled and set at the foot of the room for Baby Con to sleep in near his mum. Paddy thought about the bus journey here from Caroline's house and the shame of everyone seeing what her husband had done to her. Trisha would insist that Caroline go back to John. She'd make her go back again and again until she complied enough and demeaned herself enough and supplicated herself enough to make it work. Marriages couldn't fail in their family. Divorce was for other people, Protestants, movie stars.

Paddy looked at the house. Better to marry than burn, they said. She'd rather burn.

A gentle wind nudged the branches of a tree in the street behind them, shifting the dim lights on the road and houses around them into a moving landscape of black and grey.

Burns turned to face her, the leather squeaking beneath him. 'So this is where you live.'

The atmosphere between them was thrilling and unkind.

'Yes,' she said stiffly, wondering why she didn't just throw open the door and get out. 'Where do you live, with your wife?'

He tried to smile. 'You're very interested in my wife.'

'I'm interested in the fact that you wear a wedding ring at work and not when you're out at the pub.'

He sighed patiently and cupped the gearstick with his hand. They both looked at it: if he flexed his fingers the tips would be inches from her thigh. 'You don't know what the police are like. It's important to fit in. You can't tell everyone in the canteen that your wife's mentally ill and you're frightened to go home.'

He glanced up at her to see if the lie had taken but she was sceptical. 'Your wife's mentally ill?'

'What do you think would make a woman do this?' He lifted the waistband on his jumper and undid two buttons on his shirt, pulling it open and baring his stomach. The skin was as smooth and shiny as toffee. She could see the outline of his muscles. A suggestive seam of black hair crept down under his waistband.

'Look.' He touched a patch of perfect skin.

'Where?' she said, glad of the excuse to keep looking.

'There.' He touched himself again.

'I can't see anything.'

'Here.' Reaching over to take her hand, he pressed her fingertips to the warm skin. Her hand slid across his stomach, taking in a small scar.

'There?'

'Yeah. A bottle-opener. She came at me with a bottle-opener.'

He thought she was a mug and was using the cheapest lines on her, insulting his absent wife to trick the knickers off her. Yet she still felt her fingers glide across his silken skin and her mouth began to water. His hand covered hers, pressing the fingers deep into the skin.

'I think you're a liar,' she whispered.

His free hand slipped along her thigh. She didn't care if he felt the fat there. He didn't deserve a thin girlfriend.

'You've got me all wrong,' he said breathlessly. 'I'm a good guy.'

The dark night pressed around the car, blacking out the windows, seeping in through the cracks and filling the tiny cabin with the moist, musky scent of night time. Unbidden, Paddy's hand slipped up to his chest and her fingers felt an erect nipple, a tuft of hair on the breast plate, a heartbeat so forceful she could almost hear the echo of it in the car.

He reached inside her coat, cupping her soft round stomach, his thumb brushing the underside of her breast. Her hand slid back down to his stomach, feathering the powder-soft skin, making his eyes roll back in his head. He was melting into his chair when she pulled her hand away.

'Not outside my parents' house.'

Burns sat upright. 'Where is there around here?'

Paddy leaned back. 'Out on to the main road and go right,' she said.

They took the old road to the steelworks, a defunct metal-purifying facility that once occupied two square miles of land. It had been closed down, leaving a devastated landscape where the sulphurous scent of the devil still clung to the ground.

Burns found a potholed turning off the main road and cut his lights as they drove down it.

Moonlight illuminated a churned field of discarded rope and jagged shards of metal. When they were far enough not to be seen from the road he stopped the car, turned the engine off and looked at her.

Paddy had cooled a little, caught her breath and she wasn't sure now, but Burns's fingers brushed her ear.

'Your neck,' he whispered, pulling her scarf. It fell away, unravelling like a snake uncoiling from a branch.

There were reasons why this was a bad idea but Paddy struggled to recall what they were. He pulled a small square packet from his hip pocket, a condom, and set it on the dashboard with a smug certainty that made her despise him. Oblivious, he reached across with his other hand and took her by the waist, pulling her to his lap, sliding her skirt up her legs. His hot hands were on her thigh, on her arse, on her bare breasts, his lips wet and ardent.

The last conscious thought in Paddy's mind was a note of caution so distant that it seemed to relate to events far away.

She leaned back and handed him the condom, leaving him to pull it on as she wrestled her tights and knickers down over one ankle, graceless and desperate, leaving them to dangle off her left foot. She straddled him, kissed him, pushing his shirt up and pressing bare skin to bare skin.

When Burns pushed himself into her he still had the strip of the condom packet in his mouth. Paddy felt her eager cunt flowering out to greet him, a giant fleshy rose.

She couldn't focus or see anything but the hairs on his neck, the maze of wrinkles on the leather headrest behind him. She couldn't control her breathing. She held his shoulder tightly, perhaps hurting him, she didn't know or care, pulling herself back and forth, stroking her clit with her free hand.

She was nothing but an overwhelming urge and couldn't stop now if she needed to. Suddenly her cunt spasmed, her legs shutting as she jackknifed into his chest. Every pore on her skin shuddered and a cold wash swept over her.

She could feel something warm dribbling down her bare thighs. The skin between her legs was wet, not slimy, and she was sure she had urinated into his lap. Ashamed, she stayed stiffly where she was, feeling ridiculous and naked and vulnerable. His large hand was suddenly obscene on her damp buttock. She shifted her weight, extricating her trembling legs, but Burns stopped her, making her wait where she was while he kissed her neck with an open mouth and breathed her name.

She didn't look at him as she climbed back into the passenger seat. She stared out of the window, pretending to be engrossed in the flat, ruined land, wondering what the hell had just happened to her. Her knickers and tights were still around her ankles but she pulled her skirt down primly, wondering how she could get them up and cover herself with any dignity.

Next to her Burns pulled the condom off and tied a knot in it, smiling to himself in a way that made her feel excluded and stupid and angry. The windows were opaque with condensation. Burns ran a finger down the windscreen and smirked again. Turning on the engine, he sat back, waiting for the windows to clear, and tapped his knee patiently. He reached forward to the radio but Paddy panicked, thinking he was going to touch her again,

'We should go,' she said unnecessarily. 'I'm tired.'

It was half two and she worked the night shift five days a week. She would be awake all night and they both knew it. Burns gave half a smile and stumbled across a station playing Lionel Richie's 'Running With The Night'. A childlike pleasure came over his face until he heard her snigger, and his fingers flicked onwards to another station and Echo and the Bunnymen.

'Better?'

'I don't like Lionel Richie, but put it back if you want to hear it.'

'No, I don't like him either.' He cringed at his obvious lie. 'OK, I do like him. Is he not cool?'

She smiled. 'Lionel Richie?'

'Yeah? He's not, is he?' He bit his lip.

'Burns, what age are you?'

'Twenty-three.'

'You're only a year older than me. How come you dress like Val Doonican?'

He sat back and smiled at her, pulling his V-neck straight. It wasn't his usual toothy matinée-idol smile but a coy asymmetric face crumple. 'I'm a polis. This gear is cool in the polis. You like this crowd?' He pointed to the radio.

'I like Echo and the Bunnymen, yeah.' She didn't really, but she wanted to.

'See, I just think that guy can't sing.'

They each nodded hesitantly, looking unguardedly at each other. She imagined him dressed well for a moment, without the severe haircut and the terrible outfit. He had dark eyes and a big, character nose. He scratched his neck. 'I want to see you again.'

Paddy smiled at the euphemism and then laughed. 'Is that what we just did? "Saw" each other?'

'Yeah.' He gave a satisfied sigh. 'I gave you a seeing-to, yeah.'

She felt unbelievably relaxed and calm as she yanked her tights up, pulling her coat around her hips for privacy, and fell back in the seat, grinning. 'Take me home, Burns.'

They drove back listening to the radio. 'Killing Moon' finished and the DJ announced a change of pace and played a Madness record. They sang along – even though they were a teenyboppers' band, somehow they knew every word. It didn't take them long to get back to Eastfield.

'OK.' Paddy gathered her things together. 'I know a lot of policemen. If you ever tell anyone about this I'll phone your wife.'

He clutched his chest prudishly. 'Listen, I'm as ashamed as you are.'

She didn't want to smile or look at him again in case she stayed. Opening the passenger door, she stepped out of the car and watched him drive away, leaving her alone on the broken pavement.

If her mother had seen them pull up earlier and then drive away she'd say she forgot something at the comedy club. Her scarf. And they went back for it and stayed for another drink.

She watched him drive away. Burns didn't look back but she could tell by the inclination of his head that he was watching her in the rear-view. It was only then that she saw the red Ford Capri parked outside Mrs Mahon's house. She looked carefully, though it was in the shadow of the street lamp, but couldn't see anyone inside. She was being paranoid. Cars could park on the roundabout without her permission.

It wasn't until she was lying in her bed, reliving every touch and caress of the night, that she remembered the Ford hadn't been there when they first got home. Mrs Mahon was in her seventies. She wouldn't be receiving visitors at one thirty on a Friday night.

Paddy sat up, pulled on her dressing-gown and padded silently down the stairs, looking out of the front door into the silver frosted street.

The Ford was gone.

17

Subjects Not Objects

I

Bernie sipped cold tea from the plastic flask mug and glanced at his watch. It was late but he was into the rhythm of the work now, lost in it. The jack was well fitted under the car, he had his tools fanned out around the boogie board so that he could reach them easily without having to get up. It was a complicated job, requiring concentration, and any cracks or crevasses in his thinking were filled with the jabber of a phone-in on the radio.

The tea was bitter but he drank it down, hoping to sate his hunger. He hadn't eaten for six hours but didn't want to go back to his flat for food and sit, wide awake, thinking about Kate and Vhari and glancing down at the 'sorry, sorry' message on the newspaper. Vhari dead and Kate gone. The police had left him in no doubt as to how Vhari died, either. They spared him no detail because they suspected him, briefly.

When the police made him look at photographs of a bloody trail though the house and Vhari crumpled at the end of it Bernie sobbed so hard that he threw up. The policeman made him breathe into a paper bag and the smell of his own vomit got stuck around his nose and under his chin.

He frowned at his watch. It was two thirty. If he worked on until three or four he'd be so tired when he got home that he might even sleep.

He was sliding back under the car when the radio discussion turned to the morality of private schools. He remembered waiting at the bus stop with Vhari and Kate on wet winter mornings, fighting with each other as a way of keeping warm, the girls' bare legs mottled pink from the cold. He remembered the journey back as well, standing at the bus stop, hoping hard that none of the kids from the local comprehensive would come past and see them there in their blue Academy uniforms. He was the only boy at their bus stop until Paul came to the school. He came in the fifth year and everything changed for ever.

Paul Neilson had been expelled from Fettes boarding school for stealing. They all knew that even before he started because someone's brother was at Fettes and told them. A lot of the girls had decided not to talk to him. All the good girls. Vhari said it was wrong to treat people meanly because of rumours and she would try to be kind to him. Kate, he noted at the time, said nothing.

But then Paul arrived and everyone changed their minds. Paul wasn't just handsome, he was cool as well. He wore his rugby shirt with the collar turned up and exuded a vague sense of rebel threat. Kate, the prettiest girl in the school, was captivated from the first bus journey. She watched him introduce himself to the group, invite questions, tell them where he lived, that his dad had a business importing from South Africa and what the turnover was every year. She watched him with her pretty grey eyes, curling a blond tress of hair behind her ear. By the time they stepped off the bus at Mount Florida she deigned to smile at him. He walked up the road with them even though his house was in a different direction. By the next morning Kate and Paul stood apart from the waiting crowd, backing up against the wall, talking privately. If Bernie had known what would happen he would have dragged Kate away by the hair.

Down in the darkness under the engine, tears rolled down Bernie's temples into his hair and he shook his head. She'd stolen a fucking car from him. Even for Kate that was very bad. The Mini wasn't worth much but he didn't have much. Just as well it wasn't a punter's car, in for a service. Everyone she knew had more money than him, but then he was quite glad she had chosen to steal from him and not them. The people she knew now were not people you wanted to piss off.

The discussion on the radio moved on to yuppies and tax evasion and Bernie, unable to ignore the insistent hunger pangs in his stomach, finished off re-tightening everything and slipped out from under the car. He still wasn't tired.

Trying to listen to the fuck-wit callers on the radio, down with this and up with that, he lowered the jack on the car slowly, bringing the front wheels back to the floor, and pulled the jack out from under it. A man with a Birmingham accent was railing against the South of England for inflicting the Thatcher Government on the rest of the country for a second term as Bernie picked up his spanners and began to wipe the oil off them. Old news.

Bernie walked over to the table and crouched down to open the top drawer of his toolbox. He pulled it out, sat the spanners in place and shoved it back. It didn't close. He opened it again, checking along the lip to see if anything was sticking out, but it wasn't. He tried shoving it back in but again it stuck out half an inch, just far enough for him to be able to see inside. Something was stuck around the back.

Crouched by the side of the table, Bernie waddled sideways and saw the corner of the clear plastic sheeting. He smiled, thinking it was food, something he could pick the mould off that would keep him going for another hour or so. He pinched the plastic corner between two fingers and pulled. It was heavy and bigger than a sandwich wrapper. As he pulled it kept coming until he had to reach blindly with both hands and drag it out. It was the size of a small cushion, square and heavy.

The clear plastic had been folded over many times, the inside obscured by white dust, but the much-used silver duct tape, losing its adhesiveness, had rolled off a slit in the front when he lifted it and Bernie knew what was inside. White powder spilled out into a little pile on the floor. Panicked, Bernie's breath stuck in his throat like a fish bone. He couldn't exhale.

This was why Kate was so, so sorry. This was why she loved him. Stealing a car, inadvertently getting Vhari murdered, they were minor sins in comparison to this.

II

The sharp morning wind hurtled across George Square, eddying around monuments to the forgotten heroes of forgotten wars. It was the coldest place in the city centre; the brisk wind gathered speed across the wide open plain, pushing people into side streets.

Paddy walked past the giant post-office building and crossed over to the square, in front of the turreted City Chambers, around the imposing white cenotaph and saw them: a small gathering of people dressed in white with placards at the far end of the square. Some wore white jumpers or overcoats, one a thin anorak. They were huddled together, lighting small sputtering candles with a lighter, guarding the flame carefully with their hands and bodies and coats.

She had eaten a whole bag of Lemon Bonbons on the way here, buying them as a treat for her mum from the sweetshop at the station. She had one bonbon, just for a taste, and then another and then another one after that, and again and again until the bag was obviously half empty and she either had to throw them away or eat them all and buy another bag. Her teeth were coated in sugar, squeaking from the bicarbonate in the sherbet.

Queasy with glucose and guilt, she approached across the square and spotted a familiar green sports jacket hovering in front of the pristine line, breaking it up. It was JT, notebook in hand, with his head tilted to the side, a stance that always denoted heavy questioning. He'd heard about Thillingly and beaten her to it. She stopped, sighing with defeat, shutting her eyes. The wind brushed her hair from her ear and suddenly Burns was nuzzling into her neck, his hot breath damp on her skin. She gave a pleasured shiver at the memory.

Sex had always been a bewildering fumble that she got distracted from but never lost in. She had a moment in every sexual encounter when she was lost in everyday considerations: where had she left her house keys, would her diet work, should she get her hair cut. But not this time. It was because she had no respect for Burns. She smiled and opened her eyes, finding herself flushed, remembering where she was and what she was meant to be doing here.

The green sports jacket moved along the line. Cursing, she walked up to JT and stood at his elbow, listening in as unobtrusively as she could. He was quizzing a tall woman with an aristocratic nose and thick, lush grey hair pulled back and up into a leather clasp.

'For the release of Nelson Mandela.' Her accent was soft and English but authoritative somehow, as if she was used to public speaking. 'He's a lawyer who's been imprisoned in South Africa—'

'For starting a violent uprising.' JT spoke quickly as he always did when he was being confrontational. 'Some people would say you're supporting violent criminals. What would you say to those people?'

'Well,' the woman smiled uncomfortably, 'Amnesty're not supporting his release as a prisoner of conscience. We're arguing for his right to a fair trial.'

JT's pencil hovered idly over the page. He glanced up, waiting for her to say something outrageous.

'You ought to write that down,' said the woman. 'That's an important point.'

'Don't worry, I'll remember it. There are people who say he's the head of the South African equivalent of the IRA. What would you say to those people?'

Paddy stood behind him and listened to him wittering. He wasn't asking about Thillingly at all and she wondered what the hell he was doing here. Amnesty held their candlelit vigil in George Square every Saturday, for a different named person each week. Mandela was a controversial choice because he had supported an armed struggle after the Sharpsville massacre.

'Stuck for a story?' she asked.

JT turned and looked at her suspiciously. 'What are you doing here?'

'Well, you know, I heard they were supporting Nelson Mandela this week. Just wanted to ask them about it.'

'Yeah, looking for something to dazzle Ramage with? Well you've missed your chance with this baby.' JT smiled smugly. 'I've just done it. And now I'm going back to write it up.' He snapped his notebook shut and walked away. Paddy watched him saunter across the square, shaking her head slowly, staying disappointed in case he looked back.

The Amnesty supporters formed a solemn semicircle around two posters: one the Amnesty sign and the other a typewritten summary of Mandela's case, below a slightly blurred photograph of him as an earnest young man, his afro in a side parting. Above it broken Letraset letters in purple felt pen read '20 YEARS WITHOUT A TRIAL'.

Paddy stamped her feet against the freezing cold. The protesters looked at her, distrustful, avoiding eye contact because she knew JT.

'Look, um . . .' She stepped back, keen to differentiate herself from bombastic JT. 'I don't know how to approach this. I'm very junior, not an important reporter like him,' she thumbed after JT, 'but I wanted to ask you about a man called Mark Thillingly.'

The line rippled, disconcerted. A man at the far end shuffled his feet, someone coughed. A delicate girl in the middle of the line-up sobbed suddenly, covering her face. Her neighbour put his arm around her shoulder and pulled her in to his chest, holding the back of her head as she convulsed into the cables of his white Arran knit. He looked accusingly at Paddy. 'Mark was our friend.'

'I'm so sorry,' said Paddy. 'Please, I don't want to upset anyone.'

The girl sobbed afresh, noisily gulping air. Paddy noted the grey-haired woman roll her eyes so she turned and spoke to her instead. 'I do know that Mark was a good man.'

The woman took Paddy by the elbow, pulling her aside. 'Mark was a good man, you're right. He was very committed.' She nodded back to the sobbing girl. 'Natasha hardly knew him but she enjoys any drama to the hilt.'

'I'm sorry he died.'

The woman checked she was out of earshot of the others and dropped her voice confidentially. 'His suicide was a shock.'

Paddy matched her tone. 'Why?'

The woman shook her head. 'He was here last week. Seemed fine. Upbeat. Something must have happened between then and Tuesday night.'

Paddy looked down to the cenotaph, scratching around for one more question. 'He was a lawyer, wasn't he? Where did he work?'

'The Easterhouse Law Centre.'

Paddy nodded at her boots, 'Right.'

The woman was looking at her curiously. 'You knew that already.'

It was so cold that the woman's nose blushed red, her eyes narrowed against the wind, the skin comfortable in that position, and Paddy noticed that she looked rugged, as though she spent a lot of time outside. She imagined her briskly walking around the grounds of a grand estate, small dogs yapping at her heels.

'Could it be anything to do with Vhari Burnett's murder?'

The woman nodded sadly. 'Yes, poor Vhari. She was a member as well. Mark brought her to our first meeting. They were an item back then.'

'An item back when?'

'Years ago.' She thought about it. 'Five years ago? About that.

That's when we started this.' She turned and looked back at the group, taking in the crappy poster and Natasha crying, dry-eyed. She raised an appalled eyebrow and hummed to herself.

'And Mark was married then?'

'Oh, no, he went out with Vhari years ago. They knew each other at law school. Before he married Diana. I think their families lived near each other.'

Paddy nodded. 'Why did they split up? Did she chuck him?'

She smiled at Paddy's nerve. 'Other way round, actually. He went off with the woman who became his wife. Vhari stopped coming to meetings but she was still committed. Wrote letters from home, made a financial contribution, that sort of thing.'

'Was Mark ever violent?'

'Mark?'

'Yeah, was he ever violent?'

'The police think he killed her, don't they?'

'So I've heard.'

The woman thought about it for a moment. 'Honestly, I don't think he was even fit enough to be violent. He got breathless walking up hills. He smoked like mad and was a bit . . .' Her eyes flickered down to Paddy's body but she stopped herself from looking. 'Chubby.'

Paddy nodded at her notebook, trying not to blush.

'He was sad when he split up with Vhari.' The woman spoke quickly, trying to brush over the implied slight. 'He talked to me about it, seemed to be confiding but I think, really, he was trying to get me on his side. Mark was a natural politician. Everything was an opportunity to lobby. He was very measured.'

'It wasn't a very nice thing to do, go off with someone else.'

'Well, his wife, Diana, she's the insistent sort. Vhari was much more like Mark, very even-tempered. Diana has a bit more fire.' She wouldn't look at Paddy.

'You don't like her.'

The woman smiled wide. 'No. Diana gave up work after she

married. I can't abide women who won't work if they're able. I'm like Vhari: came from money but refused to take it and worked. I've never married. I've always supported myself.'

'You've made your own way.'

'I have.'

They smiled at each other, these two working women, both keeping jobs from needy men, betraying nature by escaping the kitchen sink, these two women who were out in the world, active not passive, subjects not objects.

III

Paddy was walking calmly away, feeling smug and superior, when she thought of JT just ahead of her in the street. She bolted after him, hoping she had correctly guessed his route back to the office, and caught sight of him a hundred yards ahead, about to turn the corner into Albion Street and the office. She jogged on, losing her breath, and caught his sleeve.

'Wait, wait, JT, I need to trade for a favour.'

He turned to look at her face-on, sceptical that she had anything to offer him.

'I'll do all your library searches for Mandela on Monday in exchange for a couple of taxi chitties. You'll get your Ramage story done twice as fast. He might even kiss you with his big red face.'

His head recoiled on his neck. 'What do you need a chitty for?'

'To take a cab journey at the paper's expense,' she said, acting stupid.

'Going to see a boyfriend, no doubt.' He started a smile, trying to engage in a bit of sexual banter, but she left her face flaccid and he gave up. 'Mandela and one other search.'

'No, just Mandela,' she said flatly. It was no skin off his nose to give her chitties. They were pre-signed forms to give to the paper's taxi firm and, as chief reporter, JT had an infinite supply, never questioned by management. They were supposed to be for office business only but she saw him climb in a firm's cab on his way home most evenings.

He watched her, grinding his teeth and looking for a chink he could exploit. 'Full-time search,' she said. 'And one on his wife Winnie as well.'

He pulled a small pad out of his inner pocket and tore two yellow slips off the pad, handing them over.

Paddy took them greedily, checking to make sure they were signed.

'What's it for, then? You doing a story?'

She smiled up at him, pleased by the small wondering throb in his voice. 'I'm doing an exposé of the illegal taxi-chitty trade. And now I'm making my excuses and leaving.'

Pleased with the line she turned and walked away.

IV

Kate found herself driving the battered Mini through streets so familiar they made her feel quite sentimental. Every street corner and hedge held a memory of an event or a person or a rumour or a game. Mount Florida. As she neared her parents' house she could name the family who lived in every second house back then, recall summer afternoons spent in most of the front gardens. There was the school bus stop and the wall where she first met Paul Neilson.

She hadn't meant to come here really, but was drawn by a memory. She had her snuff box with her, had taken a good dose and knew she could do anything.

She looked at the house. Daddy's lawn was as neat as a sheet of glass, leading up to the small thirties detached house, perfectly tidy and completely unobjectionable. They could have had a bigger home. They could have had a big home in Bearsden like the one her grandfather had, with a bedroom each and a field at the back. Their parents made sure the children knew that they could have afforded a lot of things, but were being actively denied. Money was available, but the children weren't worthy of it. Their school fees were expensive. They all knew, in itemized detail, how much food cost, how much their uniform set the family budget back, how dear each holiday was. Their parents' ever-changing wills dangled over everything like a Damoclean sword, casting a threatening shadow, spoiling every banquet. It affected them each differently: Vhari stopped caring about money and Bernie refused to take a penny off them. Kate liked money though. As soon as she got some, from Paul admittedly, she splurged it on jewellery and trips and clothes, lovely lovely things.

She stayed in the car, watching her parents' house to get a measure of it as she rifled blind in her handbag and felt the cold surface of the silver snuff box. She couldn't see any movement inside the house and a suffocating sense of dread came over her. She hadn't seen her parents for three years. If she went in now she'd have to tolerate their shock at her appearance. They'd be crying about Vhari now she was dead, when they had been so nasty about her when she was alive.

A fat girl in an old green leather coat sloped past her. Kate watched her in the rear-view mirror. She looked cheap; a loose thread was hanging from the hem of the coat. She had a small rucksack slung between her shoulderblades and spiky hair, as if she'd cut it herself. More interestingly, she stopped across the road, at the gate to the Thillingly house.

Kate looked at her parents' house and wished herself back at the start of all of this. She'd play it differently if she had another chance. Moderate her intake, scurry money aside into a secret account. Now she had nothing but the pillow. And Knox. She still had Knox. And she knew where he lived.

18

A Hundred Shades of Grey

I

Paddy hesitated by the wooden gate, looking down the long lawn towards the house. She had never been sent out on a death knock. The news editors always seemed to overlook her for the task and for once she was sure it was out of kindness. Dub had been asked to leave the paper after a death knock. He was supposed to ask a decapitated man's wife how she felt about it but was seen sitting in a café reading a poetry book instead.

It was a critical moment in most people's professional development. Even seasoned journalists hated it. Whenever people expressed bewilderment over JT's complete lack of compassion someone would bring up the rumour that he had cried in the toilet after his first death knock, as if it mitigated his lack of humanity to know that there had once been some to knock out of him. More worryingly, some people took to the work: one guy who made the move to a London tabloid had a habit of getting death-knock exclusives by turning on the family on his way out of the house and insulting the dead person: it was his own fault, he'd say, prick shouldn't have been driving a shit car. The family would be so hurt they'd refuse to speak to another journalist.

It was two in the afternoon and the curtains were still drawn in the living room. Tingling with trepidation, Paddy walked up the grey gravel path across the tidy lawn and remembered the horrified cry she had heard through the hedge four nights ago. She was going to hurt the woman again, she knew it. And yet her feet kept moving, one in front of the other, falling on to the gravel, crunching it beneath her weight, displacing it to the side as she passed. She wished she had Dub's integrity.

She reached the end of the path before she was ready.

The Thillinglys' front door was sheltered from the elements by a shallow trestle tunnel hung with vines, leafless at the moment, hanging like excised veins around the door. The brass doorbell rang out a soft two-tone.

Paddy stepped back, straightened her coat and scarf and fluffed her hair up at the sides, hoping she looked like a credible journalist, or at least an adult.

She heard shuffled steps approach across carpet and the door opened. A pretty but dishevelled woman stood in the narrow crack, head bowed as if expecting a blow. Her dirty blond hair stood up on top and lay flat on one side where she had been sleeping on it.

'Are you the insurance company?' Her voice was as high and breathless as a child's.

'No, I'm sorry to bother you at this difficult time—' Paddy stared at the small heartbroken woman and wondered what the hell she was doing here and how frightened of Ramage could she possibly be.

The woman leaned against the door frame, attempting to focus on Paddy's face. 'Who are you?'

'I'm from the *Scottish Daily News*. I wondered if I could talk to you about Mark?'

A slow tear rolled down the woman's face and she stuck her tongue out to catch it. 'They said you'd come.'

' "They"?'

'The police. They said you'd come. From the newspapers.'

No one else from the press had been. 'Oh.' Paddy nodded, trying

164

to jolt the words to the front of her mouth. 'I wanted to ask about Mark's relationship with Vhari Burnett.'

Suddenly awake, Mrs Thillingly looked up, swayed, then slammed the door shut.

Paddy stood staring at the red paint. If she wasn't so tired and had her wits about her she could have sidestepped this basic mistake. Of course it was a big deal; Thillingly was accused of killing Burnett. The woman behind the door hadn't only been widowed, her husband had been slandered as well.

The rain pattered on her shoulders, dripping cold on to her scalp. What a wasted fucking afternoon, and she'd have to stay in the office on Monday morning to return the chitties favour to JT.

Paddy looked down the wet garden, wondering where she could find a phone box to call for a taxi home. Mount Florida was a long way from George Square and further yet from Eastfield. She could have spent the afternoon at home, in the garage, with the fire on, reading a book or something, warm and alone. She was imagining herself in the big armchair drinking tea when she heard a gasp followed by another loud breath. Mrs Thillingly was still on the other side of the door, her sobs escalating.

'Look, I'm sorry,' Paddy told the door. 'I'm sorry about Mark. Everyone I've spoken to says he couldn't have hurt her. Mrs Thillingly?'

After a pause Paddy heard a soft voice. 'Diana. Call me Diana. Who did you speak to?'

'The Amnesty people in George Square. Diana, are you all alone in there?'

There was a loud sniff. 'Yeah.'

'Should you be alone?'

Diana sniffed again. 'Dunno.'

'Please . . . can I come in and talk to you?'

The lock slid back and the door opened into a neat hall. A

muggy warmth floated out to caress Paddy's face, contrasting with the cold of the day.

Diana turned and walked off down the hall, padding along the carpet in her bare feet. She had the build of a child, slim-hipped and thin-ankled, wearing Capri pants and a man's grey V-neck jumper that swamped her and hung over her fingertips. She flapped her hands behind her as she walked, hurrying away from the woman she had just let into her house.

Paddy pushed the door with her fingertips and stepped inside, shutting the door behind her. The house was overheated, the air thick with fibre and dust motes from new carpets. The long hallway was papered in pink and grey, with two matching paper borders at hip and head level that made it seem even more narrow. At the far end a doorway led into a kitchen awash with grey outdoor light.

Paddy walked towards it, listening for sniffs and clues that Diana was in there. She heard the fizz of a match striking and her throat tightened with yearning for a harsh, scratchy cigarette.

The kitchen was a later addition to the little thirties house. It was a big room plonked on the back so that the kitchen cupboards ran along what was once the outside wall. At the back of the extension was a glass box with a sloping roof, overlooking a large back garden and concrete patio.

Diana was sitting at a dining table in the middle of the glass shed, puffing on a cigarette without inhaling. The table-top debris suggested she had been sitting there for hours. A blue glass ashtray on the table had been emptied but not washed, and a recently crumpled cigarette, only half smoked and smouldering, lay face down. A navy and gold packet of Rothmans sat next to a very dirty white coffee mug which Diana was clutching, the rim marred with dried brown drips.

Shedding her coat and leaving it on the empty worktop, Paddy took a seat on the other side of the table. Diana exhaled, and even through the smell of cigarette smoke Paddy could smell the sharp edge of the brandy in the coffee. Diana was as pissed as a tramp at a whisky tasting.

'I've kind of been here all day.' She took a fresh cigarette from the packet and lit it with a match. 'Watching the garden. Mark's parents owned this house. His mother left it to him a few years ago. That's why the garden's so well established. He didn't want to change a thing.'

Paddy looked out at the small lawn bordered by bushes heavy with brown globe flowers. She hardly knew enough about nature to differentiate an oak tree from a spider plant. 'Those flowers must be nice. The round ones on the bushes – they look like Christmas decorations.'

Diana looked at her, incredulous. 'The hydrangeas?'

'Is that what they are? They must take some looking after.'

'No.' She sounded belligerent. 'They pretty much take care of themselves.'

Diana was clearly going to make her work for every snippet. She wasn't, Paddy guessed, a woman you'd want to have any power over you at all.

Stopping herself from gibbering, Paddy took out her packet of ten Embassy Regal and flicked it open. Regals were a poor person's cigarette: a brand women smoked at bingo nights and parish dances; cigarettes for women who didn't know the names of flowers. She looked at the pretty, slight woman opposite her and a spark of sharp, unwarranted resentment flared in her throat. She took in Diana's delicate features and good teeth and thought that she could go and fuck herself. Fuck herself and her fancy fucking house and her lawyer husband.

Holding the stubby cigarette between her teeth, Paddy took out her notebook and flicked to a clean page, drawing the tiny pencil out of the leatherette sheath on one side and writing 'bollocking fuck' at the top of the page in indecipherable shorthand, under-lining it twice to draw Diana's attention to her world, a world of women making their own way, a world of jobs and special skills where only Paddy knew the language.

'So,' she said, pencil poised, 'd'you have any kids?'

It was the perfect mark. Diana shook her head sadly. Her hand trembled as she lifted her cigarette to her mouth.

'And Mark worked at Easterhouse Law Centre?'

'Yeah. We're all right for money. He could choose to do that.'

'The law centre isn't a money-spinner then?'

Diana snorted. 'God no. Legal Aid's peanuts compared to what you can get for private work.' She raised her hands, as if coming to the tired conclusion of a well-worn argument. 'But that's what Mark wanted – to help people. See the sort of person he was? He used to come home at night and cry, I mean sometimes he'd actually *cry* when he told me about the people he had met that day. The poverty of the people. The poorness of their lives. Terrible.'

Paddy could imagine them both sitting in their conservatory, drinking a bottle of French wine in the evening, smoking dear fags together as they looked out over the large garden left by his mother, glorying in pity for people less well off than themselves. At that moment, thinking of her brothers and father and the cheap mince her mum padded out with onions and carrots, Paddy could have leaned across the table and slapped Diana Thillingly.

'Did he see Vhari Burnett?'

Diana's face greyed. She picked up her cigarette from the ashtray and puffed on it.

Paddy filled in the space. 'I'm sorry if I upset you.'

'Vhari and Mark weren't a sore point.' She sucked hard. 'They split up and it was fine. We met afterwards at parties. She seemed resigned to it. Never went out with anyone else, as far as I know. She was well over Mark, though. They were actually quite good friends.' She gave a shaky smile, finishing on an up-note, and stubbed her half-smoked cigarette out badly, leaving it smouldering. 'He'd hardly kill her out of the blue.'

Paddy thought of Sean and how she still regarded him as hers. Maybe Vhari felt that way too. 'But he died the night after Vhari, didn't he? He must have heard about her murder on the radio. How did he react?'

Diana shook her head and looked around the table. 'I don't know.' She took a deep breath as a defence against the attack of tears, but it did no good. A convulsion started in her chest. Her face contorted, her mouth stretching wide to the sides, eyes shutting with the pressure behind them.

'Were they involved in a case together? A prosecution or something?'

Diana shook her head. 'I can't . . .' She wheezed her breath away and started again. 'I can't . . .' She sat crying at the table, disinhibited by drink, crippled by the racking pain of loss.

Paddy picked up the packet of Regals. 'Come on now, will I get you another coffee?'

Diana nodded, still struggling to speak. 'I'd . . . no, I'm OK.'

Paddy lit two Regals and gave her one. They were short cigarettes and made the hands holding them look thick and stubby too. Diana took one, rubbing her eyes with the ball of her hand, her back rounded.

'I think I should get you a brandy,' said Paddy, standing up. 'I think you need one right now.'

Diana looked around the room, feigning confusion, as if the existence of brandy was a fact she couldn't quite grasp. 'Oh dear, perhaps . . . You could try in the cupboard under the sink. I think. I remember Mark put it there. I think.'

The bottle was wet on the outside where Diana had run it under a tap earlier, and a wet, sticky ring had formed on the cupboard shelf.

Paddy took a glass from the draining board and poured a generous inch into it, sitting it in front of Diana.

'Now, I don't want any fighting from you, but I know a bit about these things and this'll calm you down.'

Diana sipped the drink as if she'd never tried it before, shivering as it slid down. 'Why don't you have one?'

'D'you know, I'm not a great drinker. I'm taking my mum out tonight and she'll be annoyed if I turn up half cut.'

'Where are you going?'

'The All-Priests Holy Roadshow. It's a stage show that makes a school nativity look slick.'

'I've never heard of it. Is it a Catholic thing?'

'Yeah. My family are Catholic. I don't believe any of it,' Paddy leaned across the table confidentially, 'but don't tell my mum.'

Diana liked her a little more now, Paddy could tell, because of the Catholicism and the brandy. She smiled weakly, and raised her glass. 'Slange.'

Paddy raised an imaginary one back. 'And yourself.'

Random arrests and torture of suspects by the special forces in Northern Ireland had given all Catholics the cachet of an oppressed minority. Paddy had never experienced any kind of prejudice other than the favourable regard of well-meaning liberals but she enjoyed the status just the same. Sometimes she let it be known that she was Catholic to prompt the benefit of the doubt Diana was giving her now.

They smoked for a while, watching the light fail outside and the colours in the garden fade to a hundred shades of grey.

When Diana finally spoke she seemed to have sobered up. Her voice was small and she addressed the ashtray, rolling the tip of her cigarette endlessly against the glass.

'Vhari Burnett hadn't been on the scene for a while. She'd been working at the Fiscal's Office, I think. She and Mark didn't see each other professionally. The night she was murdered Mark came home later than usual, about eight o'clock. He was very upset. His nose was swollen and bleeding, as if he'd been punched on it.'

170

'Eight o'clock on the night she died? That's before she died?'

'Yeah. I heard on the telly that Vhari spoke to a policeman at about half one in the morning. But Mark came home at eight that same evening.'

'Did he go back out again?'

'No, but it was a strange night.'

Paddy had assumed there was a connection between Mark's broken nose and his death but hadn't guessed that it happened so long beforehand. 'You said he was upset?'

'He was. Very.' Diana stared at the table, nodding softly, over and over, comforting herself with the rhythm. 'It was raining that night. When he came in his nose was swollen and bloody and his woollen overcoat was soaking wet down one side because he'd been pushed over.'

Paddy remembered the cold rain, the wet outside Vhari's door and her own reluctance to get out of the car. Diana touched the bridge of her own nose, as if in sympathy. 'Mark wasn't a physical person, he wasn't tough. He didn't like violence.'

'What did he say had happened?'

'He came in late, but he could be late sometimes so I wasn't worried – it was only eight o'clock. He came in and said he'd been mugged in the car park outside his office. He wouldn't call the police or go to casualty. He said it was a client, someone he knew, and he didn't want them to get into trouble.'

'Did you believe that?'

'Not for a minute. It wasn't Mark's style, to let people off things. He thought everyone should do their time if they were guilty. That's why he didn't go into criminal law; he did civil work claims against the council, unfair dismissal, stuff like that. When he said he didn't want to call the police I knew he was lying. I checked his wallet when he was in the shower and it had money in it, so I knew it was a lie. I begged him to call the police but he was determined not to.'

Paddy could see the scene: Diana half cut after a couple of glasses of wine, stinking of fags, secretly furious that Mark was home late, the implacable fury of bright women locked in houses all day long, moving objects around, wiping dust, making meals for people who grabbed a sandwich on the way home.

'I'm afraid I got annoyed.' Diana's eyes filled up again. 'In the end I went to bed, but when he thought I was in the loo I heard the bedroom phone extension "ting" and knew he'd picked up the receiver. He thought I couldn't hear him.' She looked a little guilty. 'I only listened because I thought he'd changed his mind and was calling the police.'

'Thank God you were listening.'

'He spoke to someone. He asked them who they were and where Vhari was, and could she come to the phone. I came back down then, and asked him who he'd called, but he denied calling anyone. She'd just moved house, you know, Vhari. Her grandfather had died and left her that ridiculous huge house. Mark knew where it was, he'd been there with her when they were younger.' She slumped over her glass. 'He wouldn't come to bed with me. Sat up watching *Late Call* and drinking.'

Her voice faded as she thought herself back to the evening. 'The next morning he was gone before I woke up. I think he slept on the settee and went straight to work. It was lunchtime before I turned on the radio and it was all over the news: Vhari had been murdered. I called the law centre but he wasn't there. He never came home again.'

'Do you think he killed himself?'

Diana downed the brandy, emptying her glass, pausing to catch her breath at the end. Paddy considered offering her more, but it might suggest she thought that Diana could drink more than one brandy. She made herself sit still, willing Diana to continue.

'Yes.' Diana tapped her cigarette over and over, hesitating. 'Mark was a disappointed man. He was disappointed in himself, quite . . . depressive, you know. He always said if he killed himself it would be in the river, by the footbridge. It was his favourite place in the city. His Dad's office was by the river and he used to walk there with him when he was a boy. I think something happened in that car park that he couldn't cope with and the next night he walked into the river. I tried to make him happy.' She glanced up. 'I don't always . . . you know, drink.'

'I heard he left a note in his car?'

'Yeah,' she said softly, turning the glass in her hand. 'He said he was sorry but he couldn't, you know . . . go on. He was sorry he let everyone down, that he'd let me down and Vhari. Depressive silliness. It didn't mean anything. Certainly not that he'd killed her.'

'But he mentioned her in the note?'

Diana nodded miserably. 'That's why they think he killed her.'

'What did he say exactly?'

'Sorry he'd let her down. That was it.' She shrugged. 'He put her name before mine. As if she was the one that mattered.'

Paddy sat with Diana, rolling over the same facts: Mark's nose, the car-park attack, the phone call to whoever was with Vhari, waiting for a suitable break in which to leave, knowing she was abandoning Diana to a drunken night of lonely grief.

By the time she stood up it was dark outside. The only light in the kitchen was the throbbing scarlet glow of Diana's cigarette. Paddy struggled for something nice to say but couldn't think of anything.

'Would you have a photograph of Mark I could use?'

Diana twitched awake. 'Sure. Sure I do.' She went out into the hall, navigating fluently through the thick dark, and came back with a large walnut cigar box which she opened to reveal piles of snaps. 'This is nice.' She handed Paddy a graduation photo of Mark, slim and smiling in the summer. It didn't look like him and wouldn't go with a story about a dead solicitor who was approaching middle age.

'Lovely picture,' said Paddy, laying it firmly down near Diana, letting her know that it wouldn't do at all.

Diana took out another one. Mark looking awkward at a wedding, wearing a kilt. He was standing apart from a happy trio of friends, looking lost and left out. It would be perfect for a suicide story.

Paddy stood up, ostensibly to put the picture in her coat pocket. Diana watched her pull her coat on and then looked away into the garden.

Paddy stood next to her, hoping to be dismissed. 'I'm so sorry,' she said. 'I'm sorry all of this has happened to you.'

She really meant it – she was sorry for Diana – but noted uncomfortably that the sentiment sounded exactly the same as if she didn't.

II

Kate woke up thrashing, hitting the back of her hand off the Mini's steering wheel. Her left arm was on fire. She rubbed her shoulder, hoping it would stop, but could only reduce it to pins and needles. When she had calmed down and looked up she realized that she was parked right outside her mother and father's house. They could have come out at any time and seen her sleeping there. She'd rather meet Lafferty and the dead man than her mother.

She started the car and drove off, slowing cautiously at the junction up ahead, letting the fat girl in the green coat pass in front of her before heading for Bernie's garage, obeying the soft call of the comfort pillow.

19

The All-Priests Holy Roadshow

I

It was black night outside the train window. Paddy took the same journey to work every day but found herself seeing it for the first time because Trisha was there.

As she sat across from her mum on the quiet commuter train she wondered who had answered Vhari Burnett's phone when Mark Thillingly called her. It could have been Lafferty or the good-looking man at the door. And why had Thillingly called Vhari and felt the need to lie to Diana about it? It didn't sound as if they were having an affair. It sounded as if Burnett and Thillingly were in a lot of trouble, as if he was phoning her to warn her, to tell her what had happened to him in the car park, to tell her to run. Wondering about the relationship between Burnett and Thillingly reminded her of her hot breath wetting Burns's neck. She looked quickly away from her mother.

Trisha saw Paddy frowning and squirming and smiled, leaning across the aisle to pat her knee. Paddy smiled back reflexively. Her mum looked lost outside her house or the chapel or Rutherglen Main Street, her clothes slightly threadbare. She was wearing a stiff beige raincoat and Paddy could see a cross-hatched patch on the sleeve where she had scrubbed a mark away. Below the hem she wore thick tights over swollen ankles and little black sensible walking shoes that made her look old and spent.

And Trish was well aware of being outside her usual orbit. As she watched the moonlit landscape passing the window anxious little thoughts would flare in her eyes, suppressed immediately with a blink and a glance at her handbag. Paddy guessed what she was thinking: she had the bus fare home in her purse. Whatever happened she could still get back. Paddy had already moved further out into the world than her mother ever would.

'The buffet car's open,' said Paddy.

'Don't be daft.' Trisha frowned and looked inquiringly down the aisle. 'This train's only going into town. There's no buffet car.'

'Is that right?' Paddy reached into her pocket and pulled out a crumpled white paper bag. 'Where d'ye think I got these then?' She stretched the neck open and handed the bag of her mum's favourite sweeties to her.

Trisha grinned into the bag. 'Lemon Bonbons.' The golden light from the sweets lit up her chin like a buttercup.

'Lemon Bonbons,' Paddy smiled back.

Trisha offered a couple of times but Paddy insisted she was on a diet, and anyway, they weren't her favourites, they were for Trish. It wasn't hard to resist. Her teeth still ached from her binge in the morning.

It was dark in Argyle Street as they emerged from the low-level train platform, the street wet and glistening from a shower they had missed on the way in. The *Evening Times* seller had parked his stall under the lip of the shop opposite and Paddy found herself half listening for the headline: a football special. A bedraggled man in a rain-warped wool overcoat approached them with his hand out and a desperate alcoholic look in his eye. Trisha linked arms with her daughter, anxiously steering her away from him.

She shrank during the walk through town. Paddy felt the pangs of fear rippling through the muscles on her arm. She had meant the night to cheer Trisha up, not scare her. Every person dressed in party clothes made her draw closer to her daughter, pulling her sleeve, veering her walk out to the kerb to stay in the light and always just one degree of fright from throwing her arm out and hailing a bus to take them home.

The crowds were gathering outside the City Halls. They found their way through the chatting happy throng outside and bumped into Mary O'Donnagh inside the door. Mary was the chief chapel groupie at St Columkille's, one of a number of women who did unpaid work at the chapel and graded themselves according to their closeness to the priests. Rarely seen without a pinny, this evening Mrs O'Donnagh was dressed in blue navy slacks and was sporting a big set hairdo like a hairy halo.

'Oh, Mary,' said Trisha politely, 'isn't your hair lovely?'

Mary touched her head and smiled coyly. 'Our Theresa did it for me. Ye must go to her, Trisha, she's great.'

'I will, I will, I will,' said Trisha, so adamantly that even Mary knew she wouldn't.

Paddy saw Trisha relax as they moved in through the crowd of women. Accompanying men were occasional and stayed on the edge of conversations, holding the coats, patiently waiting for their wives.

Their seats were on the balcony. As Paddy sat down and looked to the stage she could see the centre circle filling up with a sea of women just like her mother, shedding cheap coats on to the seats, bri-nylon tops in pastel shades underneath. The stage was already dressed with a drum kit, a table of props and a couple of guitars on stands. Above it hung a sagging banner with brown writing on a white background – 'The All-Priests Holy Roadshow'.

Trisha sat forward in her chair and looked excitedly down at the crowd, spotting people she knew occasionally and pointing them out to Paddy, identifying each by the tragedies that had befallen their family. Mary O'Leery – son has multiple sclerosis; Katherine Bonner – husband died of a stroke and brother run over by a train;

Pauline Trainer – parents died of flu two days apart, always had a limp at school and a brother with TB; they weren't allowed to touch her in case they caught it.

The lights went down to a recording of Holst's *The Planets*. The audience bristled, sitting back in their seats and giving an excited collective titter. Four shadows walked on to the stage and the lights rose to uproarious applause.

Four ordinary-looking men of different ages were scattered around the stage clutching instruments. Each of them wore a priest's collar and nondescript black slacks and jersey. The man at the front raised his hands to wave a hello and the audience cheered as they started into a version of 'When Irish Eyes Are Smiling', slipping quickly into 'A Mother's Love's A Blessing'. Paddy had to admit that they knew how to work their audience.

What followed felt like a very long evening to Paddy. The priestly band split up, and one of them came back on to do poor stand-up comedy with rotten material. He told a slightly off-colour joke about a baby born on the wrong side of the blankets but the audience laughed because he was a priest so it must be all right then. Whenever Ireland or Irishness was mentioned a spontaneous round of applause would erupt and roll around the auditorium, as if the homeland was a thousand desert miles away instead of forty-five minutes away on a ferry. A skinny young priest who hadn't been in the band came on and did a poor Elvis impersonation, leaving the stage to a gale of appreciation.

It was warm in the auditorium, the heat from the crowd below rising up to the balcony, and Paddy found herself getting sleepy and half thinking about Thillingly being dragged out of the water, the black river running out of him and down the cliff as he lay in the cold grass, graceless; married Burns and the other policeman making jokes about him minutes after his soul left his body; and the jagged bank ripping his face open.

Paddy nodded off in the dark warm, enjoying the close press of women around her and Trisha, content for once, at her side. She woke up as the lights rose for the interval with Trisha rustling in her handbag for bonbons, and Paddy knew that Thillingly hadn't hurt Burnett or even been at her house the night she died. He had committed suicide because of what had happened in the car park, because of some humiliation, some small scuffle that related to Vhari. To an uncluttered mind it was an obvious conclusion, and if it was obvious to her it was probably obvious to everyone else. That's why Sullivan was going behind his bosses. That's why he was asking her to meet him in dark alleys outside the morgue. Someone was working hard to steer the Burnett murder inquiry away from the good-looking man in braces at Vhari's door. This was the story that would get her off the night shift; the story she was going to write up for Ramage

The lights went up in the hall and a flock of desperate women with labour-weakened bladders bolted for the loos. Most people stayed in their seats, saving their tired legs the worry of getting back up the stairs again. The consensus from the seats in front and behind them seemed to be that it was a very, very good show. Very good. Even better than last year.

Trisha chewed the last bonbon and looked despondently into the empty paper bag. 'I don't suppose ye brought another quarter of bonbons for the interval?'

Paddy acted indignant. 'Is nothing enough for ye, woman?'

They giggled about it until the lights went back down and the second half of the show began with a priest in sunglasses singing a Roy Orbison medley.

On the way back to the train station afterwards, as they walked down the dark streets, staying close to the others all heading home to Rutherglen, Paddy found herself feeling for the photocopy of the Burnett funeral photograph in her pocket, stroking it with her finger, yearning to break away from the cautious crowd. In the

Eastfield Star Caroline would be sulkily watching television in the living room, the boys would be out and Mary Ann would be praying upstairs or reading an improving book: she didn't watch telly any more. No one would have done the dishes after tea and Trisha would don her pinny and start cleaning as soon as they got in.

Paddy felt the pull of the town and wanted to go to work, wondering what her city was throwing up tonight.

20

Sunday Bloody Sunday

I

Paddy had wasted thirty minutes looking for the address of the Easterhouse Law Centre in the Glasgow *A–Z*. She shut the book, let it drop down the side of the armchair and put both her hands on the table in front of her, like a psychic trying to conjure a spirit.

She should have been thinking about Patrick Meehan and the book, scribbling page after page of true-crime doggerel, but nothing came to her.

Meehan was from a poor family of Irish immigrants and grew up in the Gorbals during the days of the Razor Kings, when squads of young men fought pitched battles in the high narrow streets with open-necked razors sharpened to a tip. He was sent to reform school for breaking the branch of a tree in the park and learned his trade there. Petermen were safe-crackers, skilled professionals, gentlemen who knew how to cook gelignite in a frying pan and stay calm enough during a break-in to listen for the lone, distant click of a safe lock. They were respected. He'd escaped from Nottingham jail during a stint for burglary and travelled to East Germany, crossing the border on a stolen bicycle to sell ground plans of British prisons to the Communists, prompted, he claimed, by an MI5 agent provocateur. The Communists questioned him for eighteen months and then handed him back to British intelligence to serve out his sentence. Resentful and broke, he sold his story to a national paper and claimed that he'd drawn up the plan to spring the spy George Blake. He said he'd told MI5 before it happened and they did nothing, which proved they were all counter agents. Six short months after the article was published, he was charged with the brutal murder of an elderly woman in Ayr. Everyone in Glasgow knew he was innocent: the real murderer tried to sell his story to the *Sunday Express* days after Meehan's conviction. Meehan was a technician. A criminal but a craftsman, not a thug.

Paddy had been haunted by Patrick Meehan's story since she was a young girl. The accident of having the same name made her listen every time he was mentioned on the radio news, try to read the newspapers from long before she should have, assume his mantle of guilt every time a fresh appeal was knocked back. A journalist wrote a book about the flaws in the case and the appeal was reopened. Finally, after seven years in prison, Meehan was given a Royal pardon for a crime he didn't commit and was set free. For Paddy, Meehan became a symbol of attacks on Catholics, of the blindsiding hypocrisy of the British judiciary, of the triumphant value of journalism.

She knew the story inside out and it had everything: exotic locations, secret-service machinations, a shoot-out across Glasgow, a faithful wife and a beleaguered hero who triumphed in the end.

As she chewed the end of her pen, looked hard at the blank page in front of her, she felt the will to write anything about Patrick Meehan ever again slipping away from her. The only reason she'd started was that she thought it would be easy.

She reached down to the other side and picked up her notepad and the cuttings she had kept about Vhari.

The green wood-burner gave off a warm glow as she settled back in her chair, doodling in the margin of the pad, listening to the graphite scratch of her pencil. Vhari Burnett had retreated into the house after they had pulled her teeth out. She would have known by then that they were vicious enough to kill her and yet she had slipped out of view and had gone back inside. Paddy couldn't imagine anything that would induce her to martyr herself. It couldn't have been money, Vhari didn't care about that. It didn't seem to be a case she was working on either. But whatever it was, she cared enough about it to give up her only chance of escape.

Paddy looked at the blank page again and tried to imagine Patrick Meehan doing anything: meeting Betty, being questioned, standing trial. All she could see was a pock-marked man sitting at a table, looking at her expectantly, waiting impatiently for her opening gambit. But she didn't have one.

If she was ever going to write any of it she'd need to do something. McVie was the only man who could help her.

II

For reasons as deep as a volcanic plug, Scotland mourned Sundays. Churches and pubs and newsagents were the only things open. Even the telly was rubbish. By teatime most areas were shuttered and fly-blown. Cars in the streets moved slowly, as though afraid to stir up the leaden air.

The address McVie had given her was in the back lane of the old warehouses that were being renovated and sold to yuppies. His flat was down a narrow street, the high buildings on either side swallowing what light there was. On the corner of his block was a pub: a grubby, tired working men's bar, a remainder from a time when the area had a workforce and a purpose.

Paddy passed the pool of light outside the pub and made a mental note that she could run back here if anyone jumped out at her from the shadows.

The doorway to McVie's building was a grand double door set in an arched frame of pale-green glazed bricks, its splendid grandeur lost in the narrow alley. A pristine panel of buzzers with names next to them hummed. Paddy pressed the button marked 'McVie' and waited.

'Yes?'

It was a man's voice but he was English and sounded young.

'Hello?' she stuttered. 'I was looking for George McVie?'

He paused for a moment. 'Who are you?'

'I'm Paddy Meehan, from his work.'

The voice asked someone something and came back to the intercom. 'Come in. Two flights up.'

Intrigued, she pressed one of the big doors with her fingertips and it clicked open in her hand, letting her into a wood-panelled lobby with a modern staircase on the right. Above her, somewhere along the ribbon handrail, she heard a door open and the soft sound of a piano concerto playing on a radio station.

Climbing the stairs towards the sound she wondered if George might have a son from England, or a cousin perhaps. She didn't know what his domestic situation was. Before the recent change in his behaviour she'd assumed he lived somewhere middle class with grown-up children who sided with their mother, that they all lived together in a house in the suburbs that looked nicer from the outside than it did on the inside, that they were unhappy and too cowardly or unimaginative to leave each other.

A barefoot man was standing on the landing above her. He smiled as she turned the corner. He shifted his weight, resting his hip against the railing as he dried his hands on a tea towel, standing to attention as she approached, holding his hand out to her. He had a flat-top haircut, a white T-shirt worn soft with a hundred washings, and a pair of stone-washed denims with a pleated front.

Paddy took his hand and shook it.

'I'm Ben,' his said, an excited throb in his voice.

Paddy was so distracted by Ben's face she almost forgot to introduce herself: she could have sworn he was wearing mascara and lip gloss. Either that or he had just been swimming, climbed out of the pool and eaten a greasy chicken portion without licking his lips.

She took his hand. 'Paddy.'

'Hello.' Ben shook her hand and held on to it, pulling her through a small door into a low corridor and out into a large room with a strip of kitchen against the back wall. Facing the kitchen, magnificent windows ran the full length of the room. Unfortunately the view was a brick wall twenty feet away, the monotony of it broken only by a few small, dirty office windows, dark now.

Below the big windows, as far from the door as was possible in the room, sat McVie. He was in a chintzy armchair, chosen for a different sort of house, stagily holding a book as if he was reading it. Every muscle on his face was taut, creating deep inverted commas above his eyebrows.

'Georgie.' Ben spoke his name as if he was giving him a warning.

McVie looked up and pretended to be surprised. 'Oh, hello, Paddy.'

Something was going on, something homosexual, but Paddy wasn't worldly enough to know what it was. Her mother said homos were men so debauched that they had tried everything else, the implication being that nothing was dirtier than a man with a man. She'd laughed at Trisha's naivety, but the fraught atmosphere was making her wonder. The only homosexual she had seen in the movies was the lonely guy in *Fame* who had a psychiatrist and a ginger afro. Would there be nudity? Would she be expected to dance? Would she be expected to dance nude? She made a panicked face at McVie.

'What?' He stood up from his chair, rattled and frightened.

Paddy waved her open palms at him.

'What's wrong with her?' said Ben tartly.

She wanted to leave but Ben was between her and the door. She looked around the flat for an alternative exit. Everything in it was brand new but the furniture was old-fashioned. The walls were new, the kitchen looked immaculate. She doubted the cooker had ever been used.

'Nice flat,' she said, as a filler.

Ben pulled his T-shirt up at the waist to scratch his stomach. 'We just moved in.'

'Where were you before?'

'He lived in Mount Vernon. I was in a bedsit in Govanhill.' He looked accusingly at McVie. 'It was shit. I was there for months.'

McVie looked at Ben, a sweeping look that started on his bared stomach and rose, softening, until it reached Ben's eyes. She suddenly understood that McVie loved him. There would be no naked dancing, no untoward touching. Ben was the reason McVie had bought flowers, the reason he looked younger and dressed himself nicely.

'Am I the first person you've had up from work?'

Ben answered for him. 'Yes. Georgie's met all my friends from college and I've not met any of his friends.'

'Because I haven't got any friends,' explained McVie, dropping his book.

'So,' Paddy didn't want to get in the middle of a fight, 'which college are you at?'

'Royal Academy of Music.'

'Brilliant. What do you play?'

Ben smiled arrogantly. 'Most things,' he said.

McVie frowned and looked out of the window at the brick wall. Her invitation was a test. Paddy knew he had given her his address and asked her up because she didn't matter. If the visit went badly it would be a containable disaster because no one at work listened to her anyway. To be a sexually active woman in the news room was hard, but to be a poof in love would be very hell.

'McVie, I'm on my way to work but I stopped by to ask a favour. I need to meet Patrick Meehan. Can you set it up?'

McVie sat up. 'I thought you didn't want to meet him.'

'I'm trying to write a book about him.' Admitting a personal ambition was almost as dangerous as admitting to being gay. 'But it's not happening.'

186

'Take your coat off,' said Ben, pulling at her sleeve. 'This isn't a station.'

'No.' Paddy brushed his fingers from her sleeve as kindly as she could. 'I need to go to work.'

'Your friend is rude,' said Ben, spinning on his heel and walking off to the bedroom.

Paddy smiled down at McVie. 'Georgie?'

McVie grinned back, stood up, and pushed her towards the front door.

It was cold on the landing and he was wearing his slippers without socks. He tried to talk to her but she pulled his jumper sleeve until they were two flights of freezing steps down, standing close together behind the draughty front door.

They stood close, she noticed, closer than they ever had before, and McVie looked down at her, shivering but giddy with relief. 'You don't like Ben, do you?'

'No.'

They giggled together for a moment, neither quite sure why, and looked at the rows of brass mail boxes on the wall behind the door. Paddy didn't like Ben but McVie did. He liked him so much he was dressing well and buying flowers and smiling without witnessing an accident. When they first met he was the most unhappy, bitter person she had ever sat next to. He was a homosexual but she was having mad sex with married men in cars and it was making her pretty happy.

'I've known you for four years and you've been nothing but miserable and hateful. But now . . .' She looked at him – a compliment would embarrass them both. 'You're – not.'

McVie nodded at the brass mail boxes, eyes flicking across the handwritten scraps of paper shoved into the windows. 'Aye. That's a nice thing to say.'

'It is. I'm nice.' They giggled together again. 'I'll not say anything. It's not my business.'

McVie closed one eye and looked at her again. 'You really don't like him?'

'What's the difference whether I like him or not? I'm not shagging him.'

He blanched, shocked at her frankness. 'What are you talking about? You're supposed to be a good Catholic girl.'

She didn't want to talk about her own sexual behaviour. 'I'm just saying. Not being depressed has to be a good thing, doesn't it? Those instincts are there for a reason.'

'I suppose . . .' He scratched the gummy residue of a sticker off the face of one of the mail boxes. 'It was either kill myself or give in to it.'

They bridled at the sudden honesty, looking away from each other.

'Maybe you should have considered the first option more closely,' said Paddy quietly, making him smile. 'Right, I'm off. Will you set up the Meehan meet for me?'

'Sure.'

She reached for the door.

'By the way, you were asking about Bobby Lafferty? He's in Govan police station. Been there since this morning. They're questioning him about the Bearsden Bird, apparently.' He looked at his watch. 'You want to get yourself over there. They've only got another four hours with him.'

III

The street was quiet outside Bernie's garage. Kate leaned into the back seat and lifted the blue-handled wire-cutters over to the front, finding them incredibly heavy, so heavy that her wrists could hardly manage the weight of them. She sat with them in her lap, weighing down her skinny legs. She was so thin now that she could fit her fist sideways between her thighs. Taking a deep breath, she opened the door and stepped out into the street, cradling the wire-cutters in her arms as she walked along the railway arches.

Bernie had put a new padlock on the doors and she cut through the loop of metal on it, finding it harder to get through than the last one. She was getting weak. She hadn't eaten anything for days, couldn't remember what it was like to want food. The tinned, jellied ham she'd brought from the cottage stuck in her throat like a fist of dried leaves.

Unhooking the padlock, she slipped inside, feeling along the wall for the light switch, smiling to herself when she thought about the prize waiting there for her. She realized to her surprise that she was salivating, thinking about holding her pillow again, feeling the warm skin-like texture under her fingers, smelling the clean, sweet plastic. The light flickered on, a sharp brutal whiteness that hurt and she blinked several times to adjust her eyes. Each time she opened them again she thought she was mistaken but the image resolved itself in her eye and she managed to squint and keep her eyes open. The table had been pulled out, the red toolbox yanked away from the wall at one side. She hurried over to look behind it.

The pillow was gone.

Sobbing, she sank to her knees. She could stand Vhari being murdered, she could handle losing her looks, she could even, she realized now, cope with being told to get out of the Killearn mansion she had lived in for four years, but this was too much.

It had to be here. Blinded by tears, she stood up and pulled some things off the table, toppling a stack of receipt pads on to the floor before stopping, exhausted. If Lafferty had been here he would have made the same sort of mess as he had in the cottage. Everything would be broken. It was Bernie. He had stolen her pillow.

Kate walked out of the garage, leaving the doors lying open and the light on, and climbed back into the Mini. On second thoughts she decided that she would need to keep Bernie sweet if she was to get her pillow back from him. She climbed out of the car, flicking the garage lights off and pulling the doors to.

She started the engine, patting the wheel encouragingly when it started, and headed off to Bernie's flat.

21

Lafferty the Dog

I

Sullivan let Paddy lead the way into the black corridor and shut the door softly behind him. The tiny narrow room smelled of dust and sweat, the black walls around her thick to keep the noise out. She could just make out Sullivan's face in the silver gloom coming through the two-way mirror. He turned away from her, craning his neck as he peered though the mottled glass into the cream room. His belly had been pulled in as they climbed the stairs and walked to the door but now, fascinated by the scene in front of him, he relaxed, his back slouching and his belly hanging out in a way that made her think of her dad and smile.

Sullivan had warned her not to speak, that the room wasn't soundproof, but Paddy found herself inadvertently sighing an exclamation. His head was shaved and his shoulders were broad, as if he worked out in a gym. A bushel of tendons stood out on either side of his thick neck, the skin on it wrinkled, hard, knife-slash criss-crosses over thin skin where the muscles had been tensed for thirty years. He looked like a thick-necked dog. If Lafferty went for you, he'd be making contact with his teeth.

His eyes roved around the room as one of the two officers sitting in front of him asked questions. Where was he in the early hours of Tuesday the fifteenth? Had he been in Bearsden that night? Lafferty's angry animal eyes flickered back and forth across the wall and the mirror, gliding over Paddy's face and Sullivan's chest. They were dead eyes, unkind and cold, vicious.

Opening his mouth to speak, Lafferty displayed a row of broken and dead teeth. He stared straight at the mirror and demanded in a hard man's drawl to know who was asking 'theze quesjinz'. The officer ignored him and repeated himself, sounding bored, as if he'd been saying the same thing over and over for quite a long time.

'Aye.' Lafferty stood up slowly, knuckles on the table, and craned his neck towards the mirror. 'Sullivan. *Cunt.*'

The two officers were on their feet, hands out and ready to stop him if he went for the mirror, but Lafferty lowered himself back down to his seat.

Paddy looked at the man standing next to her. The dull light through the mirror caught the beads of sweat on Sullivan's forehead. He glanced at her, tipping his head back, acknowledging how frightened he was and apologizing. He clasped his hands in front of him, as if protecting his genitals, shifted his weight uncomfortably, and turned back to watch the mirror.

Paddy looked at Lafferty and imagined him in Vhari Burnett's living room. She had been a slim, slight woman when Paddy glimpsed her. Compared to Lafferty she'd seemed no more than an ethereal strip of white light.

'I wiz in the Lucky Black Snooker Club in the Calton until seven in the morning. Jamesie Tobar'll stand for me. Anyone else who was there'll stand for me. I get home at eight in the morning and went tae my bed. The missus'll tell ye.' He glanced at the mirror again. 'The fuck else d'yeez want?'

The officers sitting at the table bristled at this news, pulling their notepads towards them and starting to take notes, asking him to go over it again and again in detail, giving them times only an obsessive with a new watch would know.

'We've got your prints on an object from the house.' The officer watched him carefully. 'On the night she died.'

Paddy saw Lafferty's mask slipping as he thought about it. His lips twitched. 'Object? What's that then?'

'It puts you there that night, Lafferty.'

'What is it? Anyway it can't,' he said confidently, 'I was at the Lucky Black.'

Sullivan's hand landed gently on the small of her back, making her jump. He nodded to the door and she followed him back into the dim corridor outside and down a longer passage. Neither of them spoke until they reached the stairs.

Sullivan cleared his throat uncomfortably. 'If his alibi pans out we'll have to release him in a couple of hours.'

'He might guess it was the fifty quid his prints were found on. He'll come after me if he does. He knows where I work and everything, for God's sake.

Sullivan avoided her eye. 'Sometimes they have to go in heavy – he's much more likely to think it's something in the house.'

'If they wiped the house clean of prints they were being pretty careful. It wasn't a fight in a pub, they're going to remember what they did and didn't do.'

Sullivan nodded slowly. 'Well, we have to confront him with the evidence. If he doesn't find out now he will later. It's better to spring it on him and try to get something out of it.'

They walked down a flight of stairs and Paddy stopped him on the no-man's land of a landing. 'Sullivan, what's the story with the cops at the front door of Burnett's house? Why is the investigation being steered in completely the wrong direction?'

'I have bosses. I don't make those decisions.' Sullivan looked down the staircase, sad and a little broken, and took the banister to steady himself. 'You had to be a journalist, didn't ye? Couldn't be a meals on wheels or Avon lady.'

'You know he's not the guy I spoke to at Burnett's front door, he's not the well-spoken guy.'

'I know. We found other prints on the note. Don't worry. We'll follow Lafferty, work out who he's with and that'll give us the boss's name.'

'But if the cops at the door won't tell us who they were speaking to, all that ties Lafferty to the scene is me and the note. He'll come for me.'

'You'll be safe enough. I've told no one about the note and neither's McDaid.'

Paddy wasn't convinced, but Sullivan was and she found this comforting.

'Did you arrest Lafferty or did he come in on his own?'

Sullivan looked suspicious. 'Why?'

Paddy shrugged. 'Just asking. I don't know how these things work.'

'We called his solicitor and he drove in himself. We'd have arrested him if he hadn't. He'd know that.'

As she listened she remembered Sullivan sweating in the dark, his paunch hanging over his belt buckle, his eyes afraid of the animal in front of him. 'I don't usually swear, Detective Sullivan, but I'll say this: that Lafferty is one fucking scary bastard.'

Sullivan cuffed her playfully over the back of the head, half smiling at the gesture of sympathy. 'Language, lady.' He dropped a foot on to the step in front of him and led her down the empty staircase to the front desk.

Paddy followed him down, feeling the damp trail from his hand on the banister, and realized that he probably had a daughter her age and that this was why he was nice to her.

'Just you leave it to us,' he told her. 'You're too pretty to ask so many questions.'

She smiled back and watched him open the door to the waiting room, holding it open and ushering her through ahead of him. He definitely had a daughter her age. And she probably half hated him too.

II

Paddy hadn't gone straight back to the calls car after Sullivan saw her to the door. She'd headed across the road towards Billy until she saw the yellow slice of light on the pavement in front of her fold into black and knew the door was shut behind her. Then she turned and headed to the car park behind Govan police station. Fords and Minis and Rovers, two Mini Metros, even a Honda estate car and an old brown Morris Minor, but no BMW. Whatever Lafferty came in it wasn't one of the cars from the back of Burnett's house on the night she was killed.

Paddy sat back in the car and watched the lights outside the window, thinking about the person who owned the BMW. If his alibi panned out they'd have to release Lafferty and whoever had been at the house that night would probably die. She thought of Lafferty's neck again, of the brute force and all the harm and misery reflected in his eyes, and she could have cried. Vhari Burnett and Mark Thillingly's deaths weren't accidents. These were deliberate. People were choosing to do these things to each other.

It was a quiet night in the city. Sunday-night trouble was always nasty, personal. A raft of domestic incidents followed the pubs shutting early as weekend drinking drew to a reluctant close, leaving people with nowhere left to go but home and no one left to fight with but family.

Billy was furious about the *Daily News* lay-offs. He was even angrier about the fact that no one was doing anything about it. It wouldn't have happened in the old days, no way, they never used to let the management dictate terms like that. Letting them give Farquarson his books was the first mistake. They should all have stood up for the guy, all gone out for him.

Paddy thought Billy was wrong. The sales figures were dropping faster than a bag of bricks. If they didn't make changes the paper would go under. She had other things on her mind anyway and just nodded vaguely when he looked to her for a reaction.

The night was so quiet that they stopped early at the death-burger van for their dinner. The lateness of the hour and deplorable standards of hygiene made the food at the van ultra-delicious. Nick, the mesmerisingly fat server, used the tiny hand-washing sink to store a bin bag of buttered rolls.

Despite his enormous girth, Nick negotiated the tiny space with balletic grace. His dance began by the sink: he whipped a pre-buttered roll from the bin bag, sauced it and did a graceful half-turn to the handle of the frier, lifting and emptying the basket's contents on to the drip tray and pinching the burger or chips or sausage into the mouth of the roll. The only thing he didn't deep fry was the mugs of tea and coffee. Everything else, from fish fingers to frozen pizzas, went into the bubbling mess, creating an aromatic aura that radiated fifty yards downhill to the main road.

The van sat on a steep, empty sliproad that led from a busy thoroughfare to the park where taxis could stop easily. When Billy and Paddy stopped, around two or three in the morning, only motorized night-shift people gathered, nodding hellos, enjoying the city's calmest hours.

Usually Paddy'd get the burgers for herself and Billy, no F-plan option here, and climb back in the car. They'd sit with the radio turned down a notch sometimes in a cosy silence, sometimes sharing speculative gossip about people at work they didn't know very well. Tonight Billy was out of the car by the time she turned back, chatting to a cabbie he knew, passing on the news of the lay-offs no doubt, glad of a fresh audience to vent his indignation to. Pleased she wouldn't have to deal with him, Paddy took his burger over to him and went back to the car alone, relishing the prospect of a quiet half-hour.

She was licking the burger grease from her fingers, wishing she could have another one, when the police car drew up. For a moment her throat tightened until a door opened and the cab light went on, showing that the two uniformed officers inside were no one she knew and certainly not George Burns.

She watched them swaggering over to the death-burger van, looking around at the parked cabs, claiming the territory like cowboys entering a saloon. They accepted free rolls from Nick, toasting him before wandering over to join Billy and the cabbie. A couple of other cabbies gravitated over to them to find out what was happening in the city tonight, where the accidents were and which routes to avoid. She noticed them glancing over to her, sitting alone in the car.

Sullivan had seemed certain that Lafferty wouldn't connect her to the fingerprints, but she wasn't sure. The thought of his thick neck and mean eyes turned her stomach.

The group of men around the burger van broke up with a bit of shoulder-slapping and a final joke, and Billy walked slowly over to the car. A cabbie sounded his horn and pulled his cab a full circle, driving off, and Billy raised his hand in a slow wave.

She had never heard a door slam quite as loudly. The sudden change in air pressure made her ear drums smart. Billy stopped for a moment and sighed, his hands on his knees, before turning the key to start the engine and yanking the car in a fast, tight turn, throwing Paddy against the side of the cab, knocking her forehead on the cold window.

She shouted at him over the noise of the radio but Billy accelerated, taking the junction with hardly a glance either way. Paddy peeled herself off the back seat and sat forward, slapping his shoulder. 'Fucking calm down!'

Billy sped the car up and ran a red light, racing through a junction to the motorway. It would have been busy during the day and Paddy could imagine cars ploughing into her side. She reached forward through the seats and grabbed the handbrake, her thumb hovering over the button.

'Stop this car or I will.'

Abruptly, Billy stepped on the brakes. Good driver that he was, he tapped the pedal three times. Paddy was thrown forward, her shoulder jammed between the two front seats. The engine spluttered to a stop. Behind them in the deserted road, the cabbie who had been at the death-burger van hooted irritably and drove around them.

Paddy touched Billy's hair at the back. 'What happened there?'

He shook his head and looked at her in the mirror, a deep hurt vivid in his eyes.

'Billy?'

'You stupid cow.' He pressed his lips together and for a moment she thought he was going to cry. 'You fucked a cop. In his own car.' He reached forward and restarted the stalled engine. 'You stupid cow.'

He drove off at ten miles an hour through the bleak, dead city.

III

An hour later Paddy was still chilled and silent, sitting in the back of the car, pressed tight up against the back seat as if Billy was doing ninety. She nodded dumbly when Billy asked her if she wanted to follow up the only radio call they'd had so far, a minor domestic in Govanhill. They drew up behind two panda cars, badly parked at angles from the pavement as if something enormously important was going on.

When Paddy got out and shut the door, she paused by the side of the car to pull her scarf up around her neck. Billy didn't lift his packet of fags off the dashboard like he usually did. He sat looking at her, straight at her, hurt and angry and disgusted. Paddy bent her knees and looked in at him, gesturing for him to unwind his window. He carried on staring at her, watching as the bitter wind blew her hair hard against her head and pinched her cheeks.

She took a step back down the body of the car, opened the passenger door and shouted in at him, 'You mind your own fucking business, you ugly prick.'

Billy started the car before she'd pulled back, driving along the road for fifty yards with the passenger door swinging wildly. He stopped, threw one foot into the street, shut the passenger door and reversed towards her, slowing as he came past her to show that he was in control. Paddy lifted her leg and kicked the passing car with the heel of her foot as hard as she could, pulling herself off balance and staggering over to the side. She left a heel-shaped dent in the door. Billy sped off.

They'd sack him for leaving her there. They hadn't even done the city centre hospital calls round yet. She'd have to cover for him by getting a taxi back to the office and she wouldn't be able to claim the money back or Ramage would find out what had happened.

Furious, she entered the damp of the green close. It was dark inside – the lights were out on the lower landings and only deflected light from higher up in the echoing stairs tempered the shadows. Following the sound of voices, she climbed up to the second landing. A drunk woman was protesting, drawling 'Nah, nah, nah,' over everyone who tried to speak to her. Two policemen were trying to calm a man who was saying that she had said this and he'd said that and then she went like this and he was like that. What would you do, pal? Eh? With a woman like that. What would you do?

His bottom lip was bloody and made her think of Vhari Burnett. Next to him, hanging on the door frame and keeping them all out of the flat, was a skinny woman in stone-washed jeans and a lemon jumper that had been stretched by a yank to her neck and hung off one bony shoulder.

The policemen looked up as Paddy climbed the stairs. It was George Burns and his partner. His eyes smiled spontaneously, a warm loving grin, but he looked away immediately. He was wearing his wedding ring.

Paddy struggled to remember what an innocent would do in this situation. She took out her notebook, conscious of her hands, her neck, the way she was moving. The other policeman continued to question the woman and Paddy made a big deal of glancing around the doorway to get the right number and the names on the door-plate. She wrote everything in her notebook, working briskly as if it was a worthwhile story.

George's pal managed to convince the woman to let them go inside to talk about it and give the neighbours a chance to go to sleep. As he followed the arguing couple into the house he turned and looked at her, smirking disparagingly. Burns hung back, wait-ing until the policeman and the couple were out of earshot. He didn't get the chance to speak.

'You cunt.' She'd never used the word before and felt the hairs on the back of her neck stand up at the sound of it.

He coughed a laugh and looked astonished. 'Wha?'

'Everyone in Glasgow knows. Billy was told at the same time as a bunch of cabbies outside the death-burger van.'

Burns looked flummoxed. 'I've not said anything.'

She was so angry every muscle in her body was tense and her strangled voice was barely audible. 'Do you have any idea what this'll do to me? For the rest of my fucking life I'll be the stupid bitch who fucked a copper in his car.'

He was insistent and quite calm. 'Paddy, I didn't tell anyone.'

Weeping with rage, she turned and took the stairs on faith, holding on to the sticky banister and slowing down as soon as she was out of sight around the turn. She stopped in the dark close, rubbing her face dry and struggling to breathe in against her con-tracting ribcage. She could walk back to the office. It would only take an hour and it had been a quiet night anyway; she probably wouldn't miss any major events so no one need know. She'd take a back road so that Burns wouldn't pass in his squad car. If he stopped and tried to give her a lift she might punch him. But it wouldn't be safe if Lafferty had been released and came looking for her. It wouldn't be hard to find her on the only call of the night.

Stepping out to the street she saw the car parked right in front of the close, Billy watching the entrance hopefully. He saw her and gave a nervous smile and raised his hand. She opened the dented passenger door and fell in.

''K?' he said, turning in his seat to look at her.

'Nothing happened. 's dead anyway. Let's do the hospitals and go back to the office,' she said, dredging up the stock phrases they used each night.

'OK then,' agreed Billy carefully, seeing how upset she was. 'That's what we'll do then.'

He wasn't just worried about his job. She could tell that he was sorry for losing his temper and sad to see her crying in the street on her own. He tried to look at her a couple of times but she didn't look back.

Burns'd told everyone. It was only two days ago and everyone in Glasgow knew. He'd looked her in the eye and lied about it. She would never, ever forgive him. And she would get him back. If she had to wait for years and years and years she'd humiliate him as much as he had her.

22

Fire

I

They were parked in the darkness outside the Royal hospital. Apart from a couple of consultants' discreetly posh cars the car park was empty. Yellow lights blazed in most of the windows of the huge soot-blackened Victorian hospital, a brittle silver frost hanging in the air. Inside the warm car it was snuggle-up-bedtime dark. Paddy's heart rate had slowed so much that she was having trouble remembering why it would be wrong to sleep.

Billy opened the window a crack and lit his cigarette, but Paddy stayed in the back seat. Sundays were always quiet but the Royal's casualty department was a good place to pick up stories that missed the police's attention. Gangsters often travelled across the city if they were stabbed or slashed, sometimes coming as far as ten miles in a taxi, clutching tea towels to their wounds, because the Royal surgeons were reputedly the best in the city.

For the first time Paddy wished peace on the city. She wanted a quick return to the twilight office, to get away from Billy and lick her wounds until home time.

Billy watched her in the mirror. 'Ye not going in?'

'Yeah.' She looked across the car park to the hospital door. A thin man in a thin brown shirt stood outside the door, smoking and hugging himself against the cold air. He had a large white dressing over one ear. Paddy didn't stir. 'Can I have a cigarette, Billy?'

'You don't smoke.'

'Just to gee me along a bit.'

He gave her a disapproving look but reached across his shoulder, handed her one and lit it. She took a deep breath, filling her lungs until her fingers tingled. She felt better, a little elated, and took another little drag for good luck before giving the cigarette back to him.

'Nip that for me, will ye? I'll not be long.'

'Did it wake ye?'

She opened the door and stepped out into the car park. 'Wee bit, aye.'

She stepped carefully across the slippery frosted asphalt and passed the man with the sore ear at the main entrance. Down a drafty beige corridor, she passed through automatic double doors and into the searing white light of the casualty-department waiting room.

A motley crowd of people were scattered around the seats inside. Some looked miserable and worn, some excited and bright. From a cursory look Paddy couldn't tell who was sick and who was a chaperone. The woman behind the plexiglas was a pretty brunette with a Western Isles accent and a taste for gory stories.

'Hi, Marcelli, anything big tonight?'

Marcelli shook her head. 'Nothing very much at all, I'm afraid.'

'No gangster action tonight? No stabbings or swordplay or anything?'

'Nope. Sorry. The German's left.'

Paddy smiled. 'The German doing the thesis?'

'Aye. I'm in mourning.' If the German doctor didn't know that Marcelli fancied him he was either blind or gay or both, Paddy thought. He had been writing a thesis about the sword injuries he witnessed during his time at the Royal, arguing that the blunt heavy swords created injuries that would match those from a medieval battle ground.

'How's work? Keeping busy?'

'Aye, busy enough.'

Marcelli looked at the wipe-clean board behind her head. The morning-shift cleaning women washed the board with soapy water so the build-up of blue smudges generally expressed how busy the department had been. The board was almost pristine tonight.

'It's all colds and falls tonight, I'm afraid.'

The two women smiled at each other politely, inquired after one another's families. Marcelli's husband worked the oil rigs and spent two weeks offshore and two weeks on. She had the content, rested look she always had when he was away. Paddy guessed that they fought a lot when he was home.

She patted the counter and told Marcelli she'd see her tomorrow.

'I'll see if I can rustle up a gang brawl for ye.'

'Cheers, Marcelli.'

She walked out of the department, through the lobby and out to the cusp of the dark dark night.

The sore-eared man was smoking a fresh cigarette at the doorway. Hunched against the cold, he caught her eye and smiled, a little hopefully, mistaking her frank stare for a come-on instead of rudeness born of exhaustion. Paddy glanced away towards the calls car and saw the red winking eye of Billy's cigarette rise in the driver's window. On the far side of the car a black shadow darted towards the road.

A scorching ball of orange light seared the delicate membrane of her eyes before she had time to blink. Paddy fell backwards, tripping on a step, a hand over her eyes as she heard the back of her head crack on the stone step. Lafferty might be coming for her across the car park, he could have the hammer in his hand, the one he used to batter Vhari to death, but Paddy still couldn't make her eyes open or get up to run away. Blind as a newborn puppy, she curled into a ball and waited for him. She heard the fire in the calls car whoosh and crackle, felt the wet of the frost on the step biting her cheek.

Someone was running towards her, urgent footsteps slapping on linoleum, and a sudden wordless cry. The feet were coming from inside the hospital, and were joined by others, a lot of people, flooding into the car park. Nurses and ambulance crews were running past her to the car. Billy was in the car.

Paddy sat up, holding the wall as she pulled herself on to her feet and stood up on unsteady legs. She could still feel the heat from the fire on her face as she forced her eyes open. Every window in the car was cracked and broken, angry orange flames lapping the roof. The driver's door lay open and Billy was on the ground, his body obscured by a gathering of medics. Protruding between two sets of legs lay a charred arm, the fingers skinned red curled into a tight claw.

A shoulder bumped hers and startled her into spinning around. It was the sore-eared man standing inside the door, flattened against one of the cold marble pillars, the dressing on his ear hanging crazily at the side of his head, hinged by white tape.

She grabbed his arm and shook him. 'Did you see him? Did you see who it was?'

He shook his head at her, pointing at her lips, asking her to slow down because he couldn't hear. She pointed out to the blackness and commotion and the burning car, being tackled by porters throwing buckets of sand over it.

'A guy ran out,' he said. 'In the shadows, couldn't see his face. Dressed in dark clothes. Crept up to the car. I didn't shout, I thought he was playing a joke on his pal in the car. I looked at you and then back. Creeping up to the window. Arm up, threw something in the window. Next thing—' He made the sound of an explosion and staggered back.

'Was he a big guy? Was his head shaved?'

He shrugged. 'He looked like a big, bald bastard.'

II

Paddy sat in the canteen at the top of the *Daily News* building watching morning break over the dirty city, blankly eating her way through another chocolate bar. Sugar for shock, that's what her mum said. That's why they always made each other sweet tea in films about the war. Sugar for shock.

Her head was thrumming, her eyes kept drying out so much she had to sit with them shut for minutes at a time. She thought she might have a lot of soot in there.

She took another bite. All she could think or care about was Billy. The attacker had mistaken Billy for her, which meant he didn't know what she looked like. Billy's wife would be at the hospital now. His wife that he fought with all the time and the son he didn't like any more, standing next to him, claiming him.

They were alone in the big canteen. Scary Mary and her helpers wouldn't be in for another hour and the room was cold and quiet.

'I'm telling you again: it was Bobby Lafferty.'

The three policemen sat in a rough circle around the canteen table, nodding disbelievingly. They had been listening to her patiently for an hour and a bit, she couldn't be sure how long. Their tea was cold anyway. They all looked the same to her: a big square disbelieving face. She knew perfectly well why they were staying with her, pretending to listen to answers she'd already given them.

'So,' said one, 'let's go through this again: why would a heavy like Bobby Lafferty want to kill you?'

'I've told you that already.'

He grunted and looked out of the window. 'Lafferty didn't kill the Bearsden Bird. The guy who did that killed himself. We pulled him out of the river last week. So why would Lafferty come after you?'

'I told you – ask Sullivan.'

'And we told you that we called Sullivan. He doesn't know what you're on about either.'

Paddy took another disconsolate bite of chocolate. She couldn't be bothered chewing. The thick lump melted in her mouth, coating her tongue until she moved it and generated some saliva.

Sullivan wasn't on her side at all. She had begun to doubt him as they stood in the dark room and watched Lafferty being questioned. It wouldn't take a genius-level IQ for Lafferty to work out that she was the only witness to what had gone on in the Bearsden house, and the note was the only thing he and the good-looking man hadn't wiped before they left. Lafferty had been released shortly after she left Partick Marine. Sullivan hadn't even contacted her to let her know and now he wouldn't back her up and admit that Lafferty was a danger. She couldn't go home. If Lafferty had found her at the hospital, he'd find her home address and follow her there.

'What about the ear guy in the hospital car park? He saw someone who fitted the description.'

The officer sighed patiently. 'We've told you already that we can't find him.'

She sat up and looked at them. 'He was treated in the casualty department for a sore ear. Marcelli always takes a name and address. He waited to talk to the police afterwards. He saw the guy who did it and you're telling me you can't find him?'

The three officers each evaded her eye in turn.

Paddy felt as if she had been awake since the Middle Ages. 'What would you do if you were me?'

No one said anything.

'How long is it until your shift finishes then? Another twenty minutes?'

They glanced guiltily at each other and one of them smiled.

'So, if you sit here pretending to listen to me for another ten minutes, by the time you get back to the station it'll be time to clock off?'

The man nearest bristled at the accusation. 'Don't get smart with us, Miss Meehan.'

'Look, Lafferty threw a pint of petrol in on Billy, and I can't go home until you pick him up. I'm giving you his name. I can get his address if you like – if it would help. Am I not entitled to protection from the police? What if he hurts my family?'

The indignant one blinked slowly. 'You're a crime journalist, Miss Meehan, you're bound to piss a lot of people off. Bad people.'

'So it's just a free-for-all? Does that make me a legitimate target then? What about Billy? What did he do wrong?'

They were tired too, and so close to the end of their shift it was hardly worth their while engaging with a stroppy bird. One officer sat back, pushing himself from the table and swinging on the two back legs of his chair. 'I think you know a mate of mine. I heard you're close friends.' He snickered at the ground.

He was talking about Burns, hinting at the rumours. A hot flush crept up the back of Paddy's neck but she stared at him defiantly. The police were a tight community. They drank in the same pubs, supported the same football team. They gossiped incessantly about each other, knew who was shagging who, who drank too much, who the idealists were and who was corruptible or corrupt.

One of the officers stole a look at his watch.

'Apart from Gourlay and McGregor, I'm the only person who saw the good-looking guy at the Bearsden Bird's door that night,' she said. 'They're saying it was the river suicide, Mark Thillingly, who killed her and I say it definitely wasn't him. Doesn't that make you wonder?'

They glanced at each other, hesitant, knowing, she felt sure, that Gourlay and McGregor were men of questionable ethics. The knowing looks dissolved into apathy. Ten minutes and they could go home. They just didn't give a shit.

Paddy felt her eyes brim with big, stupid tears. 'If Lafferty kills me it'll be on your heads.'

The canteen doors opened and the skinny copy boy peered in. 'Meehan? Ramage wants to see you when you've finished here.' He looked at the unhappy group around the table and slid back out to the corridor, shutting the door noiselessly after him.

Paddy looked at the bored policemen and felt a burst of righteous fury. 'Is this what you joined the police for? To protect each other? What if Gourlay and McGregor are bent?'

She'd gone too far. One officer hissed a warning at her.

Paddy stood up suddenly on unsteady legs. 'If that animal hurts my mum I'll come and find the three of yees.'

She shouldn't have voiced the fear out loud. She stared to cry, her face convulsing as she edged out from behind the table.

As she pulled the door open she heard one officer mutter under his breath, 'That's our home time, guys.'

III

Ramage's gruff voice called out 'Come!' Paddy brushed her mouth and chin for chocolate debris, stood as tall as her failing backbone would let her and opened the door.

Ramage was dwarfed behind the enormous desk, his early-morning shave making him look young and vulnerable, a small boy in a starched shirt and tie. He was sitting back in his chair, three neat piles of papers sitting side by side, perfectly aligned on his desk. Farquarson would have looked crumpled already, the papers would have been scattered around the desktop and he'd have been hunched over them, working.

'Meehan,' Ramage said baldly. 'I want three hundred about the firebomb – this time do it in first person and make it punchy. Get Frankie Mills to take a photo of you looking like shit and then fuck off home for a rest until I call you.'

She shook her head. 'No. No picture of me. The guy who did this is after me, but so far he's only got my name. I don't want him to have a photo as well.'

'You think he bombed Billy thinking he was you?'

'Billy looks like a woman from the back,' she explained. 'He's got a curly perm. The guy crept up from behind and threw the bomb at the window. He might even think he got me. When he hears from the police that it was someone else he'll come to my house.'

Ramage smiled and widened his eyes at the mention of the police. 'You think the police are giving him information?'

'They're the only people who know I'm not saying the same thing as the coppers on the call.'

Ramage nodded at his desk. 'So,' he said to himself, 'a young lady on the brink of a big story.' He licked his thumb and reached forward, moving a sheet of paper from the middle stack to the next one. He stopped to tidy the edges of the pile. She could almost see the captions on each one: redundancy, potential redundancy, keep. She hoped she was being moved to 'keep'.

'OK then. Three hundred words and then fuck off home.'

'Look, I can't go back to my house. The police haven't caught the guy and as far as I know he already knows where I live. I keep catching the same car watching my house. I need a hotel room.'

Ramage smirked at her audacity, put the pen down and sat up straight to look at her. 'Good for you, Patricia.'

'My name's Paddy,' she corrected curtly.

He tensed his brow at her. 'Yeah, don't act the uppity twat with me.' Staring at her, he licked his thumb again and moved the sheet back to the original pile.

'Boss,' she said, though it nearly choked her, 'I'm going to get you a great story. Sell shit loads of papers. Shit loads.'

His smile was reptilian. 'We'll see. I'll shell out for a bed and breakfast, and that's only for three days—'

'No, it has to be a hotel. Bed and breakfasts make you leave during the day and I need to sleep.'

He didn't like being interrupted. He raised his hand and licked the thumb again but stopped and smiled, dropping his hand without moving a sheet. 'Three hundred words, and make it good. You'll need a driver. Know anyone?'

She remembered Sean. He'd only just taken his test but the image of his face soothed her. 'I do, but he hasn't got his own car.'

Ramage shrugged. 'Get one out of the pool. Tell them to get a new radio and fit it.' He looked her up and down. 'You're young, Meehan. Was Farquarson the first editor you've worked under?'

She nodded dumbly.

'You probably miss him and think I'm a dick.'

She wanted to nod but guessed that it wouldn't be well received. 'Dunno.'

Ramage's smile was almost genuine this time. He lifted a gold fountain pen and tapped the soft green-leather blotter in front of him in a slow rhythmic thud. They should have been up on editorial, in a noisy room surrounded by bustle where the dull thunk of a stupid ostentatious gold pen would be lost.

He shifted in his seat. 'As you go on in this business you'll learn that loyalty to dead men is a waste of time. Grieve, get over it and then move on to arse-licking the next man in charge. That's the business we're in.' He smiled faintly, as if his brutal creed was a source of pride. 'You can come with me or you can give me that uppity-cow crap and end up selling advertising space. Understand?'

Paddy nodded and Ramage dismissed her with a flick of his hand.

Paddy backed out of the room and shut the door quietly. The windows along the corridor let the weak light of the day into the corridor. She slowed to a stop, leaning on the window-sill and looking out over the roofs of the *Scottish Daily News* vans parked outside. In the future the printworks wouldn't be under the paper. They'd move to the new site and the building would be nothing more than an office. They could be selling insurance.

She looked out over the grey day and knew Billy's family would be in the hospital, waiting for her to turn up and commiserate on behalf of the *Daily News*. She should go and phone Sean and tell him he had a good paying job if he wanted it. She had three hundred words to write and tomorrow she was expected at the inquiry into the police call to Burnett's house, but still she lingered in the lemon-scented corridor, looking out of the window at the windy street, feeling one era slip into the past and another begin.

IV

Bernie knew it was Kate at the door. The whisper of a knock at ten in the morning, the tentative pause between the raps – he didn't know anyone else who would do that. He stood behind the door, sensing her on the other side, wanting to open it to her but never wanting to see her again.

'Bernie?' Her voice was as familiar as his own and he could read volumes into the timbre. She was frightened and worried that he might be angry with her. She was ill too, didn't sound strong. Her normal voice was breathy but there was no air behind the voice. 'Bernie? Let me in.'

He imagined what she'd say to him if he did open the door: there were bits of engines and old newspapers stacked all over the floor of the pokey wee hall. He had pale-blue striped pyjama trousers and a vest on, hardly appropriate for receiving such a grand guest. But Kate had deigned to come to his council house, she'd never been before, she might not be as snooty as she usually was.

'Darling? I'm cold.'

Bernie didn't even make a decision to open the door. The reflex to save Kate from any and all discomfort was so ingrained that he leaned forward and pulled the heavy toolbox away from the bottom of the door, snapped the lock and pulled it open.

He gasped when he saw her. As soon as the breath was out he knew he had broken her heart.

'You're so thin,' he said, lying to spare her.

She knew why he had gasped. He could see by the way she hung her head and looked at his feet. Her hand rose to her face, covering her nose. It had collapsed. The tip drooped over her top lip like a witch in a children's book.

The last time they'd met, at the old man's funeral, she'd looked just as stunning as ever. She'd had the sort of looks that caught the eye and kept it, that made a man feel that his hands were designed to fit around her perfect face, cinch her tiny waist. She knew what she looked like then, had the sense of absolute entitlement that truly beautiful girls have. And she knew what she looked like now.

'When did you last eat?'

She raised her eyes and looked so defenceless she could have been twelve again. 'I'm cold, Bernie.'

She had barely spoken to him for years, had been the cause of Vhari's murder, had stolen a car from him and planted a parcel in his garage that could have had him killed, but Bernie reached out and took her hand, pulled her into his modest flat, and shut the door to the world behind her.

V

The floor was incredibly dirty. Paddy had been asleep in Farquarson's darkened office for three hours, lying on the dusty floor, starting awake every twenty minutes or so at noises from the news room.

She lay awake now, knowing she should get up and phone her mum again, just to check. Her hot eyes looked along the length of filthy carpet, past the indents from the conference table to the door. Through the half-opened Venetian blinds she could see shadows moving past and the still, squat figures of the copy boys perched on their bench, waiting to be called for a chore. She should get up and phone her mum, ask if she'd seen a red Ford outside. She should apologize to JT for not getting his Mandela clippings out for him. She'd been expecting him to burst into the office all morning to give her a bollocking for not having done it already.

A perfunctory rap was followed by the door opening; a shard of bright light made her eyes smart against the brightness.

'Ramage has booked you a hotel room.'

She sat up, blinking and brushing fibres and dust from her cheek, resisting the urge to rub her eyes. It was one of the copy boys.

'Is JT about?'

'Naw.'

'Is he out on a job?'

'Naw.'

He retreated back to the bench, leaving the door swinging open.

Pleased about the hotel room, Paddy brushed her clothes clean and stepped out into the busy room. The morning conference had apparently taken place in Ramage's suite downstairs: editors and significant journalists were pouring back in through the double doors, some scowling, some buzzed up, depending on who had been lauded and who lampooned for the morning edition. She peered at them until the last few trickled back in and settled at their desks. JT wasn't among them.

She sidled up to Reg at the sports desk. 'Where's JT?'

Reg shook his head. 'Got the bump.'

She opened her eyes properly. 'But he's just won Reporter of the Year.'

'Aye.' Reg nodded miserably at his typewriter. 'Wages were too high, though. I heard you've got a hotel room.'

'Aye.' She looked at her feet, wondering if she'd been wise to ask for anything but a chance to prove herself.

23

Ugly Things

I

The furnishings were all perfunctory and worn, gleaned from cheap second-hand shops. The grey sofa and wooden chair, the smoked-glass coffee table, all ugly things, and Bernie's living room was full of bits of engines and oily rags and tools. Kate hated the room. She was glad she had never been here before and yet Bernie's company was a comfort in itself. Just the sight of his square face and cheap-barber flat-top made her feel safe, as if it was another time, as if they were still children and were back before this all began, long before it went bad.

Kate sat her second cup on the coffee table. She didn't drink tea usually. She knew what it did to the colour of people's teeth and had convinced herself that she didn't like it, like ice cream and chocolate. Now she drank it down to try and warm herself up, and then asked for more from the tarnished metal pot. Bernie brought out a packet of digestives and handed her a couple.

'Try to eat them. You're so skinny, honestly, your legs look like strings with knots in.' He pointed to her knees under the laddered blue tights and silently hoped the dried brown stuff flecked all over the back of her calves was mud.

Kate smiled softly, eyes focused somewhere far off. She sucked an edge of the biscuit and pretended to eat, indulging him. She used to get that look in her eye when she wanted to leave home but couldn't just say so. 'Have you got my pillow?'

He wouldn't have known what she was talking about if he hadn't been waiting for her to ask for it. 'Pillow.'

She smiled. 'My comfort pillow"

Bernie smiled back, but stopped when he looked at her. 'You're killing yourself.'

She stared at him wearily. She wasn't well enough to cope with a scene. Her head was bursting and she had shooting pains in her stomach. 'You take everything too seriously, Bernie. You always have, ever since you were little.'

She was saying that to make him angry, to stop him admitting he cared. Being emotional was a crime to the Burnetts. But Bernie wasn't a Burnett, he had chosen not to be, and he did care.

'Look at you,' he said, shouting suddenly. 'Look at the state of you. What he's made you.'

She picked up the cup and sipped again. 'Has he been to see you?'

'What the fuck do you think, Katie? Would my fucking skull still be intact if he'd been here? He battered Vhari to death.'

She looked down, holding her hands together to stop them trembling. 'I want my pillow,' she said when her shallow reserve of remorse had run out.

'Katie, you're going to die if you keep taking that stuff.'

He was right and she knew it. She had felt her heart weakening, the rhythm of it change at times, straining like the Mini engine to keep going.

'Bernie, I'm not an idiot. I'm going to get help, but this isn't the time.'

Bernie rubbed his face roughly with a hand. 'Katie? Look at me.' But she couldn't, so he raised his voice. 'Look at me, Katie. Fucking look at me. You won't live to get help. They'll kill you for taking that bag of coke.'

Kate could hear singing in her left ear. It was the low murmur of the dead man. He was faint, barely perceptible, singing a hymn, she thought, some old Protestant dirge about sins and sinners.

'Katie. Can you hear me?'

She didn't know if Bernie was talking to her or the dead man, so she waited.

'Katie?' Bernie, it was definitely Bernie, his mouth was moving. 'Can you hear me?'

'I can hear you, darling.'

'They'll kill you like they killed Vhari.'

'No they won't. I've got a plan.' She was beginning to shiver.

Bernie leaned forward and cupped her chin roughly. 'Listen to me.' He held her face and made her look at him. His eyes were wild with fright. 'Listen.' Kate lifted her chin to get away but he held on, digging his fingers in. 'Listen.' Seeing it was hopeless she sat still and looked at him. 'Katie, you're a feckless tit. Your plans are stupid. You couldn't think your way out of a newsagent's. You've got to go to the police.'

She laughed in his face, a genuine, sensible, spontaneous laugh, and Bernie loosened his grip and smiled back. She was like herself again and Bernie felt a wash of relief, as if he was meeting an old friend in a hostile crowd.

'But I am planning to go to the police,' she said.

Bernie watched her, reading her face, and he believed her. 'God, Kate, fucking hell, I'm so glad. If you lie low and go to the police and just don't mention the coke, everything'll be fine. Tell them you went missing and about Vhari and even if they press you don't mention drugs of any kind. Promise?'

She pouted and looked up at him. 'Bernie, dearie, I need my pillow to lie low.'

Bernie frowned, annoyed again that she had brought it up. 'You've no idea how serious this is. Mark Thillingly killed himself the other night because of this.'

'Fat Mark?'

'He's not fat, Kate. He's dead.'

'For God's sake, I'm not responsible for every death in Scotland.' She wanted the pillow. She needed the pillow. The thought of living through the next ten minutes without knowing whether she could get it back scratched at her brain. 'Can I have it back?'

Bernie looked at her sadly, noting that she hadn't asked about Mark or even why he killed himself. 'Katie.'

'Give it to me right now or I'll cut myself.'

'Tell me your plan.'

The dead man giggled in her ear and she hesitated. 'Knox. Knox.' She stared into the distance as she repeated the name like a prayer keeping her safe. 'Knox is the get-out. Paul would do anything to protect him. If I get Knox to talk to him he'll definitely leave me alone.'

Bernie leaned in and prompted her softly. 'But who is Knox?'

'Give me my pillow and I'll tell you.' She smiled coquettishly, as she used to, but her flattened nose made the look grotesque.

'You're a fucking nut-job. And you look like a tramp.'

'Piss off.'

He stood up and began to tidy, picking up the biscuit plate, sweeping crumbs from the table on to it. Kate loathed him suddenly. She knew then that she would do anything, literally the worst she could think of, to hurt him and make him give it back. 'I'll phone my parents.'

He looked down at her, the colour bleeding from his cheeks until his face was grey.

'I'll phone them and tell them your home address and where you work. *They'll come and see you.*'

The muscles on his face tightened. He looked a little sick, like he had when he was a boy and felt trapped, which was most of the time when he was at home. He looked at his watch. 'Phone your parents if you like. I haven't got a telephone and I'll be out when you get back. If they see the mess you've made of yourself you'll be in a sanatorium by teatime.'

'I could call them tomorrow,' she said, twisting the knife. 'They will come, you know.'

Bernie let the crumbs slide off the plate into the carpet and dropped his hand to his side. 'I don't fucking care, Katie.' But he did care if they came. She could see he was trembling.

'All you have to do is give me the pillow.'

'I've thrown it away.'

'You weaselly little prick.' She stood up and slapped him hard across the face, making him drop the plate. He slapped her back and felt her flaccid nose brush his palm. She toppled over, landing on the settee, holding her nose. He had made her bleed.

Kate sat up, holding her face, streams of scarlet bubbling through her fingers. She looked at him and carefully tipped to the side, letting her nose bleed itself out all over his settee. She took her hand away and smiled at her bloody palm. 'If Paul finds me without the pillow he'll kill me. My blood's all over your sofa: the police'll come here and find it and think you killed me. So now you've got to give it to me.'

He hesitated; she could see it.

'Bernie.' She sat up, holding a hand under her nose. 'Bernie, I want my pillow so I can get it together and sort this out. Please? I don't want anyone else to get hurt. If I don't sort out my own mess we'll both end up dead. You know that, don't you?'

Bernie looked at her on the sofa. 'You're going to take it all and kill yourself.'

'Look at me, Bernie. I've got a plan. I'm as tough as nuts. If the world ended tomorrow I'd be the sole survivor. I'd be looting for handbags and jewellery. Tough as nuts.' She laughed at her own turn of phrase, holding a hand over her nose to catch the last dribble of blood.

Bernie watched her, smiling sadly, loving her and wishing everything was different, that they had stayed friends and looked after each other instead of bolting from home in opposite directions as soon as they could.

As Kate laughed up at him she heard a breathy huff in her ear: the dead man was laughing as well, deep inside her inner ear.

II

Paddy was terrified to be back in the courtyard of the Royal hospital. The car park was crammed with cars and a couple of vans, every space taken apart from the corner where Billy had been parked the night before. It was left empty, scorched black from the fire. She tried not to look at it but saw it in the corner of her eye, and the soot on the buildings nearby. The car had been taken away but had left its mark on the bubbled tarmac, a great wetness on the building and ground where it had been drenched by the fire brigade.

Paddy shuddered. She had a creepy sense that most of the soot on the building must have come from Billy's body, from his skin as it burned. A throb started in her throat. She wanted to sit down on the steps of the hospital and cover her face and cry. All she could see were his feet, twitching, his heels banging off the car-park floor and the white coats gathered around him.

She looked up at the building. A hundred heart-wrenching tragedies must happen in here every day of the week, twice at weekends, and the thought brought her comfort somehow, that she was just a part of a great wave of fright and sadness. Everyone else was being brave about it. She'd be letting the side down if she wasn't too.

The doorway was busy with staff and visitors coming in and out of the building. Deliveries were being brought in for the dispensing machines in the lobby, cans of juice and boxes of crisps. Paddy stopped in the busy crowd and looked up to the signs on the wall to find the right department. It was isolated at the very far corner of the immense building.

As she walked along the corridors following the signs, she passed the Oncology ward and remembered when her friend Dr Pete had been in here, when he looked at her with a steady fearless eye and told her he was dying. She missed him. She missed Terry Patterson. When she thought about it, she missed every fucking person she'd ever known and wished it was some time other than now. She wished she was on day shift. She wished her father had a job and her mother was over the menopause and last night hadn't happened and she hadn't shagged George fucking Burns. She wished Mary Ann wasn't a religious maniac and Sean was still her boyfriend. She wished she was thin.

She tripped along the corridor, head down, so distracted that she almost walked straight past the entrance to 7H. It was easy to miss. Only a small sign sticking out of the wall highlighted the fact that the door was there. She turned, caught her breath, knowing Billy would be a harrowing sight, and opened the door.

She found herself in a short lobby painted a calming pale lilac that made her feel faintly panicky. A kind matronly woman smiled up at her from behind a desk, asking if she could help. Paddy gave Billy's name and watched the nurse's face for a reaction, revulsion or something, she didn't quite know. The woman smiled and looked at a chart on her table.

'Are you family, pet?'

'No, I'm . . . I was with him.' Paddy thumbed out to where she imagined the car park was.

The nurse looked at her, reading her face carefully. 'What we don't want is visitors who are going to get very upset,' she said in a careful voice. 'I don't want anyone to upset the patients. Do you feel able to do that? To stay calm?'

Paddy nodded, though she wasn't sure it was true. 'Are his family with him?'

The nurse nodded. 'I'm sure they'll be glad you came.' She stood up and opened the door for Paddy, pointing her down a shabbily constructed corridor of white-emulsioned cubicle walls. Paddy had been in other wards in the hospital, she knew that only the burns ward had these walls and doors. Presumably they needed them to keep visitors from staring at the boiled and blistered men in the beds.

She crept along to the door the nurse had indicated, hearing the beep of the machines and the rustle of crisp sheets against moist skin. A strong medicinal stench came from the walls, mint over disinfectant.

She knocked gently on the door, half hoping no one would answer. A smoker's voice called to come in. Paddy turned the handle and pushed the door open.

A high, metal-framed single bed sat in the middle of the room. A tiny sink was against the back wall alongside a locker with a plastic jug of orange squash and a glass.

Billy was sitting bolt upright in the bed, flanked on one side by a standing woman and on the other by a young man in a plastic chair reading a tabloid newspaper. Billy looked astonished and mortified at the same time: his eyelashes and eyebrows had been seared off and his skin scorched into a permanent flustered blush. He was dressed in a blue paper nightie, his hands wrapped up into massive white bandage mittens, like oversized Q-tips. He seemed small and then she realized: his hair was gone.

In all the time she knew him, Billy had sported the same shoulder-length wavy perm. She knew it was a perm because she watched it carefully from the back seat, night after night, the small hint of a straight root here or there and then the sudden two-week flush of distinct flatness just before he went to the hairdresser's and had it redone. The hairdo was five years out of date when she first saw it four years ago, but she had developed a grudging respect for Billy's persistence. It was a brave man who'd risk baldness out of

221

loyalty to the age of disco. Sean and her brothers were terrified of losing their hair.

But Billy was going to have to find a new look: the perm had melted. Over his left ear – away, she imagined, from the source of the fire – a bush of hair remained as it was before, but the rest of his head was bald, furnished with small tufts or pink fleshy patches.

Relieved and surprised, Paddy barked an unkind, shrill laugh and pointed at him. The wife and son stared at her blankly.

'Bloody hell, Billy.' She sidled into the room. 'I thought you were really hurt.'

Half amused, Billy held his giant bandaged hands up to her. 'This is pretty bad.'

'I know,' she said. 'I'm sorry, I thought it would be much worse.'

The wife was staring at her aggressively. She was stout, tank-like, her hands clasped together over an onerous chest and belly. The son was built like his mother; although young and footballer-fit, he looked as if he'd run to fat given a chance. He glanced at his mother, taking her cue about the stranger giggling at his burned father.

'I might never have the use of my hands again,' said Billy. 'I might never be able to drive again. And it's bloody sore.'

It was wrong of her, but she was so relieved to see him looking like himself that she laughed again.

The wife widened her eyes, retracted her lips and stepped up to meet her. 'Who in the eff are you?' Her voice was the gravel growl of a heavy smoker and even as she stepped across the room Paddy smelled a whiff of smoke.

Billy called her off with a small, firm '*Agnes.*'

His son huffed behind his hand. Billy asked them to go down to the canteen for a cup of tea and leave him alone with Paddy for ten minutes.

They gathered their things together, the wife giving Paddy a filthy look and banging shoulders with her on the way out. 'She's had a scare,' he explained when the door clicked shut behind her. 'She reacts like that when she's frightened.'

'You been married a long time, Billy?'

'Since we were seventeen.'

He was a long way from that now. Paddy took the seat next to him, still warm from his son, and realized that Billy was pretty old. In his late forties at least. They only ever met in the dark and she was generally staring at the back of his head, but she had imagined him younger.

They looked at each other and smiled. Paddy patted the bed in symbolic contact. 'Is this you from the front then, Billy?'

Billy pointed his big white mittens at his face. 'Is it bad?'

'You just look embarrassed.'

'They won't let you see yourself. That's scary.'

She looked around for a mirror, but there wasn't one so she felt in her bag and pulled out a powder compact, opening it and handing it to him. Billy peered in at himself, turning the mirror to different angles. 'Red, eh?'

Paddy nodded and grinned. 'Is it sore?'

'Oh, my hands are murder.'

But she couldn't stop smiling, 'I thought you'd be in a big tent and have all cream on everywhere and no eyelids or something.'

'That's next door.'

They nodded together for a while. She could almost hear the comforting crackle of a ghost police radio. 'When we were at the Burnett house, did you see anyone come in or go out?'

He thought about it. 'No.'

'Could you have seen anything I didn't see?'

'Like what?'

'Like someone coming around the side of the house or a car outside or the police do something?'

He took himself back to the scene again. 'No. I smoked a cigarette, saw you at the door, nothing happened.'

'Did you mention it to anyone?'

'Not a soul.'

'Right, well, I'm not as circumspect as you: I've been mouthing off all over town. I think they were after me and got you instead. Sorry about that.'

'I don't look like you.'

'They don't know what I look like. And from the back, your hair . . .' She didn't want to press the point but swept her hand down the back of her head. ''Cause your hair's long.'

'So they thought I was a woman?'

'Could be. Did you see anything before the fire? Anyone approaching the car?'

Billy thought about it. He looked down at his silly hands lying in his lap and she saw that his eyelids were completely unscathed. He looked straight ahead, glancing up at the space where the rear-view mirror would have been. 'I'm smoking and waiting for you. You've not been long. I'm listening to the radio, listening for calls. Nothing's coming. I was angry, thinking about you and the copper's car.' He looked at her reproachfully and then at his hands. He raised his right elbow to where the window-sill would have been and pointed the Q-tip at his mouth, taking in a deep breath as he looked back at the mirror. 'Smoking. I see a shadow behind me. Moving fast across the mirror. He was wearing black, whoever he was, next thing – whoosh. Flames everywhere.'

She asked him if the shadow he saw could have been of a big guy, a bald guy, but Billy said he'd only seen the guy's torso from the neck down and no, he didn't seem all that big, quite slim actually. Had Billy seen a car behind him? But Billy laughed, opening his mouth and letting out a coughing sound so that he didn't have to move his cheeks.

'He's hardly going to park his car behind me and run up and throw a petrol bomb at me, is he? Anyway there was only one car in the car park apart from us. Came in after you'd gone into the building and parked as if it had business there.'

'Was it a red Ford, by any chance?'

'No, did ye not see it? It was a BMW.'

24

Easterhouse

I

Paddy's exhaustion was making her feel queasy and the top deck of the bus smelled like a smoker's tonsils. She had a packet of crisps in her bag but was so nauseous she genuinely didn't want them. She sat still, pains in her stomach, and watched the city pass by the window.

Lafferty would be out there somewhere, looking for her. He'd know by now that she wasn't in the car and he'd be angry, prowling the city like a hungry dog. Miserable and scared for her family, she leaned her head against the window. She'd told her mum to stay in the house, asked her to stop Mary Ann from going out too much and told her to stay away from the windows. Paddy didn't tell her about the fire bomb or about Billy, she didn't want to terrify her, she just said someone was after her and might come to the house and she should call the police if she saw a BMW or a red Ford. If Trisha had been herself she would have cried down the phone to Paddy and begged her to come home, but she was in her strange temper and sounded angry instead, huffy, as if Paddy was being self-important and making a lot of silly fuss.

The housing stock along the broad Edinburgh Road was a linear map of a century of social housing, from scrubby squares of muddy grass around garden-city dreams, to high-rise machines for living. Occasionally they passed a wall of undemolished tenements, the old housing design that had worked in the city for centuries.

Easterhouse was barely twenty years old. In its short life the scheme had developed a reputation as one of the roughest ghettos in Europe. It was part of a social-engineering project that carved the socialist city up into impassable islands surrounded by motorway. The most malcontent city-centre populations had been moved to the satellite estates, a long bus ride away from spontaneous social upheaval. Without the presence of a common enemy, frustration fermented among the people and they began to eat themselves. Gangs were rife. If Easterhouse had a heraldic shield it would need symbols for drunkenness, medication and despair. A third of the estate was on disability benefit, occupying that grey area between extreme long-term poverty and illness.

It wasn't a place to wander around. Gangs were territorial and known for attacking anyone who wandered through their patch. It was worse at night: Paddy knew from taking shortcuts in the calls car that the boys hung around in packs, watching the car pass, carrying sticks and swords, alert as hyenas. She was counting on it being not as bad during the day.

As soon as she stepped off the bus she felt unsafe. The stop was at the edge of a barren field, all the houses set well back from the traffic. The few houses that were within view were boarded up with fibreglass, the light coming through from the backs of the houses making them glow like the skin of a drum. Bottles lay smashed in the street or scattered on the grass. Paddy felt a long way from the small-town cosiness of Rutherglen.

A woman pushing a pram scuttled along the mud track towards her, her anorak hood pulled up against imaginary rain, her head down. On the distant horizon, just before the houses, unsupervised children chased each other around a playground where the baby swings had been maliciously wound around the top bar and the roundabout was burned out, the wooden base charred to a sooty stump. Paddy walked along to the corner and followed the sign for the shopping centre.

She came to a row of meagre shops. Three of them were shut and shuttered against the populace. A licensed grocer and the law centre were still open. The bookie's was operating with its windows boarded over with wood, a sign declaring cheerfully 'We're still open!' inviting the vandals to have another go.

The Easterhouse Law Centre was in an unprepossessing shop unit with nothing more than a poster in the window to explain what it was. The glass on the door was covered in notices, yellow posters for an ex-offenders' support group, a change of venue for a tenants' rights meeting, notices about expenses available for prison visits.

When Paddy opened the door notices fell off and fluttered to the floor as a shop bell tinkled happily. She bent down and picked up the papers, turning back to the door and trying to find the space they had come from.

'Leave it,' said a harsh voice. 'Give them to me.'

A woman held her hand out. Her hair was cut in a wedge with dyed blond streaks, yellow on black, like a wasp. She was young, about the same age as Paddy, but her mouth was pinched bitterly and her eyes wrinkled where they were habitually narrowed. She looked Paddy over, head tilted to one side, as if she couldn't quite believe what life was forcing her to look at now.

Paddy put the notices in her hand, expecting a cursory thank-you from the woman. When it didn't come, Paddy got confused and thanked her instead. She frowned as if Paddy had just shat in her pocket. Paddy apologized reflexively, prompting another look of disgust.

The woman retreated to a desk, dropping the leaflets in the bin as though she couldn't bear to hold them any more. She sat down at a paper-strewn desk with a typewriter on it. A purple can of Tab was sitting on a stack of used carbon paper next to a full ashtray.

Paddy glanced around the office to see if there was anyone else she could speak to. There was another desk, bare of effects, but the rude woman was alone. Pulling a cigarette out of a packet of Marlboro and lighting it with a disposable lighter, the nippy woman sat back and looked Paddy over, guessing she wasn't in for legal representation. She blew an impertinent stream of smoke at her.

'Selling something?'

'No.' Paddy stepped towards her. 'I wanted to ask about Mark Thillingly?'

The nippy woman narrowed her eyes. 'Yeah, well, Mark's dead. They say he killed himself.' She shut her eyes for a moment and took a draw on her cigarette.

Paddy guessed that being brutal might pass for integrity. 'I know. I was there when they pulled him out of the water.'

The woman flinched but looked at her with renewed interest. 'Who are you?'

'I'm Paddy Meehan, *Scottish Daily News*.' Paddy held her hand out but the nippy woman declined to take it. She dragged a chair over from the other desk and sat down. 'So, Mark Thillingly—' She pulled her notebook out. 'He worked here, didn't he?'

'Yeah. He worked here.' The woman hesitated. 'He worked here . . .'

'Did he ever mention a woman called Vhari Burnett?'

'Aye, she worked here too. Mark gave her summer work when she was at uni.'

'And were you here then, too?'

'Aye. It was when Vhari and Mark were going out together. Went together until Diana came along and poached him.' She sucked her cigarette hard, breathing in deep, making Paddy's throat close at the memory of her smoking binge with Diana in the conservatory two nights ago.

'I liked Vhari better. She'd meet scum through this centre and then help them do stuff like fill out forms for the social security, stuff she wasn't getting paid for and didn't need to do. Do anything, she would.'

'Was Mark involved like that?'

'Only when she was here. They made each other nice.' The woman blushed at the silly pink word. 'Know what I mean?'

'I know exactly what you mean,' said Paddy.

They were in danger of being pleasant to one another. The woman sucked her cigarette again and narrowed her eyes at Paddy, angry that she had unilaterally overstepped the bounds of brisk rudeness.

Paddy examined her notebook to stop herself smiling. 'Do you know of any particular cases Mark and Vhari worked on together?'

'They didn't work on the same cases. They did their own cases.'

'Is there anyone you can think of who came in looking for representation who'd link them?'

She shrugged. 'Anyone who was about the office then, I suppose. Everyone knew them as a couple.'

'Who was about the office then?'

'I dunno.' She wasn't even considering the question. 'People.'

'No special cases coming through the centre, then? Gangster cases?'

'No. We don't do criminal cases in here. We just help with social-security claims and expense claims for prison visitation. Small stuff, civil cases.'

'Look.' Paddy leaned forward and put her hands on the desk. 'What's your name?'

The woman pursed her lips. 'Evelyn McGarrochy.'

'Evelyn, I take it you don't read the papers?'

'Load of lies.'

'I'm sorry to be the one to tell you this: the police think Mark killed Vhari.'

Evelyn McGarrochy melted: her shoulders dropped, her face slackened and her mouth fell open.

Suddenly Paddy understood the rounded backs of the policemen as they took the path up to Mark Thillingly's house in the middle of Tuesday night. It was a terrible thing to see.

Finally Evelyn spoke. 'Why?'

'Because he killed himself the next night.'

Evelyn looked down to her hand and saw that her cigarette had burned down to an oily stub. She dropped it into the ashtray and slowly pulled another from the packet, lethargically popping it into her mouth like a diabetic reaching for a boiled sweet. Paddy lit a match for her and held it to the end. Evelyn's forehead twitched as she smoked, and Paddy could see her disbelieving the news.

'Evelyn, do you work here every day?'

She blinked and brought herself back to the room. 'Um, yeah. Most days. 'Less I'm sick.'

'Were you working here last Monday?'

'Aye.'

'And Mark was working here as well?'

She nodded and pointed to the table behind her. 'There.'

'What time did you finish?'

'About six,' she shrugged. 'It was a busy day.'

'So did he come in early the next day?'

Evelyn shook a finger at her, scattering ash over the carbon papers. 'He didn't come in the next day.'

'Where was he? Did he call?'

'Said he was off visiting Bernie and I wasn't to tell Diana. If she called just say he was out.'

'Who's Bernie?'

'Vhari's brother.'

'Where would Mark go to find Bernie?'

'At his garage in Yorkhill.'

Paddy licked her lips as she jotted it down in shorthand. The day after Vhari's murder Thillingly skipped work to see Burnett's brother. He'd hardly do that if he was responsible for her murder.

'Do you know what they did to Vhari?' Evelyn's voice had shrunk. 'How did they murder her?'

Paddy couldn't tell her about the teeth or the money men or the two steps to safety that Vhari had decided not to take. 'They hit her, I think. The police said it was quick. They were trying to scare her, I think, and it went too far.'

Evelyn shook her head and looked hard at Paddy. 'Mark didn't murder Vhari. They stayed pals afterwards. He was a soft guy, Mark, you know? Not a man to lift his hands.'

'I went to see Diana. She said Mark was mugged outside here on Monday.'

Evelyn coughed in surprise and exhaled a stream of acrid smoke at the table. 'What?'

'Outside of here. In the car park. He went home all wet from being knocked over in the rain and his nose was burst.'

Evelyn tried to remember Monday. 'I waved to him at his car. He was just getting into it. It wasn't even very dark when we left.'

'At six?'

'Yeah. It was getting dark.'

'Did you see Mark drive away?'

She tried to remember. 'No, now I come to think of it, I didn't. I wait at the bus stop and he passes going the other way. He usually waves to me but I didn't see him that night. It was raining awful heavy and my feet were getting wet. I never saw him come past.'

'Was anyone in during the day? Was anyone hanging around the office?'

'No. I don't think so.'

'Can ye think of anything from Monday? Were there any cars parked outside or in the car park?'

Evelyn shook her head, but stopped. 'There *was* a car. It's unusual. There aren't a lot of cars around here. It was black. Shiny. It was new.'

'Any idea of the licence plate?'

'No.'

'Any idea what kind of car it was?'

Her eyes searched the table for a moment. 'No,' she said finally. 'I don't drive. Don't know anyone who drives. I'm not interested in cars.'

25

The Red Ford

I

Paddy stood at the top of the stairs. A midnight wind lifted thin wafts of dust from the empty road and grit brushed her cheek, threatening her eyes and making her hair feel gritty. She fitted her notepad into her pocket and tripped down to the street.

Sean must have been watching the door for her and already had the engine started. He pulled the car to the kerb at the bottom of the steps to meet her and she bent down to his window.

'Was there a call?'

'Eh?'

'Did an important call come through?'

He looked at the radio, nonplussed, and then back at her. 'No. I don't know. Was there?'

He was pulling up to the kerb because he was monster keen, not for any other reason.

'Never mind.' She opened the passenger door and climbed into the back seat. 'Ye were listening to the radio, though, eh?'

'I listened for police cars being called to anywhere,' he said, repeating her instructions word for word. 'Nothing.'

''K. Well done. Now we'll go to Partick Marine station.'

He looked at her blankly. Paddy tried to think where it was. She'd never had to bother before. 'Go to Partick Cross and I'll direct you from there.'

'OK.' He smiled at her. 'You're the boss.'

Sean was being subservient and helpful. It was quite eerie. He was delighted to get the job, however temporary it might be, and she had a definite feeling that when the paper got a copy of his driving licence and found out that he'd only passed two days ago they'd get a replacement, someone older who wasn't going to cost them his wage again in insurance. Still, for the very near future Sean had a job with great money. He was making nearly as much as Paddy, and she knew the wages went up the longer he stayed.

It was a newer car than the one Billy used to drive her in, a silver car with an empty-tin-can feel. The moulded metal inside was covered in plastic but the frame was visible through it. It shuddered along the road and all the instruments on the dash looked far away from each other and essential. She found herself feeling for the broken handle of the door and the small rip in the padded door of Billy's car, missing the rhythm of his flawless, smooth driving.

Sean stopped suddenly at lights, turned stiffly around corners and swore under his breath when he came across anything un-toward on the road like a pedestrian or a bus. She was glad she was the first passenger he'd had; his style didn't exactly disguise his lack of experience.

He edged through the town, stalling and swerving his way to Partick Cross, where she directed him off the main drag to the dark station and asked him to pull up outside.

'Just wait here and, like before, listen out for any calls coming over the radio.'

'OK, Boss.'

Her fingers were on the handle. 'Stop calling me that. It's doing my fucking head in.'

'Whatever you say, Boss.'

She stepped out of the car and was almost at the big door when she looked down the street and saw it: parked quite near the station, not bothering to take a nearby street or hide in the shadows, was the red Ford.

She staggered to a stop and a sudden, horrifying thought occurred to her. Sean was defenceless in the car. Heart pounding, she bolted back and yanked his driver's door open so fast she almost fell over. Sean barely had time to look startled before she dragged him out by the arm, letting go when he was kneeling on the road.

'What the fuck . . .?'

'Car,' she panted, pointing up the road. 'That car's following me.'

Sean stood up, brushing the dirt off his knees. 'Take a breath and tell me.'

'The car –' She spun him around and pointed. 'The red Ford was parked outside last Friday and before – I've seen it before then as well.'

'Those cars are everywhere.' Sean dipped at the knees and looked into the cabin. 'Well, there's no one in there now.'

'He's probably being questioned in the station.' She pulled him over by the arm. 'Just come with me.'

The waiting room was quiet, the resigned midnight calm of a clockwork night shift had descended on the station. She pointed Sean to a seat at the back of the room and he took it, but gave her a resentful look as he shuffled over to it, left like a dog at the doors of a supermarket. Murdo McCloud spotted her and raised a hand in greeting.

'Oh, pet,' he called over, 'I heard about your driver and what happened. Are you well?'

'Murdo, who've they got in being questioned at the moment?'

'Oh, now.' He shook his head at the question. She knew he couldn't answer that. Being questioned was a delicate matter that had to be kept confidential if the police were ever to squeeze useful information from anyone. Revealing the fact that a rogue had been in for questioning was the final threat the police had over people. If word got out that someone had been in talking to the police and they had anything important to tell, there was a good chance that the guy might never make it home again.

'Don't worry, it can't be a snipe,' she said. 'The car's parked right outside. Whoever it belongs to doesn't care who knows it.'

Murdo wobbled his head, wavering. 'Well, I don't know.'

'It's a big red Ford. It looks like a sports car. It's right outside the door.'

Murdo thought about it for a minute, his eyes sliding sideways to listen to the noise of the station. He nodded her towards the door. 'Right well, come on now.' He stood up, jogged noisily down the three wooden stairs and hurried across the waiting room in an old-man run, elbows high, span hardly wider than a walk would have been. 'As long as we're quick.'

They hurried to the door, opened it and Paddy stood in the street and pointed at the car while Murdo hung out and looked at it. He nodded happily and ran back in, holding his fists up to his chest, scurrying as if the elves were after him.

When Paddy got back inside he was standng behind his desk, grinning and breathless, a little excited at having broken a rule.

Murdo panted, 'That's not a crim's motor.'

'How d'ye know for sure?'

'It's one of the young officers'. He's just been transferred here.'

'Would I know him?'

'Dunno. Young fella, just moved to this station, transferred. Name of Tam Gourlay.'

Gourlay. He must have thought she'd know his car when she saw it outside her house, but she didn't know cars at all. She considered telling Sean, but he wouldn't understand why Gourlay parking out-side her house was so bad. He was trying to intimidate her before the police inquiry, frighten her into being circumspect about what she said. And now someone had transferred him to Partick Marine, the very station that Sullivan was conducting the Bearsden Bird investigation out of.

'God, of course it's Tam,' she said, trying to smile happily.

'Ah, ye know him?'

'I know Tam well. And his wife. And the baby. We're about the same age.'

Murdo was old and hadn't noticed. He screwed his eyes up at her. 'Aye, well, so I suppose.'

'Where is Tam just now, d'ye know?'

He looked wary. 'He's on night shift.'

'I know he's on night shift. We've been bumping into each other most nights for the past two months.' She leaned in confidentially. 'We were both at the Bearsden Bird's door on the night she was killed.'

Murdo rocked uncomfortably from foot to foot. He didn't want to talk about that with a journalist now, no policeman did, not until the inquiry was over and no one was found at fault.

'Naw, naw,' she said. 'I'm not interested in that; that's too big a story for someone like me. I just wanted to hook up with him later, but if you don't want to tell me where he is, I'm sure we'll bump into each other anyway.'

She patted the desk and waited, but Murdo was an old lag and had seen every ruse there was. His blank expression didn't flicker.

'Isn't it weird that he was transferred here?' She leaned in confidentially. 'Given that the inquiry into the Bearsden call's coming up and the investigation's happening out of here? Isn't that a bit unusual?'

Murdo looked her straight in the eye until she got tired of waiting and turned and walked away, feeling foolish and awkward, Sean following in her wake.

'I'm looking to meet up with one of the officers working out of this station tonight,' she told Sean outside. 'Let's follow the calls for the west as closely as possible.'

'I don't know what you're talking about, but OK.'

She went over to the Ford and looked at it carefully, skirting around to the front so that she was seeing it from the same angle as she had in Eastfield. It was definitely the same car. She hadn't even consciously remembered it but there was a car deodorizer hanging from the mirror and it was still there, a small rectangle hanging from a chain.

When she got back to the calls car and fell into the back seat, Sean asked whether Whiteinch would count as the west end.

'Absolutely. Why?'

'Just heard a call for there. A shop window got tanned.'

'Right, let's go.'

Sean swung the car in a clumsy arch across the road and headed west.

They chased calls all night, attending every smashed street light and shadow on a shop window, but Tam Gourlay stayed ahead of them. She didn't want to ask after him; if she did he'd know she was coming and she'd lose the edge. But she was glad in a way. Sean made her see herself from the outside, imagine herself being watched instead of ignored and invisible the way she usually did. She was glad that they were hanging tight to the west tonight and couldn't meet Burns together. She was afraid Sean would guess if he saw them speaking.

But Gourlay stayed beyond them. A few hours later they were called to a polite student party in university halls that had gone bad when some street boys had crashed and smashed their way through the cooking facilities. Pictures had been ripped off the walls and wallpaper scratched all the way along the hall to the front door. When Paddy got outside she saw Sean standing on the pavement watching boys not much younger than himself being rounded up by the attending policemen. He was smoking, listening to the radio through the open window, his eyes red and heavy, smiling at the show.

'Anything come over?' she said, nodding in at the radio.

'Naw,' he grinned at her. 'Nothing came over.'

239

She could see that he was loving this. She nearly told him that it wouldn't always be this much fun, he'd get as jaded as she had when the tiredness and the sameness became oppressive, but she stopped herself. She'd had that spark when she first started, and it was fun taking these small glimpses into unfamiliar lives.

''Mon, we'll go.'

She got back into the car, watching the policemen for signs of Gourlay, and it occurred to her that Gourlay had parked outside her house on Friday night. If he had been there earlier and she hadn't noticed him he could have seen her pull up with Burns. A rush of hot blood up the back of her neck made her think suddenly that possibly, just possibly, Gourlay had followed them to the waste-ground and watched them fucking in the car. And he had told everyone in the Strathclyde region. It all made sense suddenly. He was trying to discredit her before the inquiry.

'Sean,' she shouted over the noise of the radio, sounding so alarmed that he turned it down suddenly. 'Sean, give us a cigarette, would ye?'

He was a more committed smoker than she was. He pulled the car over to the pavement and handed his fag packet back to her, watching in the mirror as she took one out and lit it with his lighter.

Paddy drew heavily on the cigarette. It was an unfamiliar brand and the taste raked hard at her throat, making her heart race and her hands shake. Burns was innocent after all. Well, innocent-ish.

'Is there any point in us driving around?'

'Eh?'

Sean took a cigarette himself and lit it. 'Is there any point in us driving around if we're going nowhere? Shouldn't I just pull over and we can listen from the kerbside?'

'Aye, yeah, whatever you think.'

He parked in a street and they sat with the radio blaring between them, smoking, not speaking. Sean didn't look at her once and didn't notice how flustered she was at the thoughts rolling around her head. Sitting with him was actually more comfortable than it had been with Billy and she was surprised by that. She kept looking in the mirror and expecting to see Billy's eyes.

They followed a call to a high-rise dive suicide and stopped at the burger van, where Paddy bought Sean a Nick Special, a deep-fried burger on a bun with a fish finger and extra onions. They ate in the car listening to the radio for west-end calls. Neither of them really believed they were ever going to find Gourlay.

Paddy was gazing out of the window, looking forward to the hotel room she could never seem to get to, raking through her troubles and feeling sorry for herself, when she remembered that Lafferty was still out there and that if he found her, and she lived, she might look back on this as a high point in her life.

26

Burns

I

Her room was small, built into the attic space of the hotel, furnished with a single bed so narrow that turning over in her sleep would be tricky, and a window set deep into the roof, showing nothing but sky. The sheets were nylon and the blankets scratchy, but it was quiet and Paddy was alone. She had shared a room with Mary Ann since she was born and had never slept by herself. She could sleep naked if she wanted. She took off all her clothes and climbed into the bed, looking at the sagging wallpaper on the sloping ceiling, luxuriating in the quiet.

As she fell asleep, in her last conscious moment she listened, as she always did, for her sister's soft breathing.

She had to tell the board of inquiry about her fifty-quid bribe this afternoon, and coupled with the knowledge that Lafferty was out there somewhere, prowling for her, it made her sleep fitful and tense. Syrupy dreams bled through her mind of Billy burning in sudden bright lights and Ramage scowling and blaming her.

A knock on the door startled her awake. She sat up, hot-faced and bewildered, not knowing where she was for a moment. The officious knock came again, three raps and a pause before the fourth. A man's voice called out that he was from room service and she was suddenly conscious of being naked and alone in a quiet part of the hotel.

'I didn't order room service,' she said, sitting up, disorientated and wobbly, dragging her jumper over her head and standing up unsteadily to pull her pencil skirt on.

Someone was breathing behind the door.

There was no spyhole and no chain. She stood behind the door and listened for clues. The knock came again; the same slow rhythm sounded sinister this time. Glancing back into the room her eye fell on the trouser press, a chair, the telephone for reception. The flex was long enough for her to carry it across the floor to the door and she pulled it over, lifting the receiver and pressing '0' for reception, holding the handset behind the door as she slipped the lock and opened it an inch, keeping her foot behind the door in case the man in the corridor tried to push his way into the room.

Burns was out of uniform, dressed in a shirt and slacks so clean that they looked as if they had just come out of the packet. He gave a penitent little smile and she slammed the door on him.

'Hello, room 745?' The receptionist's voice was insistent. 'Room 745, may I help you?'

'No, it's fine, my mistake.' Paddy hung up the receiver and turned back to the door.

'Paddy,' Burns breathed. 'I didn't tell anyone, honestly.'

Paddy stood panting behind the door. 'How did you find out which room I was in? I'm supposed to be in hiding here.'

'I'm a polis.'

So was Tam Gourlay. Lafferty might be on his way up in the lift right now. She was doing his job for him, frightening herself. Paddy rubbed her face and wished she had a mirror. She'd look terrified and pink and sweaty and puffy and didn't want Burns to see her this vulnerable.

'I heard about Billy,' he said. 'I just want to see that you're all right. Can I come in?'

'I'm fine.' She brushed her hair up at the sides and composed her face.

'Please?'

She hesitated for effect before letting the door swing open a couple of inches and backing off into the room. There was nowhere to sit down but on the bed or the single chair. It would seem suggestive to sit on the bed so she took the chair and sat, one arm slung stiffly over the back, mock casual, as Burns stepped into the room and shut the door behind him. He looked very tall and broad in the confined space. He stood for a moment, awkward, his hands patting the side of his thighs, looking around the mean little room, a strangely nervous look on his face. 'I didn't tell anyone what happened between us.'

'No, I know. Tam Gourlay did it.'

He frowned. 'How would Gourlay know?'

'He's been following me, trying to warn me off about the inquiry. He was outside my house that night, I think he saw us.'

Burns's lips thinned, his eyes widened. 'Did he indeed? Ye sure?'

'I saw his car outside my house that night.'

'Right, right.' He calmed himself and looked at her. 'You think Gourlay's bent anyway, don't you? The guys who questioned you yesterday told me.'

'Well,' she said, unsure whether she could trust him. 'I dunno. We'll see. They didn't seem to be listening to anything else I told them. I said it was Lafferty who firebombed the car but they were hell-bent on not listening.'

'They don't always seem interested in the stuff that matters. It's a bit of an act.'

'Those guys weren't acting.'

Burns tapped his hands on the side of his thighs again, looking unsure. He looked at the bed and a small smile flitted across his face, suppressed as soon as it occurred to him. 'Can I . . . ?'

She gestured to him to sit if he wanted. He pushed the blankets back and perched on the side of the small bed, bouncing once and smiling again. It was her first private bed and she didn't like him colonizing it. 'Why are you here, Burns?'

'I was worried about you. You seemed upset the other night . . . and then the fire. I asked around about Lafferty for you.'

'Why won't the police listen to me?'

He sighed heavily and stroked the bed sheet. 'Look, you have to understand, the police just want this story to go away. Gourlay . . . Guys like him, they're small fry, he'll never get promoted into any position of power.'

'It's Gourlay and McGregor.'

'OK, both of them, we know about them. We're dealing with it.'

'But you don't want outsiders objecting when a murderer gets away with it?'

He grinned at her and shook his head, looked up at the sky through the small window. The low morning light suited his face, highlighting his large nose and casting a shadow from his black eyelashes over his cheek. 'Paddy, murderers get away with it all the time. Lack of evidence, no witnesses, happens every day. We'll get Lafferty. We might not get him for this, but we'll get him for something.'

'Like you got Patrick Meehan?'

'Ah, Paddy Meehan. See, now, that wasn't a police call. MI5 did that. Stupid. It was a fuck-up from start to finish.'

She sat back and glared at him. 'So the system works? You set people up all the time?'

'Our job is to make the streets safe for people like you, Paddy. The truth is the justice system doesn't work. People get out all the time, bad people, vicious men just like Lafferty. If Lafferty gets done for something and it takes him off the streets so you can go home, would you be as against the way we work then?'

'Principles matter. Doing the right thing matters even if it's against your own interests.'

He was looking at her neck, distracted, his eyes half closed.

'Burns, have you been sent here to tell me to back off?'

'You know why I came here.'

'No, I don't.'

He swung his weight off the bed suddenly and was across the room in one fluid step. He cupped her face in both his hands and lifted her to her feet until her face was tight to his, her nose to his nose, eye to eye, open mouth to open mouth. She felt the stubble on his chin scratch her lips. He hadn't been home yet, hadn't shaved after the night shift or had a wash. He smelled glorious.

George Burns stood in his flash shirt and trousers, in his adulterous Protestant shoes and explored her with his dirty, dextrous fingers, peeling her clothes off and letting them drop to the floor.

They fell on the single bed, Paddy underneath him, and they laughed because it was so narrow. They worked their way to the side of the bed and Burns's hard purple cock stuck out of his trousers as she knelt between his knees. He sighed like a slit tyre as she kissed and licked it. Lost in a fog of sensations and smells they slid on to the carpeted floor, gliding noiselessly over one another, fuck-fuck-fucking until they both came in glorious messy Technicolor.

They lay on the floor panting, occasionally flapping hands across to cover up the most damning bits of skin.

Burns caught his breath. 'Wait till I tell the guys about this one.'

Paddy grinned and flailed a lethargic slap at him with the back of her hand. She could have slept in the chair. She could have slept on a sack of jaggy sticks, actually, she was so relaxed.

Burns sighed into her hair. 'That's why I came to see you.'

'So you could get your end away?'

He shook his head and pulled her close, still breathless from the exertion. 'Don't be like that with me. Just for a minute, let's be nice to each other.'

'You haven't got your ring on today,' she said spikily.

'No, come on.' He squeezed her shoulder. 'Give it five minutes.'

She leaned heavily on Burns's chest to push herself up to sitting and pulled herself up, turning away to pull her jumper on. 'I won't back off about Lafferty, no matter how often you do that to me.'

'I *did it* to you?' he said playfully. 'You did it to me. I was just lying there.'

She lay back, resting her chin on his chest, breathing in the smell of him. A floor below they could hear the low hum of a vacuum cleaner. A car hooted its horn a mile away in the street.

'OK.' Burns looked at her, his fingers in her hair. 'Lafferty works for a guy called Paul Neilson. Neilson used to go out with Vhari Burnett's sister. He's squeaky clean, no record for anything.'

'Vhari had a sister?'

'Kate Burnett. She's disappeared.'

'Is she dead?'

'No one knows. There've been a couple of sightings but nothing solid. Someone saw her at a restaurant a few nights ago but we've heard nothing since then.'

'What about the brother?'

He frowned down at her. 'There isn't a brother. The parents never mentioned a boy. Just the two girls.'

She was sure Evelyn at the Easterhouse Law Centre had said Thillingly spent his last day with Vhari's brother. She cast her mind back over the conversation: Bernie – Evelyn said his name was Bernie and he had a garage. But if Vhari's parents wouldn't admit to him, there had to be a reason.

'What about Thillingly? Do they still suspect him?'

Burns took his fingers from her hair and sat up, hugging his knees with his arms and looking around the mess of clothes on the floor.

'Well, do they?'

He found his underpants and stood up to pull them on, completely unabashed. 'You have to understand, Paddy, the police'll do anything to protect their own. But we get the job done. We do.'

'It's not good enough.'

They looked at each other. Burns raised an angry eyebrow.

'You can't frighten me when you're standing there in nothing but your skanties, Burns.'

He ignored the comment and yanked his trousers on, pulling up the zipper like a final statement. His chest was broad with a 'T' of black hair reaching down under his waistband. The scar on his stomach was pink and puckered. It looked like a bottle-opener might well have pierced it and she wondered if he was lying about his wife at all.

'You're giving evidence to the inquiry today, aren't you?'

'Yeah.' She stood up and scrambled into her pants and skirt, anxious not to be the last one naked in the room, perching on the bed to fit her tights on over her feet. 'Are they even looking for Kate Burnett?'

'Leave it, Paddy.'

'What if she turns up dead? What if I turn up dead?'

He slipped his feet into his toggle loafers and pulled his shirt over his head without undoing the buttons. 'I was asking about the inquiry because I was going to take you there myself, make sure you're safe.'

'Oh, that'll be great for my reputation: pitching up in a flash sports car with the slag of the year.'

She meant the comment to be taken playfully but Burns mis-understood. He stared at her. 'You're a bit of a snide cow, actually, aren't ye?'

She couldn't think of an answer. Burns picked up his jacket and walked out of the room, leaving her sitting alone on the end of the mean little bed.

27

Bernie's In

I

Bernie's garage was not quite what she expected. Knowing what she did about Vhari Burnett's family background Paddy had supposed her brother's garage would be a dealership for smart new cars, but it was in a derelict area at the bottom of a sharp hill a long way from the main road.

She headed down towards the blackened Victorian railway arches. Beyond it lay the motorway and further yet the river. Blocks of tenements had been knocked down on either side of the road, leaving just their footprint on the land. A couple of shanty workshops were still operating from what would have been the back court; she could hear radios blaring and see lights on inside, occasional drills and mechanical bits turning over. A square, single-storey pub was set on the corner of a sea of dusty rubble.

The tall arches under the railway bridge had been converted into workspaces, not the ramshackle hodge-podge of organic economic development but uniform government-subsidized workshops that spoke of an economy in terminal decline. Yellow brick filled in the grand arches of blackened Victorian bricks, each with a double garage door in the middle, painted red with a unit number stencilled on to it.

Paddy walked towards the bridge and felt the damp river air clinging to the bricks. Most of the units were dark and locked, some of them permanently. Only one or two had signs denoting a business operating out of them. Unit 7 was one of the few arches with the lights on and the red doors open. It was at the far end of the lane, across the road from a scrap merchant's yard. A sign on the fence declared that the yard was 'Protected by Dog', and below the claim was a silhouette of a snarling wolf.

Wherever the Burnett family legacy was being used it certainly wasn't being invested in Bernie's business. He wasn't leaving a smart Bearsden villa every morning to come here. A warm orange light spilled out from inside the door and the sound of a pop radio buzzed. The large hand-painted sign propped up outside, Bernie's Motors, was hardly visible behind a bank of engine parts propped up against the wall. Two cars were parked outside, one with both back wheels off, the other apparently in good working order. Paddy didn't know much about cars but she could see that it was a smart green Jaguar, an old one but with a perfectly preserved chrome trim and arched roof. The driver's and passengers' seats had been taken out, leaving jagged, uncomfortable axles pitted with bolts.

She was so engrossed in the handsome car that she didn't see Bernie until she was almost standing on his toes.

'She's a honey, isn't she?'

He was looking lovingly at the Jaguar. She'd seen him before, holding Vhari's arm in the photo of Grandfather Burnett's funeral. He had a James Dean haircut and wore a ripped navy-blue boiler suit, smeared with black grease, going baggy at the knees. A red neckerchief around his neck served no purpose other than to make the oil-blackened boiler suit a fashion statement. His jaw was so square he looked as if he'd been drawn with a ruler. 'I was trying to get oxblood leather seats for inside but they're pretty hard to find.'

'Not a believer in the fashion maxim that "red and green should never be seen"?'

He laughed and looked at her for the first time, taking her in and pointing at her coat approvingly. 'Nice.'

'A quid,' she said.

He nodded, impressed. 'Top stuff.' He pointed at the Jag again. 'Two hundred quid. She looked in such bad nick when I got her that no one else bid. If you know anything about these cars it's the trim and the undercarriage that corrode. Even if she's just for parts she was an absolute bargain.'

She could find no trace of Vhari Burnett in his face but Bernie's accent seemed familiar, posh to the verge of sounding English, and she'd heard it before but couldn't place it. At work, maybe. Someone she'd interviewed for something. She could only imagine how self-possessed he'd need to be to carry the accent in such a working-class area. Talking like that in the Eastfield Star would have been an invitation to have all his car windows smashed.

Paddy stuck out her hand. 'You Bernie?'

Suddenly sceptical, he looked at the hand and took it reluctantly, letting go as soon as he could. 'Who are you?'

'Paddy Meehan. I'm a reporter with the *Daily News*.'

He shoved his hands into his pockets. 'I don't want to talk about her.'

'Neither do I.'

It was only half true but it got his attention. 'Why are you here then?'

'Thillingly.'

She startled him. 'What about him?'

'The police are convinced Mark killed Vhari.' She used his first name, hoping Bernie would mistake her for a friend. 'I think that's crap.'

His eyes were wet, she could see that even though he wouldn't look at her. 'What makes you think that?'

'He was the chair of Amnesty. He's not going to torture someone by pulling their teeth out. And I think he was a nice guy.'

He leaned over, pretending to examine the skeleton innards of the Jaguar, and nodded. 'He *was* a nice guy.'

251

'I think Mark got beaten up in the car park outside his work just before Vhari was attacked. I think he knew something and they were pressing him for information and I think that's what happened with Vhari as well, but they went too far and killed her. Where's Kate, Bernie?'

He frowned and bit his lip.

'Can I talk to you inside for a minute?'

He looked around the lane, sad, remembering his dead sister, perhaps, and looked at her, at her spiked hair and ankle boots and good coat for a quid.

'It's bloody freezing down here.'

'It is,' he said absently. 'I've got thermals on.'

She nodded inside and he turned and stepped into the garage, waiting until Paddy followed him before scraping the big metal doors shut. He drew the heavy bolt across them.

Paddy had been trapped with a violent nutter before. She felt the hairs on the back of her neck stand to attention. Hands in pockets, she slipped her index finger through her house keys, ready to rip the face off him if he came closer than a couple of feet.

She looked around and realized that her defences were pitiful. There were drill bits on the floor, metal toolboxes and spanners everywhere. If he wanted to batter her to death she was completely fucked. 'Did you see your sister that night?'

Bernie shook his head. 'I haven't seen Kate for years.'

'I meant Vhari.'

He flinched at the mistake. 'I hadn't seen her for some time either.'

If he had been questioned by the police he would have known exactly when he last saw her, would have had to work it out and could have answered immediately.

'The police haven't even talked to you, have they?'

He looked at her curiously.

'What does that tell you about the quality of the investigation,

Bernie? Doesn't it worry you that they don't even know Vhari had a brother?'

He half smiled. 'They don't know about me?'

'Apparently your parents didn't mention a brother when they were questioned.'

He tipped his head back and barked a bitter laugh that echoed around the hollow arch. He pressed his hand to his chest. 'I don't count. Adopted. There's six years between Vhari and Katie. They thought they couldn't have any more so I got drafted in, but when Katie came along I was considered surplus to requirements. They never really took to me.'

'I'm sorry.'

'Not blood, you see. "Our adopted son, Bernie." When I was wee I thought that was my full name. They offered me money to go to university, but the truth is that I'm not that bright. I wanted to be a mechanic. They haven't spoken to me for years.'

'I've got a picture of you.' She took out the clipping of the funeral and unfolded it before handing it over, watching to read his reaction.

Bernie smiled sadly down at it. 'I haven't seen this one. The Burnetts ignored me all the way through the service. They only stood next to me at the line-up by the church door because they couldn't cause a scene. Came to speak to me at the end but I scampered.' He touched a fingertip to the picture. 'And there's Kate.'

She twisted around and saw he was touching the blonde with curly hair. 'That's Kate? I thought it was Vhari. They're alike, aren't they?'

He looked away from the picture quickly. 'Would you like a cup of tea?'

'Please.'

As he walked over to a large tool table she had the distinct impression that he was trying to draw her attention away from

253

Kate. He poured tea from a tartan flask into two heavily stained mugs. A large industrial heater burned in the corner, a flat brazier of pink flame that tinged the light in the room pink, creating an expectation of warmth that was instantly swamped by the sharp, damp cold emanating from the brick.

The room was shallow but broad. A car was neatly parked against the left-hand wall, a beige MG sports car. On a table off to the right, against the red brick wall, sat an old kitchen table with jotters and receipt pads on it, above a three-tiered battered red toolbox.

'No sugar, I'm afraid. You said you want to talk about Thillingly?'

'I heard Mark came here the day he killed himself.'

'Yeah.' He handed her one of the mugs. 'I know Mark didn't kill Vhari, whatever the police say.'

The tea wasn't very hot but she wrapped her fingers around the mug for warmth. Her stomach was sore and she was feeling the cold more than usual. 'I was at the door the night she was killed. I saw Vhari with a man.'

Bernie stiffened. 'I see. Right.' He sipped his tea carefully, not looking at her. He should have asked who the guy was or at least what he looked like, but he didn't. He didn't need to. He already knew.

'It was Paul Neilson, wasn't it?' she said, watching for a reaction. Bernie sipped at his cup quickly, blinking, and she knew she was right. 'Why did Mark kill himself?'

'Mark was depressed. Often depressed.' Bernie drank his tea, his eyes skitting around the messy floor. He was lying, badly. He was unaccustomed to duplicity and it intrigued her.

They looked around for somewhere to sit but there wasn't anywhere. They couldn't even sit on the floor because it was too oily. 'Usually with visitors I just sit in a car, do you mind?' He held his hand out towards the MG. 'Passenger or driver? The seats are soft.'

'I'll be the driver.' She opened the door and climbed in, sliding into the leather seat. It was comfortable apart from a belligerent spring that jabbed her in the back if she moved about.

Bernie slipped into the seat next to her and shut the door. 'Why are you so interested in Mark?'

'I was there when they pulled Mark out of the water. The police had him convicted before he was in the morgue, and it just seems too tidy to me. Was Mark's nose burst when he came to see you?'

Bernie havered for a moment, pretending he was trying to remember Mark's face that day, but Paddy could see he was fitting the bits of lies together to see if they worked. 'Um, no, I don't know. I didn't notice.'

'He had a nose like a smashed potato and you didn't notice?'

'I can't remember.' He glanced guiltily around the garage. 'I wasn't really looking at him.'

'Right. I've been told that he tried to phone your sister the night before, that he called her house and someone else answered the phone.'

She had his full attention now.

'Who answered?'

'Mark asked for Vhari first. Then he asked the person who they were and where the hell she was. He was very upset afterwards.'

'Who told you this?'

'Diana. He said something about Kate as well . . .'

'Did he say where she was?'

'Might have. She's still missing, isn't she?'

'Dunno.' Bernie shook his head too vigorously. 'I haven't seen Kate for years. Never see her. She never comes to see me either.'

Paddy tried not to pat his arm. Bernie wasn't a good liar. 'But you did see Vhari?'

'Vhari kept in touch with everyone. Never did the easy thing and just bolted like I did.' He bit his finger and looked away through the window. 'Vhari was a lovely person. She was *good*.

That's what the papers keep missing about her. She was really *good*.'

Paddy thought of Mary Ann reciting prayers in the dark. Being away from them for a day was a glorious novelty but she couldn't imagine not talking to her mother for years and years. With the luxury of distance she could see that the Meehans were warm. Fraught but warm.

'Did Vhari keep in touch with Kate?'

'Oh, yeah. Called her every week. Called us both.'

They stopped for a moment, looking out through the dirty windscreen, seeing the garage as if they had just driven in. 'So this is all your own?'

'Every bit of it. Got the lease, even drew the sign myself. The Burnetts were furious.'

'What's Kate like?'

He smiled despite himself. 'Kate never gave a fuck. She left home at fifteen and never went back. Grandfather left her a cottage when he died, up at Loch Lomond, and she never even went home for the keys.'

'Did you get anything?'

'No.' He looked bitter. 'I'm not blood. I got nothing. Vhari got the Bearsden house. It's worth a fortune.'

Paddy thought of the old-fashioned curtains she had noticed in the big bay window on the night of the murder. 'Had she just moved in?'

'Yeah, three weeks ago. Half a mile from the folks, God help her.'

They sipped their tea, watching the still room and the pink fire ripple across the brazier surface, its light shifting the tones in the room. She glanced at Bernie out of the corner of her eye so that he wouldn't know she was watching, and saw his eyebrows furrow with worry. Every time Kate was mentioned he baulked.

'And Mark spent his last day here?'

Bernie blinked hard at his mug and shrugged. 'He was outside waiting when I got here at eight thirty, dressed in his smart suit and that stupid Midge Ure overcoat. He was bloody freezing.' He smirked at the memory but his face crumpled suddenly at the thought of Mark. He struggled for breath for a moment, the shock of emotion making him fleck saliva on to his chin. He raised a hand and wiped it off. 'I'm very sorry,' he said, his accent still as crisp as a fresh lettuce. 'It's just . . . a lot's happened.'

Paddy tried to think of something kind to say. 'I'm sorry too.'

'Mark had come to tell me Vhari was dead. He wanted to tell me. I don't have a phone at home and he didn't want me to hear from the radio.'

'Are Kate and Paul Neilson still together?'

'Dunno,' he said, too quickly. 'Dunno anything about Kate's life.'

'But you know Neilson?'

Bernie nodded. 'We were at school together, all of us, Mark and Paul and us. Mark's family only lived across the road from us. Paul lived further away, he never really hung around the house much. I didn't know him well.'

'He didn't join the gang?'

'No, just sort of took Kate away. He was nothing to do with us. After school Vhari and Mark got engaged. Big family event. We were all big pals until Diana came along.'

She had heard Bernie's accent before and now she could place it: it was a public-school accent and the last time she'd heard it was from the mouth of the man she now knew was Paul Neilson, when they were both standing outside Vhari Burnett's door.

'Where does Neilson live?'

'Killearn. Huntly House or Cottage or something – Huntly Lodge.'

'Would Neilson have known where your grandfather's house was?'

Bernie's eye flickered to her and he shifted uncomfortably. 'Dunno. Maybe.'

'But Mark would have known. They were engaged so he probably met your grandfather. He'd know where Vhari had moved to.'

'Well,' he cleared his throat unnecessarily, 'I suppose.'

Paddy nodded, making mental notes. 'Why didn't Mark go to the police?'

Bernie shrugged again; it seemed to be a herald for a fib. 'Mark was a lawyer. He didn't have a particularly high opinion of the police.'

'Was he protecting you from them?' It was a stab in the dark and not a very good one.

Bernie smirked at her. 'From the fuzz? What have I done? Been a toff in a working-class area?' The temperature was dropping between them so she decided to move on.

'Bernie, listen, Vhari had the chance to walk out of the house that night and she didn't take it.' She watched his face closely. 'Whatever secret you're keeping from the rest of the world, she gave her life to keep it. I think she was protecting Kate. Why would she need to protect her from the police?'

Bernie looked at her regretfully and rolled his head away, rubbing his hair on the window, sad that he couldn't tell her. 'I'm sorry,' he whispered.

'It's OK. Whatever it is, it's OK, Bernie. Even if she stayed for you.'

Fighting tears, Bernie rubbed his nose with an open palm. 'It wasn't for me,' he said. 'Really.'

'Did Mark give Vhari's new address to the person who beat him up?'

Bernie looked at her imploringly but said nothing.

'And then he killed himself? Because he felt he'd got her killed?'

He shook his head. Paddy felt he'd tell her if he could.

'I'll find out, you know. I will find out and tell the police. Can't you give me anything?'

His eyes wandered slowly around her face, considering what she said. 'I can't do anything that'll hurt her.'

'Kate?'

He nodded at the dashboard. 'We can't involve the police.'

'Why? Has Kate done something illegal?' He didn't answer. 'I'll protect her as much as I can, Bernie, but you need to give me something to go on, a name or a place or something, please? For Vhari.' Bernie shook his head. 'For Mark?'

He drew in a deep breath and looked around the garage. 'I don't even know who he is, but he's important.' He worked his fingernail into the seat of his chair. 'It's Knox. Look for someone called Knox.'

28

Inquiry

I

The clippings library was a pocket of calm order in the chaos of the newspaper. Helen, the chief librarian, dressed like a real librarian would, in tweed pencil skirts and jerseys. Her glasses hung on a red beaded chain around her neck. Paddy had never liked her when she was a copy boy but Helen seemed to have mellowed since she got promotion. Paddy sometimes dropped in for a chat when she was feeling beleaguered, a fellow female in the middle of a gang of nasty men. The rumours about Burns would be all over the news room by now and she wanted to linger in the safety of the library.

Helen dropped an envelope of clippings on to the counter and smiled at Paddy. 'Here's one set of Robert Lafferty clippings. We've got Neilsen the musician but nothing for a Paul Neilson.'

'Nothing at all?'

'Not so much as a birth announcement. There's so many clippings for the name Knox I'd need to let you in here to trawl through them yourself. Will I give you the first twenty sets?'

'Uch, no, Helen, I don't have time.'

'Yeah, I heard you're going in front of the police inquiry into the Bearsden murder this afternoon.'

Paddy flinched. 'Who told you that?'

'Shug Grant was in. He's covering the inquiry.'

It was bad. Shug Grant already hated her for her Margaret Mary jibe and he was a loud-mouthed bastard. He once slept with a sub ed's wife after a party and came in the next day and told everyone. If he was reporting on the inquiry half of Scotland would know about the fifty quid before the first edition went to press.

The doors opened behind Paddy and a copy boy came in and stood next to her, his hands on the partition, looking around expectantly, but Helen ignored him.

'I heard,' she said quietly, 'that the squad car took twenty-five minutes to get to the house. Someone'll get their books.'

'I thought it was a closed committee?'

'It is, but Grant knows someone on it.'

Paddy smiled nervously and lifted the envelope. 'Shug knows someone everywhere, doesn't he?'

'Seems to.'

She hesitated on the stairs but climbed them slowly, making for the news room. She couldn't dodge them for ever or they'd know she was scared.

Slipping gingerly through the doors, she settled on the nearest seat at the edge of the sports desk and took the Lafferty clippings out of the envelope.

She was listening with half an ear to what was happening around her and sensed a murmur of something strange, a kind of hysterical edge to the atmosphere in the news room. Men were smiling fixed grins, looking busy, moving fast and typing, working unashamedly hard. At the epicentre of the oddness was a man she had never seen before, a dark, small, hairy man, simian, square-shouldered and no-necked, typing hard and looking pleased with himself, an awkward angular smirk on his blue-shadowed face.

She nudged a fat sports boy sitting two seats away. 'Who's that?'

He glanced over, averting his eyes immediately. 'JT's replacement. From London. Famous hound, apparently. Going to make us all get our act together.' He dropped his voice. '*Spy.*'

'Did JT come back?'

He shook his head. 'Not even having a drink out for him. He was told by phone: don't come in. Two subs got the bump yesterday and Kevin Hatcher as well. Fair enough. They're keeping a book on how long it'll take Kevin to drink himself to death.'

Paddy hadn't seen Kevin sober since she started on the paper. He was the picture editor and miraculously managed to do an adequate job while so drunk he could hardly form consonants. The old soaks used Kevin as a measure to justify their own drinking: if they got as bad as him they'd stop, but no one ever was as bad as him.

She looked around the room at the fixed grins of fifty people moving around a room trying to look unaffiliated. When news of her fifty quid trickled back she'd be nothing more than a whisper under the breath too.

Sweating with nerves, she tried to still her mind by getting lost in her reading. Lafferty was a graduate of the Christian Brothers reform school, a brutal regime that created a common background for all of the most violent men in Glasgow. Bad boys from all over the region were sent there at twelve, their well-being and moral development left to monks who were not much more than spiteful, frustrated boys themselves. It was *Lord of the Flies* without table manners.

The cases against Lafferty tended to be assault charges for pub fights or extortion rackets. There was an unproven murder charge: a prostitute had been thrown off a multi-storey car park, according to one witness because she wasn't kicking back enough money. Lafferty was pictured outside the court, younger but no less wired than he had been when she saw him being questioned, pleased at the outcome, his tiny eyes making him look like an angry pig about to charge.

Paddy thought about the fifty-quid note Neilson had given her. Ramage would be perfectly justified in sacking her: he wouldn't even need to pay her a redundancy package.

She looked up at the news room, at the men walking back and

forth, delivering copy to their subs, typing hard on the heavy machines. Shug Grant was sitting at a desk, watching her from across the room, chewing gum with his mouth open. Fluorescent light glinted off his oily forehead. He raised his hand and pointed a long finger at her, jabbing the tip, and stood up, holding her eye as he walked across the news room towards her. 'Just back from the inquiry. Typing up my notes.'

'Aye,' she affected unconcern. 'Great.'

'You're up today, yeah? Ye nervous?'

'Why would I be nervous?'

'Tam Gourlay was in. Came over very badly. He contradicted you about the cars. Said they weren't BMWs.' She hadn't told anyone but the police about the cars. Shug was letting slip the unimportant details to let her know he was connected. It would suit the police case if she was discredited.

'So, you know someone on the inside?'

He pressed his lips together in a mock smile. If he had known about the money, he would have hinted at it. Sullivan had kept his word. The thought of being unceremoniously sacked was awful, but the idea that it might give Shug a good story stung even more.

'Who is it, Shug? It's not Sullivan. The minutes secretary? Is it the woman taking notes?'

Targeting the secretarial staff was the obvious move. Journalists would find out where they drank or shopped or danced, mine their weaknesses and pump them for information. Shug smiled enigmatically.

She waggled a finger at him. 'No, it can't be the seccy. Your information's very specific.' She picked her teeth in a way she hoped looked casual.

Perturbed, Shug frowned down at her. 'How do you mean, "specific"?'

'So,' she nodded, 'who'd want to selectively control the information coming out of the inquiry? If it's not a seccy or a clerk, there's only policemen left. How many members of the committee are there? Usually three, isn't it? Narrows it down a bit.'

Grant was professional enough to suppress his bruised ego and ask the right question. 'What is it? What are you holding back?'

She tried to smile confidently. 'You're being played, you know that, don't you?'

'Three o'clock.'

Shug watched her pack up her clippings, slip them back into the envelope and stand up. She turned to back out of the door and saw him again, a bitter twist at the corner of his mouth. He'd warn his leak that she knew and tell them to go for her.

Out on the draughty stairs she thought about Sean. Paul Neilson lived up in Killearn and she'd like to get a look at the house, see the cars outside it and get a sense of the man, but the village was well outside the city limits and she couldn't justify getting Sean to drive her there when they were supposed to be on call. Sean brought Burns to mind and she remembered him standing in the hotel room in his underpants. She wished to Christ she had slept instead. It might be her last chance for a while.

Exhaustion was creeping through her bones, making her skin feel clammy. She could have thrown up on the stairs.

II

The grey waiting room smelled of dust. Blinding low winter sun shone in through tall windows, making one half of the room un-inhabitably bright. Huddled in the shadowed half, in amongst the thick air swirling with dust motes and the scent of floor wax, sat Paddy, Shug Grant and three guys from other papers. The men chatted among themselves, sharing cigarettes, gossiping about Random Damage and the reshuffle at the *News*. JT had walked straight into another paper across town on the same day that he was sacked. He claimed that his new job paid better money but no one was sure. Kevin Hatcher, the drunkest man at the *News*, had slept on a bench in the Press Club last night. They'd have sent him home in a taxi but no one knew where he lived. This morning he left the second half of a pint on the bar, said he was going to the toilet and disappeared. Shug had a fiver on him dying in four weeks. A guy from the *Mirror* knew Kevin when he was a sober freelancer and won prizes for his photo essays. He was funny, apparently, back in those days, a clever man, educated and erudite.

A uniformed officer was stationed by the door to stop everyone talking about everything before they went in to the inquiry. For a secretive committee Paddy thought it particularly stupid to allow journalists into the waiting room, doling out cigarettes to waiting witnesses, there afterwards to take them for a friendly drink to calm their nerves. But she knew the witnesses weren't Grant's source, he knew what was coming up and what questions they were going to ask her, and the leaks were strategic, not random. They were coming from someone who wanted to control the way the story was reported.

She leaned her poor head against the wall and shut her eyes, just for a moment – she wasn't going to fall asleep, it was just to give them a rest and avoid talking to Grant. As the skin of her scalp made contact with the plaster she felt the tingling sensation of sleep creeping over the back of her head. She saw Billy in bed in hospital and smiled to herself about his hair. He might not be back at the job for a long time but he was alive and relatively unscathed. She saw the image of Lafferty in his rear-view mirror, carefully creeping up on the car, and Billy inside, smoking, oblivious.

It was warm in the room, body temperature. A veil of sleep slid down from her brow like a black cashmere blanket until a finger poked her on the shoulder. She opened her burning eyes. Grant was watching her carefully.

'Hey tubs, what're ye going to say?' he smiled.

The uniformed officer stepped forward. 'Ah, come on now, Mr Grant, you've been well warned about that sort of behaviour.'

It was as effective as a midgie trying to stop a mud slide. Grant raised a finger, telling her he'd get her later, and sat back. Paddy shrugged as if she was helpless and thought about all the journalists Ramage could have sent to cover the inquiry. He was holding on to all the hungry journalists like Shug and herself, stripping the *News* of kindness and camaraderie. The other journalists were listening for her answers.

'Who have they had in this morning?' she asked them.

A slick journalist in a cheap suit leaned forward, making Grant sit back. 'The operator who got the call for the address. And Tam Gourlay. Dan McGregor was yesterday.'

'Much of a morning, then?'

He smiled coldly. 'No, not really.'

She smiled back, baring her teeth. Shug returned the warmth. The two other journalists joined in until they were all smiling insincerely and wondering when they could stop. The inquiry-room door opened and Sullivan looked into the waiting room. He clocked Paddy and smiled wide. 'Meehan, please.'

She was so tired that her legs felt rubbery, her footfalls uncertain as she stood up and shuffled over to the door. She paused and took a breath before following Sullivan through the tall double doors, into the official inquiry.

It was a big, empty room for such a small committee. Four great long windows overlooked the Clyde River and a red marble bridge, currently choked with traffic. The ceiling was high but plain with thick, unembarrassed utility pipes snaking across it.

A long table was set to the side of the room. At the far end sat an older woman with thick glasses, head down over a notepad. Along the table were three men in fancied-up police uniforms, a strip of braiding here, some gold trim on a pocket, sitting in a little line facing an empty chair. They seemed too old to be dressed in uniform, too dignified, and would have looked as if they were in fancy dress but for the obvious quality of the material.

They didn't look at Paddy as she came in but filled up a glass of water or checked through the sets of notes they had in front of them.

Sullivan invited Paddy to sit at the table opposite the men but remained standing himself, hovering in her eye line near the door.

These three were prosperous men, working-class boys who had slowly worked their way up through the ranks. She could see in their faces a kind of rake's progress of middle age, a warning tableau of what might happen if you didn't look after yourself. The man nearest the secretary had a red complexion and puffy, blood-pressured eyes. Next to him was a thin, sallow-skinned man with a pinched mouth, bitter perhaps over some blip in his career. The third man was cheerful, glancing sideways at his companions, seeming to look for reassurance or signs of friendship, needy and ungrounded.

Paddy fumbled with her coat and it slid inelegantly to the floor. Rather than bend the four miles to retrieve it, she kicked it under the chair and sat down, putting her hands on the table, trying to shake the dozy mist from her mind.

The sallow man tapped the table in front of her to get her attention. 'Good afternoon, Miss Meehan.'

The secretary raised her pen and began to scribble.

'Hiya.' Paddy raised a hand and waved at them, felt stupid and dropped her hand to the table, stroking the wood and smiling weakly. She needed to be more lucid, her job was hanging on a shaky nail and these were not kind men.

The sallow man continued, 'As you know, Miss Meehan, this inquiry is convened to take evidence about the police call to 17 Drymen Road, Bearsden at two forty-seven a.m., one week ago. This is a closed committee. Do you understand what that means?'

She looked young, she knew that, but there was no reason to talk to her as if she was stupid. 'I do understand what a closed committee is, yes.'

'Anything you tell us will remain confidential.'

The red-faced man glanced suspiciously at Sullivan. The insecure one saw him and did it too. Paddy looked up and found Sullivan examining his shoes, poker-faced. It was a direct insult but it was from senior officers and Sullivan had to pretend not to notice. If the men worked in a news room Sullivan would have been within his rights to punch both of them.

'Yeah,' she said, feeling a defensive spark. 'It won't stay confidential though, will it? Shug Grant's got a hotline to what you're going to ask me and I know it isn't coming from Sullivan or this lady here.'

The secretary allowed her eyes to rise from the ring-binding on her notebook and stopped taking notes. The policemen shuffled uncomfortably in their seats. The uncertain one looked to his friends to see what to do.

'So, confidentiality is a worry for you.' The sallow one brushed over the comment. 'What is it you have to tell us?'

Shocked at their lack of concern, she sat back in the chair. 'Aren't you interested in the fact that there's a leak here?'

The sallow man looked surprised that anyone anywhere would dare to question him. The rosy-faced man sat forward and took over. 'Miss Meehan—'

'It's "Ms" actually,' she said, because she knew it pissed people off.

The men paused to smirk and the rosy-faced man tried again. 'We do have the authority to require you to cooperate. I can guarantee that nothing you say will be leaked.' He glanced accusingly at Sullivan again.

'You're wrong.' Paddy stroked the desk again. 'See, I know for certain that Mr Sullivan isn't the leak because I've already told him what I'm going to tell you. I also know it isn't the lady secretary because the leaks are too strategic. So, if this information gets into the press *after* this conversation then we'll know for certain that it's one of you three.'

She looked along the line of distinguished gentlemen, each of whom dodged her eye. They seemed perplexed. The very idea that they might be challenged by a plump youngster was ridiculous.

'I'm going to be frank.' She watched the table-top but her voice was strident and schoolmarmish. 'I know your name. You, the guy who's telling Shug Grant about what goes on in here. Now, I'm not going to announce your name at the *News* but I do know who you are.'

They sat still and looked at her. The red-faced man's smirk was frozen into a rictus grin. Paddy tried not to smile. It was delicious to be frightening when so little was expected: the element of surprise always gave her a running start.

The three men shifted in their seats, raising an eyebrow, tilting a chin back, twitching their annoyance. The sallow man took charge again. 'Shall we start again?' He nodded to the secretary to resume writing.

'OK then, let's introduce ourselves properly: I'm Patricia Meehan.' She looked at the rosy man, staring at him until he was embarrassed into speaking.

'Superintendent Ferguson.'

She stared at the sallow-faced man.

'I'm Chief Superintendent Knox,' he said reluctantly.

The third man introduced himself too, but Paddy wasn't listening. Knox was a common enough Scottish name but Paddy couldn't think past it. This Knox seemed a closed man, bitter and repressed, and looked like the type to misuse his position. If a chief superintendent's name was used at the door, it would explain why Gourlay and McGregor had left Vhari Burnett in her house in Bearsden. And it explained Gourlay and McGregor being transferred to Partick just as the investigation into Vhari Burnett's murder got underway. No wonder Tam Gourlay thought he could threaten her.

If Knox was on the take, the money would show: he'd have a big house, a flash car or kids at an expensive school. She could find out where he was spending it unless Lafferty found her first. But if Knox was working with Neilson, Lafferty would know she was here.

Quelling her panic, reminding herself that Knox couldn't do anything while she was in the room, she tried to concentrate.

After gentle prompting by Ferguson, Paddy told them about arriving at the house in Bearsden and finding Gourlay by the car. She repeated the conversation about the BMWs. They brought out a car catalogue and let her pick out which models most resembled the cars she had seen. Eventually, when she could put it off no longer, she told them about the man in braces pressing the fifty quid into her hand. Knox was genuinely surprised.

'He *bribed* you?' He said it as if it was Paddy's fault that he didn't know already.

'He put money in my hand and asked me to keep it out of the paper.'

'But you printed the story anyway?'

'Well, I'd've given it back but he shut the door in my face.'

'So it was a bribe,' he repeated, looking angrily at her.

Sullivan stepped forward to the table and leaned on his fingertips, looking at no one. 'The fifty-pound note was the object from the house that we found Robert Lafferty's prints on.'

The rosy joiner whose name she hadn't caught rolled his head in recognition. They'd all heard about the prints but not the note. Sullivan had kept his word not to tell. She watched him withdraw. He seemed no more aware of Knox than he was of the other two senior officers.

'Did you see any money being passed to Tam Gourlay or Dan McGregor?'

'Nothing,' she said, to their evident relief. 'I saw nothing.' Then, as if she was just continuing the story, she added, 'I walked back towards my car, passing Gourlay and McGregor, and Gourlay said,

"It's really important to keep it out the papers because she's a lawyer," something like that, and McGregor slapped him on the back of the head.'

The committee looked a little stunned. 'What do you think he meant by that?'

'I don't know. I'm just telling you what happened.'

They were pleased that she hadn't directly accused either of the officers of taking a bribe. Ferguson's eyes flickered to the secretary taking the minutes. There were two conversations taking place here, she realized: what was said or implied, and what was minuted. Only the minuted conversation would be of any consequence in future.

Ferguson offered her a drink of water and stood up, leaning across the desk and pouring it for her, diverting her attention, breaking up the line of questioning. This was a damage-limitation exercise. They weren't going to ask anything they didn't already know or pursue a wild-card line of questioning.

Knox looked at her hard. 'We've seen the notes from the first time you were questioned by DI Sullivan. You didn't mention the fifty pounds then, did you?'

'No.'

'And despite taking the money, you still printed a story about the incident in the paper the next day?'

'Which part are you objecting to? Taking the money or welching on the deal? Because I didn't really take the bribe, he shoved it into my hand and shut the door.'

'But you kept the money?' He was emphasizing the point, knowing it would be minuted.

'I couldn't give it back. He'd shut the door.'

'Wasn't there a letterbox?' Knox's despising eyes were grey and half closed.

To a young policeman his manner would have been frightening, but Paddy was a journalist and dealt with cheeky fuckers all day.

She sighed impertinently and drummed her fingers on the desk. 'We finished here? Can I go now?'

Ferguson sat forward. 'Would you say that you left the scene quite content that Miss Burnett was safe?'

This was the crunch question, the one they would be asking of everyone. It was the issue that would decide whether Gourlay and McGregor were guilty of any misdemeanour. The truth was she hadn't felt Vhari Burnett was safe. She hadn't cared whether Burnett was safe. As Vhari Burnett and her bloody neck slid back into the living room and out of view all Paddy cared about was how soon she could get back into the warm car. She had assumed things about Burnett that seemed ridiculous now: that she was rich and selfish and slim; that she consented to stay with Neilson; that they were a couple and would sort it out between themselves. There were a hundred selfish, shaming reasons why Paddy hadn't barged in and insisted Burnett leave with her, and the only way she could avoid admitting them now was to back up Gourlay and McGregor.

'No. I felt she was unsafe. And I still walked away.'

'Why did you do that, Miss Meehan?'

She was too tired to think of a lie. 'Same reason McGregor and Gourlay walked away. Because I'm a stupid wee shite.'

Sensing the danger of an unrehearsed conversation, a frisson of panic rippled along the line. The minutes secretary glanced up. Knox wound up her interview as quickly as possible, blocking Paddy from saying anything else untoward.

Sullivan saw her to the door, as if she couldn't find her own way, and slipped out with her into the waiting room. He checked that Grant wasn't in earshot. 'What you said about her being safe, that was . . . the right thing to say.'

She looked at him, trembling at the thought that Lafferty might be outside. 'I thought you were going to tell me it was stupid.'

'It was that too.'

272

He smiled down, impressed enough to hold his stomach in for her, and slipped back into the room.

Outside the street was quiet. Paddy hurried along, keeping her eyes on the taxi rank two blocks away, telling herself to stay calm, Lafferty wouldn't dare pick her up here, not outside the police HQ. A car approaching behind her made her heart leap and she broke into an ungainly sprint, yanking her pencil skirt up over her knees, belting across a busy road, running faster and faster until she leapt into the first taxi in the queue.

'*Daily News* office in Albion Street,' she said, heading for the only place she felt safe.

29

Killearn

I

It was three a.m., the dead hour, and Paddy knew she should have slept while she had the chance. Now, standing in the all-night grocer's, she felt distinctly light-headed and had to sit down to stop the colours fading from everything. The ancient bedraggled woman being questioned next to her noted the stagger in her step and ignored the police officers talking to her. She leaned over and touched Paddy's knee.

'Sick?' she said and laughed like Mother Death. Yellow mottled skin hung down over her eyes, her bulbous nose had folds of skin on it and she had a blackhead on her cheek the size of a thumbprint. By the time Paddy walked in she was sitting on a chair by the door, sipping a half-bottle of whisky that she claimed to have brought with her, being questioned about the fight and why the whisky bottle had the same sort of pink price sticker on it as every other item in the shop.

The shopkeeper was being kept away from her, in the stock-room. Paddy could hear him shouting at the officers pinning him in behind the curtain of plastic ribbons that he wasn't the criminal here. She was a whoor, a filthy thieving old whoor.

Dressed in a number of overcoats, the woman had wandered into the twenty-four-hour shop stinking of drink and TCP. She lived not far away and, according to the shopkeeper, came in most

274

nights to steal from him. She was looking for things to sell to buy drink, trying to lift the coffee or teabags. She never went for the few overpriced half-bottles of emergency drink, which were kept on shelves next to the fags behind the counter, carefully covered by a cloth out of licensing hours.

Tonight the shopkeeper had had enough and, fly to the woman and sick of losing stock, had left an empty coffee jar and box of teabags on the shelf. The woman had come in and, as usual, made straight for the coffee. She stood holding the empty jar, trying to understand, holding her coat open ready to pinch it. Finally convinced that the jar was empty, the woman turned to the shopkeeper, dropped the jar and flew at him, screaming, aiming for the bottles of drink under the cloth.

The shop keeper claimed he was simply trying to restrain her when a group of young Goths waiting at the bus stop outside the window saw him wrestle the old lady to the ground and rifle through her clothes.

There is no sense of justice quite as uncompromising as drunken night-clubbers' justice. The Goths ran in and counter-attacked the shopkeeper, pulling him off the old woman. A couple of girls sat on him while the rest helped themselves to juice and fags and packets of crisps, leaving the old woman free to roam at will for the ten minutes it took the police car to arrive.

There weren't enough officers to arrest the mob so they limited their inquiries to the two main players. Outside the heavily made-up youngsters in a mess of black and purple, genders indistinguishable, watched shiftily through the window. Littering the pavement around them were half-eaten packets of crisps and biscuits. Incriminating cans of Coke emptied themselves into the gutter.

Paddy came out of the small shop with two pages of shorthand notes, but knew it wouldn't be worth calling it in to the night subs.

Back in the car Sean was mesmerized by the crowd and desperate to hear what had happened inside. 'Man,' he smiled, shaking his head in wonder, 'you wouldn't believe these things go on until you're actually there. Will I find a phone?'

'No point. It won't make it into the paper.'

'Why not?'

'Because it's not a car crash or a murder. They don't print vignettes, just hard news.'

'Shame.' Sean started the engine. 'It was bloody entertaining to watch.'

Sensing that Paddy's job had taken her away from him, Sean had always been a bit sneery about it, cutting her off when she tried to talk about the sights in the night city. It was affirming to see him so buzzed about it. Suddenly she loved the job she'd been trying to shed for months. By the morning Shug Grant would either know or not know about her fifty-quid kick-back, depending on how the leak felt about it. If Shug had been told, everyone at the *News* would know too. Ramage would call her. She wouldn't be allowed to take her coat off. Or he might call her at the hotel later and tell her to get out of the room, she was sacked.

'You like this job then, Sean?'

He pulled the car out on to the road. 'Don't tell anyone, but I think I'd probably do it for nothing.'

Sean drove down through the empty town, a high yellow sky with a fat moon hanging low in it. His driving had improved, she had to admit, even in the single night he'd been working.

'You're less swervy tonight. You're getting the hang of it.'

'It's good practice.' He smiled to himself. 'It's great money as well.'

She didn't want him thinking he was a shoo-in for a permanent job. 'This might not be permanent, you know. When you hand in your licence they might make an issue out of the fact that you've just passed.'

He nodded. And nodded and nodded. She knew him far too well to think it meant nothing. 'What?'

'What "what"?'

'Why did you nod so much then?'

A pained panic in his eye told her something was wrong. She took a horrified breath and sat forward. 'Sean, tell me you passed your test.'

He nodded and nodded again but she knew he was lying.

'Sean, I put you up for this job. If you got it fraudulently I'll get in trouble.'

'Well, I will pass it now, won't I? With all this great practice.'

'For Christ's sake, we're spending every night chasing police cars. You could lose the licence before you get it.'

He looked at her in the mirror. 'Even if I had passed, the licence wouldn't come through for months. If I get caught I'll say you knew nothing about it, OK?'

Paddy didn't answer. Sean was prepared to get married at seventeen to please his mum. He was a prefect all the way through school. He attended chapel on every Holy Day of Obligation. Breaking the law to get a job was the most audacious thing she'd ever known him do. She looked at him with renewed interest.

'OK?' he said again.

She nodded and watched the back of his head. By now even the casualty waiting rooms would be empty. 'Let's drive up to Killearn.'

II

Radio reception gradually died as they left the city behind, the pip and crackle of calls reducing to a soft comforting buzz. Rich yellow moonlight played on sparkling frost coating the tilled muddy fields and jagged skeletons of deciduous bushes lined the dark road.

This was rich countryside, soft hills dotted with gentle copses of old trees, with picturesque villages strung along the traditional drovers' road that the Highland cattlemen had used for centuries to bring their stock down to the city. The population was growing, the tiny villages spreading into farmland on their outskirts with big new houses built by golfers posing as country folk.

On the approach to Killearn they passed houses set back from the road, new and old, sitting in big patches of lawn and elaborate ornamental gardens, some with boats parked in the driveway, most with big cars.

It was four in the morning, everyone was asleep, and the alert watchfulness that usually hangs over wealthy areas was absent: no dog barked; no expensive cars slowed at the passing places, drivers peering carefully into their cheap car, noting the faces of strangers who were hanging around and might cause trouble.

The driveway to Huntly Lodge looked like nothing at all, a small break in the bushes with a run-down gate, algae-smeared and rotting, held shut with a shiny new chain and a padlock.

Paddy told Sean to pull off the road, keep the lights off and wait for her.

'Where are you going? I'll come with you.'

'No,' she said, 'I'm just going for a look at something. You wait here.'

She wasn't dressed for it. She'd been wearing the same pencil skirt since Sunday and her jumper was getting distinctly stale. The skirt was too narrow for climbing but she had her leather on and hoiked the skirt up to her hips before clambering over the gate. At the top, when one leg was over, the unsteady gate shifted in the mud below and she felt herself falling backwards head first. She threw her weight forwards and caught her tights on the rough wood, ripping them at the knee. Thick woolly tights cost a fiver, and she cursed Paul Neilson as she climbed down the other side. Her knee was bleeding lightly through the scratch.

She limped along the mud road, pulling her skirt down, following the high ground of a deep rut where heavy cars had passed in and out. The trees closed in behind and overhead, shifting threateningly in the light wind. Paddy walked slowly, letting her eyes adjust to the dark, rubbing her knee and feeling sorry for herself.

When she turned the corner and saw the huge house she stepped nervously back into the bushes. Someone was very rich.

The house was new and vast, an ill-considered barn of a place with an inappropriately small front door and windows that would have been the right size for a semi-detached house. An attempt had been made at dignifying the door by flanking it with plaster lions, but they were too small and only emphasized the cheap look. To the left, built as an extension of the house, was a three-door garage.

Keeping to the bushes, Paddy skirted around to the side, stepping through mud carpeted in dead leaves. The ground was soft under her feet, noisily sucking the rubber soles of her pixie boots. Hoping there wasn't a dog in the house, she picked her way carefully, stepping on tiptoe, keeping as quiet as possible.

The window at the side of the garage was too high for her to look through properly. She could see the inside of the sloping roof and three skylights in a row, one over each section, but couldn't see down to the cars.

She glanced around for something to stand on but the narrow lane was tidy. Creeping around to the back of the house, she saw a large grey concrete base with a glass conservatory perched on it plonked in the middle of a large sloping lawn. Moonlight shimmering on the underside of the glass told her that it housed a swimming pool. It was not a routinely inhabited back garden: there were no old lawnmowers or toys abandoned by the back wall, no boxes or seedtrays, not even a broken washing machine like the Meehans had in theirs. There was nothing for her to stand on.

She skirted back around to the garage window again and, checking the ground beneath the window, jumped several times, piecing together the layout and content of the garage from what she could glimpse. There were only two cars in the three-car garage, a big one and a small one, exactly the shape and size of the BMWs she had seen outside Vhari Burnett's house.

A sudden rustle in the bushes made her think of Lafferty. She turned and hurried back down the drive, reckless of the noise, pulling her skirt up over her waist, and climbed quickly back over the gate. She caught her breath when she saw Sean still parked where she had left him and sped up as she approached the car. She felt so relieved as she climbed back into the warm car that she almost slammed the door on the frightening night, but remembered herself and stopped, shutting it quietly.

'Let's go.'

'Why have you taken your skirt off?'

'Let's go, Sean, and leave the lights off.'

III

Larry Grey Lips, the night editor, was looking at her regretfully, 'Meehan, you've to wait on.'

Paddy was standing by the pigeonholes with one arm in the sleeve of her coat and her scarf around her neck. 'Why?'

He flapped a yellow memo sheet at her. 'Got this last night after you went out: Ramage wants to see you when he gets in.'

Her last vestige of courage left her. Knox had told Shug about the fifty quid. Ramage was going to sack her.

Larry and Paddy had never liked each other, but he saw how hard she was hit by the news and reached out to her, thought the better of it and withdrew. 'Might not be that.'

She thought of her mother and covered her face with her hand as frustration welled up in her. 'I'm the only one working.'

'Aye, well.' Alarmed by the display of emotion, Larry moved away sharpish. 'Sorry.'

She kept one arm in her coat and slid into a chair by the door. Shug fucking Grant. Years she had given to this job, years of waiting for it to get better and now it had come to nothing.

She'd never wanted to do anything else. She didn't have the exam results to go to university. All she could see in her future was an infinity of sitting in the damp garage at home, staring at an aching blank page. She felt so defeated she couldn't even face walking across to the tea room to make a coffee or get some biscuits from the tin.

The office filled up quickly with the morning shift, the casual timekeeping of Farquarson's reign being long past. Journalists and subs poured through the door in twos and threes. Paddy hadn't worked on a day shift for five months and had forgotten the look of the office when it was full. Copy boys were kept busy fetching teas and coffees, journalists organized their work spaces for the day, setting ashtrays by their smoking hand, feeding paper into the type-writers, while subs scanned copies of the morning edition for follow-up stories and section editors issued orders.

Shug Grant arrived three minutes late with a fat editor from international news. He didn't acknowledge Paddy but stopped near her to laugh ostentatiously at his companion's joke. She didn't look up.

She stayed at the end of the desk, dully aware of the sharp scratch on her knee, hands folded across her stomach, nursing the pains she hadn't been able to shake off for days, until a copy boy was at her elbow. 'Ramage wants to see you.'

She looked around the office for anything she wanted to take with her. They might not let her back in. She had her big mug in the stationery cupboard but couldn't be bothered walking the full length of the room and passing Shug Grant to get it.

She stood up slowly and shoved her other arm into her coat. 'Downstairs?'

The copy boy nodded sadly. 'Downstairs.'

She paused at the door and looked back into the bustle and confusion. It was a sunny day outside. Shafts of golden morning sunshine sloped in through the wall of windows, settling on the dirty blue carpet. No one looked back at her. She hadn't even been told she was being sacked and already she was nothing more to them than a sad shrug, a rumour. She wouldn't be the last.

She dragged her heels downstairs and along the quiet corridor, knocking twice and slumping against the wall. Ramage called for her to come in and she found him behind his big desk, leaning back smugly in his chair. There wasn't a single sheet of paper on his leather desk-blotter, but a small brass cafetière next to a dark-green cup and saucer trimmed with gold. The rich chocolate aroma of real coffee filled the room.

'Sorry to keep you on after your shift.'

She stayed near the door and shrugged, ' 's OK.'

Ramage examined her for a moment. 'It was only twenty minutes, Meehan, you don't need to sulk.'

Afraid she would cry when he said it, she bit the side of her mouth hard.

Ramage pressed the flat of his hand on the brass plunger and pushed it down slowly, watching as the wheel crushed the coffee grains against the bottom of the glass. 'Come over here.'

She shuffled over to the desk.

'What happened to your knee?'

'Cut it. Climbing over a gate.'

He poured himself a black coffee, lifted the saucer and cup and sipped noisily, his pinkie crooked to the side. 'What's happening with the police-corruption story?'

Paddy looked at Ramage's face. He sipped the coffee again and watched her expectantly, waiting for her to speak. He wanted to talk to her, not sack her.

She perked up. 'Well, I've found the guy who owns the cars that were parked around the back of the Bearsden house. He went out with Burnett's sister but she's disappeared. I think he's looking for her, he's desperate, and I don't think it's because he loves her either.'

'He thought her sister was hiding her?'

282

'Probably. Vhari Burnett had just moved house and the dead guy in the river knew her new address.'

'So he went through him to find her?'

'I think so.'

'What about the police?'

'Well, the two officers who were at the door call in Bearsden aren't saying anything that could lead to him; they're being very careful about that, which suggests they're on the take. But more importantly they've both just been transferred to the station the Burnett investigation's based in. Everyone knows they're bent, it's highly irregular, and I think I know which senior officer okayed it.'

'He's bent too?'

She shrugged. 'I'm guessing. I don't know for sure, but his name came up a couple of times.'

'Good.' Ramage leaned back again. 'Any evidence yet?'

'Some fingerprints of a heavy who ties them all together.'

'The one who attacked the car?'

'Yeah, the firebomb guy. He's the link but I'm the only thing that ties him to the Bearsden Bird's house. I can witness that a piece of paper came out of the house that night and they've found his prints on it.'

Ramage's face didn't register a flicker of recognition at the mention of the piece of paper, and Paddy guessed he didn't know. Knox hadn't told Shug Grant, after all.

'No sign of him? Is he following you, going to your house?'

'No.' She paused. Ramage might make her go home. 'Not so far. I haven't seen him anyway.'

'Was he the guy at the front door?'

'No. The guy at the door's prints are on the paper but not on file.'

'So they'd need to arrest him first before they can take his prints for comparison?'

'Yes,' she said, forgetting to disguise her surprise that Ramage wasn't an idiot. He noticed it, his right cheek twitching in irritation, so she hurried on. 'Anyway, the police are dragging their heels about going for the right guy and keep trying to pin Burnett's murder on other people. Someone's definitely protecting him.'

'And the investigation team? They clean?'

She thought of Sullivan taking abuse from the officers in the inquiry, holding his stomach in for her because she'd done the right thing. 'As a whistle. The officer in charge knows something's fishy and he's meeting me alone, giving me tips.'

Ramage pointed at her quickly, as if she had followed his suggestion. 'Good contact. Keep him quiet, Meehan. Don't tell any of the dogs upstairs about him. He's yours.'

Relieved that her execution had been commuted, she smiled eagerly at Ramage. 'Top tip,' she said, 'thanks,' as if she needed a warning to be cagey around other journalists.

Ramage sipped his coffee again and looked a little sick, pressing his lips together and sucking his tongue hard. She guessed the coffee smelled better than it tasted. 'And how did the inquiry go?'

'They seemed determined to avoid all the important questions.'

He nodded slowly. 'So it's someone on the board of inquiry?'

Paddy was impressed again by how astute he was. 'Could be.'

'They do that. I've seen it before. Get themselves on to the board of inquiry and try to steer it.'

'Really?'

'Sure, same thing happened in a story we covered in Liverpool ten years ago. So, how much longer d'you think you'll need to pin it?'

She had no idea. 'A few days,' she said, and wondered why she had. 'At most.'

'Good. Good.' He put the cup down, glancing at it resentfully. 'I'll only pay for the hotel for another two days and I want it done by then.' He flicked a hand to the door. 'Out.'

Paddy smiled at him, a genuine smile. He was smart and prepared to pay for the hotel and he wasn't going to sack her. 'Cheers, Boss.'

Out in the stuffy corridor her tired mind sagged again. She only had two days left. Trying to marshal her thoughts, she felt in her pocket for the crumpled photocopy of the funeral photo, pulling it out and unfolding it as she walked along the pavement outside.

The dusty black toner was crumpling on the folds but Kate Burnett's face was still clear, a mess of blond hair and a small smile perched on her lips. She tied the whole thing together. Paddy had to find her.

30

The Sea Is So Wide

I

Bed swallowed her, sucking her down into a coffin sleep. She dreamed of Kate coming alive in the photocopied photo, smiling, throwing her head back and laughing at a funeral, her big hair bouncing on her shoulders. Ramage held Kate's elbow to support her and suddenly she was on fire, her hair burning as she laughed and nodded, burning hair flailing around her shoulders, spitting vicious little sparks.

Paddy sat up suddenly to the sound of the telephone burring next to her, the heat of a low winter sun spilling through the window, warming her face.

'Hello?'

The switchboard had a call for her, a man called George Burns, should they put it through?

'Meehan.' He didn't sound friendly, but she had just woken up and was too disorientated to be cold back.

'Oh, hiya, how are ye?' She checked her watch. She had only slept for three hours and it was lunchtime.

'Eh, fine, yeah, fine. I called to tell you that Tam Gourlay and his partner McGregor have been suspended because of the inquiry. I saw Gourlay leaving the Marine just after he heard. He's a shirt full of sore bones this morning.'

It took her a moment to work out why she would be interested in Tam Gourlay's shirt. 'You beat him up?'

Burns hesitated, but she could hear a smile when he spoke. 'Aye, but I'm telling you in code, for the purposes of being sneaky.'

'Did you do it in secret?'

'Em,' he sighed. 'No. I did it in a car park full of policemen.'

'So why are you being sneaky?'

'I don't know really. I thought it might impress you.'

They giggled down the phone for a moment and Paddy rubbed her hot face. 'God, it's boiling in here.'

'Anyway, you won't have any more trouble from him.'

She thought of Knox. The trouble ran deeper than Burns could possibly know. 'Thanks.'

'It's OK. I'm not far away, just round the corner, actually.'

He left a heavy pause. She could have invited him up to her room but she had two days left and felt too delicate for a repeat of yesterday's gymnastics.

'Burns, could you do me a favour?'

'Anything.' He sounded certain, thinking she was going to ask him up.

'Could you get Chief Superintendent Knox's home address for me?'

She could feel his annoyance carrying down the phone line. He clicked his tongue. 'Sure,' he said briskly. 'Sure. I'll get that for you.'

'Ye did say anything.'

'Yeah. I did. I said that.'

After she hung up the red light on the phone continued to flash at her. She thought it was a mistake at first, but picked it up to check Burns wasn't still on the other end.

'There's a visitor for you in reception.' The receptionist sounded resentful. 'You requested that no one be sent up to your room.'

She imagined Gourlay dripping blood on to the marble flooring, Lafferty standing by the desk, grinning and holding a firebrand. 'Who is it?'

The receptionist sighed and put her hand over the receiver, asking a question of someone. She came back on. 'It's your mum.'

II

The lift doors opened and Paddy saw Trisha standing, looking lost, in the middle of the reception hall. She was wearing her poor beige going-into-town mac, clutching crumpled re-used polythene bags in front of her. The heavy bags pulled her rounded shoulders down, stretching at the handles. She looked scared.

As Paddy approached, Trisha saw her and almost bowed. The handle of one of the over-filled bags snapped and Paddy's clothes spilled on to the gleaming marble floor. When Trisha saw the knickers and jumper on the floor in front of her she almost cried.

'Don't worry about that,' said Paddy and knelt to scoop the items back into the bag. She stood up, uncertain how to greet her mother, going for a kiss on the cheek but missing as Trisha turned to receive it and hitting her awkwardly on the ear.

'Hello, pet,' said Trisha quietly. 'Hello.'

'Will we get a cup of tea?'

'Well,' Trisha looked around as if they might be having it in the reception area. 'It's a bit of a bother.'

'No, it's not a problem, we can go in here.' Paddy took her arm and steered her across the floor to a set of stairs leading down into the bar.

Trisha looked shocked. 'Well, please God, no one'll see me sitting in a pub at lunchtime.'

Paddy smiled and squeezed her arm. 'Have you ever been in a pub?'

'Of course I have. When your father and I were courting. Chapman's.' She wrinkled her nose. 'I didn't like it.'

The bar area doubled as the hotel breakfast room, then turned into a lunchtime pub and at night served as a restaurant. As such it had a large steel server in the corner to keep greasy breakfasts hot and juice cold. It was dark now, the steel base of the hotplate scrubbed and sitting ready for the morning. The bar in the middle of the room was served by young men in white shirts, and waitresses skirted the tables on the floor. Chairs and benches were upholstered in purple and yellow, matching the carpet and textured wallpaper. The room smelled of cigarettes and vegetable oil.

Trisha and Paddy sat side by side on a banquette facing the large room. It was pleasant not to have to look at each other. Between them and the windows on to George Square groups of businessmen in dark suits were clustered around tables eating huge plates of chips with fish or cottage pie, washed down with pints of lager. Everyone had neon-green peas on their plates but no one seemed to be eating them.

'This looks very dear,' muttered Trisha. 'There's a café across the road.'

'I can charge it to the room. The paper'll pay for it. Would you like some lunch?'

Every day in living memory Trish had a plate of soup and two boiled eggs mashed up in a cup for her lunch. She looked at a neighbouring plate. 'I couldn't eat all that at lunchtime.'

'You don't need to eat it all, you could have some and leave the rest.'

'That's wasteful. I'll just have tea.' She slipped her coat off. She was wearing a smart white nylon blouse she usually saved for Mass.

The waitress took their order for two teas and biscuits, and a plate of chips for Paddy's breakfast, and then Trisha lifted the plastic bags on to the bench between them.

'Now, I've brought you some clean clothes and your toothbrush and a carton of soup.'

Paddy smiled into the bag at the Tupperware tub. Trisha had carried the heavy carton all the way from Eastfield. It was a vegetable broth with marrow-fat peas, flecked with pink gammon.

Soup featured in every Meehan family meal but breakfast. Recipes were passed from mother to daughter. It had a talismanic quality, the poor man's filler, source of vegetables and, because it took so much time to chop the veg and soak the peas and featured meat, a shorthand for loving concern in a family where affection was never spoken of. 'Ma, where am I going to heat soup?'

'Is there not a stove at work?'

'Come on, I'd look like a right diddy standing over a pan heating soup.' She meant to tease her mum for her eccentricity but Trisha took it as a slight.

'But I made it for you.' Her eyes filled up. She took a hanky from her sleeve and dabbed at her nose as the waitress put the order on the table in front of them.

Paddy stroked her arm when the waitress had left. 'Don't cry, Ma.'

Trish covered her mouth and cried some more. 'Why are you here?'

'I told you why, Ma, because we're working on a big story and I need to be near the office.'

'Why are you asking me to look out for that car, then? Are you in danger?'

'No.' Paddy had tried to make light of it but her mother could read and had seen the paper. 'Billy's fine. He's getting out of hospital today. They just exaggerate it to make it a better story. There's nothing to worry about.'

But Trisha carried on crying, fighting it, biting her hankie at one stage. Paddy had sat through enough of her crying pangs recently to know it wasn't really about her. She poured tea for them, putting in a sugar for her mum and stirring it, setting a nice biscuit with chocolate on it on her saucer as a prompt. She picked at the chips but didn't really want them. The smoky room made her feel a bit sick.

Trisha sighed and picked up the biscuit and looked at it. Dried coconut speckled the chocolate. 'I'm sorry for crying.'

'It's all right, Ma.'

'I don't really mean it half the time.'

'I know, Ma, I know.'

They drank their tea quietly together, watching the businessmen eating. Every so often Paddy patted her mum's leg and Trisha said 'uch aye'.

'I wish you were home.' Trisha sipped her tea. 'Will you be home the day after tomorrow? Father Marian's arranged a place for Mary Ann in Taizé. She's going to *France*.'

'I'll try. That'll be nice. France isn't that far away.' Paddy had read about the Christian community in Taizé and it looked like as much fun as could be had on a retreat. They did a lot of singing, apparently, guitars featured heavily in the pamphlets, and met other young people from abroad. They ate foreign food in a tented canteen. 'It's all young people there; maybe she'll meet a nice boy.'

Trisha smiled into her cup. 'Mary Ann's not interested in boys. She's thinking she might have a vocation. She's looked at the Poor Clares.'

Paddy had known it was coming, that Mary Ann was teetering on the brink of declaring her interest in the religious life. The Poor Clares went about at night foisting watery soup on homeless people. The ones Paddy had met always kept their eyes down and had winsome, obsequious smiles. 'She might still meet a boy.'

But Paddy knew Mary Ann would love Taizé. She'd like the discipline of prayer and the ecumenical nature of the place. She wouldn't be sharing a room with someone who bared her breasts and swore while she prayed. Paddy would miss her silent presence, her giggling, and the sound of her breath as she slept. She'd never felt the same about her brothers or Caroline. Mary Ann was exclusively hers. She thought of Kate and Vhari, two sisters, the older one compliant, the younger a defiant little spitfire who brought ruin on the others.

'How's Caroline?'

Trisha tutted and sighed.

'Not gone back to him?'

She tutted again.

'Maybe she shouldn't, Ma.'

'Well, she shouldn't have got married then.'

Paddy nibbled a coconut biscuit. 'The story we're working on – the police went to the door of a house and saw a girl covered in blood but they left and the man killed her. They thought it was her husband. John must have beat Caroline something awful—'

'She should not have married him then,' said Trisha firmly.

'But Ma, she did.'

'For better or worse.'

Paddy picked up a chip and took a bite. 'What if he kills her, Ma? What if you send her back and he kills her?'

Trisha slapped Paddy on the thigh. 'Don't talk rubbish.'

'Seriously, what if he murders Caroline? How bad are you going to feel if he does that?'

Trisha turned to look her in the eye. 'It's a *sacrament,* Patricia, a vow in front of God. Ye can't just change your mind and leave. You and your women's lib.'

'Oh, God, Mother, don't start all that—'

'Well,' Trisha put her cup down noisily in the saucer. 'You've missed your chance with Sean over a job, a *job,* for heaven's sake, and now he'll soon be married and he's got a good job and could have kept ye fine.'

Paddy was so surprised she dropped the half-eaten chip on to the floor. 'What do you mean, "soon be married"?'

'He proposed to Elaine, did he not tell ye? The minute he got that driving job he proposed and she's accepted. Mimi Ogilvy's taken up residence outside the chapel telling everyone. Did he not say?'

'No.' She tried to hide her disappointment. 'He never said.'

Elaine was a squeaky mediocre pest but Paddy could hardly

292

blame Sean. Since she broke off their engagement she'd slept with three men and knew Sean was waiting until he got married. He must have been as horny as hell. She knew how much that could warp her own judgement. Mary Ann was leaving and now Sean wasn't hers any more. For the first time ever she felt herself alone.

'Who are you going to get now?'

'I'm only twenty-one, Mother, there are other men in the world.'

'Aye, we'll see, anyway.'

They finished their tea but Paddy left the rest of the chips untouched.

At the door of the hotel she took the plastic bags from Trisha and felt she was leaving her for ever. She followed her down into the street, running after her.

'Ma!'

Trisha turned and Paddy threw her arms around her, hugging her hard even though Trisha stood stiff in her arms. Tiredness and nausea overwhelmed her and she pressed her face into her mum's shoulder, tears flooding on to Trisha's soft neck.

Reluctantly, Trisha lifted her arms around her daughter and whispered into her hair to hush. A bus rumbled past and the cold wind sweeping across the square skirled around them.

'I'm sorry, Mum. I'm sorry I'm not what ye want me to be.'

Trisha was crying too, fighting it but crying, sobs racking her chest as she stroked Paddy's hair and patted her back. 'Oh, now. Come on now, it's not so bad as all that, surely?'

She hid her face in her mother's soft neck. 'I'm not you, Mum. I can't be as good as you.'

Trisha stroked and patted her, holding her tight as if she had been hungry for contact for ten years.

Finally, Trisha broke off. 'Eat that soup, it'll do you good.' She smiled bravely and unzipped her handbag, rummaging for her change purse and her house keys, reassuring herself that she would be home soon.

Paddy wiped her nose on the back of her hand and sniffed. Trisha pulled the keys out, and Paddy saw the clear laminated plaque on her keyring and remembered the slogan. Trisha had bought it in a holy shop, an orange sunset behind a silhouette of a tiny boat and the inscription:

> Lord help me,
> The sea is so wide
> And my boat is so small.

III

The renewed vigour of the news room had disappeared now that everyone had worked out when Random would be in and out of the room. The fact that he was generally stationed downstairs holding meetings about money meant that long hours could easily be spent carelessly doing nothing or scanning job vacancies in the *News* or other papers.

McVie sloped in through the door to the tea room and stood close to her, watching the kettle come to the boil.

'How are you?' he said, uncharacteristically needy. He was too close, looming over her.

'I'm fine,' she said, scowling up at him, hoping he'd do it back.

'So, what did you . . . ?' He rolled his head to the side. 'You know, think the other night?'

She realized that he wasn't standing close to her so much as pinning her into the wall, penning her in. 'He's a nice chap.'

McVie raised his eyebrows and leaned across her, picking at a bit of dried jam on the fridge top. He seemed offended.

'I mean, he's nice enough. I wouldn't spend a lot of time with him. Not that you shouldn't. He's nice. Pleasant.'

'Hmm, pleasant . . . Yeah.'

McVie and Paddy had known each other for four years and had a bitchy, easy rapport, but now the conversation felt as clumsy as grade-one Arabic. They cringed in unison, watching the kettle come to the boil. She had overfilled it. Scalding water bubbled out from under the lid, spilling down the sides and over the flex. They grinned together as the steaming water trickled down the door of the fridge.

'That's not very safe, is it?'

'Naw,' Paddy grinned and moved her feet away. Her suede boots were ruined already but she didn't want to make them any worse. 'I don't care if you're a poof.'

McVie blinked hard at the word and rubbed his long gothic face with his hand. 'I heard you'd shagged George Burns in his car.'

Paddy felt the hairs on the back of her neck stand on end in alarm. A week before she would have been frightened of him know-ing – she'd never really trusted him sexually – but now he was the only safe man in the news room. Suddenly it seemed funny that McVie knew. She started to giggle into the wall. McVie watched her, disconcerted for a moment, and then snorted through his nose, shaking his shoulders, actually looking more miserable than before but laughing, she was quite sure he was laughing.

'What did your wife say when she found out about you?'

McVie rolled his head back at the mention of his wife and barked up at the ceiling. 'Surprised.'

'Are you two having an affair?' It was Shug Grant, standing at the door, talking loud to draw the news room's attention to them.

'Grant,' McVie spoke without a hint of aggression, 'you're about half as interesting as ye think ye are. Fuck off and shut up.' He turned back to Paddy. 'Tomorrow night we're going for a drink with Paddy Meehan. Press Bar, seven o'clock. OK?'

She nodded.

Scolded, Grant backed out of the room and McVie followed him, pointing a warning finger back at her. 'Seven, right?'

'I'll be there.'

31

The Kaffir on the Fence

I

As soon as Bernie had pulled the comfort pillow out from under a pile of bricks in the garage Kate knew she would be able to come here. Now she sat in the Mini, cold condensation forming a film on the inside of the windscreen, blocking out the view of the pub and Knox's house across the road. The tip of her right index finger was withered from rubbing high-grade cocaine into her gums.

She needed to watch the house and make sure he was in before she went across, pressed the doorbell and told him that she would go to the papers if he didn't call Paul off. He could do that. He could tell Paul to let her go. He wasn't Paul's boss or anything, no one was Paul's boss, but she knew enough to damage all of them and Knox was the cautious one. They had laughed at how careful he was, always meeting at night in the wine cellar at Archie's basement, never wanting Paul to come to his house and refusing to come to theirs.

Knox was the cautious one.

She had said it out loud, she realized. Sitting alone in a cheap car, in the damp dark, outside a nasty brewery pub with a red 'Pub Grub' neon light blinking in the window.

She said it again just to be sure, 'Knox was the cautious one,' and smiled, incredulous, at the sound of her own voice. She hadn't realized she was talking and not just thinking. She decided to practise her speech.

'Hello, Knox. I need your help.'

That was no good. It sounded subservient.

When he opened the door she'd bluntly say, 'Knox—' He'd pull her into the hall, check outside to make sure she hadn't been seen in the street. 'I want you to help me. Paul Neilson and I are in dispute and you have to tell him to leave me alone.'

Better. It sounded forceful, as if she was in charge.

'If you don't want me to go to the papers with what I know, you'll tell him to back off.'

That was it. Pitch perfect. And then shut up, don't start twittering or say anything about Vhari or anything. Perfect. She licked her fingertip and reached across to the passenger seat, running the numb skin over a fold in the plastic before lifting it to her mouth. A little engine rev and she'd open the door and go over there. But the little dab did nothing so she tried again and again. She was rubbing and dabbing and rubbing, waiting for the perfect chemical equation to occur and give her the courage and clarity to do what she needed to.

The balance eluded her. All she could do was sit and sweat and listen to her tired old heart thumping like a galley drum while her blood raced through her brain bringing thought after thought, conclusion after conclusion, details and meaning indistinguishable, red streaks of tail light in a time-lag photograph. She knew what the thoughts were about but couldn't capture any of the detail: reminiscences of childhood, holidays, dull days off school with colds, meals she'd eaten somewhere.

She dabbed again. Her tongue was terribly dry, she didn't know if she would be able to move her mouth to talk. She could go into the pub and get a drink. A spritzer. She had money. A tenner appeared in her hand.

It took her a week to pull the clammy metal door handle towards her and step out on to the soft black tarmac. Suddenly she was in the pub, by the bar, blinking hard at the unflattering light. The décor was a crime: horseshoes, brass bedpans, horrible pretend England. It was almost empty but everyone who was there was looking at her. She wouldn't have walked into a pub this brightly lit on her best day and, she remembered dimly, she looked bad, really bad.

White wine and soda, please, and Marlboro. The sweet drink washed the salty numbness from her gums, sloshing across her tongue to hit the parched spot on the back of her throat. Another one. She smoked a cigarette, looking away from everyone, trying not to be seen. Struck by a sudden pang of longing for the pillow, she put the half-drunk glass down and reeled round, heading out through the doors to the car park and back to the side of the Mini.

She looked up and found herself standing outside Knox's house. Evidently she'd had another rub and dab; her tongue kept finding its way up past her teeth to her grainy gums and running the length of them.

Knox's front garden had been paved over to make parking spaces and the front of the house seemed very close to the road. It was a small house, Kate thought, with a cheap-looking glass porch stuck on the front of it, jammed full of ugly little plants and wellingtons and so on. Outdoor accoutrements. Perhaps he had a dog. Was he married? She couldn't remember. There was only one car parked in front of the house. Next to the glass porch, on the far side, was a window into a front room, but the curtains were shut.

Kate's heart ached, not with fear but with the simple strain of keeping going. She pressed the buzzer and stepped back, watching as the light snapped on in the hall, rosy behind the cheap orange glass in the window of the front door. The door opened, spilling light into the porchway. He was wearing slippers. And a cardigan. His angry voice crackled at her.

She answered, barking the only words she could remember. 'Knox. Help.'

II

Down at the Salt Market a Volvo estate was underneath a bus. The car driver was dead, flattened inside his car. The safety windscreen had come off whole and lay on the road by the pavement, smeared with his blood. The car was such a mess that it took the ambulancemen a while to work out if they were looking at one very big car or two wee cars.

The blameless bus driver was sitting on the wet kerb, his mouth hanging open, tears streaming down his face, blankly watching the fire brigade cutting the car up with torches, trying to establish whether there had been a passenger as well.

Paddy was jotting down the statement of an eyewitness, a tipsy old man who saw the car going fast down this road, the bus coming down that one and then, kaboom, he wasn't watching, but what a bloody bang, excuse his French. She'd already written his name and address down for the story and couldn't be arsed to try and find another witness.

'Would you say you were terrified?' she said, being unprofessional and putting words in his mouth.

He looked a little sceptical. 'I suppose.'

'Have you ever seen anything like it before in your life?'

He looked even more unconvinced. 'Well, I fought in the war, at Monte Cassino, and it wasn't anything like as bad as that.'

Paddy sighed, exhausted. 'Was it like something you might have seen in the war? Could you say that?'

'Aye,' he could go along with that, 'maybe. A bit like that.'

She wrote it down: 'Alistair Sloane of Dennistoun said "It was like something out of the Battle of Monte Cassino and I should know because I was there." Is that any good?'

He looked at her shorthand, excited that he might be in the paper. 'Aye. Is that going in tomorrow?'

'It's not up to me, really, but that's how I'll put it in.'

She left the old man grinning gleefully, looking like a ghoul, and walked back towards the car, working hard at keeping her gaze away from the undercarriage of the bus. Even in the dark she could see splatters of blood on the bus wheels, pooling on the road. Her half-informed eye kept trying to reconstruct a person out of the shapes she wasn't looking at, a round object turned into a head. There was black stuff all over the road and she was certain that it wasn't oil. She was glad Sean was waiting in the car. If she wasn't being brave for him she might have followed the example of one of the police officers and thrown up.

'I heard you were here.'

At the sound of Burns's voice her already delicate stomach spiked acid. He let his pal walk on and sauntered over solo, standing between her and the bus. She had no option but to follow the line of his body from waist to face to avoid seeing an image that might haunt her.

'Burns.'

'Meehan?' He returned the bald greeting, but looked disappointed.

'Sorry.' She tipped her head to the mess under the bus. 'I'm trying not to look.'

Burns glanced back at it, unflinching. 'Yeah, messy. We've been sent over to redirect the traffic. Exciting. I love nights. Standing in the bollock-freezing cold telling nosy bastards to go left. I got that address you were after.'

'Brilliant.' He recited it for her and she jotted it down. 'Does Knox have a reputation? A flashy car or too much money?'

'Not so much that anyone's talking about it, no.' Burns shifted nearer, looking down at her mouth as if he was going to kiss her. Paddy noticed that she was salivating. His breath hit her face in warm puffs. 'You still at the hotel?'

'Did they arrest Lafferty for the firebomb yet?'

His gaze slid down her neck. 'No. He's gone abroad.'

'Abroad to where?'

'Ireland, the wife says. No proof, just her says so.'

She shut her notebook. 'Looks like I'm still in the hotel then.'

'That's safest, yeah.' He looked over at the calls car. 'Is that Billy's replacement? You found him awful quick. Is he a boyfriend of yours?'

She stumbled over the answer, hoping he wouldn't want an introduction. 'No, he's not my boyfriend. He's my . . . well, it's complicated.'

'Is it?'

She hesitated again. If she'd had her wits about her she could have made up a salving lie. 'We've just . . . known each other a long time.'

Burns tipped his chin at her, looking down his nose and sucking air in between his teeth in a sour hiss. 'I see. That's nice and cosy. I'm doing an open spot at Blackfriar's tomorrow night. Can you come?'

Dub generally booked an open-mike night once a month so it wasn't the free-for-all. Burns must have arranged an open spot with Dub, which meant he had spoken to him, independent of her. He was muscling in on her meagre social life.

'I'll try.'

A spine-chilling creak of ripping metal filled the street as the fire brigade cleaved part of the bloody bonnet away from the bus's axle. Paddy suddenly saw herself and Burns standing too close to each other, too keen to exclude others from their conversation. It was obvious there was something between them.

'I'd better go and call this in.' She backed off towards the car.

Burns watched her mouth as she moved away and she watched his. His pink tongue glistened behind the rim of his white teeth.

III

It was the middle of the night. Or day. Or night. Kate was lying down on something soft. A sofa. A sofa draped in a sheet. Her fingertips ran over the sheet and it felt marvellously comforting, familiar and kind and warm to the touch. Like skin. Soft like skin and smelling comforting, like the comfort pillow. Paul was talking to her, reminding her how much they liked each other, how it was important to be kind to each other and help each other. She felt wonderful.

Suddenly the cold realization made her eyes spring open. The comfort pillow was plastic. She was lying on a plastic sheet.

Paul was sitting on a chair next to her, his legs crossed, talking softly to her. He was dressed nicely, a tailored blue shirt and slate-grey slacks with a pleated front. He liked to dress like a businessman. He could see that she was alarmed but said she didn't need to be afraid. Everything was going to be fine. Not to worry.

He blinked slowly and Kate knew that he was lying. She knew what Paul Neilson was seeing. A woman with no nose, an underweight woman who hadn't eaten more than a tin of ham and some biscuits in weeks. He despised women who lost their looks. And she knew what Paul could do to people he despised.

They were in an unfamiliar living room with nasty décor. A varnished gas-fire surround that ran the full length of the room, small promontories for ugly ornaments: china dogs, cut crystal, some Limoges figurines in swirling skirts. Hanging from the ceiling was a bulb in a small shade. It was shining right into her eyes.

Knox was standing behind Paul's chair, watching her.

'Kate,' Paul leaned forward and used a finger to lever a tress of blond hair from her forehead. 'Katie, tell me where it is. The package.'

She didn't think it would make any difference but she had a

302

habit of deference. 'In the Mini. Across the road. It's . . . it's almost empty.'

Paul looked beautiful. His dark hair was swept back off his face, his chin smooth and shadow-free despite the late hour. He always looked expensive, groomed. His shirt was white linen, pressed by a professional, his cuffs starched and pinned with silver and tiger's-eye studs. He didn't have a tie on but the shirt was buttoned to the neck, the top button open to the hollow of his throat.

He crossed his arms and curled his lip at her. 'Why did you come here, Katie?'

She started crying, pitiful whimpers bubbling up from her tummy. Uncomfortable at scenes, Paul looked away, drawing his fingernails down his neck, leaving welts that rose and reddened as she watched. He waited until she stopped making a noise and spoke quietly again.

'I can't have you threatening our friends, Katie, it's rude.' His voice was calm but his eyes were livid. 'Where's the BMW? You've lost it, haven't you?'

She was aware of a noise behind her head. It was Lafferty and he was watching Paul, waiting for a signal, shifting his weight from one foot to the other. She craned her neck to see his big body and his muscle-bound arms. The soft plastic crinkled sweetly by her ear. A hammer hung limp from his big hand. He was here to kill her. He wouldn't be here otherwise.

Lafferty saw her looking at him and backed out of view. Kate struggled to sit up but Paul reached forward and pressed her throat firmly, putting pressure on her airways, pushing her back down on to the plastic-covered sofa.

'I came here looking for you,' she said desperately. 'I wasn't threatening anyone. I wanted to see you, to tell you I'm sorry.'

Paul tilted his head and looked her in the eye. 'You've told me you came here to threaten Knox, Kate. You've just told me that.'

'No, no I haven't.'

'You told me a moment ago. If he doesn't want you to go to the papers he should tell me to back off. You just said it.'

Kate was lost. She had delivered the perfect speech to the wrong man, hadn't negotiated or bought any time for herself. She'd just blurted it out for nothing. It was a child's voice and surprised her, rising from the pit of her stomach. 'Why did you kill my Vhari?'

Paul breathed in, puffing his chest defensively at her, sucking his cheeks in and tipping his head back, diffident. 'She wouldn't tell me where you were.'

'She didn't know. I didn't go to her.'

He loomed over her, face flushed and furious, and shouted, 'Well, how the fuck was I supposed to know that? You're the one who ran away with sixty grand's worth of car and kit. What was I supposed to do?'

'Sorry.'

He stood up off the chair to lean closer but his voice didn't drop and she shut her eyes.

'What was I supposed to do, Kate? Sit at home and wait for you to come back?'

He left a pause for her to defend herself but her voice was too small to match his. 'You hit me,' she said, keeping her eyes shut.

His voice was so loud it blew a hair from her cheek. 'You were out of it again. What kind of man comes home every day to an unconscious junkie?

'You didn't need to kill her.'

He fell back into the chair and she opened her eyes to look at him. He looked sorry. 'She was very stubborn. We had to turn the music up to drown out the noise she made but she still wouldn't tell us where you were. Lafferty got angry after the police came to the door. He doesn't like the police. They make him angry. The mess you've made, Kate, you've no idea. There's only so much I can take. And now it's over.'

'Is it?'

'Yes,' he blinked slowly, 'it's over. You know it is.'

Suddenly and completely she saw herself and how dumb she was, how ugly she had become, how worthless. And how lost. She whimpered, cringing, bringing her knees up to her chest and making the plastic rumple noisily below her.

'Please, Paul, don't make it like the Kaffir on the wire.'

He'd told her the story when they very first got to know each other. It was a turning-point story in their relationship, when they made their deal, when she agreed to accept everything about him. It happened on their estate in South Africa, outside Jo'burg. One morning before school, Paul's father spotted a Kaffir he didn't recognize standing in the garden, in full view, looking at the ground. Grabbing the gun he ran outside. The Kaffir ran when he saw a white man after him. He ran so fast Paul's father thought he might need to go back for the truck.

The Kaffir ran out of sight, across a meadow and behind some bushes. He ran straight, that's how they knew he was just in from the country. He ran straight for over a mile and into a barbed-wire fence on the perimeter of the property. The more he struggled the more he became entangled.

Paul's father watched the man ripping himself to ribbons on the wire. When he was sure the Kaffir couldn't possibly get away he walked slowly back to the house and got Paul to come with him, to see how stupid the Kaffirs were, that they would make it worse and worse and worse and not know to stop. It took the man three days to die.

Paul and Katie looked at each other for one last time. They had known each other for seven years, had barely spent a day apart. She could see disgust in the twist of his lips and his hooded eyes.

'Don't worry.' He flicked his hand in signal to Lafferty. 'It won't be like that.'

Kate Burnett shut her grey eyes and breathed out, dismayed at her stupidity, exhausted. She heard Lafferty step forward, felt the plastic crumple as she cringed ready for the blow.

A flash of electric white pain and then came a velvet darkness.

32

Knox

I

Paddy didn't know how much a chief superintendent's wage amounted to but Knox's house seemed huge to her, not as self-consciously wealthy as the Killearn house, perhaps, but a large detached house all the same, with a bit of land around it.

'Can we go now?' Sean had smoked two cigarettes and eaten the sandwiches his mother had made him for the shift.

'No. Let's wait a bit longer.'

'What are we waiting for?'

'Dunno. Just waiting.'

Paddy was expecting Sean to tell her about Elaine, but he hadn't. She was afraid to bring it up herself, worried that she might give herself away. She practised faint surprise and disinterest in her head as they sat there, watching the house. That's lovely, Sean. Good for you. You must be gagging for it; no, that sounded ungracious. You must be pleased. I'm pleased for you.

With half an eye she watched shapes of figures in the front room, behind the curtains, moving, sometimes quickly like the flurry of movement in Vhari Burnett's living room, sometimes slow shifts of light. It was two thirty in the morning and anyone with a clear conscience would be asleep. But Knox probably had a family, the house looked far too big for a single man. She hadn't looked for a wedding ring on his finger because she didn't fancy him.

She counted three dark windows on the first floor, none of them mottled for a bathroom. He could be innocently having an argument with a wayward child. A teenager could be watching television in the front room, perhaps with some friends over, they could be getting cups of tea from the kitchen, standing up to turn the telly over.

Parked at a discreet distance further down the street was the familiar shape of a BMW, but she didn't set any store by it: the car could easily be a neighbour's and Lafferty could be somewhere else, in Ireland or parked in the Eastfield Star right now, watching her mother and father's darkened bedroom window, while she and Sean idled outside the house of an innocent man she didn't like the look of.

She looked around the car park. Behind them, the pub was shut and dark, the empty hooks for hanging baskets like gibbets for midgets. The only thing between them and the big house was a rusted green Mini parked as if abandoned, looking on to the road.

Sean whispered, 'Someone's coming out.'

Paddy sat forward and flinched when she saw the shape of the man stepping out of the front door and into the glass porch. He was broad and bald and she knew him immediately. 'Turn the radio down.'

'Why?'

She leaped forward to the radio, pressing her sore stomach hard against the passenger seat. Silence fell over the car. She could hear Lafferty's feet clipping on the pavement as he swaggered down to the BMW, fitted the key in the door and climbed into the passenger seat. He left the lights off as he backed the car up the road towards them.

'Get down!' She pushed Sean's shoulder and he slumped down in the seat. 'Keep your head below the dash.'

'Who is he?'

The smooth engine burred towards them.

'The firebomber. That's the guy.'

They crouched in the dark car, blind to what was going on in the street. The engine changed tone as Lafferty managed a manoeuvre and then stopped. A door opened and shut gently. At the first click of his heel Paddy imagined him walking towards them, but the second and third footsteps headed away and suddenly became muffled. She heard the distant click of a door handle carried through the cold night air and pulled herself up enough to see Lafferty step back into the glass porch.

The front door opened, the hall darkened now. Plants obscured the glass panel. She couldn't make out what was happening inside but seconds later she saw Lafferty reappear, carrying something at his side – a rug, maybe. When he stepped out of the porch and into the street she saw that his arm was around the waist of a slumped figure. A tumble of hair had fallen over the face but Paddy recognized her anyway.

Kate was tiny. Lafferty carried her easily on one arm, her feet trailing along behind her, the toes scuffling along the ground. She looked dead, but as Paddy watched the street light caught her limp arm and the small right hand flexed as if she was in pain.

Paddy remembered Lafferty's neck. He looked enormous and brutal next to the tiny figure, reckless of her feet. Paddy imagined the muscular arm around her own waist, squeezing the breath from her. He might just be taking Kate home. He could be fed up chasing around after his boss's girlfriend.

At the BMW he opened the door to the back seat and dropped Kate into the car, taking hold of her feet and bundling her legs in after her. He turned and reached back to the door, slamming it shut just as a slim calf dropped back out to the pavement, catching the door full on the bone. Paddy inhaled sharply. The leg must have broken from the force, but Lafferty didn't flinch. He peered at the obstruction dispassionately, bent down, pushing the offending leg back into the car and watching as he shut the door again. He wasn't taking her home. He was going to kill her.

'Sean, can you follow that car without letting him know you're there?'

'Which car?' He was slumped down as far as he could go in the driver's seat, his long legs crossed in front of him, knees trapped under the steering wheel.

'Look.'

Pulling himself up to peer over the wheel he saw the BMW pull out on to the road. 'I'll try.'

'No swerving about.'

He turned the key. 'I'll try.'

The roads were too quiet to stay close without being seen and Sean hung back, making Paddy worry that they would lose Lafferty at every corner and junction. Soon they were out of the tangle of suburban streets and following the big open road to the north of the city.

Paddy clung to the back of the passenger seat, watching the distant red tail-lights, promising Vhari Burnett that she wouldn't walk away this time. Vhari had died to protect Kate, she was certain of this now, and Thillingly had killed himself because he let the sisters down. Paddy had to do the right thing this time. She couldn't take Lafferty on herself, though, and Sean wasn't a fighter; Lafferty might easily kill them both.

Before long they had left the main road and were following a winding single-track strip of tarmac bordered by vegetation. Sean was having trouble keeping the car inconspicuous, but he dropped back so that the car ahead of them was invisible, reappearing just as they turned a corner. He flicked the lights off.

'Sean, that's not safe.' Paddy had to blink hard to make out the road in front of them.

'It's OK.' He leaned over the steering wheel and peered ahead. 'I know this road. We took it last night. They're headed to Killearn.'

'Are you sure?'

'Aye. I remember that bend in the road back there.'

'Stop if you see a phone box.'

'What for?'

'I'm going to call the police.'

He drove on for a minute. 'Paddy, who is this guy?'

She didn't know what to say. 'He's a bad man. He's got a woman in there and he's going to kill her.'

Sean dropped speed rapidly until the car stopped dead.

Paddy slapped his shoulder. 'Go! Go!'

He pointed out of the passenger window. 'Phone,' he said simply.

A red phone box stood by the side of the road. The bordering hedge was trimmed carefully around it and the light in the ceiling glowed pale yellow in the dark.

Paddy scrambled out of the car, feeling in her pocket for a five-pence piece. The dial unfurled slowly after each nine and she held the coin poised above the slot. She didn't need it. The calm operator asked her whether she needed fire, police or an ambulance.

'Police,' she said, watching the blind corner ahead of them, afraid they'd lose him completely. She told the police officer that a woman was being murdered in Huntly Lodge, Killearn.

'How do you know that, Madam?'

'I've seen a man hitting her and now I can hear her screaming,' she lied.

'Uh huh.' She didn't sound at all concerned. 'You can hear her screaming *now*?'

'Yes.'

'I see, and your name is . . .?'

Her own name might be flagged up to Knox. She didn't know who she could trust. 'Mary Ann Knox,' she said. 'Please hurry.'

'Yes, Miss Knox, and you can hear her screaming?'

'Yes.'

'I see, uh huh, well, the phone box you're calling from is three miles from Killearn, so how can you hear her screaming?'

311

They weren't going to come. Paddy looked at Sean sitting in the car. 'I *heard* her screaming. Please come.'

'How do we know this isn't a hoax?'

'You don't want this to be the Bearsden Bird all over again,' she said and hung up. She was back in the car and Sean pulled off before she had the door shut.

'They coming?'

'Aye,' she said, not sure at all. 'Aye, they'll come.'

For three long minutes they drove into the dark, following the road, not knowing if he was ahead of them or behind them or already parked in a lay-by, strangling Kate in a field, burying her helpless body in a shallow grave.

'There!' shouted Sean so suddenly he made Paddy catch her breath. Red tail-lights glinted on a far hill, following the road around a corner.

The road was straightening out as they came into the dark village and Sean hung back, letting the slow BMW take Killearn Main Street alone, following it down through a dip in the road to Huntly Lodge.

They had passed the gate to Huntly Lodge before Paddy had realized where they were.

'Was that it?'

Sean was concentrating on the road. 'Was what it?'

'Was that the gate we stopped at last night?'

'Aye, it was. He's driven past it. Should I stop?'

'No.' She sat back in the seat, stunned at the enormity of her mistake. She had called the cavalry to the wrong place. 'No, keep following.'

The tail-lights led them on and Sean followed at a cautious distance. Paddy hoped that they were following the wrong car, that Lafferty had stopped at Huntly Lodge and met the police there, that the car in front of them was an innocent midnight driver, someone pleasant going home after a long night out in the city. But they saw him as he hit the top of a hill and it was Lafferty; she could see him in the front seat, his round bald head and broad shoulders clear in the moonlight.

They were out of the green soft hills now, away from the relatively flat farming land, following the road down the side of Loch Lomond. Steep hillsides rose to their right, wind-gnarled trees clung dramatically to the sheer rock. To their left the flat land led down to the gleaming waterside. Sean had to let Lafferty get lost ahead of them and for a while they weren't even sure they were on the same road.

They came to a turn in the road, passing a small cottage partially hidden behind a clump of trees. They wouldn't have noticed it if the BMW lights weren't still on. The front door of the cottage swung wide into the dark inside. The car doors lay open. Lafferty was inside.

Paddy waited until they were around the corner. 'Stop here.'

Sean brought the car slowly to the side of the road. He looked at her in the mirror. 'The police aren't coming here, are they?'

'No. They're not coming.' She looked out at the flat silver expanse of the Loch. 'We're on our own.'

33

Two Twenty an Hour

I

Paddy opened the door, stepping out into a soft muddy bank that swallowed the sole of her boots.

'Fuck.'

Sean leaned over from the driver's seat and whispered loudly, 'Should I come too?'

Paddy tutted, 'Of course ye should bloody come. This guy's an animal.' She found herself echoing Burns's words.

Sean climbed out of the car and looked anxiously back down the road. 'Sure ye don't want me to wait with the car?'

'He's going to kill her. He's built like a brick shit-house. I could do with a wee hand.'

'But the police . . .' Sean shrugged nervously. 'Can't we drive until we find a phone and tell them to come here?'

'She could be dead by then.'

'*We* could be dead.' He felt immediately ashamed and slipped her eye. 'I didn't really sign up for this.'

'OK,' she was furious, 'you just keep watch then.'

'I'm not much of a fighter, Paddy—'

'Please your fucking self, Ogilvy.'

'Paddy—'

'I'm trying to save someone's life here, I haven't got time to squabble.'

'Can't I—'

But she'd moved off already, creeping down the lane heading back to the cottage, angry at Sean and sick with fright. Reluctantly Sean tripped after her.

It was a small Victorian cottage, a miniature mansion. A low slate roof hung over the whitewashed walls, picturesque windows with black wooden shutters open at either side. The front door was low, the heavy black lintel giving it a frown, flanked by cast-iron foot-scrapes for horse-riders to clean their boots on.

Across the road Paddy and Sean hung back behind the trees. Through the front windows they could see light seeping through doorways from the hall. Lafferty believed he was alone: he didn't need to leave the lights off any more.

Paddy looked back to the Loch and saw the shape of a rickety wooden boat house down by the water. She looked around on the ground and picked up a thick branch. It was rotten and crumbled in her hand when she gripped it. There was nothing else by the roadside, no bits of metal or big round stones. She didn't even have a plan.

Sean looked over at the house, fists firmly in his pockets, elbows locked tight. He saw her looking at his hands and smiled nervously. 'Cold, isn't it?'

'I'm going in,' she said angrily. 'You do what ye like.' She crossed the road and headed around the side of the house alone.

Unlike the Killearn house, the path here was overgrown with plants. She had to negotiate her way through the branches of an old tree that had snapped and fallen against one of the windows. A bush at her feet released the smell of spearmint as she brushed through it.

Around the back the lane opened up into a steep garden, shallow, with a sheer wall of black wet rock at the back. It was neatly set out but overgrown. The only spot bare of vegetation was a big patch of turned earth at her feet.

The back wall of the house had two small windows on either side of a set of French doors leading from the kitchen. The far window was dark – a bathroom, maybe. The window next to Paddy looked in over the sink.

She crept along the wall, the soft bare earth under her feet giving at every footstep. She stood flush to the wall and looked in. It was a pretty Edwardian kitchen, beautifully crafted wooden shelves and pierced doors on the pantry, painted pale yellow and cornflower blue. An old-fashioned black cooking range sat in a large inglenook.

The kitchen had been beaten up: the wall cupboards lay open, doors yanked off hinges, the table overturned. Matching sets of plates and cups lay shattered on the black slate floor. Below the window the Belfast sink had loose tea and empty jars lying under a dripping tap and a thick black crack that snaked from one side to the other. A packet of flour had been emptied around the room, leaving a thin Christmas dusting on all the surfaces.

She didn't see the legs at first. It was the drag mark from the doorway that led her eye to the filthy stockinged feet near the window. Kate's lower calf was horribly swollen, bent at an illogical angle, the pale sheer material of her tights holding the bloody mess together. Her feet were filthy, caked in mud, and a big toenail had come off: Paddy could see the coin-sized shape and the raw bloody mark underneath.

She tore her eyes from the figure on the floor and looked for a weapon. There were no knives visible in the kitchen; a couple of copper pots lay by the doorway but they didn't look very heavy. She stepped back in the soft earth and looked around the garden. No tools. Big stones in the rockery, but her hands were too small to pick them up.

Panicking, she stepped back to the window and looked in. Something about the drag marks on the floor caught her eye. Paddy looked carefully at Lafferty's footsteps next to the twin track-marks from Kate's feet. The footsteps were confused, as if Lafferty had turned around. Not around. He'd turned back. Lafferty's footsteps doubled back, heading back out of the kitchen.

He'd gone back out to the car, to the front of the house where Sean was waiting. Paddy froze in horror. Sean was alone with him. She listened hard, every sense heightened, listening for a cry or a call or a noise.

Wind rasped through the trees on the high hill behind her, dead leaves hissed around her ankles. So rigid with indecision that she could hardly blink, she stood there, a woman dying in front of her, her own breath frosting and clearing the small panel on the window, listening for Sean's death.

A shift in the light at the kitchen doorway made her jump back into the dark and her heel sank into the soil.

Lafferty sauntered back in through the kitchen door, calmly stepping over the table to Kate, holding a large knife. He took the hem of his sweatshirt and wiped the blade with it, a faint smile on his lips.

Paddy could hear her heartbeat drumming in her ears. As Lafferty dropped to his knees in front of Kate his free hand brushed the broken leg and she saw Kate's leg twitch, heard a desperate groan through the window.

She couldn't move. She had walked away from Vhari, had stood silently in a rockery while Lafferty killed Sean, and now she was going to watch him cut Kate's throat. Suddenly she saw a shadow in the kitchen doorway.

Having come in from the dark, Sean was blinded by the overhead light and blinked hard. Lafferty was on his feet, standing straight, twisting from the waist towards the doorway, holding the big knife in front of him.

Tearing her eyes from the window, Paddy grabbed a huge stone at her feet and stood up, surprised by the weight. She swung it at the French doors. The loud shattering of glass panels and aged wood splitting into kindling hit the back wall of the garden,

317

reverberating through the doors. The French doors swung languidly inwards. They were unlocked.

Clueless as to what she'd do when she landed, Paddy jumped into the kitchen, feet skidding on the shards of glass. Lafferty spun towards her, his neck a solid flex of muscle, teeth bared. Sean swung a wild punch at the back of Lafferty's head.

Paddy watched Lafferty's face as he received the blow. His jaw slackened and the anger left his eyes for a moment. Behind him Sean retracted his arm and watched.

Lafferty blinked, hunched his shoulders and spun on his heel to Sean, lifting the knife as he turned.

The base of the copper pan was actually very heavy. The dusting of flour on the handle strengthened her grip as Paddy used two hands to lift it over her head and bring it down on his.

Lafferty paused again as the knife slipped from his fingers; the tip stuck into the wooden floor, the handle vibrating from the force.

The great bull of a man slid to his knees and toppled sideways against the leg of the table, snapping it as his chest fell against it. He reached out a big hand to steady himself and found nothing but air. He landed on his face.

Sean looked down at Lafferty's still back and over at Kate curled into a small ball by the sink. 'Fucking Hell, Paddy, I'm due more than two twenty an hour for this.'

Kate's broken leg twitched, making them both startle. She was trying to speak.

Paddy rushed over to her side. 'It's all right. You're safe now, Kate.'

Her curly blond hair was stuck to her face. She was just like Vhari apart from her nose. It looked as if it had been crushed with a flat iron. She was mumbling, desperate to be heard. Paddy put her ear to Kate's mouth but it was hard to make out the words because her voice was so faint and nasal.

'Darling,' she said. 'Lovely.'

'Lovely?' repeated Paddy, puzzled and wondering if she had heard right.

'To see you, darling. Lovely. I can hear you, darling.'

Kate's lips slid back: a front tooth was missing, her mouth hinged with sticky blood. Her breath smelled foul.

As Kate bared her teeth Paddy heard what she thought was a death rattle, a gurgle at the back of the throat. Kate was laughing.

II

The hall stand had a shallow seat on it for Edwardian ladies and gentlemen to sit on while they pulled galoshes and riding boots on and off. It was wide enough for any single bottom, however prosperous, but Paddy and Sean were squashed in side by side, thigh pressing hard against thigh. Paddy was glad of the heat. The police insisted on keeping the front door wide open to the cold night and frost was settling on the rug.

Ambulancemen worked on Kate in the kitchen. Paddy could hear her gurgling and laughing and groaning as the paramedics expressed concern and then bewilderment. They didn't know what she was laughing about either. It was no laughing matter: that leg was a hell of a mess, hell of a mess.

When the police arrived in response to Sean's call from the phone in the hallway they assumed that Lafferty was the house-holder and screamed at Paddy and Sean for a bit, putting handcuffs on them and then taking them off again after the radio confirmed that Paddy did indeed fit the description of a *News* journalist and that she should be in the car they found parked around the corner.

Lafferty was dead. There was no bleeding that they could see, no violent spills of guts or anything to make Paddy feel it was real. He had died of a massive bleed into his brain where the saucepan had hit him.

They carried him past her with a sheet over his face, but she didn't feel anything but relief that he hadn't killed Sean. She thought of poor Mark Thillingly handing over Vhari's new address after a minor scuffle. She would have stood on the bridge as well if Sean had died because of her. She wouldn't have jumped, but she would have stood there.

The police officers were gathered by their cars, one of them taking charge of the radio while three others stood in a semi-circle around the open doors, rubbing cold hands together, listening bright-eyed to the familiar buzz and crackle of the radio. One of them was still suspicious and scowled in at Sean and Paddy.

'You're engaged,' Paddy said flatly.

Sean seemed startled but nodded. 'Aye.'

'Congratulations.' She held her hand out at an awkward angle for him to shake. He took it and pumped once. 'You'll be happy.' She meant it well, but it sounded like an order rather than a wish.

'Maybe.'

Two uniformed policemen came to the front door and gestured for them to follow. 'We'll take your car,' said one, leading them past the waiting police cars.

'Are they not coming with us? Why are we going in our car?'

The policeman waited until they were out of earshot and on the dark road. 'They've found another body out the back. A man. He was stabbed in the eye. They reckon the bird killed him.'

'Why do they think that?'

He shrugged. 'It's her house, isn't it? They figure someone else came for her and she popped him.'

They took the keys from Sean and made the two of them sit in the back, even though they hadn't done anything wrong. Sean asked them to pump up the heating and turn the fan on and they drove away from the house in a sweltering wave of warmth, rubbing their cold fingers back to life and drying their noses.

The sun was coming up, climbing low over the ancient

wind-warped trees on the hillside as they drove back down the road they had come along. They passed a few other cars on the road, the police driver refusing to stop in passing places, driving as arrogantly as if he was in a police car and had the right.

They passed from the wood into farming land and looked at each other when they realized where the car was headed. They were back on the road to Huntly Lodge.

34

The Line-Up

I

The lichen-stained gate was open, shoved back against a hedge. Judging from the depth of the ruts in the muddy entrance a lot of cars had been up the small lane since they passed it earlier.

The place looked different in the thin morning light. The woods around the drive weren't as dense as they had seemed in the dark. Paddy could see through them to the mild slopes of the fields beyond. They turned the corner to the house and Paddy saw Sullivan standing by one of the three cars parked outside, wearing a thick coat and grey woolly police-issue gloves. He looked up at her, a broad, slow smile breaking over his face.

The police driver slowed to a stop and Sullivan padded over to the car.

'I'll take them from here, Kevin.'

The two policemen got out of the calls car and went over to join their uniformed pals.

Sullivan opened the passenger door next to Paddy and crouched down. His knees objected to the reckless gesture by clicking loudly but Sullivan pretended not to notice.

'You've had quite a night.' His glance flickered over to Sean.

'This is my driver, Sean Ogilvy.'

The two men made a big deal of respectfully shaking hands across her face. 'Good job you were there, young man.'

'It was me that hit him,' said Paddy indignantly.

Sullivan pointed at her but spoke to Sean. 'Greedy for glory,' he said, and she could see he was impressed without being able to say it to her face.

She slapped his hand away. 'Did you arrest Neilson?'

'Can't. We've got nothing on him. No witnesses tying him to Lafferty or the house on Loch Lomond or to the Bearsden Bird's house.'

'Well, you've got me, I saw him at Vhari's door.'

Sullivan nodded and grinned. 'And there are prints on the note. If we only had an eyewitness, that wouldn't be enough. We need corroboration, and we haven't his prints on file. It's only because you called this in that we can take him in for questioning and take his prints. That'll give us a comparison.'

'What about Gourlay and McGregor? No way they'll corroborate, seeing him there?'

Sullivan sighed and looked at his feet. 'I think we both know the answer to that one, don't we?'

She wondered about the wisdom of mentioning Knox. If Sullivan was this cagey about fingering two officers of lower rank he wouldn't want to know about his boss's boss's boss's boss. But she had to try. 'Look, we saw Lafferty bringing Kate Burnett out of a house in Milngavie; that's how we picked him up in the first place.'

Sullivan prompted her on with a head nod.

'Fifteen Ornan Avenue, do you know it?'

Sullivan's neck stiffened so suddenly that his head wobbled a little. He looked as if his kidneys had burst but he was too polite to say anything.

'There's a glass porch outside and it's opposite a pub.' He didn't want to hear what she was saying, Paddy could tell. 'An old sort of Englishy pub. With a car park.'

'Right.' He nodded tetchily. 'We'll look into that. We will.'

'*Can* you look into that?'

He gave her an imploring look. 'We've got plenty to go on as it is. Let's do what we can.'

'You're not going to, are you?'

Before he had the chance to answer, a policeman next to one of the other cars shouted over that they were ready. Sullivan tried to stand up to answer him but his knees wouldn't let him. He dropped back on his haunches and looked embarrassed. 'We're doing our best. We're doing all we can.' He took his time rising slowly to his feet. 'I'm driving.'

'Where are we going?'

'You need to pick Neilson out of a line-up. Are you game?'

'Oh, aye,' said Paddy. 'I'm always game.'

Sullivan drove carefully back to Glasgow, following the car in front. Every so often Paddy could see the back of Paul Neilson's well-groomed head in the car in front. It was the guy she had met at Vhari Burnett's door. She felt sure of it.

II

Listening to the noises through the door, Paddy was waiting in the side room, her stomach cramping with exhaustion, imagining the cause of the noises next door. Feet shuffled and men chatted casually, the sounds of men who didn't know each other passing occasional comments. Two of them gurgled phlegmatic smoky laughs.

They were gathering men who looked a bit like Paul Neilson for the line-up and she, star witness, was waiting in a dull side room, walls painted industrial beige, a table and three chairs pushed up against a wall. There was no window, just a bare light-bulb hanging overhead, throbbing sixty watts into the cupboard room.

She couldn't help but think of Patrick Meehan. His line-up for the Rachel Ross murder was the trap he didn't see coming. He might be a career criminal but he still had a naive belief in the justice system and hadn't anticipated the police tipping the witnesses off. Meehan had actually leaned over to one witness, a young girl, and told her not to be nervous, it was OK, she could say it was him, thinking she was his alibi. But in court she was called as a witness for the prosecution. Paddy remembered reading about the murder victim's husband: old Abraham Ross was kept in the room the witnesses were taken into after they had picked Meehan out. No one ever proved it, but they must have talked to each other: who did you get? I picked the guy at the end of the line, short, plump, acne scarred. I got him too, same guy, at the end of the line, sandy hair.

Sullivan had stuck his neck out and desperately needed Paddy to pick out Neilson. Driving seven miles into town with the accused man riding in the car in front had to be bad practice: she saw Sullivan watching her in the mirror sometimes, when they stopped at lights or the car in front turned sharply, hoping she'd had a good look at Neilson. But Paddy wasn't looking at the car in front. She could have picked him out with her eyes shut.

It was warm in the room. Burned dust had turned the light-bulb yellow and brown. It must have hung there for a long time. The room didn't get used much. Eyewitnesses weren't called for very often and then it was usually for robberies. She knew from the calls car that most murders were solved by arresting the blood-splattered spouse holding the knife and standing over the body.

There was a sudden absence of movement outside the door, a reverent silence fell over the waiting men and feet shuffled into place. A final check was called for and she heard a shoulder brush against the waiting-room door.

It opened and she surprised herself by standing up suddenly and finding that her legs were weak with tension. The door slammed shut.

Slowly, the door swung open again and an officious uniformed officer looked in. He frowned at her, looked her over and asked if she was ready. She nodded, nervous and hot. Letting the door fall open, he gestured for her to come out into the room.

Five men were lined up against the wall. The officer walked her along the line, watched by a group in the corner that included Sullivan and a tired-looking lawyer man in a brown suit.

Paddy and the officer walked sombrely along the line and she pretended to look carefully at each one, aware of the breathless hush from the audience behind her.

The men were all dressed the same, but she could have picked Paul Neilson out just by looking at his clothes. His white shirt was crumpled, an expensive linen shirt, probably discarded when he went to bed and thrown on again when the police came to the door in the middle of the night. The rest of the men had freshly pressed shirts on, made of a hard-wearing nylon blend, police issue, ill fitting, cuffs hanging over their wrists. Some of them had dark hair, some black like Neilson's.

She walked to the end of the line and turned back, walking to the middle. The men avoided eye contact, staring up at the back wall as if at a urinal, but Neilson still looked arrogant, a smug twist at the side of his mouth, weight resting on one foot. His haircut looked expensive.

Paddy stood in front of him, showing him she wasn't scared. He looked back at her. Behind him the lawyer coughed anxiously. She stepped towards Neilson, examining him, looking at the hands that had held Vhari Burnett's door shut, at the neck that had been speckled with Vhari's blood. He looked down and smiled warmly.

'That's him,' she said.

Paul Neilson grinned, dark-brown eyes twinkling, crow's feet spreading across his cheeks. It was as if she had told him a great joke, flattered him on his choice of clothes, asked him to buy her a drink.

The officer looked at Neilson for confirmation. 'Number two?'

Paddy pointed at him, her fingertip three inches from his chest. 'This one, number two.'

Neilson's grin spread until his eyes were almost shut.

Sullivan stepped forward. 'OK.' He took her elbow and steered her to a far door. 'That's it for now.'

III

Ramage had called the station looking for her and Sullivan allowed her to make a phone call from his desk.

She told him what had happened in detail, leaving out the fifty-quid note because that would come out at the trial and by then she would be bathed in glory. Sullivan had been dodging every mention of Knox. She guessed that he wasn't senior enough to go after him, so she didn't mention him to Ramage. They couldn't report on Neilson yet either, and would have to wait for the trial, but Ramage promised her a front page on the scene at the cottage, the lady in peril and the *Daily News*'s own intrepid reporter. The story would include details of Kate's attack and the body in the garden, and because Lafferty was dead they could defame him as much as they wanted.

She was to come in and write it up for the Saturday edition and then she could go home. He sounded pleased with her, a little in awe at the story of the cottage, and she played up Sean's part in case they found out that their new driver didn't have a licence.

'He was brilliant. Saved the day. I couldn't have done it without him.'

'Well, you can keep the hotel room until tomorrow, if you want to go out and get pissed tonight.'

Paddy thought of Mary Ann leaving for France in the morning. 'Ah, thanks, Boss, I think I'll just go home after.'

'Excellent,' he said firmly. She felt he appreciated her being cheap almost as much as the story.

She hung up and found Sullivan standing across the room, sadly chewing a hangnail, as if he'd just heard Santa wasn't real. He caught her eye and looked away.

He had heard about herself and Burns. She knew these old guys.

They liked women but if they heard any hint of scandal they'd be the first at the front of the mob with a pocket full of stones.

Paddy stood up and walked over to him. 'What?'

He shrugged guiltily, avoiding her eye.

'Sullivan, what's going on?'

He dropped his hands to his sides and his back sagged. 'We've let him go.'

'Neilson? But I picked him out. He was number two, right?'

'He was number two, but the fifty-quid note—' He bit his finger again, ashamed. 'The note's gone missing.'

35

Colum McDaid's Shameful Exit

Colum McDaid was on the verge of being sacked from a job he had dedicated his life to, but it didn't stop him being a gentleman and offering Paddy tea and biscuits.

'They're sending someone up to replace me now, calling in a retired officer from another area. I'll be out by lunchtime.'

She watched him move around the room, boiling the kettle, offering sugar, pouring in the milk first so that it didn't scald. She watched him and noted that at no time did he allow her to be in his blind spot between himself and the evidence cupboard or the safe. The only chair in the room other than his own was bolted to the floor just inside the door.

He handed her the cup with two bourbons perched on the saucer and took his own seat back behind the desk.

'So it's gone?'

McDaid nodded into his tea. 'I'm here all the time, I check everyone on the way out. I don't understand . . . they'll say it's because I'm old.'

'It's just gone?'

'It's gone. I stayed last night until three thirty in the morning looking for it. It's gone. It's not in this room or the next room, there's no sign of a break-in and I didn't leave the room once the day before without locking up.'

'Couldn't someone just have nicked the key and come in? There must be a spare set of keys in the station.'

McDaid shook his head. 'No, see, I do what my predecessor did.' He looked a little shifty. 'There's an element of temptation in this job, you know, for the young men. They've got families, wee babies and the basic pay's not much. We older ones, we take it on ourselves to guard the young men against that. There's money about, people who want favours and so on. It's harder for a young man to say no. That's why we have the key.'

'What key?'

'Well, it's a secret, but there's no point in not telling you now: I have a key to the safe that I don't leave at the station. People think it's here but it's not. No one can get in there without it, which means they must have taken the note during the day when I was here. Sitting in this very chair.'

She thought of Knox. 'Do very senior officers know about the key?'

'No, just me.'

'And you know for certain that the note was here yesterday morning?'

'Definitely.'

'So, who came in yesterday?'

He pulled a blue notebook out of his top drawer and reluctantly pushed it across the desk to her with his fingertips. 'I'm one year short of my full term,' he whispered. 'I won't even get my pension now. Mrs McDaid'll . . . I don't know how we'll manage.'

Paddy read down the list of three and there, first off, at nine ten in the morning, was Tam Gourlay's signature. He must have gone in just before he was suspended, before Burns found him in the car park and beat him up. She showed McDaid the page and tapped the name.

'Him. Did he go into the safe?'

'Sure, he put a production in there. First thing.' He checked the seven-digit number next to Gourlay. 'A shoplifting production. Straightforward case. But I know for certain it wasn't him because he came in in his shirtsleeves and I watched him the whole time.'

'How did he stand?'

McDaid got up and leaned towards the safe with his bum in the air. 'Summary charge productions go on the bottom shelf.' He adjusted his stance and they both realized that Gourlay's hands would have been obscured from McDaid's vantage point at the desk.

McDaid stood up, looking broken. 'But he was in his shirtsleeves and I would have heard him fold it if he took it. A fifty's a very big note. It was new. I'd have heard it.' His eyebrows furrowed with self doubt. 'I'm old, I know I am, but I'm alert. I'd have heard it.'

II

Paddy stepped back out into the cold morning street, feeling sick as she remembered Neilson's wide crocodile smile. The missing note was good for her, though; her bribe would never come to light or be mentioned and she could still run her story with Lafferty as the sole villain. Without the note it was actually a better story, there would be no codicils or information held back until the court case. But Paul Neilson had walked, gone back to his vulgar villa in Killearn to take leisurely swims in his pool. It was all wrong.

Crossing the supermarket car park to the train station, her stomach spasmed and she doubled over, throwing up the cup of tea McDaid had made her at the station. She leaned over the brown puddle to see if more would come, waiting for her head to stop spinning, and deep inside she realized.

She stood up slowly, blinking at the light, and spoke aloud without meaning to. 'Oh, shit.'

III

It was because she had so much to avoid thinking about that the words came so easily, flowing through her fingers straight on to the page, perfect paragraphs in the new, punchy *Daily News* house style.

It was an exciting story to tell: the lawyer who had died to protect her sister from a crazy ex-boyfriend, beautiful Kate in terrible danger, the view from the garden window in Loch Lomond. She had to throw in a few comments from 'sources', facts framed as speculation so that the lawyers would pass it for publication, but she knew the police wouldn't object. They came out of it looking good too.

Paddy stopped at the end of her seven hundred and fifty words and wondered why it had never been this easy before. Maybe exhaustion brought her down to the right level for this style of writing; she was usually too considered to bang out reams of short sentences, one fact in each, top-and-tailing the article with what she was going to say and a summary of what she had just said. Sullivan had given her a couple of on-the-record, ascribable statements to hang the whole thing on. It read perfectly well, but she thought of everything she had to leave out: Neilson, Knox being the most important. She knew that although it satisfied as a *News* article and Ramage would be pleased, it didn't satisfy her.

She looked up from her desk. Three copy boys were perched on the bench, scanning the room for the faintest signal. The news room was packed with men going about their business but every-one seemed altered. The energy of the room seemed to move around her and the scoop she was writing up. No one came near her desk. Shug Grant and Tweedle-Dum and -Dee were over at the sports desk, keeping their backs to her. A photographer looked away as she glanced over at him. The news-desk editor caught her eye and smiled. A copy boy leaped to his feet and jogged over to her, gesturing with a phantom mug, asking if she wanted tea.

This was the respect of her peers. She ran her tongue over her teeth. It tasted metallic, like faintly sour milk.

36

Patrick Meehan

I

The smell of tired men on a Friday night hit her nose, a mingling of sweat and disappointment. The Press Bar was no longer a nice place to drink. Most of the powerful movers wanted to get away from the politics of the *News* on a Friday and drank in the Press Club a mile away, where the drink was union subsidized and the staff from other papers gathered as well.

A thin smattering of drinkers were hanging around the bar or sitting at the tables, reading or staring. No one was talking much. Behind the bar, McGrade was cleaning glasses and greeted Paddy with a welcoming nod.

McVie was alone at a small table and Paddy was relieved that Patrick Meehan hadn't turned up. She stood up straighter and walked over to the table. 'Did you get a dizzy?'

'Eh?'

'A disappointment. Did Meehan not show?'

McVie nodded behind her and she turned to see him walking back from the toilet, checking his fly as an afterthought. He was small and dressed in a heavy black overcoat. His skin was acne scarred and yellow and he looked pissed off. He arrived at the table, looking down his nose at Paddy.

'Hiya,' she said.

'You're just a girl.'

She couldn't really argue with that. 'I am, aye.'

McVie intervened. 'This girl's one of the brightest young journalists in Scotland.'

Patrick Meehan stuck his tongue in his cheek. He looked Paddy over again and stuck his hand out to her.

Given that he had just come from the lavatory, she didn't really want to take his hand but she forced herself. He squeezed it a little too hard, letting her know he was strong. His shortness and arrogant demeanour, the russet hair and short legs, suggested that he had never been very attractive to women and she suspected he had the resentment she met all the time from men like that, as if she was responsible for every knockback and slight every woman had ever given him.

'I'm Paddy Meehan too,' she said.

He nodded at McVie. 'He said that. You've got the same name as me,' he said, picking a stubby cigarette off the packet on the table and lighting it.

'Aye.'

He looked her over. 'Meehans from Eastfield? Where are your people from?'

'Donegal, I believe, around Letterkenny.'

'We're from Derry.'

'Most of the Meehans are, eh?'

'Aye.'

He seemed to trust her more, now that they had established which Irish county their great-grandparents fled from. 'Will we sit?'

'Aye.' She shook herself awake. 'Let me get you a drink, Mr Meehan.'

Appreciative of the courtesy, Meehan pulled a chair out and sat on it. 'I'll have a half and a half.'

Paddy looked at McVie but he frowned, indicating that he'd like to make the meeting as short as possible, or duck out before it finished.

The barman, benign McGrade, smiled as she came towards him. 'See you're interviewing a local celebrity over there?'

Paddy smiled and ordered. 'I think I've been pipped at the post by just about everyone else in the paper business.'

He put the large whisky and half of beer down next to each other. 'Ah, there's always something new to say, isn't there?' he said, letting her know that even he knew the Meehan story was dead in the water.

The round cost her more than four pounds.

They sat and smoked and Meehan talked, telling his story. He started when he was arrested for the Ross murder. She didn't want to hear about that, but he wanted to talk about it.

'I was particularly interested in your time behind the iron curtain,' Paddy said at last.

He gave her a slow, warning blink. 'As I was saying, the line-up was a fix.' And he continued from where he'd left off. By the time of the trial McVie got up and left, leaving Paddy to listen to the end.

During her painfully earnest childhood Paddy had read and re-read every article and book ever printed about the Meehan case. She recognized some of the phrases from the articles. He'd clearly given the speech a number of times. His eyes clouded over and, at times, even he didn't seem very interested.

Finally he came to a stop and they looked at each other. His beer glass was half empty. It would have been polite to offer him another, but she didn't have enough money.

Paddy explained that she wanted to write a book about the case, not focusing on the Rachel Ross murder, but on his time as a spy, the year and a half behind the iron curtain and his part in the Blake escape.

'I told them how to do it—'

'I know.'

He gave her a slow blink, a curl in his lip that meant it would be a bad idea to interrupt again.

'Yeah, I told them the way to get the radio in to him. You knew that, did ye?'

He was a man used to being listened to and Paddy spent her professional life appeasing men like that. 'I did, kind of, but I'd appreciate it if you'd tell me again.'

He picked up the shot glass and dropped the whisky into the half-empty beer glass. It was a perfectly measured manoeuvre: the beer fizzed a little, rising up the glass and bulging over the rim, threatening to spill but contracting back down again.

'Old man's drink,' said Paddy thoughtlessly.

Meehan liked that. He smiled at her. 'I was in a prison in East Germany. They wanted me to tell them how they could get a two-way radio in to a prisoner and I thought about it, mulled it over in my mind. I'd drawn them maps of every prison I knew. It's easier to get about in a prison than most people think, you know. A lot of screws are corrupt, you can move around all you like. But the problem is high-security prisoners, and that's what they were talking about.

'I told them: send a radio in to the high-security prisoner. Just a normal radio, nothing to attract attention.' He leaned across the table. 'Get a radio that looks the same in to a low-security prisoner, but make it a two-way radio. They wouldn't check it, he's low security, see? Do you see?' He waited, making her say yes. 'D'you know what a pass man is? A pass man is someone the screws trust, a prisoner who's an *inside* man.' She thought of Tam Gourlay. 'Get two radios into the prison then swap them. That was my idea. Get the pass man to swap them, see what I mean?'

She did see. She understood perfectly.

'When George Blake escaped from prison, what d'ye think they found in his cell?'

Paddy nodded. 'A two-way radio.'

'A two-way radio,' Meehan agreed. 'Hidden in a tranny. And they'd checked the tranny's inside the week before.'

Paddy stood up abruptly. 'I'm sorry. I have to go. I need to call someone.' She shuffled out from behind the table.

Meehan looked up at her, offended.

'Mr Meehan, I want to write a book about you.'

'There's been enough books about me.'

'No, not a trashy book about the Ross murder, just a book about you. About the Communist Party and the agent provocateur who sent you to East Germany and the life of a professional criminal in the fifties. A good book. Will you let me buy you lunch one day next week and we can talk about it?'

He hunched his shoulders. 'But I'm here now.'

'I'm sorry, I've got to make a call.'

Meehan looked at his half-empty glass. 'I don't know about that. Maybe I'll write my own book.'

'I'll phone ye.' Paddy pulled her coat on as she opened the door to the street. 'I'll call ye.'

II

She took her place at the news desk and lifted the phone, calling McCloud at the Marine.

'Cloudy? I need to talk to Colum McDaid.'

'Ah, wee Meehan, is it yourself?'

'Aye, it is. Any chance I could get his home number?'

'McDaid's? Here, he's not your boyfriend, is he?' McCloud laughed at the thought until someone came to the desk to ask him for something. 'Aye, aye. Not now, no. Hello? Meehan?'

'Still here.' She had her pen poised above the page.

McCloud gave her the number, a local Partick number.

She called it and got Mrs McDaid. 'Aye, he's here, dear.'

She called out in Gaelic and McDaid came on the phone.

'PC McDaid, Paddy Meehan here. The note's still in the safe.'

'Eh?'

'Gourlay didn't take it out at all. It's in the safe and I'll bet it's

337

tucked inside another production.' She could hear him grunting. 'What are ye doing?'

'Putting my coat on. I live around the corner from the station. Are ye there? Can ye wait by the phone for an hour or so?'

'Aye.'

'I'll call ye back.'

III

The news room was busier on a Friday. The calls-car relief shift were playing cards over by the picture editor's office, eating fish suppers and drinking indiscreetly from a half-bottle of whisky. When she first started everyone drank at the *News* but she hadn't seen a bottle in the office since Farquarson left. She read a book while she waited, aware that Dub would be introducing the open spots now, that Burns would be sweating at the back of the dark room, nervously running over his set.

McDaid phoned back on the direct line after forty minutes. He didn't even greet her. 'Got it. The bugger tucked it in the back of another envelope. The shits were going to wait until I'd given the keys over and tidy up the cupboard themselves.'

'Will you phone Sullivan?'

'I would be delighted.'

'Have a good night, PC McDaid.'

'And yourself, Miss Meehan.'

IV

The club seemed busier than usual. Lorraine wasn't guarding the door and it had just been pulled shut, not secured at all. Paddy slipped down the stairs and watched the stage. Dub was on and the atmosphere was bristling, his voice was high and he was talking fast, pointing at the audience, riding a wave of love.

Lorraine was standing by the bar and sidled over, forgetting to pretend she didn't recognize Paddy.

'He stormed.'

'Dub?'

'Burns. He absolutely fucking stormed.'

Dub came off to a roar of applause, running down the fifteen-foot aisle too fast and coming to a gangly stop at the back wall. He was sweating with joy.

When he saw Paddy he threw an arm around her neck, pulling her roughly over to the far end of the bar. She grinned, despite the wet on the back of her neck from his armpit, and staggered across with him to the four square foot that counted as backstage.

He let go of her and she stood up. Burns was standing at the bar with his long, suburban policeman's drink, smug and wired at the same time.

'You did well?' said Paddy.

Burns looked her up and down. 'I looked for you, in the crowd. You weren't here.'

Paddy waited for a punchline that never came. Finally she muttered, 'Sorry about that. I had a lot of work on.'

He poked her in the chest, and let his finger linger there, making a slow climb up her long neck. 'I wanted you to see me, could have done with your support.'

She took hold of his hand and pushed it away. 'I'm not much support, Burns. I'm a jinx for open spots anyway, you didn't want me here.'

'That's right,' he fell back a step, 'you're a headliner, not a sideshow, aren't you?'

A member of the audience came over and took Burns's elbow. 'You were brilliant, pal. That was the funniest thing I've seen in ages and I come here all the time.'

Burns's eyes lingered on Paddy's neck until Lorraine fought her way through the crowd and stood by him. Swaying, she began to bump her tits on Burns's arm. Burns put his hand around Lorraine's waist, watching Paddy for a reaction.

She grinned at him. 'Oh, I wish I'd come now. You're making me so jealous.'

Dub draped his arm over Paddy's shoulder so they were standing in a foursome. 'We were all great tonight. It was so fluid. Perfect night, one act just built on the previous one. There were no shifts of tone, no break in the atmosphere, you know, like there normally is? None of that.'

'Yeah?'

Burns shot her a dirty look and steered Lorraine away by the waist, leading her over to a table. Paddy watched them canoodling and shook her head.

'That guy is an out-and-out prick.'

'You think so?'

'He's a fucking arsehole.' Burns was looking straight at her and she hoped he could lip read.

'He's fucking funny, though, Paddy. If we get him as a regular it would do the club's rep a ton of good. Anyway, where were you tonight?'

She told him about Loch Lomond and Meehan and whispered about McDaid and the note. They drifted away from the crowd over to the audience chairs, sitting on the stage when the barman took their chairs to stack them up with the rest of them by the wall. Between them and Burns's table the audience pulled on coats and finished drinks, talking too loud because they sensed the excitement in the place.

Dub listened intently, his face inches from hers, and she was loving talking to him. She didn't feel worried when Dub was there. She never felt fat or naive or imperfect with him.

He was leaning close, the better to hear her, and she looked at his big nose and the swirl of his ear, at his powdery white skin. She didn't know why, it was nothing to do with Burns being there, but she wanted to kiss his cheek. He sat back and looked at her, his eyes clear and appreciative. 'You're fearless. I don't know anyone like you.'

She was shocked by how much she wanted to kiss him. It would be easy, all it would take was for her to lean forward a few inches and her mouth would dock with his. Their eyes locked. He was her only friend. She sat back and slapped his leg. 'God,' she said, focusing on his knee, 'I feel as if I haven't seen you for ever, Dub.'

'And you. Even if he is a prick, thanks for bringing him here.' Dub smiled wide, glancing at her. For the first time she saw a trace of disappointment in his eyes. He had looked at her like that before, she realized now. She had seen him with that look many times over the years they had known each other and never understood it before.

She smiled back, glad she hadn't kissed him. 'You're my best friend, Dub.'

Dub nodded at his feet. 'I am.'

'Going to walk me to the station?'

Dub glanced over at Burns. Lorraine was almost sitting on his lap, her mouth firmly clamped over his. Burns had his hand halfway up her T-shirt. 'Aye, I'll walk ye.'

37

Sick

It was the best sleep she had ever had. Ten and a half hours of solid sleep, unconsciousness, broken only when she woke up and listened for the steady metronome of Mary Ann's breathing.

Caroline was refusing to go back to John and tonight she was due to move into Mary Ann's bed. She was sulky and depressed and snored because she smoked.

Mary Ann woke her up with a cup of tea and a warning that her train to London was from Central at eleven so she'd be leaving soon. Paddy sat up in bed, sipping the milky tea and watching as her sister checked through the pale-blue cardboard suitcase, making sure she had everything she needed for a month away in France.

She had seven pairs of pants and vests, two bras, three tops and skirts and a dress. The rest of the space in the suitcase was taken up with prayer books and rosaries and a French phrasebook Con had bought her in a second-hand shop.

When Mary Ann clicked the lid shut and set it on the floor her suitcase looked very small.

Paddy carried it down to the station for her. They waited for the train into town in silence. Paddy was afraid to talk in case she cried because she was going to miss her so much and Mary Ann was afraid she'd cry because she was afraid.

'I've never been further than Largs,' she said, her chin wobbling as she looked down the track.

'You'll love it,' said Paddy, as if she'd been any further. 'I'm mad jealous.'

The train arrived and Paddy swung the suitcase on to the carriage for her. Mary Ann climbed aboard and stood between the open doors, looking out at her wee sister. Paddy couldn't hold back any more. She started to cry.

'Goodbye.'

Silently, Mary Ann grinned and raised a hand and began to cry herself.

'Say hello to God for me,' called Paddy.

The doors slid shut between them but Paddy held Mary Ann's eye as the train slid off into the future.

She stood on the platform watching the tail of the slow train creeping down the track, hoping Mary Ann would be happy; that she was wrong to be worried; that she wasn't about to break her poor mother's heart.

She walked to Rutherglen in the rain to get to the chemist's. Luckily the pharmacist was no one she knew. She took the package over to the public toilets behind the Tower Bar. It smelled of carbolic soap and urine and was freezing because the door was always left open.

Ten o'clock Mass would be coming out soon. When it did there would be a queue of women with pelvic floors ruined from carrying too many children, running over after the fifty-minute Mass. But not yet.

Paddy locked herself in the far cubicle and took the stick out of the packaging, reading the directions and following them to the letter. She didn't dare watch it during the four minutes but stood with her forehead pressed against the cold wall, begging a favour of a God she hadn't spoken to since she was seven.

Outside the cubicle she heard approaching voices, familiar women's voices. Mass was out and everyone she knew would be gathering outside. She'd have to talk to them when she came out, act natural what ever the result. She didn't know if she would be able to.

Daring herself, she turned and looked at the white stick on the cistern. Two faint blue lines had formed, one in each window.

There was no mistake about it: she was pregnant.